CLEARING
THE DARK

HANIA ALLEN

Constable • London

CONSTABLE

First published in Great Britain in 2019 by Constable

1 3 5 7 9 10 8 6 4 2

Copyright © Hania Allen, 2019

The moral right of the author has been asserted.

A CIP catalogue record for this book
is available from the British Library.

ISBN: 978-1-47212-549-1

Typeset in Bembo by Photoprint, Torquay
Printed and bound in Great Britain by
CPI Group (UK), Croydon CR0 4YY

Papers used by Constable are from well-managed forests and other
responsible sources.

FSC
www.fsc.org

MIX
Paper from
responsible sources
FSC® C104740

Constable
An imprint of
Little, Brown Book Group
Carmelite House
50 Victoria Embankment
London EC4Y 0DZ

An Hachette UK Company
www.hachette.co.uk

www.littlebrown.co.uk

Hania Allen was born in Liverpool, but has lived in Scotland longer than anywhere else, having come to love the people and the country (despite nine months of rain and three months of bad weather). Of Polish descent, her father was stationed in St Andrews during the war, and spoke so fondly of the town that she applied to study at the university.

She has worked as a researcher, a mathematics teacher, an IT officer and finally in senior management, a post she left to write full time. She is the author of the Von Valenti novels and now lives in a fishing village in Fife.

By Hania Allen

The Polish Detective
Clearing the Dark

Clearing the Dark

CHAPTER 1

The ball soared over the slatted fence, disappeared into the trees and landed with a dull thud.

'*Cholera*,' Dariusz shouted. A devout Catholic, he didn't usually swear, but they'd just started the game and someone would have to climb over.

His companions were looking at him expectantly. Antek glanced at his watch, letting him know more eloquently than words that, if they wanted a football match, he'd have to get a move on. The weather was on the turn. Although the clouds weren't the ones that dropped rain, the speed with which the cloud-shadows chased each other over the fields suggested the wind was strengthening. It was the last game of the season because the field in which they were playing was about to be spread with fertiliser, readying it for planting with potatoes the following month.

Dariusz wiped his hands down his heavy-duty jeans and started to climb, his irritation mounting with each step. He hadn't gone far when he heard a furious barking. Louie, the farm's black-and-white Border Collie, had decided to join in and was leaping up and crashing against the fence. Dariusz called to the others to hold the dog back but they shouted to Louie to keep jumping. Idiots. What were they thinking? After months in their company, Louie

1

still couldn't understand a word of Polish. The dog gave up and scrabbled at the loose earth under the slats.

Dariusz continued to climb, feeling the fence sway under him. Fortunately, there were places where he could get a finger grip, even with hands as huge as his. Finding somewhere that would take his workman's boots was another matter. He reached the top, swung his legs over and plunged the three metres to the ground. A mistake, as he landed in dense gorse, scratching his face and neck as he struggled to maintain his balance.

He knew this was a private estate because he drove past it every day. Curiosity had led him to check it out on Google Maps. He'd been surprised at the extent of the land. Bushes fringed the perimeter all the way to the ornamental metal gates, behind which a hedge-lined gravel driveway curved off to the left.

He pushed into the woodland, savouring the clean, resinous smell. The trees were mainly conifers, but there were also silver birches, just coming into leaf. He loved those trees as they reminded him of his native country, where they grew tall, the outer layers of bark curling in woody tatters. When he'd arrived in Dundee, he'd searched for the white storks' nests, like huge crowns; he'd assumed there'd be storks in Scotland. He saw them everywhere in Poland, where they were much more common than the national bird, the white eagle. Every year, the same pair, Kleo and Klekotka, came to Lower Silesia to nest on his father's farm. They were such a feature that his brother had installed a webcam above the nest and beamed the images to the rest of the world. Dariusz had proudly shown the footage to the other Poles. Antek, who'd been there the longest, had said storks were almost unknown in Scotland. A few pairs arrived but they never nested. He had added, grinning, that they were said to bring fertility, so what did that say about the Scots?

Dariusz was glad he'd made the journey to Scotland. The

climate, the rain especially, was similar to that of Poland. Farm work was plentiful, and he was used to the hard physical labour and early mornings. Most of all, he was overwhelmed by the friendly attitude of the Scots. The only thing that worried him was the looming shadow of Brexit. Like many, Dariusz hated uncertainty.

A moment later, the trees thinned, giving him a glimpse of a lawn overgrown with coarse grass. In the distance he could see a great grey stone structure. Breek House, the farmer boss had called it. 'A place to steer clear of, if you know what's good for you,' he'd added, with a knowing nod. Curiosity had always been a weakness of Dariusz's. He waded into the grass, his attention not on where he was putting his feet but on the house with its black windows, like gaping mouths. There was something forbidding about it, a feeling that it was watching, perhaps for an unsuspecting guest. What wasn't evident, because of the rise in the ground, was that, on the other side of the house, acres of land stretched to the horizon. A farmer's paradise, if the soil was as rich as it was on the farm where he worked. But he'd heard that the house had lain empty for over a decade as no buyer could be found.

There was a sudden yapping. Louie had succeeded in tunnelling under the fence. He bounded over to Dariusz and gazed up expectantly, his tongue lolling from his open mouth. Dariusz ordered him first in Polish and then in English to search for the ball. Louie listened attentively, then cocked his head and darted back into the trees, sniffing at the ground. Suddenly, he went berserk and started scrabbling furiously.

The other Poles were shouting from behind the fence, asking what was keeping him. So where was the ball? If it had landed in the knee-high grass, he might as well give it up. He dropped down on all fours and ran his hands over the ground. Behind him, Louie was still digging, his back paws flinging pine needles and rotting leaves to left and right. Maybe he would reach Australia before Dariusz found the ball.

He sat back on his heels, wondering if money was to be made in inventing footballs with electronic chips that were detectable with a mobile phone, when Louie dashed over. His jaws were fastened on something large and round, something he set on the ground.

Shock surged through Dariusz. '*Jezus Maria*,' he murmured, crossing himself.

The skull was missing its teeth and lower jaw. Bits of soil clung to the yellow-brown bone and had collected along the sutures. Dariusz stared at the vacant eye sockets and nose cavity with a mixture of horror and fascination. He prodded the skull. The pale light from the March sun touched it, making it glisten as though wet.

Louie rushed back into the woodland and continued to dig. What the hell was he doing now? Dariusz leapt to his feet and ran over, stopping short as he saw the long bone poking up through the soil.

He grabbed Louie's collar and dragged the struggling animal away. Ignoring the frenzied yapping, he snatched the phone out of his pocket.

DS Honor Randall pulled up at the forbidding wrought-iron gates. 'This must be it, boss. Breek House.'

'Do you know this area?' DI Dania Gorska said.

'Nope. It's pretty, though.'

This was Dania's first visit to Burnside of Duntrune, a hamlet on the outskirts of Dundee. After passing acres of farmland and the odd white-painted farmhouse, they'd arrived at a picturesque bridge. To the left there was a low stone aqueduct over water that flowed into a mill dam, the Fithie Burn, according to the sat-nav. They veered left, getting a better view of the aqueduct, and reached Breek House a short while later.

Honor was stifling a yawn. A sharp-featured Londoner with wild dark hair, she was stick-thin, despite having discovered the delights of Scottish cuisine. Since making sergeant, she'd revamped her wardrobe and now wore Debenhams trouser suits, which never seemed to fit properly.

'What time did you get to bed this morning?' Dania said.

'I'm not sure.'

'New man?'

'I'm not sure about that either.' She grinned. 'You know I only have eyes for your brother.'

Dania was glad to have Honor in her team. She'd worked with her, a straightforward and straight-talking officer, on her previous murder case and had come to the conclusion that Honor was someone she could depend upon. The two women had recently been promoted and Dania had almost had to beg on her knees to keep Honor in the squad. Fortunately, the DCI had recognised that the women working together were more than the sum of their parts. Dania knew little about Honor's private life except that she was fond of cats, lived alone but seemed to enjoy a gloriously active sex life.

'You should have let me drive, Honor.'

'It's okay, boss. I can keep my eyes open if I have to.'

'Wait here, and I'll see if we can get inside.'

The padlock was hanging open. Dania pushed hard at the gates, prepared to put her back into it, and was surprised at how easily they opened. The Polish worker had told them the place was abandoned. Yet a quick examination revealed that the hinges had recently been oiled.

Back in the Skoda, she signalled to Honor to turn into the

grounds. The driveway was flanked on either side by low ever-green shrubs, which looked as though they'd been hastily trimmed. They crunched along the gravel, following the left turn, and, a minute later, reached a clearing with the house beyond. A short flight of steps led to the front door, above which was a stone crest with the Latin inscription: 'ABSIT INVIDIA'.

'Crikey,' Honor said reverentially. 'That's some pile.'

The house, its stone darkened with age, was built on three levels, and had a gable roof tiled with slates. It might have been described as handsome were it not for the general air of neglect. And the bars on the ground-floor windows. An attempt had been made to tackle the ivy by lopping it near the roots, but the curling strands were still creeping skywards, and it was simply a matter of time before the plant claimed the house.

'Where did the guy tell you he'd be waiting?' Honor said, cutting the engine.

'By the woodland. Which could mean anywhere. We should check first whether someone's at home.'

They hurried up the steps. When there was no reply to Dania's ring, she signalled they should try at the back.

'Look!' Honor said, as they rounded the corner. 'There he is.'

In the wooded distance, a man was standing hunched over, waving an arm. He was shouting something they couldn't catch.

They made their way across the grassy wasteland as quickly as the terrain allowed. The ground, Dania discovered, was littered with hidden stones that slowed their progress. As they approached, she saw that he was gripping a black-and-white dog by the collar. The animal was straining to free himself, his attention on some-thing in the trees behind.

'Are you Mr Dariusz Baranowski?' Dania said.

'Yes. You are police?' His English was heavily accented, much more so than her own. He had messy hair, the same blond as her brother's, and eyes that were a faded blue. If he straightened, he would tower over her, no mean feat as she was nearly six foot tall.

'I'm DI Gorska and this is DS Randall,' she said, pulling out her warrant card. 'West Bell Street station.'

'You are from Poland?' Dariusz said in Polish.

'I am, but we'll need to speak in English as my colleague doesn't understand the language. So, can you tell us what happened?'

'We are playing football.' He gestured to the fence, visible beyond the bushes. 'We kick the ball over here. I climb the fence to find it.' He glanced at the dog. 'Louie came too. I look for the football and not see that Louie is digging. He carry to me the head. It is in the field over there. Then I see that he finds this.'

Dariusz gestured behind him. Scattered around a pile of earth was an assortment of what looked like human bones.

Dania squatted beside the mound. She was no expert, but she recognised the curve of a ribcage.

'I am afraid Louie messes everything when he is digging.'

'Do you reckon it's an ancient grave?' Honor said, picking at her lip.

'It looks too shallow. But it may be.' Dania straightened. 'We'll need Professor Slaughter. Can you call it in?' She glanced towards the house. Seen from the side, it seemed distant and forbidding. Who lived there?

'Mr Baranowski, will you show me where the skull is? The head,' she added, when he seemed uncertain.

His expression cleared. 'It is just here.' He tried to drag the dog, but the animal had other ideas.

'Honor, can you take Louie?'

'Sure, boss.' The girl took hold of the collar, but lost her grip, and the dog made a dash for freedom. A few metres from where they were standing, he started to scratch at the ground. A damp earthy smell reached Dania's nostrils. Dariusz made to go after him but she grabbed his arm.

'Let him do it,' she said quietly.

A minute later, they saw it.

'My God,' Honor said, her voice faltering. 'What is this place?'

'Pull him away, Dariusz,' Dania shouted in Polish.

He caught Louie and held his collar firmly. The blood had drained from his face. He was praying softly. *Święta Maryo, Matko Boża.* Holy Mary, Mother of God, pray for us sinners now and at the hour of our death. Amen.

'Honor, can you take Mr Baranowski to the car and get a statement? I'll wait here for Forensics.'

'What about the dog?'

'Take him as well. Otherwise he'll keep digging.'

'You think there are more of these?'

'Who knows? We'll need to get Nelson out here.'

Nelson was the unit's cadaver dog, trained to uncover human remains, including skeletons. He could detect the chemical signature of death even when the bones were buried.

Dania watched the Pole drag Louie away. The dog probably spent his time herding sheep. Given he'd already found two graves, perhaps he'd prefer a change of career.

As the figures dwindled into the distance, she felt a twinge of apprehension. If these graves proved to be recent, this would be her first big case since becoming DI. Although she had a good team behind her, she was only too aware that any failures would be attributed to her. She remembered what one of her colleagues at the Met had told her: the higher up the greasy pole you climb, the harder it is to hang on. All officers of her rank and above knew this to be a fact.

As the freshening wind sucked at the leaves, lifting and

scattering them, she stared at the graves, wondering what sort of grip you needed to hang on to a greasy pole.

The area round the graves was cordoned off with blue tape. Markers had been placed to form a corridor, and officers were moving back and forth in solemn lines.

Dania approached the tall man with the expertly barbered hair. He was standing surveying the graves, his expression suggesting that, not only was he in charge, everyone needed to know it.

'I'm DI Dania Gorska.' She hesitated. 'I had expected Milo Slaughter.'

'Milo's on sabbatical. I'm Professor Jackson Delaney,' he said, stressing the title. He had soft brown eyes and knew how to use them to best advantage. 'But everyone calls me Jack,' he added, holding her gaze. He spoke with a polished English accent.

'I'm afraid the graves were disturbed by the dog. We've still to find the skull from the first. I think it's somewhere in that grass.'

'I take it you've sent photos to CAHID.'

CAHID was Dundee University's Centre for Anatomy and Human Identification. As well as running courses in forensic anthropology and anatomy, it supported the police in their forensic-science work, including offering a 'bones service'. Police sent in photos of bones found by the public, and one of the responders, a specialist in human anatomy, would identify them as either human or animal. Knowing that a bone was animal saved the police huge costs in terms of time and resources. Although Dania had been as sure as she could be that the remains were human, she'd needed an expert's opinion. The reply had come back in minutes.

'The bones are human, Professor. We wouldn't have called you out otherwise.'

9

'In that case, let's get gowned up.' He shouted to his assistant, a plump, auburn-haired girl in her twenties, to bring the box of over-suits.

Dania dressed quickly, glad that she'd worn her trouser suit. It had cost a small fortune but was worth it as it fitted her perfectly. Finding clothes was always difficult, but she'd discovered a boutique in Edinburgh's Grassmarket that catered for tall women. Since then, she hadn't looked back, and much of her salary disappeared into the shop's coffers. Most of the rest went on the rent.

They ducked under the tape.

'Where did you say the skull was?' Jackson said.

'Somewhere in that field.'

'Go and find it, Steph,' he said to the assistant.

The girl lumbered away, the set of her shoulders revealing the extent of her irritation. Dania guessed she was still in training, or she wouldn't have put up with Jackson's manner so readily.

They squatted beside the first grave. 'Can you say how old the bones are, Professor?' Dania said, breathing in the leaf-rot smell.

'It depends on dampness and soil acidity. These bones are hardly degraded, but I'll need to get them back to the lab to be sure.'

'Best guess? I won't quote you,' she added, when he seemed reluctant to continue.

'Not ancient.'

'And how old were these people when they died?'

'If I had the teeth, I could narrow it down from the X-rays. Comparing the stage of tooth formation with known dental growth gives a pretty accurate age determination.' He picked up a piece of bone. 'This is the lower jaw. But it's missing every tooth.'

'Don't you find that strange?'

'Very.'

'Could it be an elderly person who's lost teeth over time?'

'Possibly. It's not a deal-breaker because bones also have markers that can give you the age.' He rested his gaze on hers. 'Have you used CAHID before?'

'Just their bones service. I've only been here a year.'

His mouth formed into a smile. 'I did some of my training there. We'll have dinner together tonight, and I can fill you in on what they do for the police.'

'We'll have dinner tonight, Professor, but not together. Now, what can you tell me about the second victim?'

His smile glazed over. He got to his feet and loped across to the grave. The Forensics staff stepped back as he approached.

He examined the skull. 'This one has upper and lower jaw intact.'

She said it before he did. 'No teeth.'

'They may have fallen out over time, as you suggested.' He stared into the distance. 'Is that an old people's home, by any chance?'

'I've no idea. It's called Breek House.'

'Never heard of it. But if it is a care home, it might explain the missing teeth. I'll have the investigators sift through the soil just in case.'

'There's another explanation.'

'I'm sure there is. Tell me your theory, Inspector,' he said, in the tone a lecturer would use.

'They've been pulled out.'

He frowned. 'Torture?'

'Maybe we'll find evidence when the skeletons are examined.'

'Good luck with that.' He glanced across at the photographer, another young-looking girl, whose hair was dragged back into a ponytail. She was hunched over the first grave, snapping away, while Jackson's staff conducted the exhumation. 'Johanna, we need you here when you're finished,' he shouted.

The girl looked up and nodded sullenly.

'There's no evidence the bodies were clothed,' Dania said.

'Good point. And why do you think that is?'

His manner was starting to annoy her. 'The perpetrator might have left his DNA on the clothes. Or they might have been removed because they gave a clue to identity.'

Steph had found the skull. She strolled over to the first grave and tossed it to one of her colleagues.

'What the hell are you doing?' Jackson shouted. 'They may be dead but they're still human beings. They have the right to dignity.' He pointed at her. 'You're on report for that,' he added angrily.

The girl stared at him, open-mouthed.

He muttered something Dania couldn't hear, then turned his attention back to his work. 'So, what's your current thinking, Inspector?'

'There may be more graves. We'll have to search this place thoroughly. I'll call it in.' She got to her feet. 'How much of this area will you need to examine?'

'How long is a piece of string? We won't know until we've begun. Sometimes you find human fragments some distance from the body. It's my responsibility to recover them all.' He looked around. 'Pity about the leaves. It makes it impossible to see differences in plant growth and colour. Those can be helpful when excavating graves.'

She pulled off the protective clothing and nodded to the duty officer, who was keeping a log of arrivals and departures. Hunched against the growing wind, she set off in the direction of the Skoda.

Honor was in the car with DC Laurence Whyte, a young, boyish-faced officer. When Dania had first worked with him, she'd found him pathologically shy, his green eyes constantly avoiding her gaze. Like many women, she was drawn to shy men, and had

had to remind herself of the difference in their ranks. But it soon became clear that his affections were directed towards the station's technical department. Honor, who had a great rapport with him to the extent that he was the only officer with whom she'd share her toffees, claimed to know which girl he had his eye on, but was saying nothing.

The two officers were interviewing the last of the farmworkers, a nervous, close-shaven giant. Dania waited for him to leave before filling in her colleagues on what Jackson had found.

'Know what I'm thinking, boss?' Honor said, chewing her thumb. 'Those missing teeth. Some of the Dundee gangs like to do nasty stuff when they play with their victims.'

'That's what I thought. And there might be more graves. Laurence, can you see what's keeping Nelson?'

'Yes, ma'am.' He reached for the car radio.

She signalled to Honor to get out of the Skoda, and they walked slowly down the driveway.

'What did you learn from the farmworkers, Honor?'

'They don't know anything. They had a game of footie and the ball was kicked over. There was one thing I found strange, though.'

Dania looked at her expectantly.

'They all have this grey smudge on their foreheads.'

She felt her lips curve into a smile. 'That's ash.'

'Ash? Why do they have it? Some sort of weird initiation?'

'You could say that. They're Roman Catholics. Today's Ash Wednesday.' She lifted her heavy fringe. 'I have the same. See?'

'Okay,' Honor said, drawing out the word.

'I'm assuming the workers aren't here on a permanent basis. Have you spoken to the farmer?'

'He's away on a buying spree, according to Dariusz. They're about to start planting spuds.'

'Where's the collie?'

13

'Dariusz took him away.'

Dania looked past the gates towards the road. 'Will you watch out for the Canine Unit? I'm going to take a quick look round the grounds.'

Dania struck out across the grass, wishing she had more appropriate footwear. Although she was wearing boots, they didn't grip well enough, and the last thing she wanted was to sprain her ankle. In the distance, the white-suited figures of Jackson and his team were bent over the graves. They were making good time. The first lot of remains was being taken to the gates where the mortuary van was waiting.

She turned left without any firm idea of where she was going or what she was looking for. The ground grew more uneven, the lawn, if it could be called that, morphing into a stony brown field dotted with patches of grass. The smell of woodsmoke reached her from the adjacent farm.

Only now did she appreciate how extensive the grounds were. After walking for several minutes, she reached more pine trees and yellow gorse bushes, and the same wooden fence skirting the perimeter. If she followed it to the right, she'd arrive at the graves. The opposite direction would take her to the metal-gated entrance.

She retraced her steps, rounding the corner of the house to find Honor and Laurence chatting to a man holding a black and gold German Shepherd on a leash. Dania recognised Nelson and his handler, a hunky smiling Irishman she knew only as Christy. He had long dark hair and was wearing his usual ribbed blue jumper and baggy camouflage trousers. The dog was straining to get loose, which was a good sign.

'Hello now, Inspector,' Christy said cheerfully. 'What's the score today, then?'

'We've found two graves close to one another, and I need to know if there are more.'

'What's the land like?'

'Flat and grassy, with trees and bushes on the boundary. That's where we found the bones.'

'Not bodies?'

She shook her head. 'That won't be a problem, I take it.'

'Ah, sure it won't. I trained Nelson well. He's that good, he can alert you to remains under running water.'

She knew that cadaver dogs can detect residue scents even after a corpse has been removed. They'd have to steer him away from the excavated graves. 'We should wait until Forensics have finished,' she said.

Christy tilted his head. 'What shall we talk about in the meantime? A second referendum on Scottish independence?'

Honor groaned. 'Oh, please, anything but that.'

'If Scotland leaves the UK, it'll be all right for the likes of me, I may say. I'm from Dublin.'

'You sure you won't be kicked out along with us English?' Honor said.

'Me? Kicked out of Scotland?' He rolled his eyes in mock horror. 'The women of Scotland can't live without me, so they can't.'

Dania smiled. 'Shall we see how the professor's getting on?'

'Would that be Professor Jackson Delaney, by any chance?'

'It would.'

Christy's eyes narrowed. 'I wouldn't give that man the steam off my porridge.'

'Oh? Why not?'

'He told me he can't stand dogs.'

She hesitated. The last thing she needed was a confrontation between two alpha males.

'It's all right, Inspector. I know how to behave in public.' Christy ran his fingers behind the dog's ears. 'And so does Nelson.'

She nodded to Honor and Laurence to stay by the house, then led the way round the back.

'Would you look at this place?' Christy said, stopping and gazing around. 'It goes all the way to the next county. Who lives here?'

'We've still to establish that.' She gestured towards where the professor was working. 'Right now, all I'm interested in is what's out there.'

Jackson Delaney was getting to his feet. Moments later, two Forensics staff headed away from the woodland, carrying a large box with the second lot of remains. As they passed, Nelson pulled frantically at the leash.

Jackson was heading in their direction. He glanced at Nelson, then nodded curtly to Christy. 'I'm taking these to CAHID,' he said to Dania. 'I'll have Harry get in touch when he's ready.'

'Harry?'

'Professor Harry Lombard. He's assistant director there.'

'Only the assistant?' Christy said cheekily.

'The lady who runs the place is away just now.'

'Did you find the teeth?' Dania said quickly, as the men continued to glower at one another.

Jackson shook his head. 'We sifted the soil pretty deeply.'

'I'd be grateful if you waited around in case we find more graves.'

'All right, but I need to make sure these get processed. Hold on.' He hurried to where his staff were waiting and spoke to them, then returned.

Nelson let out a low growl and would have leapt up at Jackson, had Christy not calmed him with a word.

'I'll thank you to keep that animal away from me,' Jackson said sharply.

'It's because you've got the smell of death on you. Perhaps you should wait over there with your staff.'

Jackson thought about this, then turned on his heel and walked off.

'Cheerful bugger, isn't he?' Christy said, not too quietly. 'We'd better get going. If I don't release this mutt soon, he'll take my arm off.'

'So how do we do this?' Dania said. 'Shall we start at the gates and work our way through the woodland systematically?'

'It'd be quicker to wait for the second coming of Christ. No, we just let Nelson loose.' He walked towards the woodland and took Nelson off the lead. The dog stood to attention.

'Go, Nelson!' he shouted.

Nelson dashed into the trees, Christy following.

'Is that his signal?' Dania gasped, trying to keep up.

'I've trained him that way. All handlers have their preferred method. Sometimes it's a code word, like "Geronimo" or "Popeye".'

Nelson had reached the woodland and was padding around the trees, his nose brushing the ground. Suddenly, he stopped and lay down, his ears pricked.

'That's where we found the first grave,' she said. 'You need to move him on.'

Christy took a biscuit from his pocket and fed it to the dog. 'Go, Nelson!' he said.

The dog jumped up and ran off, sniffing the ground. Seconds later, he found the other grave.

After feeding the dog another biscuit, Christy said again, 'Go, Nelson!'

Nelson dashed off into the woodland. He sniffed around and under the gorse bushes, then ran on, leading them further from the graves.

Dania was beginning to think that two sets of remains were all they were going to find when Nelson sat down beside a gorse bush, his heavy tail thumping the ground.

She felt her throat tighten. 'Okay, I'll mark the spot and get the professor to take a look.'

Christy called Nelson. At his signal, the dog disappeared deeper into the trees. They were now diametrically opposite the metal entrance gates.

It was when Nelson sat down for the fourth time, looking expectantly at his handler, that Dania realised the site might be one massive graveyard. And what would push her investigation into the well-nigh-impossible category was that the fence the dog was sitting beside was no longer made of slatted wood but of rusted barbed wire. Anyone could have slipped into the grounds with a body and buried it. The realisation that this investigation could either make her or break her twisted the knot in her stomach. She closed her eyes. Perhaps leaving the Met hadn't been such a good idea after all.

CHAPTER 2

The ball soared into the air, disappeared into the trees and landed not far from where Marek was crouching. Normally, he'd have stepped out of the bushes and kicked it back. But he had a good reason for staying hidden: the man in the navy tracksuit, running towards the ball, was someone he'd been tailing for the past two weeks, and he wasn't yet at the stage where he wanted to show himself. The man had long dark hair, with no signs of grey, and was heavily built. And he was hardly breaking sweat. Not bad for a fifty-five-year-old. Marek steadied his camera and took several high-resolution shots, capturing him in a variety of poses, but all of them showing him on his feet, which was the purpose of the exercise.

He decided to leave them to finish their seven-a-side in peace, as they were pretty rubbish anyway, and wait near the cars. It was a quarter to two and he reckoned that the kickabout would end soon as most of the men had jobs to go to.

He slipped out of the bushes and hurried along the track. Apart from the time he'd come with Danka to see the Bonfire Night fireworks, this was his first visit to Lochee Park. It was a welcome green space to the north of Balgay Hill, and had once been owned by the Cox family, who'd made their wealth from jute. He was well impressed by its size and particularly by the number of sports

19

fields. Perhaps he could persuade the guys at work to get up a couple of teams.

He positioned himself behind the trees near the white Renault Mégane.

Minutes later, he heard chatter and laughter from the direction of the park. He was tempted to take more photos but he had a fortnight's worth, more than enough. As the men split up and made for their cars, he stepped out on to the track.

'Hello, Ned,' he said, keeping his voice friendly.

The man called Ned had reached the Mégane and was opening the driver's door. He wheeled round and, seeing Marek, his mouth dropped open into a perfect O. The wind gusted, dishevelling his hair. But it was his eyes that commanded attention: they shone with a hard, metallic glint.

'Gorski,' he said. He had a breathy voice, which Marek knew was due to fear rather than his exertions on the pitch.

'Where's the wheelchair, Ned? You forget to bring it?'

The man's demeanour changed. 'I ken how this looks, Marek.'

'I ken how it looks, too.'

'I can explain.' There was desperation in the voice.

'So can I. You've been claiming benefits, saying you're in a wheelchair. Which you're clearly not. That means you've been defrauding the Department for Work and Pensions.' He held up the camera. 'And I have the proof here.'

'It's not what you think. The pain comes and goes. This morning I felt well enough to try a few steps.'

'And, miraculously, you were able to play football for nearly an hour,' Marek said, with a snarl. 'You don't fool me.'

'Look, I swear to God—'

'Don't do that,' Marek interrupted, with a shake of his finger. 'Because you don't fool Him either.' He turned on his heel and walked towards Glamis Road.

With this last lot of photos, he had everything he needed to finish his piece on false benefits claimants. His editor had been hurrying him, but Marek knew it would be worth the wait. And Ned McLellan was a prize catch.

The piece had started as an investigation into how well the DWP was working for the people of Dundee. Marek had interviewed several claimants but something about Ned McLellan had rung a warning bell. It was still ringing after he'd made some enquiries. What he'd discovered suggested he should give the man in the wheelchair a wide berth. Not only did he have an ugly temper, rumour had it he was into a variety of shady deals he skilfully concealed from the authorities. As to the nature of these deals, Marek was none the wiser, since everyone he talked to clammed up when he pressed them. So he'd asked Ned for a second interview. The traffic had been lighter than usual, and he'd arrived at the man's house on Berwick Drive earlier than expected. And seen him walk past his living-room window. It was in that instant that Marek decided to redirect the thrust of his article.

He was setting down the camera on the back seat of the Audi Avant when he heard the sound of running. He'd half expected Ned to retaliate: the man had been defrauding the DWP for nearly a year and was unlikely to let Marek go easily.

As Ned's reflection appeared in the wing mirror, Marek made a rapid calculation, remembering that objects in the mirror are closer than they appear, and sidestepped as the man reached him. Ned tripped on a raised piece of paving, crashed headfirst into a lamppost and bounced off with a thwack.

Marek watched him roll on the ground in agony, clutching his head. 'What were you going to do, Ned? Grab the camera? These aren't the only snaps I have. I've been following you for the past two weeks.'

'Damn you, you fucker,' the man said, through clenched teeth. 'Now that we're Brexiting, you'll be thrown out. That's if my brother doesn't get to you first.'

Marek crouched beside him and gripped his jaw. 'Is that a threat?' He peered into Ned's eyes, his face so close he could smell the stale mouth odour. The man had had a nasty bump, but he wasn't concussed. Still, he should be checked out. Marek tugged the phone out of his jacket. 'You know, Ned, the reason benefits have been cut for people who really need them is because of the rising number of fraudulent claims. I've met your type before, scum who aren't prepared to get out of bed in the morning for something as trivial as work.'

'Ach, what do you know? You're nothing but a dirty foreigner. You haven't even bothered to wash your face.'

'If you're referring to this,' Marek said, touching his forehead, 'today is Ash Wednesday. Shall I tell you what I'm giving up for Lent?' He paused for effect. 'Bastards like you. Now, which emergency service shall I phone first? Ambulance?' He smiled serenely. 'Or police?'

CHAPTER 3

After the discovery of the fourth set of remains, Dania's boss, DCI Jackie Ireland, authorised full forensic deployment. Rows of uniforms systematically scoured the grounds of Breek House, finding nothing but broken beer bottles, a few coins and a torn pair of Marks & Spencer knickers. Christy and Nelson continued their hunt for human remains, finally convincing Dania that there were no further graves to be found. Jackson Delaney left to take everything to CAHID.

It was now after six and the last vehicles were away, Laurence with them. Dania and Honor were about to follow in the Skoda when they heard a car on the gravel.

'Looks as if the owners are back,' Honor said.

Dania threw her a glance. 'Let's hope so. I have a few questions for them.'

'They must have passed the professor and his crew on the road.'

'So they'll have a few questions for us.'

The noise of the engine grew louder and, a second later, a large yellow car rounded the corner and pulled up beside the Skoda.

'Wow, boss,' Honor murmured. 'That's a vintage Chevy.'

The door opened and the driver stepped out.

She was in her late thirties or early forties and would have been of average height but her heeled shoes added another three inches.

Her wide-brimmed hat was identical to the one worn by Ingrid Bergman in *Casablanca*, the colour exactly matching the brown of her flared woollen coat. In her gloved hands was a crocodile skin clutch bag. Rita Hayworth's face with perfectly plucked brows, red lipstick and a hint of rouge stared out at them.

'May I help you?' she said, forming her lips into what Dania suspected was a well-practised smile. The accent was Home Counties English.

'We're police,' Dania said, showing her warrant. 'Are you the owner?'

The woman frowned. 'Yes, I'm Valentine Montgomerie.'

'Valentine's an unusual name for a girl,' Honor said.

The woman smiled faintly, as if to indicate she'd heard this many times. 'I was born on February the fourteenth. But everyone calls me Val.'

The passenger door opened and another woman emerged. She was dressed in a red coat, with matching hat and gloves. The hat, worn at an angle, was in the style of a flat pillbox, and the stiff veil, which was dotted with tiny red hearts, came down over her chin. Her hair, the colour of dark honey, fell to her shoulders in the waved style known as a Victory Roll.

'This is my sister, Robyn,' Val said.

Robyn came forward, lifting the veil over her hat.

Seeing the women together, Dania detected little of a family resemblance. They were the same height, with creamy complexions enhanced by good-quality foundation. But, where confidence shone from Val's brown eyes, Robyn's green ones darted from one detective to the other.

'How do you do?' Robyn said, pulling off a soft kid glove and extending her hand. She had the same accent as her sister.

'DI Dania Gorska,' Dania said, taking the outstretched hand.

24

'This is DS Honor Randall.' She glanced at Val. 'We need to ask you a few questions.'

'In that case, you'd better come in.'

Val took a key from her bag and sprinted up the steps, giving the officers a view of shapely legs in seamed nylon stockings. Her perfume was an expensive blend of jasmine and sandalwood.

They followed the women into a spacious hallway.

One wall was covered with a detailed map of Dundee, glued to the plasterwork. On the opposite wall, a gilded mirror hung above a varnished table, next to which was an umbrella stand with a single tired umbrella. The mirror was wide enough that both Val and Robyn could stand side by side, remove their hatpins and take off their hats. Val's hair, slightly darker than her sister's, had been pinned up in a mass of curls that would have required time and patience. Dania thought of her own morning routine, which involved dragging a comb through her thick shaggy bob.

The women removed their coats and hung them up. They both wore patterned V-neck dresses, which swirled as they moved.

'The living room's through here,' Val said, opening a door to their right.

The large room was papered in dark green, giving the place a slightly gloomy air. The women had tried to dispel this by installing lamps with fringed shades. Given the absence of ceiling lighting, these would provide the only night-time illumination. Most of the furniture looked bought at auction, and some was spotted with woodworm. A pair of Chinese vases stood at either side of a dead fireplace, which, Dania guessed from the tattered paper fan in the grate and the modern radiators under the windows, would continue to remain dead. She also guessed that the sisters weren't readers: the floor-to-ceiling built-in shelving covering one wall was empty, apart from a lonely set of *Punch* in blue-cloth bindings. The strong scent of lemon polish suggested that whoever cleaned this room either had no sense of smell or simply didn't care.

Her gaze was drawn to the horn gramophone on the window table. Next to it was an old-fashioned Bakelite phone. Seeing the women in this room, she had the strangest sensation that she'd stepped back in time.

'Please make yourselves comfortable,' Val said, gesturing to the squashy sofas with their lace antimacassars. 'May I offer you some refreshment?'

Dania thought of the limp sandwiches Laurence had scrounged up for lunch, all she'd had since breakfast, but she guessed it was drink that was being offered. 'No, thank you.'

'You don't mind if we do? We've had a long drive and we always have whisky and splash when we come in.'

'Please go ahead.'

Val sashayed across to the mahogany sideboard and searched for the whisky among the decanters. After pouring two generous measures, she squirted some liquid from an ancient-looking soda siphon.

'Are you just back from a fancy-dress party, or something?' Honor said.

Val laughed lightly. 'No. Why do you ask?'

'Your clothes.'

'We always dress like this,' Robyn said.

'We just love the period, you see.' Val handed her sister a glass. 'The nineteen forties.'

'You mean you wear these sorts of clothes all the time?' Honor said incredulously.

'We do now we've moved up here. It was harder in London. We could only do it at weekends.' She glanced at her sister. 'We both worked in the City as investment bankers,' she added, taking a seat on the chaise longue. 'So, what can we help you ladies with?'

Dania opened her notebook. 'Earlier today, we uncovered human remains on your land.'

Val paused in the act of bringing the glass to her lips. Robyn sat bolt upright, her eyes wide.

'We found four graves. We don't yet know enough to treat the area as anything other than a crime scene.'

'How did you find them?' Val said, setting her glass on the table.

'The workers in the next farm kicked a ball into your grounds. One of them climbed over to fetch it. Somehow, his dog got in and started to dig.'

'And found the four graves?'

'He found two. The man called the police. We searched the grounds and found the others.'

Robyn was staring at the detectives with an expression of horror. 'Who are they? Were they murdered?'

'We can't say any more at this stage. You said you own Breek House. When did you buy it?'

Val pushed a curl off her forehead. 'It was last year. June. I can get the exact date for you, if you need it.'

'Who was the previous owner?'

'The local council.'

Dania exchanged a glance with Honor. What would the council be doing with an old house like this? 'And did the sale include the land?' she said.

'As far as the eye can see. In fact, we wouldn't have taken it without the land.'

'Why is that?'

'We want to get our plants in. We need to get our business up and running.'

'Did you move in straight away?'

'Pretty much. The house had been empty for ages, and we spent the first few months getting it shipshape. Some of it, anyway.'

27

'Have you any idea why the council owned it? And why they wanted to sell?'

'They wouldn't say. I had the impression from the agency handling the sale that they wanted to do something with the place. But they ran out of money and decided to sell what had become a white elephant.' Val took a gulp of whisky. 'The estate agent seemed to think the council had owned the place for decades, certainly as long as he'd been in business.'

Robyn was fidgeting. 'Inspector, you said this is now a crime scene. Does that mean we have to move out?'

'That won't be necessary,' Dania said, with a slight smile. 'Forensics went through the grave sites pretty thoroughly. The area is no longer locked down.'

'And where are these graves exactly?'

'I'm not sure we want to know, Robyn,' Val said firmly.

'You'll find them if you go looking,' Dania said. 'Although the tape has been taken down, you can see where the earth has been disturbed.' After a pause, she added, 'You mentioned you're starting a business. Is it something horticultural?'

'Gin is having a revival, so we're making and selling it. We've installed our still in what used to be the banqueting hall, according to the estate agent's blurb.' A look of amusement came into Val's eyes. 'I'd describe it more like a large dining room.'

'You're making gin?' Honor said.

'Perfectly legally. We can show you our distiller's licence and approval document. To begin with, we'll be buying in all the ingredients, but our aim is to cultivate the land and grow the botanicals ourselves.' She looked at Dania with interest. 'Do you drink gin, Inspector?'

'I don't, I'm afraid. I prefer vodka.'

'Maybe we can entice you away. What brand of vodka do you drink?'

'Żubrówka.'

'Ah, I know the one,' Val said, nodding. 'It's pale green, isn't it?'

'That's right.'

'Once we're up and running, you must let me show you our distillery.'

'I'd be very interested.'

'You, too, of course, Sergeant,' Val said, addressing Honor.

'Great.' Honor paused. 'Can I ask about the bars on your windows? Did you have them put in?'

'They came with the house. I've no idea why the council wanted them in. Why would you do that? To keep people out?'

'Or perhaps to keep people in,' Dania said, thinking of Jackson's comment about the care home.

'Like some sort of asylum?' Val shrugged. 'I suppose the remoteness of the place makes it ideal for that.'

Dania glanced enquiringly at Honor, then said, 'Well, I think that's all for now. We may have more questions as the investigation progresses.' They got to their feet.

Val opened her bag and took out a business card. 'This has our numbers,' she said, handing it to Dania.

'You're not planning to be away, I take it?' Dania said, giving Val her own card.

'The odd shopping trip. We'll be around otherwise.'

'Thank you for your time, Miss Montgomerie. We'll let ourselves out.'

As they left the house and strolled towards the Skoda, Dania said, in a low voice, 'Honor, can you do a background check on those women?'

'You think they might be involved?'

'Not necessarily with the graves. But there's something about them, especially the quiet one, Robyn. I've a gut feeling something's

29

going on there.' She glanced back, hearing the front door close. 'And if there's one thing I always do, it's to act on my gut feelings.'

At the living-room window, Val stood watching the car drive away.

'Do you think this will scupper our plans?' Robyn said. 'Bodies found on our land?'

Val took the packet of Lucky Strike from the window table and ran a finger over the red bullseye design. '"Lucky Strike means fine tobacco",' she murmured, taking out a cigarette and twisting it into a holder. 'Want one?' she said, turning to Robyn.

'No, thanks.'

She lit the Lucky with the Zippo lighter she'd bought on Covent Garden Market, and inhaled deeply, holding the smoke in her lungs before letting it out.

'So?' Robyn said. 'What do you think?'

'Too early to tell, darling.'

'But why would those bodies be there?'

'The remains may be ancient.'

'What if they're not?' Robyn closed her eyes briefly. 'What if they were buried on our land after we bought the place?'

'Don't get into a state over it,' Val said, going over to her. She lifted the woman's hair back and kissed her neck lightly. 'The police will tell us in due course.'

'Do you think the local council are responsible? Maybe one of them is a murderer.'

Val pulled on the cigarette, studying her. Of the two, Robyn had been the smarter when it came to playing the markets, and the money they'd made had gone into starting the gin business. They couldn't have done it otherwise, given that banks were unwilling to lend, these days. But Val knew she had the edge when it came to finding clients and handling them. She was better with people, and Robyn, recognising this, had more or less let her take the reins of the business. Val had even come up with the name: Ginspirations. They'd absorbed the tight regulations and Customs and Excise requirements with little difficulty, thanks to the consultant they'd engaged. With luck, they'd be in business in a matter of months, weeks even. The man had suggested they take on someone to help with the process of making the gin but, once they were up and running, they could manage everything themselves.

They'd been incredibly lucky with Breek House, getting the building and, more importantly, the land. But this discovery of buried bodies might well put a spanner in the works. On the other hand, the notoriety could work for them. The papers would mention Breek House and she would ensure that Ginspirations was always in there. All part of the marketing strategy, take every opportunity. But Val would have to keep an eye on Robyn's jitters. Especially in view of their situation. It wouldn't do for their secret to come out. They'd have to keep a lookout for people snooping in the grounds.

'I told you this house has an atmosphere,' Robyn said petulantly. 'Now I know why.'

Val pressed her cigarette into the ashtray. 'The last time you said that, you were convinced it had to do with the room at the back. You said it looked like a torture chamber.'

Robyn shuddered. 'Don't remind me. We've still got to decide what to do with it.'

'I thought we could store our bottles there.'

Robyn seemed undecided. At least her look of alarm had gone. 'Shall we listen to some music, darling? Take your mind off it?'

'How about Benny Goodman?' Robyn said brightly.

Val selected a vinyl disc from the collection under the table, placed it on the turntable and wound up the gramophone. The opening bars of Duke Ellington's 'In A Sentimental Mood' filled the room.

'Shall we?'

Robyn got eagerly to her feet.

Val put her arms round her and danced her about the room in a slow foxtrot. It would be all right. Whatever had happened in this house would be forgotten once the gin started to flow. And, with luck, no one would rake up what they'd left behind in London.

The music came to an end. Robyn lifted her head from Val's shoulder and gazed smilingly into her eyes.

CHAPTER 4

'Four corpses with their teeth missing? Sounds like a serial to me, right enough.'

The speaker, Detective Constable Hamish Downie, a sullen, newly arrived officer from Glasgow, was sitting slouched on the table. They were in one of the smaller rooms at West Bell Street while the main incident room was being refurbished with new hi-tech touchscreens. Until it was made ready, Dania and the team had to squeeze into a space usually reserved for interviews, which smelt of plastic. At least it had a window, even though it was painted shut.

'Technically, they're skeletons, not corpses,' Dania said. 'But the missing teeth may be our best clue,' she added, not wanting to discourage him.

He nodded acknowledgement, crossing his arms.

'Do you think they could be ancient graves and the teeth were pulled as part of a ritual?' Laurence said.

Dania ran a hand through her hair. 'As for ancient, it takes about two years for flesh to decompose completely underground, so all we know is that the remains have been in the ground at least that long. As for ritual . . .' she shrugged '. . . your guess is as good as mine.'

'About that, boss,' Honor said, jumping in. 'I checked with

33

Dundee's archaeological societies. TAFAC, that's Tayside and Fife Archaeological Committee, knows of no ancient graves in that part of Tayside. Historic Environment Scotland say the same.'

'What about the university? Do they have a school of archaeology?'

'Nope.'

'If the graves aren't ancient, then two years or more in the ground means that any vital clues will be long gone,' Hamish said.

'I'm afraid you're right. It's now down to CAHID.' Dania studied the map pinned to the whiteboard. All four graves were clearly marked. 'Let's assume the burials are recent. I'm wondering whether the location is significant.'

'Woodland in the middle of nowhere,' Honor said. 'Barbed wire that's easy to get under. Anyone digging those graves couldn't be seen from the house.'

'Yes, but then why weren't all four bodies buried together near the barbed wire? Two of them were found a distance away where there's proper fencing. If someone got in under the wire, why drag those bodies all that way?'

'Maybe enough time had passed after the first two,' Hamish said, after a pause, 'and the perp forgot where he'd buried them. It doesn't explain the distance from the barbed wire, right enough, but it might explain why they weren't all buried together.'

Dania pointed at him. 'Now *that's* a working theory,' she said, with enthusiasm.

The corner of his mouth lifted, which she suspected was what passed for a smile. He was a stocky, bald man, who looked as though he'd squeezed into the same size suit he'd worn as a teenager. She'd heard good things about his ability, although they made her wonder why, at forty-seven, he hadn't got beyond the rank of DC. Having the reputation of a killer whale might have had something to do with it, but he never showed her anything other than respect. And if he was good, she was keen to encourage him, regardless of personality, something she'd learnt on her inspector's course. She was aware of the attitude of Glasgow cops to their counterparts elsewhere, but Hamish didn't have it. He seemed keen to fit in, although the others, Honor particularly, had yet to treat him like one of their own, something Dania was hoping would happen soon. It wasn't clear why he'd come to this part of the world but, after a few discreet enquiries, she'd discovered he'd been born in Dundee and was so homesick for the place that he'd requested a transfer. She should have realised he was a Dundonian from the way he spoke, although she wasn't always good at differentiating between the various Scottish accents.

'What did you uncover about the Montgomerie sisters, Honor?'

'Laurence and I have been doing a bit of digging. They worked in Montgomerie Investment Bank in London. It's a boutique bank.'

'Which is what when it's out?' Hamish said.

'They're smaller banks that specialise. In this case, it's mining, oil and gas, but also cleantech.'

'*Montgomerie* Investment Bank?' Dania said. 'Did the sisters start up the company?'

'It was a Lucien Montgomerie. But he wound it up shortly before he died.'

'Presumably the Montgomerie girls are related to him.'

'I think it's a safe bet, boss. Anyway, the sisters made enough and wanted to start up their gin enterprise.'

'I doubt it'll make them the money they got in London,' Hamish said, scratching his neck.

Honor frowned. 'Maybe it's not about the money. When you've got enough, why not follow your dream? And, besides, they're into all that cool nineteen-forties shit. At the bank, they'd have to wear modern suits.'

'Interesting they wanted to follow their dream here and not in London,' Dania said. She put the cap back on her pen. 'Okay, until I've been to CAHID, there's not much more we can do. They said they'll be ready for me this afternoon.'

She watched the team file out, thinking not about her forthcoming meeting at Dundee University but about the Montgomerie women. Two sisters giving up banking to make gin. Nothing wrong with that, especially if, as Honor suggested, they were following their dream. And yet as Dania thought about her encounter with them, she was forced to the conclusion that there was more to the sisters than met the eye. Much more.

Dania's meeting wasn't until two p.m. After a rushed spicy meatball sandwich at Frankie & Benny's in the Overgate shopping centre, she made her way to the ground floor. In front of the curved windows and not far from the steps leading down to Costa Coffee, someone had placed a white lacquered baby grand.

Since moving out of her brother's flat in the New Year, she still hadn't got round to buying a piano. She'd found a shop on Castle Street, not far from the Caird Hall, which sold musical instruments as well as sheet music. Digital pianos and home keyboards were on the second floor and, if business was slow, the manager let her play. It was less than ideal, but if she didn't practise, her fingering went to pieces. It was just like going to the gym, she'd told Honor. Two days off and she was awful. As if the sound of a digital piano weren't awful enough.

But then she'd stumbled across the baby grand. To her amazement, it was a Steinway, which, for some inexplicable reason, had been painted a white-cream colour, then varnished. She asked around, but no one could tell her who'd put it there or why, but they reckoned anyone could tickle the ivories if they wanted to. She sat down, opened the lid, and played Scott Joplin's lively ragtime two-step, 'The Easy Winners'. The tone's dynamic range wasn't as good as that of a new piano but there was no comparison with the digital pianos in Castle Street. She was considering what else to play when she noticed that the general hubbub around her had tailed off. She glanced up to see shoppers standing with their mouths open.

A little boy who couldn't have been more than four disentangled his hand from his mother's and ran over. 'Play some more, play some more!' he commanded. Without waiting for an invitation, he climbed on to her lap and looked up at her expectantly. She'd played some more, peering over the child's head and hoping he wouldn't fall off. The Scott Joplin was followed by her own embellished rendition of 'The Teddy Bears' Picnic'. There were cheers and applause, and a couple of bystanders asked where they could leave the money.

Since then, she hadn't looked back. Whenever she had a rare half-day off, she'd learn a new piece here. Her technique was simple: at home, she spent days poring over the score and running the entire piece through her head until she knew the notes by heart. Only when she felt she was ready did she approach the Steinway. During those learning sessions, the Costa staff would supply her with endless cups of cappuccino.

After a time, she viewed playing the Steinway as entirely natural, and did chores, like shopping or cleaning the flat, in the evening when the Overgate was closed. After a couple of weeks, an article had appeared in the *Courier* about the mystery pianist who threw free concerts. The grainy photo showed her in profile, and a couple of follow-up articles appeared but, so far, her identity had remained a mystery. DCI Jackie Ireland, in a rare moment of humour, had drawn her attention to the articles with a wry smile, asking if she was thinking of a change of career. Dania had explained with a straight face that playing helped her think things through – in fact, some of her cases had been solved at that piano – and perhaps West Bell Street might consider installing one. Although the DCI looked sceptical, Dania's remark about letting her mind roam free as she played happened to be true. On those occasions, she would both surprise and dismay the listeners by stopping abruptly and hurrying away.

Now, she adjusted the stool and lifted back the piano lid. Before beginning, she gazed out of the window at the City Churches. The clouds parted, and sunlight touched the building, lightening the grey stone.

Her fingers needed a workout, and it had to be a piece that would exercise them all, especially the fifths, which on her were abnormally long. There were plenty of compositions that fitted the bill, but today it would be Liszt's Hungarian Rhapsody No. 2 in C sharp minor, a piece that, with its dark and dramatic opening, followed by the energetic *friska*, taxed even a virtuoso. In workout terms, this was the equivalent of a Shock and Awe high intensity, and she had still to play it without making mistakes although, given its whirlwind speed towards the end, only the most discerning listener would pick up the errors. That Liszt himself had had little difficulty playing it was down not only to his technical ability but also to the shape of his hands: his fingers were long and narrow and lacked their connective tissue. This allowed him to stretch his hands to span an unbelievable thirteen notes. In addition, his fingertips were more square than tapered, so he could grip the keys better than most. It irked many pianists, including herself, that he wrote pieces he could play relatively easily, but they couldn't.

To applause, which was louder than usual, she finished with the famous series of octaves, ascending and descending to cover almost the entire range of the keyboard. She smiled, nodding her appreciation, and got to her feet. A couple of shoppers approached, applauding.

As she chatted, she became aware of a man leaning against the wall, watching her. He was tall and fair-haired, with seductive blue eyes and an aristocratic appearance. His well-fitting navy suit and striped blue and white tie suggested he was a businessman, but she happened to know he was an investigative journalist. Seeing her glance in his direction, he smiled and clapped his hands soundlessly.

The shoppers drifted away.

He straightened and strolled across. 'Liszt?' He raised an eyebrow. 'I thought in public you only played Chopin,' he said in Polish.

'Hi, Marek,' she said, smiling.

'You played it without any mistakes, I see.'

'Actually, I made several. All in the second half.'

'Ah, well, I doubt anyone noticed.'

'Can I buy you a quick coffee and cake?'

'There are things a man won't do, Danka, and one is to take money from a woman. Especially his sister. His twin sister, at that.'

'It's hardly taking money. Anyway, the Costa staff usually let me have coffee for free.'

'I would love to, but I can't stay. It's Friday afternoon and I'm due in court. Come on, I'll walk along with you.'

Dundee Sheriff Court was next to the police station, which Dania had found unbelievably convenient. At the Met, she'd had to schlep halfway across London to attend court hearings.

'So what have you done wrong now?' she teased, as they left the Overgate.

'I'm testifying. It's a civil case, so it won't interest you. Maybe we could meet up afterwards for a drink.'

'I'm not sure I'll be free. I'll text you.' She lifted her face to the sun. 'By the way, I'm assuming you won't be out of town on your name day.' Like the majority of Poles, Marek didn't celebrate his birthday but, rather, his name day, which fell on 13 March. And it was a tradition that on those days each planned a celebration – the details of which were kept strictly secret – for the other. Although she could rein in her curiosity, delayed gratification wasn't something Marek had learnt when it came to name-day surprises. His question therefore was one she'd anticipated.

'So, are you going to tell me what we'll be doing?' he said eagerly.

'Absolutely not.'

They walked along West Marketgait and stopped at the junction leading to the court building, a fine golden sandstone affair, with pillars and a pediment, very different from the blue Lego box where she worked. West Bell Street might be a building with an uncompromising exterior, as befitted a police station, but it lacked the charm of the court house.

'This is me, I'm afraid,' he said. 'Call me when you're free, Danka.'

'I will.'

She watched him go, relieved he hadn't guessed that his name-day festivities were nowhere near the planning stage. And, with her workload, she was unlikely to find the time to organise the kind of celebration he deserved. But she'd have to be inventive. A meal in a restaurant simply wouldn't cut it.

Marek left the court building and headed westwards towards Perth Road. He was glad he'd run into Danka, and even more glad he'd managed to keep from her what had been preying on his mind since he'd returned to his flat on Union Place late the previous evening to find the lock broken.

It wasn't the first time he'd come home to a ransacked apartment and it was unlikely to be the last. The damage wasn't too bad: kitchen drawers emptied on to the floor, the contents of cupboards strewn everywhere, books thrown around and pictures slashed, although they hadn't touched the one of the Syrenka, Warsaw's sword-carrying mermaid, in his bedroom. As usual, there would be no forensic evidence so he didn't bother calling the police. What was the point? He knew who was behind this. Archie McLellan. And he knew why. Ned, a firm believer in the philosophy that one bad turn deserves another, had made good on his promise of having his brother 'get to him'. But by trashing his flat, he'd succeeded only in strengthening Marek's resolve.

He wondered if Archie himself had done this or whether he'd ordered one of his soldiers. The latter, more likely. Although Marek had never met the man, he'd heard enough to know he was someone to avoid. Even more so than his brother. When it came to the McLellan brothers, where Ned was a Jack Russell terrier Archie was a pit bull.

He hadn't bothered clearing up the mess. He'd made something to eat, turned the slashed mattress over and put new sheets on. And then gone to sleep. A friend at work had given him the name of a cheap, reliable locksmith the first time the lock had been broken. Marek had called the man after breakfast.

He'd finished his piece about benefit cheats the morning before and filed it with his editor. It would appear in the Saturday edition of the *Courier*. The thought gave him a sense of satisfaction that was almost palpable. When he got home, he would spend a couple of hours tidying the flat, then see if he could take Danka out for dinner. They didn't spend nearly enough time together now she'd moved into a place of her own.

He was approaching the Nisa Extra supermarket on the corner of Perth Road and Union Place when a white stretch limo with blackened windows drew up. The doors opened and two men got out. One had a tattoo in the shape of a black ace of spades on his face. The other had dyed dark hair gelled into spikes. Without seeming to care whether anyone saw them, they threw a blanket over Marek. He felt his arms grabbed on both sides. Then he was bundled into the car and pushed up against someone on the back seat. The smell of warm wool and expensive leather filled his nostrils. He started to drag the blanket off but froze when he felt something hard pressed against his groin.

'I wouldn't do that, son. Not if you want to keep your stones.' The voice was smooth. Marek was in no doubt that its owner meant every word.

'We're going for a ride, Gorski. A friend of mine wants a wee blether.'

CHAPTER 5

'Inspector Gorski?'

'Gorska,' Dania said automatically. She turned to see a tall man in a short-sleeved blue tunic hurrying towards her. He had warm brown eyes, a shy smile, and an open, honest face. She put him in his mid-thirties, young for a professor.

'Oh, I'm sorry, Inspector. I was expecting a man.' He hesitated. 'I'm Harry Lombard.'

'If you were expecting a man,' she said, wanting to put him at his ease, 'I hope I haven't disappointed you.'

His smile vanished and he stared at her, his mouth slightly open. She wondered if she had crumbs on her face. He seemed to remember himself then. 'You managed to find us all right?'

It was her first visit to the College of Life Sciences and, after trying to negotiate the rabbit warren around Dow Street, she had returned to the main road and asked a student for directions. But she wasn't going to tell him that. 'I walked along Perth Road and up Miller's Wynd,' she said. 'It was steep enough to give me my workout for the day.'

He chuckled. 'Next time let me know, and I'll arrange a car-parking spot for you. So, shall we make a start?'

'It's good of you to see me. You must be in the middle of teaching.'

'Indeed. But we always make time for the police.'

He made no attempt to move, and she was wondering what was odd about her appearance when he reached across and opened a door on her left. As she passed him, she caught his after-shave, a blend of medicinal and aromatic, but maybe it wasn't aftershave and all forensic anthropologists smelt like that.

Inside the low-ceilinged room were several trolleys. Although the strip lights provided adequate illumination, each trolley had a large Anglepoise clamped to one end. On the wall was a similar map to that pinned up in the station's incident room, showing the grounds of Breek House, the graves clearly marked.

Her gaze was drawn to the nearest trolley where a skeleton was laid out. The hands were rotated outwards, palms upwards and thumbs pointing away. She was struck by how clean the bones were: the last time she'd seen them, they'd been covered with soil and leaves.

'This is the skeleton found at Site A,' Professor Lombard said, nodding at the map. Site A was the location of the first grave. 'It's been arranged in the standard anatomical position. I was hoping to have all four sets laid out by now, but we've been terribly busy, and our main laboratory is being used for another case.' He ran a hand over his cropped black hair. 'I'm so sorry about that. As soon as we can, we'll get them all together. It will be easier to spot any differences.' He hesitated. 'I have another confession to make and it's that I haven't yet had a look at these remains. I had intended to do it before you arrived, but something came up.'

'So it wasn't you who arranged this skeleton?'

'One of my students. I'll make a preliminary examination now. You may find the process interesting.'

'Should I make notes?'

'No need, Inspector. I'll provide a written report in due course.' He pulled on a pair of blue gloves, smiling self-consciously.

He bent over the skeleton, studying it and frowning in concentration, giving her the opportunity to study him. He had toned, muscled arms. His tunic with the colourful University of Dundee crest was spotless, and she found herself wondering if someone at home looked after his clothes. No wedding ring, but that meant nothing. He could be married and not wear one. Or he could be married, wear one, and take it off at work. She smiled to herself. She really ought not to think like a detective the whole time.

'All the bones seem to be present,' he said, straightening, 'but I'll double-check the record.'

'And this is a man?'

'Indeed. An adult male.'

'How do you know? I'm genuinely interested,' she added quickly, in case he thought she was being cheeky. 'Think of me as one of your students.'

'All right. So, first of all, men's skulls are larger. But the best indicator is the pelvis. A woman's has evolved to create a larger space for childbirth and has a circular opening. A man's is narrower and more heart-shaped, like this one.'

'And how old was this man when he died?'

The professor's shyness evaporated as he continued his explanation. 'Teeth are by far the most accurate indicators but, as there were none found, we'll have to determine the age from the bones. Now, the growth process is complete at between seventeen and twenty-five years. By then, you're as tall as you're going to be.' He hesitated, and she guessed he was trying to avoid language that was too technical. 'When you're born, the ends of the long bones of the arms and legs are mainly cartilage. As you grow, the shafts get longer, and bone gradually replaces the cartilage. Therefore, looking at the shape of the ends of the different bones can help us estimate age. In this case, the man was older than twenty-five.'

'So to be more precise you have to look at other markers?'

He seemed pleased by her interest. 'A good indicator is the sagittal suture.' He bent over the skull, inviting her to join him. 'You see this squiggly line here? By age thirty-five, it's completely fused.'

'Like this one?'

'That's right. Now this line across the front of the skull is the coronal suture. It doesn't fuse fully until about age forty.'

She looked up, only then seeing how close his face was to hers. The strange thought came to her that, if she leant forward, she could kiss him. 'It looks completely fused to me,' she said. 'So he's older than forty?'

'And that means I'll need to examine the other bumps and grooves and compare them against a database of standard markers.' He straightened slowly. 'It will take time.'

She sensed he wanted to be left alone to get on with it, but she had more questions. 'What else can you tell from bones?'

'We can look at the mineral content. The isotopes give us an indication of diet. And bone is a great source of DNA.'

'What would be really helpful to know right now, Professor, is *when* this person died.'

He gazed at the skeleton. 'Bones are subject to continued decay after death so I can make an estimate. But, to be more precise, we'll need radiocarbon dating.'

She could see he wanted to wait and give her an accurate figure. 'Your best guess,' she said. 'I won't hold you to it. I just need a ballpark figure. Five years? Fifty years? Five hundred years?'

'The bone isn't flaky or crumbly, so not even fifty years. This man was put into the ground more recently than that.'

She let out a breath. These weren't ancient graves, then. 'Once I have the data, I'll be able to input it into our missing-persons database. It may give us some answers.'

'I suppose the absence of teeth suggests something horrible was going on.'

She knew she was pushing her luck, but she had to ask. 'Any chance of cause of death?'

'That's difficult when all you have are the bones.' He paused. 'But there's one thing you should know now. It may help your investigation. There are a number of fractures.'

'Fractures?' she said slowly. 'Where?'

'On the arms and legs.'

She stared at him. 'What kind of fractures?'

'Mainly hairline, but one that's deeper.' He indicated a region of the left leg. There was a significant crack in the bone.

'Could the dog have done it when he was digging?'

'I'm afraid not. There's evidence of healing. The body starts to do that within hours of a fracture. However, this man died before the bone could heal completely. I'll arrange for a CT scan at Ninewells. Then we'll have a clearer picture.'

'Thank you, Professor. Have you any idea when the full report will be ready? I suppose you must get that question all the time,' she added, with a sheepish smile.

He pulled off his gloves. 'Indeed. But I'll do my best to have something for you in a day or two. Shall I call you at home if I finish before Monday?'

She gave him her card. 'If you don't catch me at home, try West Bell Street.' She smiled. 'Like you, I often work weekends.'

Marek felt the car pull up, and heard the driver cut the engine. A second later, the heavy object placed against his crotch was removed. He was bundled out of the car and marched along what felt like a cobbled street before being pushed through a doorway so roughly that he stumbled against the side. The blanket was whipped off his head.

He blinked in the semi-darkness. From the smell of oil, he guessed he was in a garage but, before he had time to take in his surroundings, his arms were grabbed, he was pulled through an opening and dragged up a flight of steps.

'Through there,' one of his captors said gruffly, indicating the open door at the end of the corridor.

As his arms were held tightly, he had little choice but to comply.

The view through the picture window was of the Tay, the position of the bridge telling him that he was well east of his apartment on Union Place. The room shrieked of new money: showy furniture, tasteless prints on the wall and the sort of thick-piled carpet you could trip over. There was a cloying smell of bodies, as though the windows had never been opened.

The men released him. He made a show of brushing down his arms as if there were dirt on the sleeves. As he did so, he cast a glance around, scoping the room. An angular man in a pinstripe suit was lolling against the far wall, playing listlessly with his mobile. His glasses kept sliding down his long nose and he kept pushing them back. At one end of the red leather sofa, a youngish woman with unfeasibly large breasts, wearing tight black denims and pointy shoes, was sitting in a daze with the TV remote in her hand. She was watching one of the shopping channels. At the other end sat a great brute of a man in a Dundee United foot-ball strip. But it was the figure in the armchair by the window that drew Marek's attention.

He was watching the Pole with calculated interest in his eyes. It was hard to tell what sort of build he had because he was wearing baggy jeans and a cream-coloured zip-up cotton sweater that looked two sizes too big. His hands were large, like a butcher's. He had a puffy face and thick lips, and his hair was pure white and almost gone. He smiled then, the rubber lips stretching. Marek thought that, if he hadn't been slightly cross-eyed, which gave him an air of menace, he would have looked like somebody's grandfather.

'Mr Gorski, is it?' He was softly spoken, which somehow added to the air of menace.

'It is. But I'm sure you already know that.'

'Aye, I do. But I like to begin with the formalities.' His accent was Dundee, but not as strong as some Marek had heard.

'Well, I don't like being kidnapped and generally manhandled.'

At the word 'kidnapped', the woman looked up, startled. She wore the sort of make-up usually seen on fashion models.

'Angie,' the man said, 'why don't you take yourself off for a wee bit of retail therapy? There's a good girl.' He looked at the ape in the football strip.

That was all it took, a glance, and the man sprang to his feet and waited at attention. The woman switched off the TV, picked up her pink pebble-leather handbag and hobbled out of the room on high heels, the man following.

'Kidnapping is too strong a word, Mr Gorski. Bringing you here seemed the easiest way.' He cracked his knuckles. 'I somehow doubt you'd have come if I'd sent you an invitation.'

'And why is that?'

He frowned. 'You don't know who I am?'

Marek was tempted to say, 'I neither know nor care,' but his professional interest was piqued. 'I'm afraid I don't,' he said politely.

'I'm Archie McLellan.'

Marek tried to keep his expression unchanged, but he felt his throat constrict. Everyone in Dundee knew the name Archie McLellan, and what it stood for, but not everyone had set eyes on its owner. The man tended to keep out of the public eye and photos of him in the press were usually from a previous era. Marek tried to see the resemblance to Ned but found none, except perhaps in the roundness of the face. It said something about Archie's brass neck that he'd sent a limo for Marek that people stopped and gawped at.

'Was it you who trashed my apartment?' he said quietly, determined not to be intimidated.

Archie stared blankly. 'Your apartment, Mr Gorski? May I call you Marek, by the way?'

'Threats don't scare me off.' He held the stare. 'Quite the opposite.'

There was silence for a moment, then Archie stretched his lips into a broad smile. 'If your apartment's been burgled, laddie, it's nothing to do with me. Why would I do that?'

'You want me not to expose your brother's benefits scam. Well, it's too late. The article's coming out tomorrow.'

For a second, a look of genuine incomprehension crossed Archie's face, and it dawned on Marek that he might have made a mistake.

'Sorry, Marek. Not with you.'

'You didn't wreck my place because your brother told you I've been checking up on him?'

'I don't give a toss what my brother's been up to. We've never got on.'

'So it wasn't you?' Marek persisted.

Archie waved his hand as though bored with the conversation. 'Then why am I here?'

'I've a wee proposition for you.'

'Not interested.'

'Aye, but wait till you hear what it is.'

'If you think I'm going to give you the time of day, you're mistaken.'

'Try to control that hot Russian temper of yours, and just listen.'

'It's my hot Polish temper. I'll thank you to remember that.'

'Marek, Marek,' Archie said, laughing and shaking his head. 'I'm about to offer you something that will turn your life round. Ah, *now* you're interested.' He got to his feet and loped over to the drinks cabinet, scuffing the carpet with his white trainers.

He chose a bottle from the array on the cabinet. 'I thought we could get to know each other as professionals, so I've bought some proper vodka. Stolichnaya,' he added, mispronouncing it.

'I don't drink that Russian piss,' Marek said with disdain. 'I drink Polish vodka and nothing else.'

For an instant, Archie seemed at a loss. 'I thought all vodkas were the same.' He must have seen Marek's expression because he said quickly, 'Aye, all right. What about whisky, then?'

'It'll have to do. What have you got?'

'Balvenie.'

'Fine.'

'Ice?'

Marek shook his head.

Archie brought the glasses over. He set Marek's on the coffee table and resumed his seat in the armchair. 'I'm forgetting my manners, Marek. Please sit down.'

Marek perched on the edge of the sofa, trying not to look as though he were about to make a dash for it.

'*Slainte*,' Archie said, lifting his glass.

'*Na zdrowie.*'

Archie smiled as if he understood the Polish toast. Given the number of Poles in Dundee, perhaps he did. He settled himself, resting his head back. 'So what made you become a journalist?' he said, his gaze wandering lazily over Marek's body.

'I like the variety. Always different people. Always a different story.'

'You been successful?'

'I find that people open up to me.'

'I bet the lassies do.'

'Not especially.'

'A bonnie lad like you?' Archie grinned, showing misshapen teeth. 'Don't give me that.'

Marek had better things to do on a Friday evening than exchange pleasantries with Archie McLellan. He wondered if the scoop the man had hinted at would be worth his time.

As if guessing his thoughts, Archie said, 'I want to tell you a story. About my family. You'll find it interesting.'

Marek listened despite himself. He often found himself in this situation, unable to record a conversation or make notes. It was just as well he had an excellent memory.

'I come from simple farming stock,' Archie began. 'My father and his ancestors worked the land north of Dundee for generations. Aye, and they made a good living too.'

'But you're not a farmer.'

'I chose another path. Real estate. I manage a number of properties in and around Dundee.'

And a few other activities on the side, Marek thought.

Archie took a mouthful of whisky. 'I wasn't here when my dad passed away. It's one of my deepest regrets. Do you know how he died, Marek?' Without waiting for a reply, he said, 'He put his Parker Hale shotgun into his mouth and pulled the trigger.'

Marek paused, his glass halfway to his mouth.

'He was surrounded by the dark, you see. Completely. Couldn't find a way out of it. And no one could clear the dark for him.'

'What do you mean?'

'He had a mental disorder. Severe depression, you'd call it.' Archie gave his head a little shake. 'In the end, he lost interest in everything, the farm, the family, even having a blether and a few bevvies with the other farmers, something that had given him pleasure all his life. It started when he complained of pains across his body. Got checked out, but the doctors could find nothing physically wrong. Then he began to see and hear things. Visions. Ghosts of people he'd known.' Archie swirled the whisky round his glass. 'Our lovely cuddly NHS prescribed antidepressants. Worse than useless. My mother was tearing her hair out, trying to keep the farm going.'

'And did you help her?' Marek said, his tone a challenge.

Archie held the whisky to the light, examining the golden colour. 'When I was around, which wasn't often. Soon after I turned twenty, I was detained at Her Majesty's pleasure. It was then that my dad took his life.'

Marek was about to make one of those meaningless comments about being sorry when Archie said, 'The same happened to my uncle Keith.'

'He killed himself?' Marek said guardedly.

'He fell into the dark. Just like my dad. Same symptoms exactly. But Keith was cured. Aye, his dark was cleared.'

Marek was wondering where this was going when Archie said, 'After getting nowhere with the shrinks, he had a course of hypnotherapy.'

'On the NHS?'

'They said no. Gave the same old same old about not having enough scientific evidence to show it's worth the money. No, Keith had it privately. He came to see me after a few sessions. The difference in him was unbelievable. It was as if someone else had walked in, right enough. He was blethering away without pausing to draw breath, just like he used to. Still wasn't cured, but he was sticking with the treatment. The doctor said there was every chance he'd make a full recovery.'

'And how many more sessions did it take?'

'A few, over several weeks. But there was improvement after each one. I saw Keith just once after that first time. It was a couple of months later. We ran into each other in town. He said his treatment would be over in a wee while and, when it was done, he'd be retiring. He was sorting out the paperwork. After a lifetime of digging roads, he was taking his savings and backpack and going off to see the world, something he'd always had a mind to do. He intended to live out his days on a beach somewhere. I admired him for that. We said our goodbyes, and I wished him all the best.'

'And you want me to write a piece about hypnotherapy and all its benefits. Is that it?'

Archie shook his head. A look of what might have been panic crept into his eyes.

And, seeing his expression, Marek understood. A father and an uncle both showing the same symptoms, falling into the dark. Archie was terrified the same would happen to him. Perhaps the process had already begun. But why was he asking a journalist for help?

'I want you to find the man who cured him, Marek.'

'You want *me* to find him? Are you serious?'

'As serious as a heart attack.'

'Why?'

'Do I have to have a reason?'

'But why *me*?'

'Okay, I read your piece earlier this year. How you tracked down that arsewipe who interfered with children.'

'You didn't need to be Sherlock Holmes to do that. He'd more or less told everyone where he was going.'

'Aye, but it was when he flitted the second time that you found him. You succeeded where the polis failed.'

The case was one that had gripped Dundee. A football coach who molested children had escaped the police. He'd been pursued by Marek, who'd interviewed the man's girlfriend and learnt of their bolthole in the Highlands. There'd been no skill involved. Marek had simply been lucky. But, for a brief period, he'd been a minor celebrity.

'Have you thought of contacting your uncle? He may know of this hypnotherapist's whereabouts.'

'Och, Keith never was one for keeping in touch. I haven't a scooby where he is now. Or even if he's still alive.'

'What about hiring a private detective? They're much better at this sort of thing.'

The pinstripe leaning against the wall stopped playing with his mobile and glanced up. 'We've tried that, Mr Gorski. We bought the best that money can buy.' He came forward, giving Marek a better view of the lived-in suit, the tie hanging loose round his neck. He took a seat on the sofa. No offer to introduce himself. He looked like the family lawyer.

'I'm offering you a tidy sum, lad,' Archie said. 'Down payment in cash.'

'And if I fail to find him?'

'You can keep the down payment.' He rested his gaze on Marek. 'But you won't fail.'

'Can I think about it?'

'Aye, of course. I'm a reasonable man. Take as long as you need.'

'How will I get in touch with you?'

'Don't worry about that, laddie.' Archie smiled. '*We* know how to get in touch with *you*.'

CHAPTER 6

Marek lay on the sofa, going through his conversation with Archie McLellan. *You can keep the down payment. But you won't fail.* He knew little about Archie himself, but he did know of his reputation as a hard man who was none too soft on his enemies. Failure, therefore, was not an option. There was nothing for it but to get the details and press on with it. How hard could it be to find this hypnotherapy doctor?

He wondered if Danka could help him and, more to the point, would be prepared to. He tried not to get her involved in his investigations, although now and again they did each other small favours. But he was sure about one thing and that was that under no circumstances would he tell her it was Archie McLellan who'd given him this assignment. If the man was as bad as his reputation, his sister would put her energies into dissuading him. And certainly wouldn't help him. The sensible half of him told him to steer clear of the man. But the professional half told him otherwise. It wasn't the money, which might prove not to be as much as McLellan had hinted at, although, if it were, it would go some way towards the mortgage Marek was constantly thinking about. No, it was that by getting close to the man he might stumble upon the scoop of the century. His article about Ned McLellan was in the day's *Courier*. How much better would it be if he could follow it up with an article about the man's more in-famous brother?

It was early on Saturday afternoon and Dania was at her desk at West Bell Street when the phone rang. She listened carefully, then grabbed her jacket. Honor and Hamish, the other officers on shift, must have seen her expression because they sprang to their feet.

'What is it, boss?' Honor said.

'Someone's just reported a shooting.'

Shock registered on their faces. Shootings were uncommon in Dundee.

They hurried outside, and headed towards the response car, a blue and yellow Vauxhall Astra.

'So, where are we going?' Hamish said.

'Dock Street. Not far from the Holiday Inn. We can't miss it, according to the caller. What's the quickest way?'

'Nethergate and then Union Street,' he said, getting behind the wheel.

'Switch on the siren.'

The sun was past its peak, its light changing rapidly with the motion of the clouds. She was glad they were heading east. Heading west was a nightmare. The Perth-bound inside lane of Riverside Esplanade was closed until the following year while external cladding and landscaping were done at the Victoria & Albert Museum of Design. Tours of the new museum were planned for 1 April as part of Open Doors Week, but when she'd tried to get a ticket, she'd found the event sold out. The £1 billion waterfront regeneration had propelled Dundee up the tourist ratings. If this shooting was the first of many, the city would find itself relegated.

The multi-lane A991, a hassle to navigate at the best of times, had become a total misery because of the roadworks, and it was hard to believe that the area had once been teeming with inebriated sailors. Hamish seemed unfazed by the lane changes. Dania was impressed, as she found it difficult to keep her eye on the traffic while simultaneously reading the lane directions painted on the ground.

They saw the pale green façade of the Holiday Inn Express near the turnoff to the Tay Bridge.

'Doesn't take long for a crowd to start forming, does it?' Honor said sourly.

They scrambled out of the car. From the distance came the wail of sirens. Dania pushed her way through the onlookers and flashed her warrant card at the harassed-looking uniforms.

Lying in a heap on the pavement, his head resting against a tree, was a man in his twenties. He had sandy-blond hair, shaved close at the sides, and blue eyes that stared vacantly. His face was chalk white, as though powdered, in stark contrast to the blood darkening the pavement. But it was neither the spreading puddle nor the bloody hole in the leather jacket that drew Dania's gaze. It was the nail hammered into his forehead. A thin trail of blood had leaked on to the bridge of his nose.

'God Almighty,' Hamish said softly.

A seagull landed beside them and paddled its claws in the blood. She shooed it away, watching the droplets fall as it flew off. Something to warn Forensics about. 'Call it in, Honor,' she said. 'The works.' She glanced over her shoulder. The uniforms were having a hard time keeping people back. 'And find out if anyone in the crowd saw anything.'

The sirens grew louder. First to reach the scene was the photographer, a short jowly man with a permanent frown. Scenes-of-crime officers spilt out of the other vehicles, and the process of securing the scene began.

'We meet again, Inspector.'

'Professor,' she said, nodding at Jackson Delaney.

He bent over the victim. 'So, what have we here?'

'Someone rang the station, saying they'd heard shooting.'

'One bullet, from the looks of it. Straight into the heart.'

'At close range?'

'Hard to tell without checking for gunshot residue.' He signalled to the photographer, who set about capturing the scene with professional efficiency.

Minutes later, protective suits on, they knelt beside the body. The sharp coppery odour of blood was now so strong that you could taste it.

'Am I right in saying it's the gunshot that killed him, Professor?'

'You are. That nail was hammered in post-mortem. There'd be more blood otherwise. There's no rigor,' he added, feeling the victim's neck. 'He died within the hour.'

She thought the statement unnecessary, as the blood hadn't yet congealed, but Jackson was just being thorough.

The victim's jacket was zipped up to the chin. Jackson undid it carefully. The blue waistcoat and white shirt were stained red.

'Smart clothes to be wearing on a Saturday afternoon,' he said, indicating the black bow tie.

'Maybe he wore them on a Friday evening and he was just coming home.'

'And is *this* something you'd wear on a Friday evening?' Jackson said, pulling the jacket wide.

Tucked inside the waistband, only the matt-black handle showing, was a pistol.

'What's with the nail?' Hamish said. They were watching Jackson Delaney placing bags over the victim's head, hands and feet, prior to supervising the loading of the corpse into the mortuary van. The photographer was snapping away, recording the crime scene. Dania wondered how he'd landed this job. Not everyone had the stamina.

'He's called the Nailer,' Honor said. 'His signature is the nail through the forehead. Never heard of him in Glasgow?'

Hamish shook his head.

'Some of his tentacles spread that far.'

'Tell me about him.'

'Not someone to mess with. He went over to bad when he was still at school. Started out with tyre-slashing but he soon moved on. Convicted of premeditated murder when he was twenty. I'll spare you the details as I'm likely to lose my lunch. He was given a sentence that would have seen him leave prison an old man, but his conviction was overturned a few years later.'

'On what grounds?'

'It was found to be unsafe. Can't remember the details. My guess is his family found a fancy-schmancy lawyer. Anyway, he met some unsavoury types in prison and started his criminal empire.'

'In prison?'

'In prison.' She lowered her voice. 'He learnt how to handle himself, how to use a knife properly. The warders were terrified of him. His dad died while he was inside but he was allowed out to attend the funeral. If you look on the Internet, you'll find the photos. He helped carry the coffin, handcuffed to a police officer. When he came out, he hit the ground running and didn't look back. Some of his soldiers he met in prison, others at school.'

'Why haven't we put him back in prison?' Hamish said, frowning.

'It can be a bit tricky when you've no evidence. Don't forget that people like him are stepping further and further back into the shadows. Tying them to the crimes is a huge challenge. We

60

thought we'd nailed him – sorry about the pun – a while back, but a credit-card receipt as well as the shopkeeper's testimony put him in another city on the date of the crime.'

They all knew that anyone could have used the credit card and the shopkeeper's testimony could have been bought, but hard evidence of it was needed to convince a jury.

Hamish was picking at the scab on his knuckles. 'What's the nature of his empire? The usual?'

'He runs working girls. He deals class-A substances. Now and again he tries something new. Last year, it was credit-card skimming. It's never the same thing twice.'

'What does he do that's legit? Or appears to be?'

'He owns properties, which he launders his money through. He's opened a casino not far from here.'

'And the nail? Is he taunting us, or what?'

'He honed that skill in prison too. He doesn't do it to just anyone. It's intended as a warning. Anyone who's crossed him, or hasn't delivered, gets the treatment. Either before or after he's been killed, depending on how the Nailer's feeling that day. But, like everything else, we've never been able to tie him to it. And he's consistently denied he's ever done it.'

'Aye, okay, so he's known as the Nailer,' Hamish said, in exasperation, 'but what's his real name?'

It was Dania who spoke. 'His real name?' She looked into the distance, to where the clouds were massing beyond the Tay Bridge. 'Archie McLellan.'

CHAPTER 7

Jackson Delaney was in his office, mounting the X-ray images on the light box. As offices went, his was on the large side with room enough to accommodate several people, which Dania suspected was intentional since Ninewells was a teaching hospital. She'd expected the same antiseptic smell she'd encountered in similar offices and was pleasantly surprised by its absence.

From the effects in his pockets, they'd been able to establish that the victim of the Dock Street shooting the previous day was one Brodie Boyle, with an address on Lochee Road. Despite their best efforts, no next of kin had been found, and the procurator fiscal had authorised the post mortem without delay.

'We took these yesterday evening,' Jackson said, inviting Dania, Honor and the fiscal to step closer. 'There are no broken bones except the sternum. The point of entry was directly over the heart and the bullet ripped right through, taking bone with it.'

His mention of broken bones reminded Dania of what Harry Lombard had found on examining the first Breek House victim. And also that he hadn't phoned her. It was now late Sunday afternoon. Which meant that either he'd not yet made a start on the other three sets of remains, or the process was taking longer than expected. Probably the latter. Perhaps it was just as well. She now had something else to worry about.

'There was nothing under the fingernails, which were well manicured,' Jackson said. 'There's something else you'll find significant. We took swabs. The rectal indicated lubricant, recently applied. It suggests the victim had sex shortly before he died.'

Dania glanced at Honor, wondering if the girl was thinking the same, that this was the result of a lovers' tiff. Tempting to come to that conclusion, but the nail in the head, Archie McLellan's signature, suggested otherwise.

Jackson was studying the X-rays taken from the side. The nail was visible as a thick white streak. 'You can see the bullet track clearly on this one. The trajectory suggests he was standing when he was shot.'

'In the middle of a busy street,' the fiscal said, shaking her head. 'With bairns watching.' She was a slim woman with neatly cut dark hair. Dania had worked with her before and found her to be a no-nonsense but sympathetic woman.

'Shall we get gowned up? It'll be late by the time we finish. I do hope you ladies have had something to eat. I don't want you fainting.'

Dania wondered if he was being facetious. Few people ate before an autopsy for fear of throwing up. She was someone who could watch flesh being cut without it affecting her appetite. In fact, she'd managed a large pepperoni pizza before arriving at Ninewells.

They followed Jackson to the robing room where they pulled on aprons and overshoes.

The assistant, a worried-looking girl with fair hair wound round her head, was waiting for them in the main cutting room. They gathered round the table where a naked Brodie, eyes closed now, was lying as if asleep, his penis flaccid in his ginger-blond pubic hair. The loss of several litres of blood had given his mottled skin a pale bluish tinge. Dania gazed at the toned body. If it hadn't been for the wounds in his chest and forehead, he could have been a statue by Michelangelo.

'The victim is a white male in his late twenties,' Jackson said in the cadences of a public speaker. 'X-rays indicate that he has been shot once through the heart.' He pulled down the magnifying glass and bent low over the victim's chest. 'Come and look at this, Inspector,' he said, stepping back.

Dania peered through the lens at the star-shaped entry wound, with its radiating lacerations. It was neither clean nor neat, as the bullet had forced not only bone but fragments of leather and cloth into the flesh. 'I can see black fibres. And something else.'

'The bullet went through the mobile phone in his breast pocket. The glass is alkali-aluminosilicate. There are also bits of metal and plastic in the bullet track.'

The huge bloody tear in the back of the leather jacket had pointed to the bullet exiting the body. A lost bullet was the worst-case scenario, as they needed it to match it to a firearm. But they'd been in luck: a SOCO had found the projectile embedded in the trunk of the blood-spattered tree.

'What can you tell us about the nail?' the fiscal said.

'Only that there's no evidence of vital reaction round the wound. It means it was inflicted post-mortem.' He nodded at the assistant, who handed him a pair of pliers. After fastening the jaws on to the nail's head, he pulled it out with a sharp vertical tug. It looked surprisingly clean apart from one or two tiny gobs of pink-grey matter. Dania was impressed. The nail was at least two inches long and she doubted she'd have removed it as easily. Or as neatly. Perhaps Jackson was a dab hand at DIY. Then again, given he had perhaps seen Archie McLellan's handiwork before, he might be well practised. He dropped the nail into a metal dish.

'Okay, Lavinia, let's turn him over.'

A minute later, Brodie Boyle lay on his front. Dania was familiar with the concept of exit wounds, and how the bullet either expanding or tumbling on its axis results in an exit wound with greater diameter than an entry wound, but she was still surprised at the damage. After Lavinia had taken several photographs, she and Jackson turned Brodie on to his back.

Jackson took a scalpel from the instrument tray and made a T-shaped incision. He pulled back the flesh, revealing the shattered sternum.

Honor was clenching her teeth and staring at the ceiling. Everyone knew what was coming next. Dania didn't know which was worse, the electric Stryker saw, or the shears, which Jackson preferred, given the dust when a whirring blade slices into bone. With decisive movements, he cut through the ribs at the sides of the chest, then lifted out what was left of the sternum and attached ribs. As he laid them on the table beside Dania, a meaty stench filled the room.

'Now for the lungs. They look in good shape. Not a smoker, then.'

He lifted them out and placed them on a tray, which Lavinia took to the scales. She read out the weight.

'The left atrium and pulmonary artery have been severely damaged,' he said, peering into the chest cavity. He removed a piece of mashed flesh.

This wasn't Dania's first autopsy and she knew what to expect but, had she not known that the heart came next, she'd have been hard pressed to identify what Jackson was holding. The organ was so badly damaged that part of it had disintegrated. As he continued to work, he spoke quietly to Lavinia, who shifted between weighing the organs, note-taking and bringing over dishes and instruments.

Dania's thoughts drifted to her briefing of the evening before. The first twenty-four hours gave police the best chance of picking up a lead, so shifts had been reorganised and leave cancelled. Honor and the team had begun the process of knocking on doors and interviewing people. As the crime had taken place in broad daylight, they'd hoped to find credible witnesses but, since most people shopped in the city centre on a Saturday afternoon, only three people had seen anything. Fortunately for the police, they'd come forward.

'The liver is in good condition. Can you weigh it, please, Lavinia?'

The witness accounts had been remarkably similar. A young couple had been walking in an easterly direction when they'd heard a loud bang immediately behind them. They'd wheeled round in time to see the victim slump against the tree and slide to the ground. A figure leant over him and, a second later, straightened and ran past them, heading east. The third witness, a middle-aged woman, had seen everything, but from the other side of the street. It was she who'd reacted quickly and called West Bell Street.

'The stomach is almost empty. I'd say he hasn't eaten for nearly four hours.'

When asked for a description of the killer, the witnesses could say only that he was well built and wore white trainers, blue jeans and a shiny black parka with the hood up. And he was carrying a handgun. On that point, the accounts diverged: one witness placed the gun in the killer's gloved left hand while another swore it was in his right. The third witness hadn't seen the gun at all.

'I'm about to remove the intestines and irrigate them.'

None of the witnesses had seen the killer's face, but they all confirmed that he'd disappeared into Commercial Street. When pressed, they weren't even sure that it had been a man.

'The kidneys look normal. The tray, please, Lavinia.'

It had been nearly midnight before Dania sent her staff home, advising everyone to get a good night's sleep because the following day would require them to be at their sharpest. She'd lain in bed in her Victoria Road flat, making mental notes while listening to the hot-water pipes ticking behind the wall.

Jackson's voice, followed by the whine of the Stryker, woke Dania from her reverie. 'Now for the final part. You ladies still with me?'

He had pulled the scalp from the skull in two flaps, which hung front and back. She was tempted to lean forward and take a look at the sagittal suture, which for someone in their late twenties should be only partially fused, but decided this might be viewed as ghoulish behaviour. Especially since Honor and the fiscal were looking everywhere but at the corpse.

Jackson cut a neat cap in the skull. He examined the brain *in situ*, then reached in with a scalpel and made some sawing movements before lifting out the organ. He took it to a side table and examined it.

'The tox report will be a few days yet but, from what I've seen, he was a healthy young man.' He pulled off his gloves. 'Cause of death: single gunshot wound to the heart.'

And exactly what Dania had expected . . .

'Take a gander at this,' Kimmie said. 'You might have to adjust the focus.'

'Well, that's a fair bet. At this hour on a Monday, my eyes are pointing in different directions.' Dania squinted into the microscope. 'What am I looking at?'

'It's the slug that killed your bloke. Here, I'll get it up on the screen.'

Kimmie, the station's chief forensic scientist, tapped at her keyboard and transferred the image of the bullet to the large wall screen. The copper-coloured slug was distorted, but not so badly that a ballistics expert couldn't identify it. Fortunately for West Bell Street, Kimmie was such an expert.

A cheerful Australian, her expertise was wide-ranging, and Dania had often wondered what kept her in Dundee. After a couple of boozy, girly evenings at the station's local pub, Kimmie had confessed she'd come to Scotland to escape an abusive boyfriend. She'd worked in an almost entirely male environment in Canberra, and her man had begun to suspect that her long hours away from home weren't spent at work. A spell in hospital after a beating had convinced her she had to get away. Far away. And anywhere in Australia wouldn't be far enough. After laying a few false trails, she'd taken the next flight to Scotland, but it was a long time before she could sleep with her bedroom door unlocked, she'd told Dania after a few beers. And she still hadn't reached the stage where she'd let a man touch her, although she was slowly getting her confidence back. Dania was tempted to accelerate this process by engineering a meeting between Kimmie and Marek. With her blue-green eyes, creamy skin and dark curly hair, Kimmie was Marek's type. And maybe he was hers.

'It's a nine mil,' the girl was saying, 'the most common calibre for handguns. Also known as the nine by nineteen millimetre, or nine millimetre Parabellum. You know the saying, right? *Si vis pacem, para bellum.* If you want peace, prepare for war.'

'Yes, I've heard it,' Dania said, staring at the screen.

'And here's the jacket the SOCOs recovered from the crime scene.' Kimmie pressed a key and the image changed to a gold-coloured cartridge case. 'Rimless and slightly tapered. It's unmistakable. The nine mil is a popular calibre.'

'What's the recoil like?'

'Muzzle velocity is eleven hundred and twenty feet per second so the recoil is moderate. A woman would have no difficulty.'

'What else have you found?'

'First of all, no dabs on the cartridge case.'

'Our perp was careful.'

'Bit of a bummer. But here's the snag. There are no rifling marks on the slug. It means I can't specify the make and model of the firearm.'

'No marks at all?' Dania said slowly. 'How is that possible?'

'The barrel of the gun that fired this slug isn't grooved. My suspicion is that it's a converted replica. One that once fired blanks, and now fires live ammo.'

'The lack of rifling explains why he was shot at close range. The rounds wouldn't have fired in a straight line.'

'Spray and pray, huh? But it gets more interesting.' She gestured to Dania to follow her. '"Come into my parlour," said the spider to the fly.'

The adjacent room was Kimmie's workshop. It looked a mess, tables laden with lathes, drills and machine tools, but Dania knew that there was method in the girl's madness. On the far table lay a handgun. It had a matt-black handle and a silver barrel.

Kimmie took gloves from a box and handed Dania a pair. 'This is the gun that was in Brodie Boyle's waistband. It's a Zoraki Model 914.' She held it up, letting Dania see the words: ZORAKI-MOD .914. 'The only fingerprints on it are his. And they're on the handle and barrel. It's *also* a blank firer that's been converted.'

'How do blank firers work exactly?'

'Right, so most replica manufacturers place an obstruction in the barrel to prevent a solid object escaping. Just in case something goes wrong. Because the only thing that should escape is hot gas, which comes out through vents at the top or the sides. But here's the thing. *Some* replicas are made to vent from the front, and they don't have an obstruction in the barrel.' She turned the Zoraki over. 'This little beaut is one of those. It's made of zinc polymer, not the usual crap that blanks firers are made of, so it's ideal for conversion. And whoever converted it didn't bother rifling it.'

Dania had little direct experience of firearms. Her homicide cases in the Met had usually been beatings or knife crimes. But she knew that converted firearms are untraceable because the blank firers from which they're made are not subject to the same rules and regulations as real firearms. That includes the absence of serial numbers. The lack of rifling, which etches a bullet as it's expelled and creates unique ballistic marks, might just sink her investigation.

'What ammo does the Zoraki have in the magazine?'

'Also nine mil Parabellum.'

'Could the perp have killed the victim with it, then stuck it into the waistband?'

'I thought of that, but no. Not only is the magazine full, but a round has been chambered, and another round added to the magazine. That little trick gives you one extra shot.'

'So no point doing a test fire.'

'I'm relieved I don't have to. Replicas often don't work after a few uses. The barrels aren't made to withstand the pressure when a real bullet is fired. Some replicas even explode in your hand. Others are difficult to fire. And then, once you get them to go, you can't always stop them. But this Zoraki has never been fired.'

'Never? No gunshot residue in the barrel?'

'Or anywhere else. Even if the gun is cleaned, it leaves traces behind.' She looked at Dania quizzically. 'Why do you think the perp shot the bloke, then put the gun into his waistband before legging it? Why bother? It would slow him down, for one thing.'

'It's a possibility, that's all. But from the witness statements, I doubt he'd have had time to shoot Brodie, hammer the nail into his head, stick the gun into his waistband *and* zip up his jacket.'

'So, we have a converted replica in his waistband, and another converted replica that killed him. They may not work well, but they don't cost the big bikkies the real things do. And they're disposable and largely untraceable. All attractive features. I wonder how they're coming into Dundee.'

'How difficult is it to do? The conversion of a replica, I mean.'

Kimmie snorted. 'There are tutorials on YouTube. And the tools aren't hard to get hold of.' She glanced round the room. 'I could do it with what I have here. Easily.'

'Who manufactures Zorakis?'

'The Turks. But the cartridges loaded in your bloke's were made in Slovakia. The headstamp is ZVS. I won't attempt to pronounce it. And ZVS was also stamped on the cartridge that killed him.'

'Another link between the firearms.'

'I tested his jacket for GSR. The quantity and distribution of cordite suggests the gun was pressed against his chest. It means there'll be blowback. The spray coming back from the front of the victim is much finer than blood spatter, and you need a lamp to see it. If you find the perp and he hasn't had his jacket dry-cleaned, I'll find the blood.'

'If you need a lamp to see it, he may not realise his jacket's got blood on it. That could work for us.'

'And if he stopped to hammer in the nail, he may have stepped in the blood without noticing. Did you find any bloody footprints?'

Dania shook her head. 'Anything useful on the nail?'

'I've still to pick it up from Ninewells.' She paused. 'Do you think it's the Nailer? Has all the hallmarks.'

'Could be. But guns aren't his style.'

'Maybe he's pushing the envelope.' Her expression changed suddenly, and she laid a hand on the other woman's arm. 'Watch yourself, Dania.'

CHAPTER 8

'It's early and it's a Monday, so I've got you all something.' Dania set the Styrofoam tray on the table. 'Help yourselves.'

She'd bought the coffee and scones at the café opposite the Sheriff Court House. The owner, a stocky hulk of a man with a seamed face, whose name she'd discovered was Jock, had buttered the scones hastily. He usually made a start on her full Scottish and pot of builder's the instant she came through the door. On this particular day, she'd returned to the café after her session with Kimmie.

'Twice in the same day, lass?' He raised a bushy eyebrow. 'So, same again?' He said it with a straight face.

She'd collected the order, which she stressed was for her colleagues, and hurried to West Bell Street, ducking the spitting rain.

'Thanks, ma'am,' Hamish said, nodding appreciatively. He picked out the biggest scone. No two were the same, since Jock made them himself, not bothering to cut the dough but simply ripping it into scone-sized pieces. 'You not having one yourself?'

She smiled. 'I've already eaten.'

'So have I.'

Ah? Was that a grin? Maybe she'd found the secret to what made Hamish lighten up.

They were in the same makeshift incident room, and wall space was getting tight. Dania had been promised somewhere larger but so far there was no sign of it.

'Let's make a start,' she said. 'Where are we with house-to-house?'

'Still at square one, boss.' Honor licked the butter off her fingers. 'No one in the shops or restaurants on Dock Street saw anything. One or two heard the gunshot but thought it was a car backfiring. And there are no buildings on the other side of the street, just that wall with those arty photos.'

'We were lucky there were any witnesses at all. Has the DCI updated the press?'

'She did it yesterday morning.'

'Then we should brace ourselves for the calls to start coming in.'

'We got a photo of the victim from Passport Control. The posters are now up all over that area.' Hamish took a gulp of coffee. 'We also interviewed along Commercial Street, where the killer was last seen. No luck there. But someone rang in yesterday afternoon to say he saw a man in a black hoodie running into one of the street's side alleys. It's behind the Holiday Inn. Leads to Gellatly Street. Forensics went over the place but found nothing.'

'We need the CCTV trail to establish the killer's movements. Both before and after the shooting. Same goes for the victim. I want to know where Brodie was all of Saturday.'

'I'm on it, ma'am.'

'Is it worth looking at traffic cameras?' Honor picked up the last scone and examined it. 'The shooter may have driven into Dundee. If we're lucky we'll see him getting out of a car.'

'Good point. Thanks for volunteering,' Dania said, trying not to smile. When it came to donkey work, wading through traffic-cam footage was the task they liked least. 'Right, let's talk about Brodie Boyle. What do we know about him?'

'Lived on Lochee Road,' someone said. 'Just past Dudhope Park.'

Dania knew the park with its steep slopes and white-walled castle, one of Dundee's many green places, because she and Marek had once played tennis there. 'Did he live alone?'

'Seems that way. Only one set of everything in the bathroom. Nothing fancy in the way of furnishings. There was one thing, though. He had more of the same clothes he was wearing on Saturday. Dark trousers, white shirts, and a couple of those blue waistcoats.'

'About that, boss,' Honor said. 'There was nothing in his flat to tell us where he worked, but he could have been a waiter.'

'It's worth checking the bars and eating houses. What about visitors?'

'His landlady never saw him bring anyone home. He was out nearly every evening.'

'Any progress on his mobile?'

'Laurence is still on it with Tech, but it's not looking good. My guess is the mobile's a write-off.' The girl popped the last of the scone into her mouth. 'And we've still to hear from his bank. That's the problem with weekend crimes.'

Dania rubbed her face. 'Okay, my turn now.' Briefly, she told them what she'd learnt from Kimmie. 'I know very little about converted firearms,' she finished.

'They're used in military training,' Hamish said. 'Or bought by gun collectors. They're not such a big thing in the US as you can buy the real item in any corner shop. But in the UK we've seen a steady rise in converted firearms since real firearms were banned in nineteen ninety-seven. Most of the ones used by criminals here are converted replicas, right enough.'

They looked at him in silence.

'I saw many in my time in Glasgow,' he said, with a crooked smile. 'One of the syndicates started buying in replicas from Lithuania at typically two hundred pounds each. The conversions went for about two thousand apiece. Sometimes more. They sold them all over Scotland. We shut the syndicate down, but there are others.' His expression hardened. 'If converted replicas are coming into Dundee, we've bought ourselves some trouble, and no mistake.'

'We need to find out why Brodie Boyle had one in his belt. And that means finding out everything we can about him.'

Honor brushed the crumbs off her jacket. 'You think the Nailer's started up another of his little enterprises?'

'Aye, and maybe Brodie was in on it,' Hamish added. 'Or he stumbled across the scam and decided to steal a piece and sell it himself. Double-crossing the Nailer would account for what we found in the lad's forehead.'

'There's one way to get some answers. We could ask the man.' Dania glanced at her watch. 'Now's as good a time as any.'

'I'll come with you, ma'am,' Hamish said, springing to his feet.

'I need you all to get on with your own investigations.'

'But he's Archie McLellan, boss,' Honor said, letting the words drift.

'And I'm a police officer.' She saw their stares. 'All I'm going to do is ask him a few questions. Politely.'

They looked at her as though she came from Mars.

Donnan's casino nightclub was further along Dock Street, not far from Candle Lane. There was no flashy sign above the entrance, but Dania knew it was the right place because the word 'Donnan's' was etched into the polished brass wall plaque. At eleven a.m. on a Monday, it wasn't open for business, but when she tried the wide revolving doors she found them unlocked.

To her right was a low counter and cloakroom. A couple of men in the same blue waistcoats worn by Brodie Boyle were loitering in the short hallway, the taller resting his backside against the counter. As Dania came inside, he stepped forward, smiling.

'You're a bit early,' he said, with a nasal drawl. He gestured to the large door at the end of the hall. 'Please go through. Mr McLellan won't be long.'

Early for what? Dania wondered. No matter. She was about to find out.

The door opened on to an empty room, all mirrors and lights and stylish blue furniture. Her eye was drawn to the low platform and microphone. And the black-lacquered grand piano, its lid open. She sauntered across and ran her fingers lightly over the keys.

'I can't tell if it's in tune,' a soft voice behind her said. 'I'm tone deaf.'

She turned to see a heavy, broad-shouldered man, with a round face and wispy white hair. He was standing by the side door, leaning against the wall. His clothes were smart: a charcoal-coloured tailored suit and a blue silk tie. She recognised Archie McLellan from a recent photograph, having done a search of the police databases.

'You're here for the audition, I take it? It's not till twelve. And I had hoped you'd be wearing something other than a dark trouser suit. But you're here now. So please play something.' He spoke as if he'd been rehearsing each line. His accent was local, with the *i* sounding like *eh*. 'Hold on,' he added, 'I'd like to watch you play.' He came forward and eased his bulk into a chair.

She was about to pull out her warrant card, but something made her go along with it. She sat at the piano and adjusted the

76

stool. A few moments later, she brought her hands down on the keys. The piece she played was Paderewski's Caprice-Valse Op. 10 No. 5. A lively, challenging piece, it covered most of the keyboard and told her immediately that not only was the piano in tune it had a delightfully soft, mellow tone.

'It's fine,' she said, looking up. 'It doesn't need tuning.'

Archie McLellan had been joined by a man with an ace of spades tattooed on his face. He was standing behind his master, frowning under thick, dark eyebrows.

'Is that the sort of thing you usually play?' Archie said.

'Pretty much.'

'Who wrote it?'

'Paderewski. It's from his Album de Mai.'

'Paderewski? Who was he, then?'

'He was many things – a composer, a pianist, a politician. He became prime minister of Poland.'

'Your accent's Polish.'

'That's right.'

He settled back. 'Play some more. Something sad. I'm feeling sad today.'

She studied the keyboard. It would have to be Chopin's Nocturne No. 20 in C sharp minor. *Lento con gran espressione*. A dreamily romantic composition, she played it more slowly than usual, making it last nearly four and a half minutes. It was a piece that occupied a special place in the heart of most Poles as it had been played in the last live broadcast for Polish Radio on 23 September 1939, while the Germans were bombing Warsaw. It was played again when the station reopened in 1945.

She finished, lingering on the final chord, which Chopin had written in a major key. Archie was slumped in the chair, a hand over his eyes. He lifted his head, and a pained expression appeared on his face. He seemed suddenly to shrink.

'If you're needing a job, lass,' he said quietly, 'you can do better than be a nightclub pianist.'

'Actually, Mr McLellan, I've got a job.' She drew out her warrant card. 'DI Dania Gorska. Specialist Crime Division at West Bell Street. I'm here to ask you a few questions.'

He got slowly to his feet, frowning. 'You're a DI?' he said, ignoring the card. 'And you play like that?'

'It's a hobby.' She nodded at the piano. 'That's a beautiful instrument. You were lucky to find it. Not all Yamahas sound like that.'

He stared at her. 'May I offer you coffee? Or something livelier?'

'Thank you, but no.'

'You can leave us, Col,' he said, without turning round.

The man with the tattoo sloped out of the room.

'Aye, DI Gorska, you said?' He hesitated. 'I saw your husband's article about benefit cheats in the *Courier*. A cracking wee piece. He writes almost as well as you play.'

She opened her notebook. 'He's my brother, not my husband.'

'Well, if you want to ask me some questions, we'd better make ourselves comfortable. Please,' he said, indicating the vacant chair at the table. He waited until she'd sat down before resuming his seat.

'Mr McLellan, I'm here about Brodie Boyle.'

'Aye, I read about it.' The pained expression again. 'Awfy business. Shot, the newspapers are saying.' He shook his head. 'I hope he died quick.'

'How well did you know him?'

'What makes you think I knew him?'

'He worked here.'

'And you know this how?'

'He was wearing the same blue waistcoat as the men in the corridor. I'm assuming it's the house colour,' she added, glancing at the tabletop.

Archie inclined his head, as if to acknowledge the point. 'Blue was my father's favourite colour. I named this casino after him.'

'How long had you known Brodie Boyle?'

'Only since he started working here.'

'And that was when?'

'Shortly after the place opened.' He paused, as if thinking. 'That would have been six weeks ago, right enough.'

'What sort of a person was he?'

'I didn't know him well enough to say. He was punctual, I give him that.'

'Do you know if he had any enemies?'

'I don't even know if he had any friends, Inspector. I saw him only at work.' His expression lightened. 'I mind now that I did see him once with a gym bag. The logo was from that place in Gallagher Retail Park. I reckon that's where he spent the rest of his time.'

'Why do you think that?'

'He had a good body on him. All my boys do. And my girls. I have certain standards.' Archie shrugged. 'I mentioned the gym because you asked about friends, and he might have made some there. Now there's something I'd like to ask you, Inspector.'

'Go ahead.'

'The press release said he'd been shot. Do you know what kind of weapon it was? The make?'

The DCI had been careful not to say anything more than the witnesses had told the police: the victim had been shot, a nail hammered into his head, and the killer had legged it. 'I can't tell you which make it was,' Dania said. 'Why do you ask?'

'Gun crime is rare in this part of the world.'

'Do you own a gun, Mr McLellan?'

He hesitated. 'Why would I?'

'Do you happen to know if Brodie owned one?'

79

'Brodie?' he said, widening his eyes. 'He wasn't that kind of lad.'

'You told me you didn't know him well,' she said, watching him. 'How do you know what kind of lad he was?'

'I'm good at reading people. With Brodie, there was an innocence about him.' His eyes took on a faraway look. 'He had that soft Irish lilt to his speech.'

'And where were you on Saturday, Mr McLellan? At two p.m.?'

'I was at home, Inspector.' He nodded at the ceiling. 'I live above the casino.'

'Were you alone?'

'Aye, I was.'

'And you were at home until when?'

'Until it was time to open the casino. That would have been six p.m.'

'Can anyone corroborate that? Did anyone come to visit you?'

'No one. I was alone the entire morning and afternoon. I had a long nap. I find I need them, these days.'

It was only minutes from Donnan's to where Brodie had been murdered. That and the nail in his forehead made Archie McLellan the prime suspect. Yet, this man, who had spent a lifetime fabricating alibis, was freely admitting to not having one. Yes, there was nothing to place him at the scene of the crime, but there was nothing not to place him there either, and he'd know that.

She gestured to the side door. 'Is that the way up to your apartment, Mr McLellan?'

'Aye. There's also a way in from the Lane. Means I don't have to go through the casino.'

'Candle Lane?'

'That's it.' He smiled. 'Would you like a wee look around?' he said, in a helpful tone.

'I would, if you don't mind.'

'I don't mind at all.' He got to his feet.

The side door opened on to a corridor with a flight of stairs immediately to the left. He stood back, letting her pass in front of him. It was a strange sensation, walking up the steps knowing that Archie McLellan was behind her. But, so far, he'd been courteous. And helpful. A million miles from his reputation as a thug and a killer. Yet she'd be a fool if she didn't keep in mind what sort of man he was.

She stopped at the first-floor landing.

'That's the living room,' he said, motioning to the door on the left. 'And down there, on the right, you can see the stairs leading back down to the corridor. At the bottom, there's a door. You can get out to Candle Lane that way.'

'And who has keys to that door?'

'Only myself, Inspector. Keys and keycode.' His gaze held hers and then he said, 'Are you sure I can't offer you a wee bevvy now you're here? I know Poles don't drink Russian vodka but I have a fine Balvenie.'

'I'm afraid I'm on duty.'

'Och, well, another time, then.' He paused. 'Perhaps you could give me some advice. We get Poles coming to the casino and I'd like to offer them a good brand of vodka. Could you recommend one?'

'You can't go wrong with Wyborowa. It's a *czysta*, a clear vodka. You'll find it in supermarkets. My advice would be to keep it in the freezer.'

'Thank you.'

She was turning to go when he said, 'It's not far from this place to where Brodie was shot.'

'That's correct.'

'You think the killer came from here?'

'It's possible.'

'Is that why you've come, Inspector?' He didn't wait for a

reply before adding, 'But it's only me you're interviewing. Now why is that?'

She was conscious she was alone with this man and could disappear without trace. Archie would tell her colleagues that, yes, she'd come to interview him, but had then left. She looked directly at him and said, 'There was a nail hammered into Brodie's forehead.'

'And, because of the name some people have given me, you think I did it.'

'Did you?'

'I didn't. I've never done it. I don't know how I got that reputation.' The silence lengthened. 'I understand you're involved in another case, Inspector. The bodies at Breek House.'

She wondered how he knew, but then remembered that her name had been in the evening paper. 'I am. But we found bones, not bodies.'

'Have you been able to tell how long they've been there?' he said slowly.

'Not yet. Forensic examinations take time.'

He nodded, his expression suggesting he didn't believe her.

'Why the interest, Mr McLellan?'

'As someone who lives in this fine city, of course I'm interested if there's any foul play going on.'

She wondered if he was being facetious, but his face was without expression. Apart from being moved when she'd played Chopin, he'd been skilful in masking his emotions.

'Is there anything else you'd like to ask me, Inspector? It's just that the lassies will be arriving for the audition. I'm looking for a piano player, you see.'

'Nothing for the moment. But I may have further questions.'

'Aye, well, you know where to find me.' He touched her elbow lightly. 'And do please visit Donnan's. You'd be most welcome.'

'I might do that.'

'I run the place myself, so I'm around most of the time. Needs must when the devil drives.'

She nodded, not quite getting the gist.

He followed her down the far set of stairs to the ground floor. As they passed an open door, the sounds of quarrelling came from within. Two men were arguing loudly. Dania glanced inside, seeing a room with a desk and black leather swivel chair, a large filing cabinet and a corner table, with an expensive-looking PC. There was no window; the illumination was provided by two bright strip lights. The man with the ace-of-spades tattoo was pushing someone in black and orange football clothes against the wall, knocking over the industrial-strength air cooler. Archie strode in. The effect was transformational. The men stopped and stood to attention.

'Boys, remember your manners,' he said sharply. He threw Dania an embarrassed grin. 'We have a guest in the house.'

The men glared at her. The one with the football strip let his gaze slide down her body.

Archie left the office, closing the door loudly as if to signify that the rumpus was nothing to do with him. Without another word, he escorted Dania back through the nightclub and into the corridor. A group of girls in short cocktail dresses were chatting to the men in waistcoats.

He stopped at the entrance. 'It's been a pleasure, Inspector. I wish you luck in your investigations. Ah, I see the sun's coming out.'

'I have one final question, Mr McLellan. Why were you feeling sad earlier?'

He replied without hesitating: 'Because I'll have difficulty replacing Brodie. The lad was quality. Aye, he was my best croupier.'

★ ★ ★

Dania left Donnan's wondering what, if anything, she'd learnt. Okay, so Archie had no alibi but, if it came to it, he would rustle up someone who'd testify he was in the apartment and had never left it all afternoon. But wouldn't Archie already have set this up? Wouldn't he have been expecting an early visit from the police? It made no sense.

She glanced back through the revolving doors, seeing him lurch down the corridor, the girls following. But the visit hadn't been a complete waste of time: she had the name of the gym Brodie attended. First, though, there was something she needed to do.

The caller to the station had reported a man in a black hoodie running into the alley behind the Holiday Inn Express. The hotel was a short walk away. And the rain had exhausted itself.

The alley directly behind the hotel connected Commercial and Gellatly streets. If the man in the black hoodie was Brodie's killer, where would he have disappeared to on reaching Gellatly Street? She imagined she was the shooter, and walked the short distance down the alley, re-emerging on Gellatly Street's pavement. A lorry was parked on double yellow lines, the men emptying the bins clustered behind the hotel. Gellatly was one of those streets that led up to Seagate, one of Dundee's main shopping streets, and it was more than likely that the killer had legged it there and lost himself in the shops. The CCTV started at the car park opposite the Oriental supermarket so, if he had taken that route, they'd find him. But could he have disappeared into one of the nearby build-ings? That would be the smart move. She made a mental note to have her team knock on a few more doors.

She was about to head up Gellatly Street when she remem-bered that Candle Lane was the next street along.

The two concrete bollards at the entrance to the lane said it all – this wasn't a place to enter unless you had business. It was gloomy and chilly, with mould darkening the narrow pavements, and it was hard to believe that there had once been a thriving candle-making workshop here. The double yellow lines on both sides were something of a joke, as the bollards made it impossible for anything other than a bicycle or pushchair to enter. A short way along on the left was the back of Donnan's. The sturdy door was fitted with a keycode entry system.

She squinted through the tiny window, seeing little through the grime. Was it a garage? It would be impossible to manoeuvre a car through the narrow door, although there was evidence there had once been a wider entrance. What was this place Archie sometimes went through to get to his casino?

She walked slowly back to West Bell Street, deep in thought.

CHAPTER 9

'We'll never get a search warrant,' DCI Jackie Ireland said, frowning. When she was angry, her west-coast accent became more pronounced. 'We tried it before when we found victims with nails in their heads, and the fiscal made it abundantly clear that, unless there's firm evidence, we're not to do it again. McLellan threatened to sue last time. And I've no doubt he'll make good on it.'

'He has no alibi,' Dania said.

'Neither has most of Dundee.'

She tamped down her irritation. 'I know he's guilty.'

'What we know and what we can prove are two different things. I don't need to tell you that.' Her expression changed. 'Aye, we know fine well that he did it, Dania.' She leant forward, her pen raised. 'I understand your frustration. But your job is to find some hard evidence. And then we can put the fucker away for good.'

Dania had never heard the DCI swear, and the surprise must have shown on her face because the woman looked away. She'd have had her own meeting with the super, who would have said much the same. Only even more colourfully.

Dania was just getting to know her superior. As bosses went, she'd experienced worse. Jackie Ireland's reputation as an obnoxious cow had been honed in the military and had followed her to the force, although Dania had seen little evidence of it, finding the woman's even-handedness a refreshing contrast to what she'd experienced in the Met. Her blonde hair, turning grey, was swept back off her face in a short, elegant style. She had that classic Helen Mirren-like beauty that must have done her no favours as a lieutenant colonel. But when she spoke to the press, turning her laconic smile and china-blue gaze on the assembly, no one dared interrupt her.

'What did you make of McLellan, Dania?'

'He wasn't exactly charming, but he was perfectly polite. And he didn't duck my questions.' She hesitated. 'He asked about the Breek House investigation.'

'I'm surprised the public haven't forgotten all about that. Brodie Boyle seems to be the only show in town. What do you think the motive is for his murder?'

'It must have something to do with the firearm.'

'Aye, so that's where you concentrate your effort. In the absence of evidence, the motive is the key.'

Dania left the office, her thoughts spooling in her mind. The team were either out or at their desks, hammering their computers. She felt wrung out. Having worked through the weekend, what she needed was a good dollop of R and R.

She pulled out her phone.

'And how long will you be staying, madam?' the girl said, with a vacant smile. She had long auburn hair and looked new in the job.

'Just the one night.' Dania was tempted to add that it would be only for the afternoon, but the last time she'd said that, the receptionist had taken her for a prostitute.

'You've stayed with us before?' the girl said, frowning into her computer screen.

'Dania Gorska.'

'Ah, yes.' She glanced up. 'The usual suite?'

'If it's available.'

'It is.'

'I'll be joined by a gentleman. He should be arriving within the hour.'

'No problem.'

'And could you send up a bucket of ice and some champagne?'

'Of course.' She scrolled down. 'I see you have an account with us. Do you wish me to charge everything to it?'

'Please.'

The girl tapped briskly, then handed Dania a keycard. 'Your room key, Miss Gorska. I take it you know the way?'

'I do.'

Inside the lift, she pressed the button for the top floor, humming softly to herself. The mechanism was so smooth that she almost didn't feel the slight increase in heaviness.

The suite was as she remembered: a spotless cream-walled room hung with oil paintings and furnished with heavy Victorian pieces, the air scented from the roses on the table. Each room was different, or so she'd been told, but she always took this suite because of the stunning view. She strolled across to the window. The gardens were arguably the hotel's best feature, as the first owner had landscaped the area, building gazebos and fountains and even a maze. The watery sun broke through the clouds, casting faint shadows on to the grass.

She'd chosen this hotel near Invergowrie as it was reachable from Kingsway West, the northerly part of the A-road that ringed Dundee. Fortunately, the man she was about to meet had a car, although when they met here he came by taxi. The idea to use the hotel had been his and, she had to admit, the location was ideal: it was off the beaten track and none of her colleagues knew about it. Which was as it should be.

There was a soft knock at the door.

'Come in,' she said, raising her voice.

The door opened and an elderly, sunken-cheeked man shuffled in, wheeling a trolley.

'Thank you. Could you put it over there, please?' she said, indicating the alcove by the bay window.

'Yes, madam.'

She slipped him a generous tip. He smiled hesitantly before closing the door behind him.

She threw off her shoes, plumped up the pillows and lay on the four-poster bed.

Half an hour later, there was another knock, loud and confident.

She sprang to her feet and opened the door.

'Hello, Quinn,' she said, smiling at the tall, well-built man in the dark suit.

He smiled back. 'Dania.'

Before closing and locking the door, she hung the 'Do Not Disturb' sign on the handle.

He stood at the window, hands in his pockets, watching her. 'It's been a while,' he said. 'Too long.'

'Champagne?'

'Why not?' He picked up the bottle and, with the thumb of the same hand, teased off the cork slowly enough not to lose any of the liquid. It was a trick she'd tried but hadn't mastered, despite her strong fingers. He poured two generous measures. 'What shall we drink to?' he said, handing her a glass.

She looked into his dark, hooded eyes. 'A successful afternoon?'

'And a successful outcome,' he added, with a roguish smile.

She laughed. 'Always that.'

She sipped slowly, wondering if he had any idea what was in store for him. Probably not.

He glanced at the bed, crumpled from where she'd been lying. 'So,' he said, loosening his pink tie, 'shall we get down to business?'

She motioned to the armchair.

They sat for a while, drinking, and then she said, 'You were a croupier in London, I understand.'

'That's right.'

'Were you good?'

'The best.' He smiled disarmingly. 'If I say so myself.'

'I need you to go undercover. Do you know Donnan's night-club?'

'The new place on Dock Street?'

'That's the one.'

'Hold on. It's Archie McLellan's.' They looked at each other for a long moment. 'I can't do it,' he said finally.

'Why not?'

'Because I can feel myself dying.'

She tried to keep the pleading out of her voice. 'You're my best informant. If anyone can do it, you can.'

He put the glass down. 'All right if I smoke?'

'Of course.'

He took a packet of cigarettes out of his pocket. The design with the two-headed eagle told her these were what he always smoked: Black Russian Sobranie. He opened the pack and shook out a gold-tipped black cigarette. She watched the familiar movements, how he flicked a match with his thumbnail and bent his head to the flare. His dark hair, always superbly cut, faded behind the cloud of smoke.

She said what she always said when she saw him smoking. 'Those things are going to kill you one day.'

He smiled as though at some private joke. After dragging on the cigarette, he said, 'What do you need me to do? I'm not promising,' he added quickly.

'I'll give it to you straight, Quinn. The man shot on Saturday worked at Donnan's. He was a croupier. There's now a vacancy, although there might not be one for long.'

'And you want me to apply?'

'Nothing's been advertised yet. What you'll do is go in asking if there are jobs of any kind because you're out of work. You'll add you've worked in casino nightclubs before. They'll ask what you did. You'll say you worked as a croupier.'

He narrowed his eyes against the smoke. 'You've thought this through.'

She inclined her head.

'Okay, so what do I do once I'm in?'

'I want you to be my eyes and ears. In your various disguises, you've been my eyes and ears on the streets of Dundee, and you've been superb.' She glanced at his toned body. 'And this time you won't have to go in disguise.'

'What do I look for? Evidence of money laundering?'

'I doubt you'll find it. It's his accountant who'll have two sets of ledgers in his safe.' She took a sip. 'I think Archie is bringing in firearms. Replicas that have been converted. Have you heard anything on the street?'

'I have, as a matter of fact. There's talk of a place where you can get them. The Howff.'

'The old burial ground?'

'Friday night is the time. The rest of Dundee is drinking itself legless, so it's a safe bet you won't be disturbed. The person to ask for is Dougie.' He drew his brows together. 'You think Archie's selling them there?'

'Unless he's stockpiling them for a gang war. Although I don't know who'd be foolish enough to take on the Nailer.' She leant forward. 'So here's what I know about Donnan's. There are a couple of men there that belong to Archie. One has a tattoo on his face. He's called Col. The other wears football clothes. They may or may not be in on any scam. It's worth trying to make their acquaintance.'

Quinn nodded, staring at her through the smoke. She could see he didn't like what he was hearing.

'In the nightclub, the door to the left of the stage opens into a corridor. Halfway down on the right-hand side, there's an office. It has a filing cabinet and computer. Might be worth a look if you can get in. There are flights of stairs at both ends of the corridor. They lead up to Archie's apartment. Four doors off the first-floor landing. I'm guessing living room, bedroom, kitchen and bathroom. Now, right at the end of the ground-floor corridor, there's another door. From there you can get out on to Candle Lane by going through what looks like a garage. But the door on to Candle Lane itself is locked, and you'll be unlikely to get out that way if you're in a bind.'

'You think he stashes the firearms there?'

'He may do. And one of them may be the gun that killed Brodie. Although only a complete idiot would keep a murder weapon around. But if you do get in and find any cartridges, see if you can pocket some. I'm looking for ones stamped with ZVS.'

'Dania, it's a truth universally acknowledged that people who cross Archie McLellan wind up dead as mutton.'

'It's not without risk, which is why you'll get twice the going rate.'

'I've heard that song before.'

'That you'll get twice the going rate?' she said in surprise.

He exhaled loudly. 'That it's not without risk.'

'So, do we have a deal?' she asked, when the silence grew awkward.

He stubbed out the cigarette, leaving the black butt smouldering. 'How do we keep in touch?'

She pulled a phone out of her bag. 'This is an unregistered. It has a number you can call me on. And a few numbers that don't go anywhere except to voicemail, in case someone takes it off you. There's nothing to link you to me. And it goes without saying that you don't take your own phone into Donnan's. We'll use code names. How shall I address you?'

He thought for a second. 'Laszlo.'

'And I'm Lloyd.'

'I take it meeting up is out of the question?' he said with a faint smile.

'If they suspect you, you may find yourself tailed.' She got to her feet. Seeing the look on his face, she relented. 'We might be able to set something up. But I'm also running the Breek House murders case, and I'm pushed for time.'

'Stay and have another glass with me,' he said, standing.

'I have to go, Quinn.' She squeezed his arm. 'Finish the bottle.' She glanced at the bed. 'And ruffle the sheets. We have our reputations to preserve.'

Quinn watched from the window as Dania made her way across the grounds towards the taxi rank, moving in that brisk, determined way of hers. He was glad he'd made the move to Dundee, taking up his old job as her informant, or Covert Human Intelligence Source, as they're officially known, although, apart from a few minor assignments, this was the first time she'd seriously called on his services. In London, she was constantly giving him things to do, sending him to watch people and infiltrate gangs.

His mind drifted to how they'd met. It was one of those fuck-ups the police occasionally make. Dania, not long out of training and still a DC, was working undercover as a journalist, tasked with getting a story on a Mr Big. The man owned a string of upmarket eating houses and used them to launder the proceeds of his less legal enterprises. Quinn's 'day job' was working as a male escort, but his main occupation was informant to a DI from another division. Acting on a tip-off that Mr Big was going to close a deal with a rival gang boss in his main restaurant, the Hanging Judge, Dania's boss sent her there to sniff around. As she needed an escort, she contacted the company Quinn worked for and requested a man for the evening, little knowing that it would be an informant whose job was also to get close to the same Mr Big.

Things started well, but when the operation went tits up and both Dania and Quinn nearly lost their lives, it was his own boss who was hung out to dry. By that time, his role as informant had been exposed and none of the other officers would touch him. Except Dania. Whether she felt sorry for him or simply recognised his potential, he never knew. What he did know was that his growing feelings for her were not those an informant ought to have. Apart from that first night, where they'd returned to her place after the failed operation, drunk too much vodka, and somehow found themselves in her bed, nothing further had happened. Ah, but what a night it had been. He closed his eyes, remembering the smell of her skin, her passion as they made love, the excitement of sex with a near-stranger. And they do say that a brush with death enhances the experience. But the following week, when she'd offered him the opportunity to work as her informant, she'd made it clear in a friendly but unequivocal manner that their relationship had to be strictly professional. He'd been impressed. A lesser woman would have skirted the issue, embarrassing them both.

They'd been a good team. And still were. He poured himself another glass and sipped thoughtfully before throwing it back. Of one thing he was certain: he was determined not to let her down. They went too far back for that.

CHAPTER 10

It was Wednesday before Dania heard from Harry Lombard. The phone call came at around ten in the morning.

'Is that Inspector Gorska?'

'Professor Lombard?'

'I must apologise for not getting back to you before now. I'm calling to say that we have all four skeletons laid out together. And I'm further forward with the profiles. Would you be free to come over?'

'I'm on my way.'

'Splendid.'

Was that enthusiasm in his voice? Best not to read too much into it, she decided, as she left the office. He might simply be keen to make his report and get the case off his hands.

It was a crystal-clear sunny day, rare for this time of year, with only a few puffy clouds hanging in the sky. It was more the absence of wind than the absence of rain that she was thankful for.

Twenty minutes later, she entered the building and saw him waiting at the door.

He came forward, smiling shyly. 'It's so nice to see you again, Inspector.'

'And you,' she said, returning the smile.

He ran a hand over his hair. 'We're in the main room now. It's this way.'

He took her along several corridors to a larger version of the room they'd been in before. The skeletons were laid out on four trolleys in what she remembered was the standard anatomical position.

'Inspector,' he began.

She interrupted him. 'Please call me Dania.'

He flushed slightly. 'In that case, you must call me Harry.'

'All right, Harry, so what have we got?'

'Right, the two skeletons on the left are from Sites A and B. If you remember, A and B were close together but C and D were further away.' He nodded towards the nearest skeleton. 'This is the first one found. I'll call him Victim A.'

'The adult male over forty?'

'Well remembered, Inspector. I mean Dania,' he added quickly.

'And you found fractures.'

'And not just with Victim A, but with Victims B and C. There are breaks in both tibia and fibula, the bones in the lower leg. Best if we look at the results of the CT scans. I've got the images up for you on the desk.' He indicated the large screen behind her.

She gazed at what looked like three-dimensional X-rays. 'Are there no fractures in the upper legs?'

'The thigh bone, or femur, is the strongest bone in the body and it takes a lot to break it. In the case of Victim A, the left patella, or knee bone, has also been smashed. See here?'

'Wow, that looks nasty,' she said slowly.

He pressed a key and the images changed. 'These are the scans of the arms. Again, we see fractures in the lower bones, the radius and ulna. They're thinner than the upper arm bones, and consequently easier to break.' He glanced at her. 'I should add that all these fractures occurred before death as there's evidence of healing in every case. And they occurred over a relatively short period. The degree of healing tells us that.'

'So Victims A, B and C have fractured arms and legs.'

'But not Victim D. He's very different from the others. Take a look at this last image.'

The single scan showed the skull from the side. It didn't need an expert to see what had happened.

'The parietal bone at the back of the skull has been caved in,' Harry said. 'Not only that, but the frontal bone has been crushed too. I can say with a degree of confidence that the parietal trauma occurred first. The blow was from behind and in a downward direction.' He lifted his arms to demonstrate. 'The second blow, to the front, came from a horizontal direction.'

'Hold on a minute, Harry. The first blow would surely have floored him.'

'Agreed.'

'So the second blow was delivered by someone standing over him? Or straddling him?'

'That's my conclusion. As he fell, he must have hit something that caused him to fall face up. His attacker brought an object down on his head, presumably to finish the job.'

'And that blow would have killed him?'

'Undoubtedly.'

She stared at the scan, wondering at the strength needed to cause such damage. 'Can you tell what sort of instrument did this?'

'These are blunt-force injuries. From the nature of the damage, I'd say it was something this size.' He held up his hands. 'And heavy.'

'Could a woman have done it?'

'Unlikely. But not impossible.' He frowned. 'From your experience, do women kill like that?'

She thought of her grandmother's accounts of life under the

Occupation. And what women in the Home Army had been prepared to do when weapons were scarce. Whether her grandmother
had done them was something she'd never asked, knowing that
the woman would never have told her.

'If the circumstances are right, Harry, women can kill like that.
So, we have three victims with fractured arms and legs, and one
with a smashed skull.'

'And the teeth are missing in every case.'

'The three with skulls intact, can you say what killed them?'

'I'm afraid not.'

She returned to the trolleys and studied the skeletons. 'What
else can you tell me?'

He opened the folder lying next to the screen. 'I've written it
up for you, but I'll go through the main points. Victim A was
aged between forty-eight and fifty-five when he died, Victim
B between thirty-two and forty. Victim C was a woman, also
aged between thirty-two and forty.'

'A woman?' Dania paused. 'And the one with the smashed
skull?

'He was between thirty-eight and forty-four.'

Her mind was racing. Three men and one woman. Her theory
was that they'd been tortured before being killed. Had they been
tortured for information? How long could you hold out if your
legs and arms were broken and your teeth pulled? But could they
have been tortured for information they didn't have? The thought
was chilling.

'We've still to do the bone mineral analysis and the radiocarbon
dating. I've not had time, I'm afraid. I do apologise.'

'There's really no need.'

He gazed at the floor. 'I have to say that there's one advantage
in not finishing this yet.'

'Oh?'

He looked up, a smile playing on his lips. 'It means I have an excuse for seeing you again.'

The phone rang as Marek was finishing shaving. He towelled his face, then hurried into the hall. The mobile was lying on the previous day's edition of the *Courier*, the paper open at the page with a picture of Ned McLellan under the headline 'Fraud Office Investigates Archie McLellan's Brother'.

He picked up the phone. 'Marek Gorski.'

'Marek! Archie McLellan here.'

He fell into the chair.

'Are you there, laddie?'

'How did you get this number?' Stupid question. This was Archie McLellan. He'd found Marek's address. He'd have found his number just as easily.

'It's been a week,' Archie said.

'Has it?'

'Aye, it's Friday today. I reckon it's time for another wee blether. I'll send the car round.' He rang off, leaving Marek staring into the phone.

A quarter of an hour later, there was a sharp knock at the door. Marek was finishing his coffee and decided not to be rushed. The knocking again, louder now.

'I heard you the first time,' he shouted.

He picked up his jacket and went to open the door. The thug with the ace of spades on his face was standing grinning.

'So, no blanket over my head this time?' Marek said sarcastically.

'Not if you don't behave like a dafty.'

'I never do that.'

'Let's go, then.'

The same tasteless white stretch limo was waiting on the corner of Perth Road and Union Place. To Marek's surprise, Archie was sitting in the back. He was dressed in a sharp navy suit and red and white striped tie. Marek took the seat next to him, breathing in the man's smoky cologne.

'Grand seeing you again, lad,' Archie said.

'Where are we going?'

'To the casino. It's not open for business, so we won't be disturbed.'

Marek said nothing.

'Something wrong, Marek? You've got that face on.'

'Well, what sort of face should I have on?' he said, with ill humour.

Archie held up his hands. 'Aye, all right, then. No small-talk.'

They travelled in silence along Perth Road, swinging right and reaching Dock Street in record time. The traffic peeled away on either side. Maybe it was something to do with the fact that the limo was instantly recognisable and no one wanted to get in Archie McLellan's way. Or perhaps it was simply that, for Archie's driver, an amber light meant speed up, not slow down.

They cruised to a stop in front of Donnan's and Tattoo Man cut the engine. He opened the door for Archie, who got out briskly. No one opened the door for Marek. He was struggling to find the handle in the squashy beige leather when the door opened and Archie thrust his head in. 'Come on, laddie. We've got business to discuss.'

This was Marek's first time at Donnan's, and he was less than impressed. He was used to casinos that advertised themselves with a bit of style, but the name wasn't even over the entrance. For all he knew, the building could have been a small department store.

Archie pushed through the revolving doors. Tattoo Man stood back, letting Marek go first. More to ensure he didn't do a runner than out of politeness, he thought cynically.

A couple of men in black trousers and blue waistcoats were lolling against the wall. Seeing Archie, they straightened immediately. 'Morning, chief,' one said.

Archie nodded without replying.

At the end of the short corridor, a door stood ajar. The sounds of a piano drifted through. Someone was playing 'Beautiful Dreamer'.

Archie strolled in, opening the door wide as a signal that the others should follow. 'Natalie, sweetheart,' he said, in a soothing voice. 'Run and get yourself a manicure or something.'

'Sure, Mr McLellan.' The blonde slipped off the piano stool. She was wearing a sleeveless red dress and had warm brown eyes. As she left, she threw Marek a backward smile.

'My new pianist,' Archie said. 'Lovely lass.' He nodded to the nearest table. 'So, take a seat.'

Marek pulled out a chair. Archie exchanged a few words with Tattoo Man, who took up his post at the door.

'Well, now,' Archie said, sitting down opposite Marek. 'Have you come to a decision? I've given you a week to think on it.' When Marek hesitated, he added, 'We haven't talked about your fee. How much do you want?'

He was taken aback. He'd expected Archie to suggest a figure and then they'd haggle. 'That depends on how long it takes. I've no idea till I hear the details.'

Archie waggled a finger, his mouth breaking into a wide smile. 'Fifty dollars a day plus expenses, eh, laddie? So you can string it out as long as possible?' His smile vanished. 'I don't make those kinds of deals.'

'Well, what do you think the job's worth?' Marek said in irritation.

Archie studied him. Marek returned his gaze unflinchingly.

'Ten grand, Marek. Take it or leave it.'

'Then I'll leave it,' he said, getting to his feet.

Archie gripped his arm. It felt like it was in a vice. 'Let me put this in capital letters, Marek. You're not leaving it. We're arriving at a mutually acceptable figure. Twenty grand.'

He wondered how far the man was prepared to go but decided not to push it. 'All right. But there's a condition. As well as the money, I want an interview.' He watched the emotions come and go on Archie's face. In the man's forty-five years as a career gangster, no one had succeeded in getting him to grant an interview.

'What's it to be about?' Archie said slowly.

'How you got to the top. What motivated you to go into business.'

Archie looked at him steadily.

'It's an opportunity to set the record straight,' Marek said, wading in. 'People think you're a gangster. You're telling everyone you're not.'

For a second, he thought he'd gone too far, but Archie said, 'I get to see the article before it goes to press.'

'Of course.'

'That wasn't a question, lad.' He nodded. 'Aye, all right. And to seal the deal, we'll have a wee swally.' He jerked his head at Tattoo Man. 'Col, fetch the vodka.'

Marek was about to protest when Archie raised a hand. 'Patience, Marek, patience.'

Col shambled over to the bar and returned a moment later with a bottle of Wyborowa and two glasses. A rime of frost had formed on the bottle. A good sign. It had been in the freezer.

'Polish vodka,' Archie said. 'I always take good advice.'

Marek inclined his head in acknowledgement.

Archie poured two glasses and handed one across.

'*Na zdrowie,*' Marek said.

Archie raised his glass. '*Na zdrowie.*' He watched Marek down it in one but didn't try it himself. 'Were you born in the UK, Marek?' he said, sipping slowly.

'Warsaw.'

'And did you get British citizenship?'

He shook his head.

'I reckon you'll be worried that EU nationals may have to leave this fine country of ours.'

'It's possible.'

'Another vodka?'

'No, thank you.'

Archie put down his glass, having drunk less than half the measure. 'Col, the dossier,' he said, without turning round.

Col disappeared through the side door and returned shortly with a buff-coloured folder. Inside was a brown envelope and a single sheet of paper.

Archie pushed the envelope across. 'That's the down payment. As I said, you keep that, regardless.' He handed Marek the sheet. 'The man I want you to find is called Peter de Courcy. This is all we have, courtesy of the detective I hired to track him down. There's not much, right enough. Read it and tell me what you think.'

Peter de Courcy and his wife, Anamaria, had arrived in Britain in 1975. They'd lived in a villa in Roxburgh Terrace where de Courcy had set up the De Courcy Clinic and practised as a hypnotherapist. The couple had moved away in 1985. Destination unknown.

Marek glanced up. 'What did your investigator do to try to find him?'

'He talked to folk who knew him. There weren't many. He tried to get his new address, but the man's vanished off the face of the earth, and no mistake.'

'Do you have a photo of him?'

Archie shook his head. 'But if you read on, you'll see the statements from the neighbours. Most of the residents have moved on but one or two are still there. They remembered him. There's a description.'

Marek read aloud. 'Dr de Courcy was a short man who wore half-moon reading glasses. And he had an old scar on his cheek.'

'I reckon that's the most helpful bit.'

'Dark hair, all over the place.'

'It'll be white now.' Archie stretched his rubber lips into a smile. 'Like mine.'

Marek turned the sheet over. It was blank. 'That's it?' he said, in dismay.

'Aye, not much to go on.'

'De Courcy. It's a French name.'

'He came from Austria, a neighbour said. Vienna.'

'Have you considered he may have gone back to Vienna?'

'Then find his address there.'

'Have you considered he may have died?'

'Then find his grave.'

Marek stared at the man opposite, his thoughts swirling. De Courcy had left Dundee more than thirty years before, and this sparsely typed sheet was all that a trained investigator had dug up. What Archie was asking of him was beyond his capabilities. He pushed the envelope back.

'No you don't, laddie,' Archie said.

'I haven't the skills. You need a professional.'

'I want you to do it.' He looked steadily at Marek. 'You could always ask your sister for a few pointers. A detective inspector, right enough.' He paused. 'And intelligent, from what I remember.'

'You've met her?' Marek said, feeling the blood drain from his face.

105

'Just the other day. She called in.'

He didn't like the look in Archie's eyes. Ignoring the potential consequences, he leant forward and said slowly, 'Listen to me, McLellan. If anything happens to my sister, you're looking at someone who'll spend a lot of time taking care of the person who did it.'

Archie's look of surprise was replaced by one of delight. He clapped his hands slowly. 'It's a long time since anyone squared up to me like that, laddie. I like a man with a bit of spunk.' He picked up the envelope and, leaning over, pushed down the expertly folded handkerchief in Marek's breast pocket, and stuffed the envelope in. 'We have a deal.' He said it in a tone that brooked no contradiction.

Marek couldn't risk anything happening to Danka. Archie had him.

'Anything else, Archie? Or can I go now?'

'Stay and have another vodka.'

'No, thank you.' Marek got to his feet.

Archie stood up slowly. 'I'll get Col to drive you back.'

'There's no need.'

'Why not visit the casino one evening? I've invited your sister,' he said, in a way that suggested that if she were coming it made it all right. 'And you needn't worry,' he added, ushering Marek to the door. 'I won't breathe a word to the detective inspector that you're on my payroll.'

Marek glared at him.

In the corridor, the blonde pianist was chatting to one of the bouncers.

'Natalie,' Archie said, slipping an arm round her shoulders, 'may I introduce Mr Marek Gorski?'

The girl smiled. She had a face few men could ignore.

Marek held out his hand, palm upwards, and the girl put hers in his. He lifted it to his lips and kissed it lightly. 'It's a pleasure,' he murmured, raising an eyebrow.

The girl smiled dreamily. 'Likewise.'

Col was standing staring, a stunned expression on his face.

'We'll be in touch,' Archie said, as they reached the entrance. 'Aye, and don't forget to visit.'

Archie watched the tall Pole push his way through the revolving doors. He wondered whether the man would be able to find de Courcy when a professional investigator had failed. But his reasons for having Marek do it were simple: not only had he tracked down the piece of filth who'd been molesting wee bairns but he had a sister in the force – a sister who had access to data, and methods for finding missing persons, and who knew what else? Aye, Marek had been the right choice. And Archie's remark that he'd met the bonnie detective inspector, and his veiled hint, although he'd been careful not to be explicit, that her well-being depended upon Marek's cooperation, had clinched it. As he'd known it would.

He dragged himself up the steps to his apartment. His energy seemed to have evaporated. Maybe he wasn't getting enough kip. These days, he had difficulty drifting off to sleep and then, when morning came, he could hardly bring himself to haul his carcass out of bed. He was aware he was constantly snapping at his staff. That wouldn't do. He'd need to watch himself. And, on top of everything, his eejit brother was about to be lifted for being a benefit cheat. As if Ned didn't have enough money. Archie paused halfway up the steps, leaning against the banister. He'd have to have a wee word with his brother, and soon. Aye, the twat needed to get a hold of himself.

He reached the apartment and staggered into the bedroom.

Without bothering to take off his shoes, he threw himself on to the bed, and stared at the ceiling. What he feared in his marrow was the dark. Not the dark that came and went with the passage of the sun, but the dark within. It could appear any time, and anywhere. He'd be enjoying a wee bevvy with his pals, and then he'd feel it creeping over him, like a black fog. Other days, it came more quickly. When that happened, he could do nothing but find a quiet corner somewhere and curl up, sobbing. Was that how it had been for his dad? Had the man found it impossible to face the fact that no one could clear the dark for him? Archie tormented himself by imagining what had gone through the man's mind as he put the shotgun into his mouth.

He closed his eyes, clenching his fists against the suffocating pressure in his chest. Sweat trickled down his temples. He lifted his hands to his face, feeling the skin tight with fear. Blackness closed in with a rush and, not caring if anyone heard him, he cried out in anguish.

CHAPTER 11

Saturday morning saw the team assembled in the incident room. Dania had finished describing her visit to CAHID.

'I agree, ma'am,' Hamish said, rubbing his jaw. 'Fractured arms and legs look like torture, right enough.'

Laurence had joined them for the briefing, having given up working with the Tech boffins who'd declared Brodie Boyle's mobile beyond redemption. 'Maybe they were tortured for the fun of it,' he said. 'It's not the first time that's happened. Some sicko who likes to see people suffer.'

'More likely to extract information,' Dania said. 'And the information was so important that the victims tried to hold out. I suspect the teeth were pulled first.'

'That would have been enough for me,' Honor said, with a pained smile. 'Actually, one tooth would have done it. Nope, scratch that. They'd just have to show me the pliers and I'd tell them everything. Even things I didn't know I knew.'

'The question is, though, what killed them? The first three, I mean.'

'They could have had their throats cut,' Hamish suggested.

'Or been poisoned,' someone said.

There then followed a discussion of how to kill without leaving evidence on the skeleton. The favoured method was to tie up the victim and tape a plastic bag over his head.

'This is getting us nowhere,' Dania said. 'Harry promised biological profiles. That might give us something. Slow poison that gets into the bone, for example. We'll have to wait for his report.'

Honor tilted her head. 'Harry?' she said, with a knowing smile.

'Professor Lombard.'

'Professor Lombard to me, but Harry to you, boss?'

'Exactly,' Dania said, keeping her expression blank. 'Now let's move on to Brodie. We know he hadn't eaten for four hours and he'd had sex shortly before he died.'

'We've got a lead on that,' Hamish said. 'We found his green Volkswagen Beetle at Gallagher Retail Park. He was a member of the gym there. The manager confirmed he was working out from eleven a.m. till twelve fifteen p.m. on the Saturday he was killed. Once we got the VW's licence number from the DVLA, we found him on the traffic cameras. He left his flat at around ten forty-five a.m., drove down the Marketgait, and then swung left on to Dock Street, following the road until he reached Gallagher's car park.'

'Good work. Now, no food for four hours. He was killed at roughly two p.m. And I'm guessing he didn't eat for at least an hour before exercising.'

'Which means he had no lunch. That's when he must have had sex, boss. After he left the gym.' Honor frowned. 'Personally, I don't like to do it on an empty stomach.'

'Could he have had sex at the gym?'

'The cameras say no, ma'am. I saw the footage. He was there the whole time, lifting weights and slogging away on the treadmill.'

'What about the changing rooms?'

Hamish smiled wryly. 'There are no cameras there, but we did

110

catch a few people who remembered him. They're prepared to testify he simply showered and left.'

'And the cameras in the car park?'

'Showed him leaving the building just after twelve fifteen p.m. He threw his gym bag into the boot of the car – we got a clean close-up shot of him doing that – then walked out of the car park and turned right into East Whale Lane.'

'Hold on.' She ran a finger across the wall map. 'Let me find it.'

'Halfway up the lane, there's a hotel,' Hamish said. 'You'd miss it if you didn't know what it is. Brodie went inside.'

'You saw this on the retail park's camera?'

'It's just out of view. It was a member of the public who told us. She saw Brodie's image on one of our posters and remembered seeing him going in.'

There was a buzz of excitement at this piece of news.

'It took us a wee while to figure out how it all works.' Hamish glanced at his colleague. 'It was Honor who finally cracked it.'

'All I did was pick up a leaflet in the foyer,' she said dismissively. 'The hotel is one of these new places where everything is done online. You pay in advance electronically, and you're emailed a room number and a PIN that is activated for the time you've bought. You arrive, find your room, enter the code and you're in. You don't check out. You just leave. When the time's elapsed, the PIN changes and someone comes to clean the room.'

'Breakfast? Room service?'

'There's a machine downstairs where you can buy bottled water.'

Dania felt her heart race. 'Was it Brodie who booked the room?'

'We finally tracked down the guy who manages the system. Brodie Boyle had it booked until six p.m.'

'We checked with his bank,' Hamish chipped in. 'It was Brodie who paid, no question.'

'Damn it. I'd hoped it would be the person he was meeting. What about email? Maybe that's how they communicated.'

'No joy, boss. Brodie had a dormant account full of junk and spam. And we couldn't find him on social media.'

'I don't suppose the hotel has CCTV?'

'Nope.' Honor scratched her neck. 'We contacted the other guests, but no one saw anything.'

'By now, the room will have been cleaned,' Hamish said. 'And the sheets and towels changed.'

Dania stared at the map. Something niggled. 'So Brodie leaves the hotel before two p.m. Did the car-park cameras show him going back to the Volkswagen?'

'They didn't, boss.'

'He walks down East Whale Lane on to East Dock Street. And then on to Dock Street proper, where he meets his killer. And in his waistband is a Zoraki Model 914. Could he have picked it up from his car when he threw in the gym bag?'

'Not a chance, ma'am,' Hamish said. 'We got clear images.'

'Okay, so he doesn't go back to the car to pick up the gun.'

'And he wouldn't have taken a firearm into the gym,' Honor said, her eyes gleaming, 'because someone could have found it in his bag and, anyway, he could easily have left it in the car and picked it up afterwards. So . . .'

'. . . the person he met in the hotel, and had sex with, must have given it to him.'

'Bingo,' Honor said softly.

'*Cholera!*' Dania slammed her hand against the wall. 'No receptionist. No guests. And no hotel cameras.' She was conscious of their stares. After a moment, she said more quietly, 'Why would Brodie want a gun?'

'To kill someone?' Honor said.

'Or?'

'To sell it.'

'Could this guy he met at the hotel be from Donnan's?' Hamish said suddenly. 'I reckon that if Archie McLellan is importing firearms someone from the nightclub could have got wind of it and stolen one. He and Brodie could have started up a wee operation of their own.'

'Good point. Did anyone talk to the staff?'

'I've spoken with them all,' Laurence said. 'The interviews are now on the system. I've still to cross-reference, but basically all I learnt is that Brodie was a nice guy. Very popular with the lady gamblers.'

'Did he have a boyfriend there?'

'I was careful to say "girlfriend or boyfriend". But the staff looked surprised when I asked that. They never saw him with anyone. And, apart from taking him out for a drink when he first arrived, no one socialised with him.'

'Why was that?'

'He kept himself to himself.'

'Maybe he wanted to keep his sexuality a secret, ma'am.'

'There was a new guy there,' Laurence said. 'Just been taken on to replace Brodie. He had nothing to say, unsurprisingly, as he'd never met him.'

'That was quick,' Honor said. 'Replacing him like that.'

So Quinn was inside, thought Dania. She'd need to let the DCI know. 'Did you get anything else from the bank? Was Brodie in receipt of large unexplained sums of money?'

'Everything was in order, boss. Salary in. Rent out. Nothing major with his credit card. He wasn't in debt. Little in the way of savings, just a tiny cash ISA. Selling a firearm might have looked like an attractive proposition.'

'Donnan's has been open only a few weeks. Where did he work before?'

'The place just across the road,' Honor said, nodding towards the window. 'Laurence and I talked to them too. They were sorry to lose Brodie, but McLellan was offering over the odds. Brodie was well liked. But they didn't really know him.'

Before Dania could reply, the door opened and a constable poked his head in. 'Ma'am, the chief inspector wants to see you.'

'Now?'

'Now.'

There was something in his expression that didn't fill Dania with confidence.

'So where are we with the Brodie Boyle killing?' DCI Jackie Ireland said, placing her palms together.

Dania recognised the gesture as one of barely contained impatience. Briefly, she gave an account of what they had.

'And this informant,' the DCI said, 'is he in character?'

'Very much so. He's my best.'

'Are you sure McLellan is bringing in these guns?'

Dania knew the DCI was simply testing the evidence. Like everyone at the station, she had Archie McLellan down as prime suspect. 'We've no evidence, but it's the sort of thing he'd do. Like his credit-card skimming, it may not make him a fortune, but that's how he operates. Nothing so big that we'd waste our time on it.'

'You're saying firearms aren't big?'

'I'm saying he may not be bringing them in in large numbers. It makes it harder for us to track.' She gnawed her bottom lip. 'I wonder why he'd bother. His casino nightclub will surely bring in enough.'

'Maybe he likes to keep his hand in. Or he wants us to see that he can still cut it.' The woman played with her fingers. 'I wasn't long in this job when our paths first crossed. Aye, and I knew immediately what sort of a man we were dealing with. Not your usual gangland kingpin controlling a huge syndicate, but a small-time criminal who's equally deadly. He's obsessively careful not to leave any trails. And that's why he's so dangerous.'

'And yet he has no alibi for the time of the shooting.'

'He doesn't need one. What evidence do we have that points directly to him?'

'Our best lead was the nail in Brodie's forehead, but I've heard from Kimmie that the only DNA on it is Brodie's.'

'Exactly. McLellan wouldn't have made a mistake like that. He knows we've never been able to link him to any crime where nails have been hammered into foreheads, right enough.' She massaged her temples. 'So, what about the shooter's movements, prior to and after the killing?'

'No black jackets on the CCTV. We've put up posters with a description and knocked on doors on Gellatly Street. Hamish checked out the cameras further up beyond the car park. There's nothing.'

'Traffic cameras?'

Dania thought of Honor, her eyes red-rimmed from staring at the footage. 'We haven't found anyone in a black parka getting out of a car,' she said wearily.

'Aye, par for the course.'

'Do you know if Archie McLellan's married?'

The DCI looked surprised. 'Not as far as I'm aware. I've heard tell he's gay, although it's not something he advertises. He keeps a bit of fluff around but, if he is gay, it will be for show. Why do you ask?'

'I'm wondering if he's close to anyone.'

'The Archie McLellans of this world are too canny to leave themselves open to kidnap and blackmail. Children or a significant other leave you vulnerable. His brother, Ned, is the same. He's never married.'

'Shortly before he was killed, Brodie had sex in a hotel in East Whale Lane. It could have been with Archie.'

'Go on.'

'If the man wants to keep his homosexuality a secret, he'll use a place like that discreet hotel. Convenient. Easy to get to. That Saturday, after the sex, he would have told Brodie they shouldn't be seen leaving together. He'd have left first, taken the back roads to Candle Lane and waited for Brodie to walk past.'

'You think he'd risk having the murder weapon on him? And the nail and hammer?'

'He would have left them in the garage on Candle Lane. There'd have been time to fetch them before Brodie came by.'

The DCI considered this. 'It's a working hypothesis. So, anything else to report?'

'I got a call from CAHID.' Dania opened the folder, prepared to go through Harry's findings.

'Leave it with me. And one more thing, Dania. What I said earlier still stands. Unless you have firm evidence against Archie McLellan, don't move against him. Not an inch. Understood?'

Dania held her gaze. 'Understood.'

CHAPTER 12

'I must say, Danka, this place is a bit of a mess.' Marek was gazing round his sister's living room. It doubled as a dining room, with a table and mismatched chairs at one end. Packing crates were pushed up against the ribbed cast-iron radiators, and boxes of books were stacked in tottering piles. More alarming than the clutter was the faint smell of mildew. 'You still haven't unpacked,' he added.

'I don't have time,' Danka shouted from the bedroom. 'When things settle down at work, I'll get on to it.'

Knowing his sister, she would set up her laptop on the dining table and eat out of cartons. He sauntered into the tiny kitchen and opened the fridge door. Half a cucumber, a packet of tomatoes, some *kiełbasa* and a block of orange cheese. A glance inside the large bin confirmed his suspicions. Plastic wrappers from ready meals. The window opened on to a narrow street, which accounted for the gloom. Outside were dustbins and more dustbins. He lifted the sash window only to close it against the stench. Still, Danka liked living here because it was within easy reach of the police station and, if he was being honest, his Union Place flat wasn't much tidier. When the two of them had lived there, they'd kept the apartment in reasonable condition, but since his sister had moved out, somehow things had gone downhill for them both. It probably had to do with the fact that neither had a partner.

'I'm nearly ready,' she called.

In the end, they'd had to celebrate his name day on the Saturday because Danka was on shift on Monday evening. And festivities on a Sunday were out of the question because, as Marek had jokingly pointed out, they'd need a dispensation from the Pope. His sister had been unable to find a Polish restaurant in Dundee, so had booked a table at the brasserie in the Dundee Repertory Theatre. Not only was the food excellent but, as it was a theatre restaurant, they offered early sittings, which would give them time to do something later. What exactly that something would be, he still didn't know.

He ambled back into the living room.

'Can you help me with my zip?' she said, hurrying out of the bedroom.

'Wow, you look fabulous,' he murmured.

She turned her back so he could do her up. 'You've seen this dress before,' she said. 'It's the only one I have that's suitable for where we're going.'

The royal-blue shimmery dress, coming to just above the knee, hugged her figure. A shorter woman would have worn stilettos but Danka's shoes had small heels. Any higher and she'd tower over most men. Her blonde-brown hair was pinned up around her head with no visible signs of support. He tried to work out how she'd done it but failed.

'Can I ask you something, Danka?'

'Of course.'

'How do the police trace a missing person?'

She turned and gazed at him. 'We check hospitals, call car-rental places and airlines. We put up posters, appeal to the public. Something that may work is to flag the person as missing on the PNC.

That way police in other parts of the country are alerted.' She thought for a moment. 'I once found someone who'd made a long-distance phone call on his landline. We traced the person at the other end and took it from there.'

'This is someone who disappeared thirty years ago.'

'Most of the trails will have gone cold. What did this person do for a living?'

'He was a medical practitioner.'

'He could still be a member of a professional body. You could ask at Ninewells. Milo Slaughter is on sabbatical but, if he's still in Dundee, he might know where to start.'

'That's a good idea,' Marek said brightly.

She picked up her jacket. 'Are you considering a change of career? Becoming a private investigator?'

'Not really. It's part of an ongoing story. I'm hoping it'll be a great scoop.'

She looked at him steadily. 'There's one thing to keep in mind.'

'Oh?'

'Whoever you're looking for may not want to be found.'

'Can you call us a taxi, please?' Dania said to the man at the desk.

'Of course. And did you both enjoy your meal?'

'It was excellent. We'll be coming back.'

He beamed and picked up the phone.

Marek was coming out of the Gents. 'So, where are we going, Danka?'

'You'll have to wait and see.'

When the cab arrived, she leant in and spoke softly to the driver so that her brother wouldn't hear.

'Keeping me in suspense?' he said, settling in beside her.

'Patience never was one of your virtues, Marek.'

119

A few minutes later, they cruised to a stop. He reached over to pay while she got out.

'What's this mystery venue, then?' he said, shutting the cab door.

He turned and, in the soft darkness, she caught his look of anxiety.

'Donnan's?' he said.

'I hear their cocktails are excellent.'

'This is Archie McLellan's place.'

'That's right.' She made to go to the door when he grasped her arm.

'Danka, are you sure you want to go in?'

'Why wouldn't I?'

A look of understanding crossed his face. 'Is this to do with the shooting? Are you here to check the place out?'

'I've already done that. I'm here to have a good time. With you.'

And also to see how Quinn was getting on. It had been five days since he'd agreed to go in and she'd heard nothing from him. She needed at least to check he was still alive.

Marek took a breath. 'Fine, let's go.'

'Is that all right? We can try the casino on the Marketgait if you prefer.'

He smiled. 'Absolutely not.'

She studied his face. This wasn't like him. Was he afraid? Perhaps he was afraid for her. She smiled reassuringly and pushed against the revolving doors.

The men in blue waistcoats were greeting people and ushering them on.

'Your jacket, madam?'

She handed it over and received a token in return.

'Nightclub or casino?'

'We'll start with the nightclub,' she said, glancing at Marek for confirmation.

He nodded. 'Fine by me.'

They were directed into the large open salon. It was hard to believe this was the place where, just a few days before, she'd sat and played for Archie McLellan. The room was almost full, and an expectant hum rose from the guests. At the back, the lights glittered in the glasses at the bar.

A girl with a glued-on smile came forward and escorted them to a free table. They ordered cocktails, a margarita for Dania and a whisky sour for Marek. As they waited, they chatted about cards and roulette, and which gave better odds on winning.

The lights dimmed and two women walked on to the stage. One, a young blonde in a glittering black dress, sat at the piano while the other, an older woman with dark curls framing her face, adjusted the microphone. She sang a few songs, then she and the pianist left the stage. They sauntered to the back where one of the barflies bought them drinks.

The voice came from Dania's left. 'Detective Inspector.'

She turned to see Archie McLellan dressed smartly in a suit and red tie.

'Mr McLellan.'

'I'm so glad you were able to come, Inspector,' he said, casting a glance at Marek.

'Let me introduce my brother, Marek Gorski. Marek, this is Mr Archie McLellan.'

'It's a pleasure, Mr Gorski,' Archie said, pumping Marek's hand. 'So, are you celebrating a special occasion?'

'It's my brother's name day.'

'And that is?'

'The feast day of his patron saint.'

'I see,' Archie said, in a tone that suggested he didn't. 'Well, I hope you'll visit the casino.'

'We intend to look in,' Marek said.

'Excellent, excellent. Now, if you'll excuse me?'

They watched Archie weave his way across the room, nodding at the customers, stopping here and there to exchange a word.

'So you've met Archie McLellan,' Marek said quietly.

'I came to question him about the shooting. He told me he was feeling sad and asked me to play something.' She looked at the stage. 'On that piano.'

'You played for him?' Marek said, frowning.

'He thought I was auditioning.'

Marek regarded her. 'Would you trust McLellan?'

'To do what?'

'Nothing in particular. I'm just wondering.'

She finished her drink. 'Let's forget Archie McLellan. We're here to have a good time. Shall we go to the casino?'

He smiled. 'Why not?' He got to his feet and pulled out her chair.

There was something in his manner and the way Archie had looked at him that piqued her interest. As she left the room, she thought that, if she hadn't known better, she'd have sworn the two men had met before.

The casino was back along the corridor, next to the cloakroom. The noise hit them as they entered the room.

People were crowded round an oval table, cheering loudly. At the far end, a fleshy woman with mouse-grey hair was throwing dice towards a backstop as though born to it.

Dania caught sight of Quinn at the card table. He glanced up, but gave no indication he knew her, and carried on dealing. 'What do you fancy?' she said to Marek.

'Roulette, I think. You?'

'I may watch the cards.'

'Do you intend to play?'

'You know how I hate losing money.'

He laughed. 'I'll find you later, then.'

She strolled over to watch Quinn. One of the people playing against him was Val Montgomerie. She was wearing a short-sleeved satin gown in a deep jade and long white gloves. Her hair cascaded in waves to her shoulders and was pinned at the side with a silk flower in matching jade. She was so immersed in blackjack that she was oblivious to everything around her.

Dania watched as she won and lost and won again. She got to her feet, tipping Quinn generously before leaving, her long gown sweeping the floor behind her. Her perfume was a subtle, powdery blend of violet and carnation.

'Miss Montgomerie?' Dania said.

'Inspector.' Val's eyes widened. 'What a pleasure. Come and have a drink with me. I've just won at blackjack.'

Dania was hoping to have a word with Quinn, but he was setting up the next game. 'Why not?' she said.

At the bar, they perched on stools and gave the barman their order. 'Is your sister here?' Dania said.

'Roulette's her game.' Val inclined her head, her gaze taking in Dania's dress. 'I'm assuming, dressed like that, Inspector, you're not here on business.'

'I'm on a night out with my brother. He's also at the roulette wheel.'

'I'm wondering how things are going with the case.'

'Which one?' Dania said, sipping.

'The graves found on our land.'

'All I can tell you is that enquiries are ongoing.'

'I suppose these things take time. And you must be involved in that awful shooting. The newspapers said a nail was hammered into the poor boy's forehead. Is that right?'

The comment reminded Dania that what the police knew one

day, the press too often knew the next. 'That's correct. But I'm afraid I can't tell you any more.' She glanced at the card table. Quinn was playing with a new set of guests. She wondered when his break was due. 'What about you, Miss Montgomerie? How is your business doing?'

'Our new still is in,' she said, excitement in her voice. 'We made a trial batch yesterday. Look, why don't you come over and have a look? The process really is most interesting.' Her mouth curved into a smile. 'Even for a vodka drinker.'

'You've got a good memory. Yes, I'd like that.'

'We want to get visitors in to see how our gin is made, so you'll be a sort of dummy run. I hope you don't mind?' she added quickly.

'Not at all.'

Her eyes shone. 'We've got all sorts of plans. We're going to make up bespoke batches as corporate presents.'

'In return for sponsorship?'

'And we're thinking of having a team-building day where you make your own gin and we send the bottles across when they're ready. Maybe the police station might like to do it,' she added coyly.

'I don't know what the chief super would say about that. But it sounds as though you're well on your way. I expect the Polish farmworkers will be round for tastings before too long.'

'We've already made friends with them. A few have offered to help in the grounds, provided there are no more skeletons. They're unbelievably superstitious.' Her expression changed. 'You know, one of the Poles told me he has a brother who drives coaches from Warsaw to the UK. He said there used to be twenty people a day travelling to London, but now there's not a single one going the whole way.'

'Because of Brexit?'

'There's a widespread perception that Britain is no longer a friendly place. Do you feel that?'

'I've not experienced anything personally.'

'Surely the UK needs Polish immigrants. Despite all this stuff about "taking back control", I don't think there'll be any real difference in the long term.'

'It's the short term that will be problematic. EU nationals are getting worried.'

'You're not thinking of going, surely?'

'I'm not planning to. But anything's possible.'

'That would be a great pity, Inspector.'

They finished their drinks in silence.

'Well, I'd better find Robyn before she fritters away the family silver,' Val said, getting to her feet. 'So, I'll expect your phone call?'

'Next week.'

Dania watched her glide across the casino as though she owned the place, her jade gown rustling as she moved.

She was finishing her cocktail when her gaze fell on the man at the end of the counter. At the rate he was drinking, he'd be quicker taking it intravenously. Seeing her watching, he turned and grinned, giving her a view of his dark hair, long and tangled, and a round face with an unhealthy complexion. A wine-coloured bruise decorated one half of his face.

He must have taken her apparent interest as an invitation because he picked up his drink and sauntered over.

'Can I get you another?' he said, pointing to her empty glass.

'No, thank you.'

He sat down. 'You here for the cards?'

'Not today. You?'

He winked. 'I'm here for the spinning wheel.'

'Good luck with that.'

She glanced towards the roulette table. Marek was chatting to a woman in a full-length sparkly black dress. As she turned to say something to the croupier, Dania recognised Robyn Montgomerie. Val was nowhere to be seen.

'You don't fancy a wee go at roulette yourself?' the man was saying.

'I've never won. My game is cards. *Chemin de fer.* But they don't play it here.'

'There are other casinos in Dundee. What say you and me go and check them out?'

She smiled, shaking her head. 'I make it a rule always to leave with the man I came with.'

'I'm trying to place your accent. You're not British, are you?'

'Polish.'

'Aye, that's it.'

'Please excuse me.' She got to her feet. 'I wish you success at the wheel.'

She strolled towards the roulette table just as Marek was getting up.

'How did you get on?' she said, taking his arm.

'I always quit as soon as I break even.'

'I've just been talking to Ned McLellan.'

Marek shot her a glance. 'I didn't know you knew him.'

'I recognised him from his picture in the *Courier*. Your article, actually.'

'Was he in a wheelchair?'

'He wasn't.'

'He's no longer bothering with the pretence.' Marek sneered. 'I hope the Fraud Squad throw the book at him.'

Quinn was exchanging words with a similarly dressed man. The man took his place at the card table, and Quinn made for the door.

'Marek, would you excuse me for a moment? There's someone I need to talk to.'

'Okay, you'll find me trying my hand at blackjack.'

She followed Quinn out of the casino. He stopped a short distance away and leant against the wall. The wind of earlier in the day had died and a strange calm lay over the city. She walked past him and stood in the shadows.

'I see you got the job,' she said quietly.

He pulled a pack of Sobranie out of his pocket and shook one out. 'Mmm–hmm,' he said, without looking at her.

'Anything to report?'

'Nothing,' he murmured.

'The room that leads to Candle Lane?'

'The door at the end of the corridor is bristling with locks. I couldn't get in.'

She swore silently.

'I'm pals with Col and Murray,' he said.

'Murray?'

'The one who's football mad.'

'Did they give you anything useful?'

'They don't strike me as being the sharpest pencils in the box. I reckon they're just Archie's heavies.'

'You don't think they're involved in a firearms scam with him?'

He blew smoke from his nostrils. 'A man like Archie simply wouldn't risk it. And they're too thick to branch out on their own.'

'Have you had many dealings with Archie?'

'We've chatted a couple of times.' He smoked for a while, then threw the stub on to the ground. 'Seems an okay guy. I'd never have made him for a master criminal if I hadn't known his reputation. The gangsters I've run across in London are nowhere near as polite.'

'Have you been able to get into his office?'

He ground the stub under his heel. 'I tried, but Archie and either Col or Murray are always in there.' He lowered his voice. 'There's a lavatory next to the office. It's got a ledge at the bottom of the shared wall. Right above the wash-basin is an air-vent cover. If you balance on the ledge and put your ear to the vent, you can hear everything.'

She felt her heart race. 'And?'

'And nothing. Archie talked about operations at the casino, drumming into his guys how he expected them to behave, stick to the dress code, that sort of thing. I had the impression he'd said it all before. But not a word about firearms.'

'Okay, keep at it. If you do get a chance to peek into the office, it would be good.'

She made to go but he said, 'Stay a bit, Dania. Just a couple more minutes.'

'All right.'

He flicked a match with his thumbnail and lit another Black Russian, exhaling a cloud of smoke.

'Those things are going to kill you one day,' she said.

'Not a bad way to go.'

He finished the cigarette, smoking in silence, and lit another.

'I have to go, Quinn,' she said, after a while.

'Me too. My break's over.'

'You go first.'

He puffed furiously, apparently determined to extract as many toxins as he could from the Sobranie. Then he dropped the fag end and left.

As she walked back through the slipstream of smoke, savouring the rich chocolate-tea smell, she wondered, as she did every time she met Quinn, why Black Russian Sobranie smelt so good.

Marek was still at the card table, looking as though he might be winning. Perhaps she should warn him to stop playing now that Quinn had returned, or he'd fall into the red. Standing nearby, watching closely with frowns on their faces, were Col and Murray.

She returned to the nightclub. The lights had been turned down, and the only part of the room that was illuminated was the stage. The blonde was at the piano, accompanying the brunette, who was crooning something unintelligible in a husky voice.

Dania edged furtively along the wall until she reached the side door. If she opened it, light would flood into the room. She waited until the song had finished and the lights went up. With every-one's attention on the two performers, she opened the door and stepped into the corridor.

Archie's office was towards the back. Faint voices were coming from behind the closed door. As quietly as she could, and rehears-ing her excuse that she was looking for the toilet, she slipped into the adjacent lavatory. A row of cubicles stood on the right, and three wash-basins on the left. The tang of urine hung in the air.

She stepped on to the ledge and, gripping the water pipe to steady herself, angled her head up towards the air vent. The voices were clearer now. One was a woman's.

'And you're sure this is enough?' Archie was saying.

'Absolutely, Mr McLellan.'

The person speaking was Val Montgomerie.

Dania held her breath. Papers rustled, and then Archie said, 'Right, let's do it.'

'How long before it goes through?'

'You should expect it within twenty-four hours.'

'Excellent. Where do I sign?'

'Here.' More rustling. 'And here.'

'Fine. Well, I think that's all, Mr McLellan.'

'Pleasure doing business with you. As always.'

More rustling. Then a door closing, and voices in the corridor.

129

'Please go ahead, Val. I'm just going to pay a visit to the little boys' room.'

Dania sprang off the ledge and looked around wildly, but already the door was opening. There was no time to rush into one of the cubicles.

The door opened wide, trapping her between the wall and the wash-basin. Miraculously, she heard Archie walk straight to a cubicle without bothering to shut the lavatory door. A second later, the cubicle door closed and she heard the lock slide.

As silently as she could, she stole out from behind the door and into the corridor. To the right was Archie's office and, at the end of the corridor, the locked door that led to Candle Lane. She turned left and, making no attempt to disguise what she was doing, opened the side door and walked confidently into the nightclub. Without stopping to look around, she made her way to the bar.

'What are you having?' the barman asked. He had wavy red hair and an easy smile.

'Żubrówka,' she said, indicating the tall bottle with the bison label.

'Ice?'

'No, thank you.'

She sat on the tall stool, sipping the vodka, before risking a glance round. Val had vanished, and Archie was nowhere to be seen.

'You smoke Sobranie,' the man said, polishing a glass. It was a statement.

Dania looked at him in surprise.

'They're hard to get.' He replaced the glass on the rack. 'There's one guy here who smokes them, too. The new croupier.'

At that point, a girl in a blue waistcoat came up and put in an order for one of the tables.

Dania continued to sip at her drink until she heard Marek's voice. 'So this is where you're hiding, Danka.'

He was always relentlessly cheerful when he'd won at cards, so she didn't bother to ask how he'd done. 'Ready to go?' she said, smiling.

'If you are.' He glanced at the drink. 'Unless you want another?'

She shook her head and slipped off the stool.

At the front entrance, as she was waiting for her jacket, she ran through the events of the evening. Quinn's intel had proved to be disappointing, but overhearing Val's conversation with Archie meant that the evening hadn't been a complete waste of time. The challenge now was to figure out what was going on between the two of them.

'Detective Inspector. Leaving us so soon?'

'I'm afraid so, Mr McLellan.'

As the cloakroom attendant arrived with her jacket, Archie reached for it and shook it out. She put her arms through the sleeves and let him lift and arrange it round her shoulders.

'Thank you,' she said.

He was looking at her thoughtfully. Lurking behind him, also watching her, was his brother, Ned.

'I hope we'll see you both here again?' Archie said, with a question in his voice. This was directed at Marek.

Marek said nothing, inclining his head, which could have meant anything.

Archie glanced at one of the attendants. 'Call a taxi for these good people.' When Marek started to protest, he lifted a hand. 'It's no trouble.'

While Archie waited with them, he made small-talk, which he was surprisingly good at. If he kept this up, thought Dania, he'd make a great success of Donnan's.

The cab arrived a minute later.

'Enjoy yourself?' Dania said, as they sped away.

'My wallet's much fatter than it was at the start of the evening.'

'Any plans for what you're going to do with your ill-gotten gains?'

He didn't reply but, in the darkness of the cab, she thought she detected a smile creeping on to his lips. She knew what that meant: he intended to put the cash towards that mortgage he was always talking about.

CHAPTER 13

'Okay, boss, so what are we looking for?'

Dania scrolled through the recordings list. 'I want to follow the camera trail myself. And I need a second pair of eyes in case I miss anything.' She studied Honor. 'Although one who's not half asleep would have been my first choice.'

The girl grinned. 'It's my new toy. I was with him last night.'

'A new toy? I hope he's still intact. Anyway, I thought you only had eyes for my brother.'

'How do you know your brother isn't my new toy?'

'Because *I* was with my brother last night.' She tapped at the screen. 'Right, so here we are. Saturday, March the fourth, the date Brodie was killed. I want to see if we can find the killer.'

'But Hamish has already looked.'

'He may have missed something. So, what do we know for certain?'

'The killer was seen running into the alley behind the Holiday Inn Express. He was wearing a black hooded jacket and gloves.'

'Right, that alley leads to Gellatly Street. There's no CCTV till further up by the Manchurian restaurant.'

'But Hamish looked through the cameras on Seagate, where the perp would have come out, and didn't find him.'

'The killer can't have disappeared into thin air,' Dania said, as though stating a scientific fact. 'Which is why we're taking another look. With our minds open.'

'Okay, boss,' Honor said wearily. 'Let's fire it up.'

Dania typed quickly, and the screen filled with images from the CCTV. She recognised Gellatly Street, and the area round the Oriental supermarket. 'This is from the camera outside the car park. Let's go back to just before Brodie was killed.'

Honor rubbed her eyes. 'Are you sure this isn't a waste of time?'

'Double-checking is never a waste of time.' Dania glanced at her. 'How do you account for the killer's vanishing act, then?'

'He went into one of the apartments near the alley. And the owners are lying to us. They'd have been well paid by McLellan to keep their traps shut.'

'Let's assume he went up the street. And let's think about the timing. He kills Brodie, hammers the nail in, then runs along Dock Street and takes a left into Commercial Street. I'd say less than a minute to get to the alley behind the Holiday Inn.'

'Agreed.'

'And then he runs along the alley into Gellatly Street.'

'Fifteen seconds?'

Dania cast her mind back to when she'd visited the area. 'Much less.'

'And then he runs—'

'No, he'd walk.'

'Okay, Gellatly is not a long street so maybe thirty seconds to get up to the supermarket. The footage should show him walking past.'

Dania wound a strand of hair round her finger. 'We'll start at one forty-five and go on till what? Two thirty? That will give us a large margin of error.'

They went through it, frame by frame, keeping an eye on the time code across the top of the screen.

'There are loads of people coming and going, boss. I guess it's Saturday and the supermarket's busy. And the car park. But I don't see any black jackets.'

'Wait,' Dania said suddenly. She zoomed in on a figure loping up Gellatly Street away from the camera. He was wearing an off-white fleecy jacket, baggy jeans and white trainers. No gloves. His blue baseball cap was on back to front.

'Okay, I've clocked the baggy jeans and white trainers,' Honor said, 'but it's not the right jacket. The witnesses said "shiny black parka".'

'Let's follow him,' Dania said softly.

It took some juggling with the CCTV and traffic cameras, but they found him on Seagate, heading east.

'Is he going to the bus station?' Honor asked.

'No, look, he's turning into Candle Lane.'

'Candle Lane?' the girl murmured. 'But Candle Lane leads into Dock Street. If he'd wanted to get there, why bother going *up* Gellatly Street? Why not simply go back *down* it?' She paused. 'Unless he lives there. There are a few car parks off the lane, come to think of it.'

But Dania could think of another reason – near the bottom of Candle Lane a door led into the back of Donnan's. The theory that she'd discussed with the DCI was fast becoming a certainty.

'What interests you about this guy, boss?'

'It's his posture and the way he's walking. I've seen that gait before.'

'Where?'

'At Donnan's.'

'Crikey! Yep, it's the Nailer,' Honor said triumphantly. 'Archie McLellan.'

'The question is: why would Archie walk all the way up Gellatly Street, along Seagate, and down Candle Lane to get into Donnan's the back way? After killing Brodie, he could simply have sprinted back along Dock Street, into Candle Lane, and been inside that garage in a matter of seconds.'

She thought about her visit to the area, the lorry parked on double yellow lines and the men emptying the bins behind the Holiday Inn. And, suddenly, it was blindingly obvious.

'You've got that look, boss,' Honor said impatiently.

Dania ran her hands through her hair. 'He wore that white fleece under his parka and had the baseball cap scrunched up in the pocket. Along the alley are the hotel's bins. He ditched the hammer, gloves and black jacket, and possibly the firearm, and put the baseball cap on back to front. Then he ambled up the street – what's that English expression? – as though butter wouldn't melt in his mouth.'

'Woah, we need to check out the bins,' Honor said, jumping to her feet.

Dania grasped the girl's arm and pulled her down. 'Forget it. They were being emptied while I was there. It was over a week ago.'

'Can we pull him in?'

'No magistrate would accept that that's Archie McLellan. Not once do we get to see his face.'

'But the way he walks . . .'

'His lawyer has a reputation for being the best. He'll drum up several men who walk that way and they'll testify to having been there, on that date and at that time, wearing those clothes. The DCI's made it clear we don't move without irrefutable evidence.'

'And how do we find it?'

'Let's go through the possibilities. From the beginning. The first possibility is that it was Archie who had sex with Brodie. He left the East Whale Lane hotel before Brodie, legged it to Candle Lane via the back roads, avoiding the cameras, fetched his equipment from the garage, and waited for Brodie at the corner of Candle Lane and Dock Street.'

The girl considered this. 'Strange MO. Why would he give Brodie a gun and then kill him?'

'That's the snag with this theory. I'm inclined to ditch it.'

'And the second possibility?'

'Brodie had sex with someone else. Someone who gave him the gun. Archie knew where they'd be that Saturday, and when they'd be there. He lay in wait at that Candle Lane corner.'

'And he killed Brodie because he found out he was double-crossing him?'

'It would account for the nail in the head.'

But there was a third possibility, one that Dania couldn't ignore: the killer might have been someone else.

After a silence, Honor said, 'Shall we double-check the cameras near Dock Street again? See if we can find Archie?'

'I've already done it.'

'So where did he come from?'

'My bet is he left Donnan's the back way and came out of Candle Lane into Dock Street. There's no CCTV between there and where Brodie was killed.' She glanced at Honor. 'By the way, talking of Donnan's, I ran into Val Montgomerie there last night. She and Archie went into his office, and I overheard them concluding some sort of a deal.'

Honor's eyes widened. 'The plot thickens. You think she's in this firearms scam too?'

'Seems hard to imagine.'

'Maybe, like most start-ups, they have a cashflow problem. Mind you, I can't see how they'd get much from firearms. This thing with Archie has to be something else. Maybe she's going to supply Donnan's with gin. I'll keep digging, boss.'

As she watched the girl head back to her desk, it struck Dania that the obvious place to dig was Breek House itself.

CHAPTER 14

Tuesday morning saw Marek directed to Professor Milo Slaughter's office at Ninewells. He'd spent the previous day reading everything he could find online about depression and hypnotherapy. None the wiser, he'd taken Danka's advice and contacted the professor, explaining who he was, and that he was looking for a man who'd practised as a hypnotherapist. The professor, picking up on Marek's surname, had enquired warmly after Danka before suggesting he come in the following day.

'Mr Gorski?' the professor said, in a deep voice. He had thinning hair, large hooded eyes and a wide smile. 'I'm Milo Slaughter.'

They shook hands.

'It's good to finally meet you, Professor Slaughter. Danka's told me a lot about you.'

Milo indicated the chair opposite. 'Oh? And how is your sister?'

'Busy, as always.'

He nodded, but didn't press Marek. Which was just as well: he knew little about his sister's current investigations. It had been a different matter when they'd shared a flat.

'Thank you for agreeing to see me, Professor. I'll come to the point as I know you're busy. I'm trying to track down someone, a medical practitioner.'

'Who also practised as a hypnotherapist, you said?'

'That's right. I've done an Internet search using "hypnotherapy" and the man's name as the search terms but got nowhere.'

'I couldn't find Peter de Courcy on our staff lists. I went back to nineteen seventy-five, which is when you said he'd arrived in the UK. But, if he practised hypnotherapy privately, I wouldn't necessarily expect him to have worked here in another capacity.'

'Could he be a member of a professional body?'

'There's a large number of such organisations. Apart from hypnotherapy, do you know what Dr de Courcy would have specialised in?'

'That's just the problem. I know almost nothing about him.'

'In that case, you'll need to try them all.' Milo removed a couple of sheets from a folder and handed them to Marek. 'I've highlighted the professional bodies I'm a member of. Feel free to use my name when you contact them.' He smiled. 'It should open a few doors. There's also the National Hypnotherapy Society. I've put their contact details there.'

Marek ran his eye down the list. He had a long road ahead of him. Fortunately, an investigative journalist was used to hard graft. Especially the kind that led nowhere, he thought glumly. 'Thank you, Professor,' he said, glancing up.

Milo played with his pen. 'What do you know about hypnotherapy, Mr Gorski?'

'Call me Marek, please.' He placed the sheet on the desk. 'It can be used for breaking smoking habits, losing weight, that sort of thing.' He chose his words carefully. 'The person who's asked me to make this search told me that hypnotherapy was used successfully to cure his uncle's depression. Do you know anything about how widespread that is?'

Milo frowned. 'My colleagues in the Neuroscience Division would be better placed to answer, but what I can tell you is that there's little evidence to support it. I've no doubt it might work in a few cases, but it may simply be a placebo effect: patients who think that hypnotherapy will cure them, and then it does.' He clasped his hands together. 'It's not regulated in the UK, and anyone can set themselves up as a practitioner. Let me have that sheet.' He went down the list, marking it. 'I've put an asterisk next to the organisations that deal with psychotherapy and complementary healthcare.'

'I'm in your debt.'

'Not at all. I only wish I could have been of more help.' He got to his feet. 'Do remember me to your sister,' he said, adding wistfully, 'It's a while since we worked together. That's what a sabbatical does. Cuts you off from what's going on.'

'I'll pass on your regards,' Marek said, smiling. 'And if I can ever help you, you only need to ask.'

The road to Breek House was much as Dania remembered it. After leaving the city centre, she took the Pitkerro Road, cruising through the suburban sprawl of north Dundee, and, in a matter of minutes, reached the open land with its cut-up fields. Temperatures were expected to touch the high teens, although she'd seen enough weather forecasts not to take this at face value. As she drove along the unfolding country road, she thought again about Val Montgomerie and what the significance of her conversation with Archie McLellan might be. And how she would broach the subject when she met the woman.

The wrought-iron gates of Breek House were standing wide this time, as though inviting a passer-by to drop in. Dania eased up the driveway and veered left. Strangely, the house seemed to have a more lived-in look, which she put down to knowing that it was inhabited since the exterior was exactly as it had been before, down to the bars on the ground-floor windows.

As she puttered to a stop, the front door opened and Val appeared. She was wearing high-waisted baggy navy trousers with white buttons down the sides, and a short-sleeved white blouse. Her hair was hidden under a blue and white spotted turban, only the large curl over her forehead showing. This must be what passed for working clothes, Dania thought. She could only admire the woman's style.

'Inspector,' Val said brightly, 'I'm so glad you could come. When I received your call yesterday, I must say I was mildly surprised. Given everything that's going on, I thought you might leave it a week or two.'

'I'm allowed some time off, Miss Montgomerie,' Dania said, smiling.

'Do come in.'

'Your sister not at home?' she said, when they were inside.

'She's away buying. We now know which botanicals we want to use, so we need to get them in.' Val hesitated. 'If you're not on duty, perhaps you'd like to sample our new batch?'

'Just a tiny sip. I'm driving.'

'Of course.'

She led Dania down a long corridor and through a door on the left. A huge metallic structure, which looked like a copper kettle attached to a set of organ pipes, dominated the room. The lemon-polish smell that had greeted Dania as she entered the house was masked here by an aromatic blend of scents she was hard-pressed to identify. Crates of empty bottles lined the walls.

'This is our still room,' Val said, with pride in her voice. 'And this is the still,' she added, indicating the structure.

'How does it work?'

'Steam comes in here and out here,' she said, running a hand along the kettle. 'The pipe at the top goes to the botanicals basket, which holds the plants.'

'The alcohol vapour condenses in that?' Dania said, nodding at the tall cylinder.

'And the liquid finally ends up in this tank with the tap at the bottom. Then we bottle it.'

'Sounds straightforward.'

'The hard part is getting the botanicals right. You can make, for example, elderflower gin, then raspberry gin and so on, and blend the liquids. But what we do is add all the botanicals in one go.'

'Must have been quite a job getting all this equipment in.'

'We had to put in stronger floorboards.'

'What made you decide on gin, Miss Montgomerie, not beer or whisky?'

'The gin renaissance is the main reason for becoming a gin-smith. You can be up and running incredibly quickly. As soon as the stuff's made, it's ready to go into the bottle. Not like with whisky, where you have to wait ten years to age it.'

'Surely whisky is more popular in Scotland.'

'Gin sales are predicted to outstrip whisky sales all over the UK. And did you know that Scotland now produces most of the gin drunk in our lands? Micro-distilleries like ours are on the increase.'

'Did you have to go on a course?' Dania said, genuinely interested.

'I have a friend in London who's in the trade so I picked his brains. Like me, he knew nothing about distilling when he began. It took him six months to design and build his still.' She threw Dania a crooked smile. 'We bought ours in. Neither Robyn nor I have the skills to design anything. But we learnt from him exactly what needs to be done. One thing we decided to do at the outset was to future-proof the business so we bit the bullet and bought a bigger still.'

'And can you run the operation with just two people?'

'You don't need a lot of staff to run a distillery, Inspector. It's the setting up that takes time.'

'How long does gin take to make from scratch?'

Val rubbed her chin. She had long nails, painted in a blood-red varnish. 'A batch will take about five hours. That'll make two hundred bottles. It's why many whisky distillers also make gin. And vodka. Otherwise, they'd be cash poor very quickly, and would remain that way for a long time.'

'So what are the botanicals that go into gin?'

'The exact composition is a trade secret,' Val said, smiling, 'but you can't classify it as gin unless it's flavoured with juniper. We're going to plant our own and see how it goes. We're still at the stage of trying out different recipes, but we think we've cracked it. A bit more tweaking, and we're ready to produce in bulk.' She inclined her head. 'Are you ready to try it, Inspector?'

'Never readier.'

She took a bottle from the side table and poured a finger of pale peach liquid into a glass tumbler. 'Ice and slice?'

'I'll try it neat.' Dania lifted the tumbler to the light, then took a gulp, holding the liquid in her mouth the way she did with flavoured vodka.

'So, what do you think?' Val said nervously.

'Surprisingly good.'

'Better than your green vodka?'

'Now that's like comparing apples with oranges. But the fact the gin is flavoured is probably why I like it.' She took another sip. 'Has anyone else tasted it?'

'You're the first. But we'll be taking samples round the bars and asking the bartenders to try. After all, what Robyn and I like, and what bartenders think customers want, may be entirely different. That's the hard part – making something that will sell.' She poured herself a glass. 'Robyn's doing some competitor analysis. It would be fatal to produce a flavour that's already out there.'

'So where do you plan to sell? Locally?'

'To begin with, yes. There are plenty of independent bars and clubs we might be able to interest.'

'And export?'

'We're not that far along yet.' Val smiled enigmatically. 'But never say never.'

'Maybe you could sell to Donnan's,' Dania said, watching the other woman over the glass. 'I noticed when I was there on Saturday that they have loads of malts, but a poor range of gins.'

Val's eyes widened. 'Now *that's* an idea.'

'I'm sure the owner would be interested.'

'Who is the owner?'

'Archie McLellan. He was there on Saturday, doing the rounds of the customers. Did you not meet him?'

'I'm afraid I didn't,' Val said, finishing her gin. 'I was too busy playing cards.'

After a pause, Dania said, 'So, what's through there?' She motioned to the door at the back. 'Another still?'

'It's too small for that. Come and look.'

The door opened on to an empty room. The bare walls could have done with a coat of paint, and the floor with a carpet. And the same bars were on the windows.

'We've not done up this room, mainly because we don't know what to use it for. We were looking for a room we could use as a showroom, but this is too small. Our current thinking is to store the bottles here.' Val stood at a spot away from the door. 'It's very quiet in this part of the house.' She gazed out of the window. 'So quiet you could hear the corn grow. Robyn's terrified to come in here. I can't say I blame her. This room has an atmosphere. Don't you feel it?'

'I'm not susceptible to things like that.'

'She said she heard babbling lunatic laughter the first time she walked in. It came up from the ground, just where you're standing. And then it was freezing in the room.'

As if on cue, Dania felt a sudden drop in temperature. The cold seeped up from the floor, closing round her. She shivered involuntarily.

'I've noticed that happen, too. I think the Fithie Burn runs under this house, and that causes the temperature to fall occasionally. If you wait a few seconds, it'll get warm again.'

'Interesting phenomenon. And the rushing water might explain what your sister heard.'

'The temperature fluctuations shouldn't affect the gin after it's bottled.'

'Have you thought of pulling up the floorboards to have a look?'

'Not so far. But if it turns out the water from the burn does run under the house, we could use it in the gin.'

As they returned to the distillery room, Dania noticed marks on the door, as though a sign had been hastily removed.

'Ah, Miss Hayes,' she heard Val say, 'you're early.'

A tall, severe-looking woman with prematurely greying hair was standing frowning at them.

'Miss Hayes is our cleaner. Miss Hayes, this is Inspector Gorska from the police.'

The woman stared at Dania, her mouth stern. If Val hadn't said she was the cleaner, Dania would have guessed from the smell of lemon polish that came off her in waves.

'Miss Hayes,' she said, smiling and extending a hand. 'I hope I'm not disturbing you.'

The woman's expression softened. She transferred the duster she was clutching in her knobby fingers to her left hand and shook Dania's. 'Is that a Polish accent, Inspector?'

'It is.'

'When I was a wee bairn, my granny used to speak fondly of the Poles. Aye, very gallant, she said they were. She lived in St Andrews during the war.' She paused. 'I could tell you some stories about the soldiers.'

'I'd like to hear them some time.'

Val's mobile rang. She pulled it out of her trousers pocket. 'Will you excuse me?' she said to no one in particular. 'I really have to take this.' She hurried out of the room.

'What brings you all the way out to Breek House, Inspector?'

'Miss Montgomerie offered to show me how she makes gin.'

'Mother's ruin,' Miss Hayes said, grinning. Her smile faded. 'My mother used to work here. She was the cleaner when this was a farmhouse.'

Dania nodded, hoping her smile would encourage the woman to talk.

'Then, after the old gentleman passed on, God rest his soul, things went downhill.' Her eyes took on a strange expression, as though seeing the events that had happened then as if they were happening before her now. 'Breek House.' She sneered. 'Bleak House more like it, my mother used to say. She saw what was happening.'

'And did your mother carry on working here?' Dania said, when the woman seemed reluctant to continue.

'Aye, we needed the money. It was regular work. I'd come with her sometimes.' She turned slowly to look through the window. 'I used to play outside, on that patch of waste ground where there's hundreds of dandelions. I loved the puffballs. They'd all come at once, and when the wind blew, it was like snow falling.'

They heard Val approaching. Dania slipped her card into Miss Hayes's hand. 'Can you call me?' she murmured.

'I'm so sorry about that,' Val said, hurrying into the room.

146

'Business calls are the worst,' she added, smiling ruefully. She looked from one woman to the other expectantly.

'I need to be going, Miss Montgomerie,' Dania said. 'But thank you for showing me round.'

'Thank you for coming.'

She smiled at Miss Hayes. 'A pleasure meeting you. And I'd really like to hear your mother's stories about the Poles.'

The woman nodded, saying nothing. But Dania caught the gleam in her eyes.

Val accompanied her to the front door. 'I do hope you'll bring your colleagues here when we start up our team-building days, Inspector.'

'I'll pass on your invitation.'

As she started the car, she glanced in the rear-view mirror. Val was at the front door, smiling. But it was the figure standing beside and a little way behind her that intrigued Dania. Miss Hayes might turn out to be a mine of information. Most of it interesting. And all of it relevant.

She saw what was happening.

And what would that have been, then?

CHAPTER 15

A couple of days later, Dania was staring at her computer screen, paying little attention to the report she was reading. Her thoughts were constantly on the Brodie Boyle case. Everyone was out, talking to the shoppers at Gallagher Retail Park, the members at Brodie's gym and anyone who used the nearby Olympia swimming pool, a task she didn't envy on such a dismal, rainy day. They had contacted the regulars at the hotel Brodie booked as, after a bit of digging, Hamish had discovered that the Saturday the lad had been killed wasn't the first time he'd paid for a room. But these investigations were proving to be a total waste of time. No one could tell them anything. She and the team were no nearer finding the man he'd had sex with.

Kimmie had rung to say there was nothing of interest in Brodie's Volkswagen, and all the usable dabs on the interior and exterior of the car were his. There was only his gym bag in the boot, with his sweaty kit inside. For the sake of completeness, she'd checked the car for gunshot residue, but found none. Dania was conscious the cost of the investigation was mounting, which would not please the DCI. They were running out of leads, and out of ideas. It was time to do something about that. And, anyway, it was lunchtime.

After leaving the station, she ran the short distance to the

Overgate, keeping half an eye on the rain clouds. An elderly man was seated at the Steinway, picking out one-handed the theme tune of *Game of Thrones*. She leant against the wall of the shoe shop opposite and settled herself to wait.

'Dania?' The voice came from her left.

'Harry! How nice to see you.'

Harry Lombard hurried towards her, beaming. He was wearing brown trousers, and a tweed jacket over an open-throat shirt. And the same aromatic aftershave. This was the first time she'd seen him in anything other than his blue scrubs.

'Are you on your lunch break?' she said.

'Sort of. I usually grab a sandwich and eat it at my desk. But I heard there's a smashing pianist who plays classical music here the odd lunchtime. I've come for the last few days but haven't been lucky.' He frowned at the man at the Steinway. 'And it looks as though I'm not lucky today.'

'If the pianist were here, what would you like him to play?'

'It's a lady, actually.' He ran a hand over his hair. 'I'd love to hear Mendelssohn's Rondo Capriccioso. Do you know it?'

'I do. It starts off all slow and dreamy. And about a third of the way in it changes to something more energetic.'

He nodded happily. 'And then it becomes wild, especially towards the end, with all those loud chords.'

She knew the piece well. In her sheet music, it was marked as *presto*, which she'd always thought was something of an understatement.

The man at the piano had come to the end of his tinkling and was pushing the stool back.

'Excuse me a minute, Harry. Don't go away,' she added quickly. 'I'm coming back.'

Before anyone else could take the empty seat, she sat down and adjusted the stool.

She paused briefly to fill her mind with the music. The Rondo Capriccioso was about seven minutes long, but she played the first part more slowly than usual to make the contrast with what followed more marked; she felt sure that was what the composer had intended.

She finished to enthusiastic applause. Harry was gazing at her with humour in his eyes.

'What a marvellous surprise,' he said, coming over. 'Not only are you a detective but you're a pianist, too. And the mystery pianist, to boot.'

'I've no piano of my own, so I come here to play.'

'Don't let me stop you, if this is your time for practising.'

'I try not to practise on an empty stomach. Have you had lunch?'

'Not yet,' he said eagerly.

'Shall we get a sandwich?'

'Excellent idea.'

They took the steps down to Costa Coffee and bought their food and hot drinks.

'I'm so glad I ran into you,' he said. 'I was going to ring you this afternoon. I've got some more data on those skeletons.'

'Ah? What have you found?' she said, cutting into her mushroom toastie.

'First of all, two of the victims, the ones at Sites A and B, showed evidence of having worked with their hands.'

'How can you tell?' she said in surprise.

'Where the muscles attach to the wrists and have pulled over the years, it creates bony ridges.'

'And the other two? The ones buried further away?'

'They show no such wear and tear.' He sipped his tea. 'We also did an analysis of the isotope ratios. Victims A and B had a relatively high proportion of carbohydrate and fat in what they'd eaten.' He smiled. 'It's what you might call a typically Scottish diet. The other two had eaten more protein.'

'So Victims A and B could have been what? Farmworkers, perhaps.'

'That would be my guess.'

'I don't suppose you could tell if they came from around here?'

'We compared the strontium isotope levels in the bones with values for this area. That told us all the victims were locals. Or, rather, that what they ate and drank was locally sourced.'

'Now for the million-dollar question – did you manage to establish how old the remains are?'

'I was waiting for you to ask that. We sent collagen from the bones to the Scottish Universities Environmental Research Centre in East Kilbride. They do the radiocarbon dating.' He gazed at her steadily. 'We were lucky with these remains.'

'In what way?'

'Anyone who's lived in the nineteen fifties and nineteen sixties has an enriched carbon-14 signal because of all the nuclear weapons' testing that was done then. The carbon-14 found its way into the soil, and from there into humans via the food chain. Younger generations don't have the same signature because this testing has now stopped.'

'So what did you find?' she said impatiently.

'The remains date from between nineteen seventy-five and nineteen eighty-five. I can't be more precise.'

She put her toastie down slowly, her spirits sagging. It was impossible to get away from the fact that, with remains that old, the trail would have gone cold.

'You look disappointed,' he said.

'It's just that the older the crime the harder it is to investigate.'

She injected a note of cheerfulness into her voice. 'But it's still enormously helpful to have the date narrowed down.'

'The fine details are in my report at the office. Shall I have it sent over?'

'Thank you.'

His gaze moved over her face. 'So where will you go from here?' he said softly.

'The first step is to see who was reported missing in that period.' She pushed the remains of the toastie away. 'I'm wondering if the time has come to request DNA profiles. The DCI may decide against it. Or to hold off until we've checked MisPers.'

He nodded sympathetically. He would know how stretched the budgets of public services were.

'Well, do tell me if there's anything else I can do to help.' He stared at the table. 'And I wondered if you'd like to go for a drink sometime.' He looked up at her and smiled. 'Or do the police not fraternise with the lower orders like us scientists?'

'A drink would be great,' she said warmly. 'I have some late shifts coming up, though. I'll give you a ring in the next few days.'

His smile faded, and she realised he might think she was fobbing him off. 'Let me play something for you, Harry,' she said, putting her hand over his. 'What would you like?'

He flushed. 'Gosh. You've put me on the spot, now. How about some more Mendelssohn?'

The piece she chose was 'Sweet Remembrance', Op. 19 No. 1, one of the composer's *Songs without Words*. The elegantly simple melody in the right hand was underscored by the left hand's arpeggios. Most pianists played it in just over three minutes but she preferred it slower.

As she finished, she looked up to see Harry surreptitiously wiping a tear from his eye. She wondered if this piece held a unique place in his heart. Maybe he'd heard it with someone special at a concert. Or perhaps it was simply that he was like her – moved by the beauty of romantic music.

Marek threw the phone on to the sofa. He felt exhausted and depressed. Two days of calls and he was no further forward. He'd contacted half the organisations on Professor Slaughter's list, with mixed results. Some of those replying, especially when he declared he was a friend of Professor Milo Slaughter's, were happy to check their archives, and got back in due course to say that, no, they had never had a Dr Peter de Courcy as a member of their organisation. Others checked first with Milo before replying to the same effect. The rest were deeply suspicious that a foreign-sounding journalist was contacting them and asking for details of their membership. The most defensive was the secretary of the National Hypnotherapy Society, who flatly refused to check the society's databases, even threatening Marek with the police. He felt too dispirited to continue.

He wandered into the kitchen and looked inside the fridge. Disaster. He was out of Wyborowa. How had he let that happen? He opened the tub of pickled herring. *Śledzie*, in Polish. Hard for non-Poles to pronounce. And for Poles who'd drunk too much. He picked out a small piece and chewed slowly. It tasted much better with vodka. He replaced the tub in the fridge.

The cure for his headache was obvious: ring Danka, fall upon her mercy and ask her to help him. But that would give him a bigger headache: she'd need certain details, and those details would inevitably lead her to the discovery that Marek was working for Archie McLellan. He'd never be able to keep that from her, as she was by far the cleverer of the two. She'd worm the information out of him. And hate herself for doing it. And he'd hate himself for putting her in that position.

He returned to the living room and flopped on to the sofa. And, slowly, as he stared at the ceiling rose with its faded pink and white plaster swirls, he remembered his conversation with Archie.

He came from Austria, a neighbour said. Vienna.

Have you considered he may have gone back to Vienna?

Then find his address there.

It was just possible that de Courcy, having retired from a career in hypnotherapy, had returned to his home city to live out his final years.

Marek glanced at his watch. It wasn't too late.

The caller picked up after two rings. He recognised the housekeeper's voice.

'May I please speak with Herr Harti Gassinger?' he said, in fluent German. 'It's Marek Gorski, phoning from Scotland.'

'One minute, please.'

A few moments later, he heard Harti. 'Marek! It's been a long time. How are you, my friend?'

'Excellent. And you?'

'Oh, you know. One manages. How's that beautiful sister of yours?'

'She a detective inspector, now.'

'Women are ruling the world. We need to get equality of the sexes back.'

Marek laughed. 'Listen, Harti, I need a favour.'

'Then you've come to the right man.'

'I'm trying to find someone. An Austrian called Peter de Courcy. He's a hypnotherapist.'

'And he's in Vienna?'

'He may be. He and his wife, Anamaria, came to the UK in nineteen seventy-five. We lost track of him in nineteen eighty-five. We think he lived in Vienna before he came here, and it's possible he's returned.'

A pause. 'That's a long time ago. Over thirty years.'

'I know.'

A longer pause, in which Marek resisted the urge to flatter Harti by telling him he was an excellent investigative journalist and this should be a breeze for him, given his contacts in the Austrian police. But Harti was not one for flattery.

The men had met a couple of years previously in Copenhagen at an international conference for investigative journalists. The talks were pedestrian but, as is the case with conferences, the value of attendance, and of the attendance fee, lay in the contacts made. Harti, a giant of a man with stiff brown hair, had been propping up the bar of the Scandic Palace Hotel, waving a chubby hand and enthralling the delegates with his stories of how he'd infiltrated an Austrian neo-Nazi group and brought the leader to justice.

Marek had stayed drinking with him long after the others had gone to bed. It was as they were thinking they should call it a night that the attack came. Two men who'd been sitting quietly in a shadowy corner rose and walked over. It was Marek who saw the knife in the hand of the taller man. For one frozen instant, he realised the target was not himself but Harti, whose back was turned. In the split second it took him to decide to do something about it, the assassin had stepped forward, his arm raised, his eyes glittering with malice. Marek gripped the arm and swung his fist into the man's face. He staggered back, the knife clattering to the ground. Another blow to the face and he collapsed and lay still. Marek turned to see Harti grinning at him. The second assailant was on his knees, spitting teeth into his hand. A kick to the head from Harti rendered him unconscious.

Marek had picked up the knife. The black handle was emblazoned with an eagle and swastika, and on the blade were the words: *Meine Ehre heißt Treue.*

'"My honour is loyalty",' said Harti, seeing the knife. 'The motto of the SS.' He reached across and gently took it from Marek's hand. 'Unless you want to keep it?'

'Absolutely not,' Marek said in disgust.

Harti riffled through the would-be assassin's shoulder bag and found the black and silver scabbard with its decorative chain.

'What are you going to do with it?' Marek said. 'Give it to the police?'

'Oh, I don't think we need to involve the police, do we?' Harti said, running a thumb across the blade. He lifted his head and his gaze met Marek's. 'We'll end up drowning in paperwork. And I'll miss my plane.' He threw a glance round the empty lounge. 'No one saw anything and, by the time the maid finds these men, assuming they haven't recovered and staggered out of here, I'll be on the early-morning flight to Vienna.'

'But they intended to kill you.'

'It's not the first time. And it won't be the last.' He pulled himself up, almost standing to attention. 'Your quick thinking saved my life, Marek. I'm in your debt. Let's keep in touch,' he added, handing Marek his card.

And they'd kept in touch, meeting a few times in London when Danka was working there, which gave Marek the opportunity to get to know Harti better. Sometimes the Austrian would bring his wife, Gerrit, a slim woman with a boyish haircut and lively brown eyes. An interior decorator, she spoke little English, so their conversations were in German. The four of them spent several merry, boozy evenings together in the bars around Leicester Square. Although Harti could put away enough to floor an ox, he remained stone-cold sober, his gaze constantly wandering around the room and flying to the door whenever it opened. Marek, noticing that he made a point of sitting with his back to the wall, wondered if there had been further attempts on his life. By mutual consent, neither spoke to Danka about the Copenhagen incident, and Marek suspected Gerrit had also been kept in the dark. It was some time afterwards that he learnt more of Harti's past from a Polish historian friend. Harti's grandfather had been a high-ranking official in the security services of the Austrian SS.

'Have you got a physical description of this de Courcy?' Harti was saying.

'He was a short man. And he wore half-moon reading glasses. In the nineteen eighties, he had dark hair, which was all over the place. It will be grey or white now. Oh, and he had an old scar on his cheek.'

It was a while before Harti spoke. 'Leave it with me, Marek. But next time I'm in Scotland, you must let me take you and your sister to the best Michelin-starred restaurant in town.'

Marek laughed. 'It's a deal,' he replied, knowing that Harti was unlikely ever to make it to Dundee. 'But only if you bring Gerrit.'

He ended the call. Harti's comment about Scotland lingered in his mind. Maybe he should send Harti and Gerrit a firm invitation to visit in the summer. Danka had to have some time off, and they could show the Austrians round the Dundee clubs. It was a nice thought.

CHAPTER 16

'So that's the list of the long-term missing from this area,' Dania said. 'Over the ten-year period nineteen seventy-five to nineteen eighty-five.'

Honor and Hamish stared at the screen.

'These are the ones for whom the cases have gone cold,' she added. 'I've filtered the results to those in the relevant height and age group.'

Hamish ran a hand over his face. 'How many does that leave, ma'am?'

'Four hundred and fifty-eight.'

'*How* many?'

'I suppose DNA testing is out of the question?' Honor said tentatively.

'Assuming we can find living relatives. But that number of tests would bankrupt Police Scotland. The other thing to factor in is that one or more of our victims may not even be on this list. They may have had no immediate family to report them missing. And their friends may have concluded they'd left the area.'

'That's just dandy,' Hamish said gloomily. 'What about farm-workers? Or the construction industry? Professor Lombard said two of them had worked with their hands.'

'There are fewer than a dozen of those. I'd be inclined to start there.'

'I sense a "but",' Honor said.

'Something tells me it's a wasted effort. I think we need to look at this in another way.'

They waited expectantly.

'The problem is that I don't yet know what that way is.'

Her phone rang. She stiffened. 'I need to take this.'

The others left the room quickly.

After the door had closed, she yanked the prepaid out of her pocket. She didn't need to look to see who had called. 'Laszlo?' she said.

'Lloyd, I'm in Donnan's.'

She drew in her breath sharply. Quinn was taking a hell of a risk.

He spoke quickly. 'We're having a fire drill, and everyone's outside. I'm in Archie's office. Nothing in his desk, and his PC is password-protected. But his filing cabinet's open. Lots of stuff about getting Donnan's up and running. But, right at the back, I found an old folder. It's labelled Breek House.' A pause. 'Hello? Are you there, Lloyd?'

'How old is this folder?'

'Everything in it goes back to before the seventies. Mainly letters, and invoices for livestock and farming equipment.'

Her mind was spinning. Why did Archie McLellan have a folder with all this paperwork for Breek House? 'Anything else?'

'There are no firearms in the office. Unless they're in the wall safe. Some of those cartridges stamped with ZVS might be there too.' A pause. 'Look, I've got to go.'

'Okay. And thanks.'

But Laszlo had already rung off.

★　★　★

Honor and Hamish were in the corridor, deep in conversation. They looked up in alarm as the door burst open.

'Breek House,' Dania said breathlessly. 'Who owned it before the council?'

Honor threw Hamish a glance. They hurried into the room.

'Do a search,' Dania said, sitting down and motioning to the chairs. 'Now.'

'Okay, Registers of Scotland first,' Honor said. 'Then I'll try the Register of Sasines.'

Dania watched as the girl's fingers sped across the keys.

'Here it is, boss.' Her eyes widened. 'Crikey,' she murmured. 'The previous owner was Archibald McLellan.'

In the growing silence, Dania heard herself say, 'And when did he sell the house to the council?'

'July two thousand. I don't get it. Didn't Val Montgomerie say the council owned the place for as long as anyone could remember?'

'It's what the estate agent thought. But this changes everything. How did Archie get to own Breek House?'

A few seconds later, the girl said, 'The previous owner was Donnan McLellan.'

Blue was my father's favourite colour. I named this casino after him.

'That's his dad,' Dania said. 'Can you check if he had any children other than Archie and Ned?'

A minute went by while Honor worked her magic. 'Nope,' she said finally. 'Donnan McLellan had Archibald and then, ten years later, Edward was born. Donnan died in nineteen seventy-five. Suicide. And Breek House passed to Archibald, the older son.' She paused. 'I know what you're thinking, boss. Those bodies were put into the grounds of Breek House between nineteen seventy-five and nineteen eighty-five. And that's when Archie owned the place.'

'And he was out of jail in nineteen seventy-eight.'

'Broken bones look like Archie McLellan's handiwork. He isn't above resorting to that kind of torture.' The girl smiled. 'And if we can establish the identities of the victims, and show that Archie had had dealings with them . . .'

'. . . then we might be able to nail the Nailer.'

'And that would be a good day out,' the girl said softly.

Hamish was frowning. 'There's one thing I don't get. Okay, there are broken bones. But no nails, or holes that could have been made by nails, in any of the skulls.'

'Fair point,' Dania said. 'But think about it a minute. A nail in the forehead is Archie's signature. He intends the victim to be found, and everyone to know who did it. But the four buried in the grounds of Breek House were just that. Buried. Out of sight. Had it not been for the farmworker's dog, they might have lain there for decades. Centuries, even. If Archie had no intention they would be found, why bother with nails?'

'So who were those poor bastards?' Hamish said in frustration.

'If we can find that out, and link them to Archie, we'll solve the Breek House murders.'

And, thought Dania, her excitement mounting, they might be able to solve the murder of Brodie Boyle into the bargain. Although they had only a few pieces of the puzzle, and no way yet of fitting them together, she was rapidly coming to the conclusion that whatever linked Archie to the bones victims linked him also to Brodie.

It was just after midday when Dania pushed through the revolving doors of Donnan's. The rain of the day before had eased, leaving behind a slab of grey sky. She'd expected to have to ask one of the bouncers to take her to see Archie, but he was in the corridor, talking on his mobile. He was dressed casually in large jeans, white trainers and an off-white zip-up sweatshirt. Her immediate thought was that all he needed was the blue baseball cap and he'd be a dead ringer for the figure they'd caught on Gellatly Street's CCTV.

Seeing Dania, he said quickly into the phone, 'Got to go. I'll catch you later.' He ended the call.

'I'm sorry if this is an inconvenient time, Mr McLellan,' she said.

'Not at all, Inspector.' He pulled his thick lips back into a smile. 'Is this business or pleasure?'

'Business.'

'In that case, let's go to my office,' he said promptly.

He led the way into the nightclub, which was empty except for a couple of card players. One was Ned McLellan, his gaze moving rapidly over his cards as if that might improve his chances. The fading bruise on his cheek now had more yellow in it than purple. He seemed an unlikely guest at Donnan's, with his unwashed hair and his worn navy suit, stained at the lapel. The grey-haired woman opposite looked in her eighties. She had a pallid face with huge bags under the eyes. Her liver-spotted hands were clutching her cards to her blue ribbed jumper, and as Archie approached, she pressed them tighter to her chest, watching him with a stony expression.

'Mother, may I introduce Inspector Dania Gorska?' Archie said.

The woman lifted her gaze to Dania and studied her openly, her expression not unfriendly. If she thought it strange that a policewoman would call on her son at his nightclub, she gave no indication.

Dania smiled. 'Good afternoon, Mrs McLellan.'

'Inspector,' the woman replied, nodding. Her voice was the

harsh rasp of a fifty-a-day smoker. She turned her attention back to her game.

'And have you met my brother, Ned?'

'Aye, we met the other evening. At the bar,' Ned said, his eyes on his cards.

'While we're here, Inspector,' Archie said, 'may I offer you a drink?'

'I'm on duty.'

'A cigarette, perhaps?'

'Thank you, but I don't smoke.'

He ushered her through the side door.

'Please have a seat,' he said, when they were in the office.

He took the swivel chair and she sat opposite. From the corner of her eye, she glimpsed the filing cabinet, but resisted the urge to look directly at it.

'I take it you're here about young Brodie,' he said. 'Are you any further forward?'

'We're following several lines of enquiry, Mr McLellan, but I'm not here about that.'

He inclined his head quizzically.

She pulled out her notebook. 'It's about the remains found at Breek House.'

For an instant, a guarded expression crossed his face.

'The first time we met, you asked me how long the remains had been there,' she said. 'I can tell you now. The bodies were put into the ground between nineteen seventy-five and nineteen eighty-five.'

The silence hung between them, and then he said, 'And you'll have checked who owned Breek House at that time.'

'You didn't think to mention it.'

'Why would I? I reckoned the burials were more recent. Nothing to do with me.'

'But you can't say that now.'

'But I can.' He nodded at the notebook in her hand. 'For the record, I know nothing about those bodies.'

'Why should I believe you?'

He shrugged, evidently not angered by the implication that he was lying. 'Anyone could have buried them on my land. It's a braw location. Isolated, surrounded by woodland that's easy to get into.'

'How isolated is it, though? Was it not a working farm then, surrounded by other farms? Workers coming and going?'

'Not every hour of every day. Workers have to sleep. And only a complete bampot would dispose of bodies during the day when he could do it at night.'

'What made you sell Breek House to the council?'

'It was losing money hand over fist, like many farms. I wasn't always around to manage things.' He played with the folder on his desk, lifting a corner, then flattening it. 'To be honest, I'm not much of a farmer. When I got out of prison, I was more inter-ested in building my property business. Word on the street was that the council were looking for somewhere they could convert into a care home. I contacted them and they jumped at the offer.'

'How many people did you employ at Breek House?'

'I forget now, it was a long time ago. It would have been the usual number for a farm that size.'

'You wouldn't happen to remember any names?'

He looked hard at her. 'Are you thinking those poor bastards buried in the grounds were workers at the farm?'

'It's possible.'

It was a while before he spoke. 'Most were casual labourers. We took them on as and when we needed them. I don't remember any names.'

'Do you still have records from that time?'

'I had a big clear-out when I sold the place. I reckon I've not got a lot left.' He nodded at the filing cabinet. 'It'll be there, if there's anything. Do you want me to look?'

'If you wouldn't mind.'

He rummaged through the bottom drawer of the cabinet and produced a tattered beige folder, which he placed on the desk. The words 'Breek House' were scrawled on it in blue biro.

He opened it and swivelled it round. 'Go ahead and have a look,' he said, pushing it across. 'Take your time.'

She flicked through the papers. There were letters between Donnan McLellan and his bank, invoices and receipts for feed and farm equipment and copies of returns to the Inland Revenue. She went through everything a second time.

'It's all dated from before nineteen seventy-five,' she said, glancing up.

A pained look crossed Archie's face. 'Aye, that was when my dad died.'

'And it was when you took possession of the farm.' She paused. 'So where are the papers dating from your time as owner?'

'As I said, I cleared everything out when the council bought the place.'

She pushed back the folder. 'But you kept this.'

'For sentimental reasons. It was all I had left of my dad.'

'And who owned the house and farm before your father?'

'My granddad. Breek House had been in the McLellan family for generations.'

She gazed into Archie's eyes, seeing something there that she didn't expect, a look of great sadness.

'I often wonder whether I shouldn't have tried to make a go of it, Inspector. For my dad's sake. Aye, he wouldn't have wanted the farm to go under.' He shook his head sadly. 'But farming simply isn't in my blood.' He gestured at the wall behind her. 'That's my dad, there.'

165

The framed photo was of a man in his thirties, leaning over a barred gate and gazing unsmilingly into the camera. There was a faint resemblance between him and his son, Ned, but she saw nothing of Archie in him. The man's pinched lips and troubled eyes made her wonder if he resented having to quarry the land for a living, the way his forebears had done. At least it was an honest, if hard, way of life. What would he have made of the path Archie had followed?

As if reading her mind, Archie said, 'I've put the photo there so he can watch me getting on with running my businesses. I may be a bit of a numpty when it comes to farming but I'm making a success of the casino. I hope he can see that from wherever he is.'

She was tempted to ask about the circumstances of Donnan McLellan's suicide, but the look on Archie's face stopped her.

'I think that's all for now, Mr McLellan,' she said, getting to her feet. 'Thank you for your time.'

'Only too happy to help. I hope I've demonstrated that.'

As she left Donnan's, she cast a look behind her. Archie McLellan was standing watching through the doors, a strange expression on his face, as though he weren't looking at her, but at something that had happened in his past. And was still very much in his present.

CHAPTER 17

Quinn was tidying away the playing cards. The casino had just closed, and Dundee would be stirring in an hour's time, its citizens waking to a sleepy Saturday morning and wondering if it was worth dragging themselves out to do their weekly shop. He, on the other hand, was going home to crash out. And not before time, as he was well and truly knackered.

He was one of the last to leave, taking the left turn into Candle Lane and heading towards the bus station on Seagate. The first glimmer of dawn told him that the sun was rising. He imagined the light lifting in from the horizon and touching the tops of the buildings, warming the air and dispersing the damp odour from the river. It would be a while before its rays reached Candle Lane, and he kept his eyes on the cobbles so as not to lose his footing.

He was so absorbed in scanning the ground that he didn't hear the soft footfalls behind him until it was too late. A blanket was thrown over his head, and his arms were gripped. Struggling was futile, as the men holding him meant business. He tried to quell the rising tide of panic as he was marched up Candle Lane and bundled into the back seat of a car, colliding with a person sitting there. The pulling back of a handgun's slide, and the pressing of something hard against his head, caused him to freeze.

'That's it, laddie,' a quiet voice that sounded like Archie's said. 'Sit nice, and everything will be fine.'

The car pulled away.

Quinn tried to work out where they were heading from the direction of travel and the mental map he had of Dundee, but the car made so many turns, some back on itself, which he guessed was done deliberately, that he soon lost any sense of where he was. Some twenty minutes later, they pulled up and the driver cut the engine.

'Out,' the man beside him said. As if to reinforce the message, he prodded Quinn roughly in the ribs with the handgun.

His heart was thudding painfully. He felt for the door, but a hand grabbed him and dragged him out. The absence of traffic and the cawing of crows suggested he was in one of the villages skirting Dundee. The arms gripped him again and he was bundled away, feeling the deep ruts under his feet change to wooden floorboards. The blanket was whisked off and he smelt mildew, overlaid with earth and manure, but before he could take in his gloomy surroundings, an oily rag was tied over his eyes.

'Put him there,' the soft voice said.

Hearing it more clearly convinced Quinn that his hunch was correct, and the speaker was Archie McLellan. And who else knew he'd be making his way home from Donnan's at six in the morning?

'Tie his wrists and ankles,' Archie said.

He was pushed down on to what felt like a canvas bed. His wrists were seized, and plastic cable ties slipped over them and pulled tight, securing his arms to the bedframe. He struggled fiercely in the grip of a bowel-churning fear until he felt the handgun against his temple.

'Uh, uh,' Archie said. 'That'll do you no good, lad.'

His legs were pulled apart and his ankles tied to the frame.

'Right, boys, you can go.' A rustle of paper. 'Here's something for your trouble.' Footsteps receding, and the sound of a door being opened and closed.

A chill spread through Quinn's chest as he realised he was totally at Archie's mercy. 'What the hell do you want, McLellan?' he said through gritted teeth.

'Just a wee blether. I've got a few questions for you.'

He tried to settle his mind. This might be simply routine, something Archie did now and again to keep his employees in line. The man didn't intend to kill him. If he did, why bother blindfolding him?

'Let's get on with it then,' he said, with a bravado he didn't feel.

'That's more like it.' A pause. 'Let's start with Breek House. What's your interest in it?'

'Breek House? I've never heard of it.'

'It's been in the papers, those human remains found on the land. I ken fine well you've heard of it. So I'll ask you again. What's your interest in it?'

Quinn tried to keep his voice businesslike. 'I've no interest in it.'

'Is that right, now? Then why were you snooping around the main office yesterday morning, eh? When we had fire practice.'

He felt a plunge in his stomach. Had Archie crept back in? And heard his conversation with Dania? He'd closed the office door so his voice wouldn't carry. Maybe this was a bluff and Archie had nothing on him. He decided to brazen it out.

'I wasn't snooping. You're mistaken.'

'I heard your voice, lad.'

'It must have been someone else. I was with the others the whole time. Except when I snuck round the corner for a quick fag.'

A long sigh. 'You know, Quinn, you're doing yourself no favours by lying.' There was courtesy in the voice. 'I heard it all.

Including what you said about firearms. Aye, and what's your interest there, I'd like to know?'

He felt his guts turn to water. There was no point denying it now. But he needed to keep Dania out of this. He had a sudden flash of inspiration. 'I'm looking for a gun for someone.'

The voice was close to his ear now, so close he could smell the sour breath. 'And you reckoned you'd find one in the casino, is that right?'

'Word on the street is that you're bringing them in.' He took a deep breath, trying to keep his voice steady. 'I thought there'd be one in the office.'

'Just lying around.'

'Or hidden in the filing cabinet. That's how I came across the folder on Breek House.'

'And decided to take a wee keek inside.'

'As you said, Breek House has been in the news. I was curious.'

'And did you find anything of interest?'

'Just old stuff about the farm.'

'So who were you talking to on the phone yesterday?'

'The man who wanted to buy the firearm.'

'Name?'

Archie had heard it. Now was not the time to lie. 'Lloyd.'

'And who's Lloyd?'

'Someone I've known for a long time.'

He felt a hand slide up the inside of his thigh and grip his crotch. 'Your boyfriend, perhaps?' came the murmured voice.

Strong fingers kneaded his balls. 'He's not my boyfriend,' he gasped. 'Just a mate I want to help out.'

'A girlfriend, then?'

The zip was slowly pulled down. A second later, the fingers were inside his trousers, searching for his genitals, rubbing, squeezing.

'It wasn't my girlfriend.' Despite his fear, he felt his penis start to harden.

Archie removed his hand. 'Let's cut to the chase, laddie. Lloyd is Detective Inspector Dania Gorska, am I right?'

'Who?'

'Did the two of you have a cosy wee chat that evening she came to Donnan's with her brother, eh?'

'I've no idea what you're talking about,' he said thickly, feeling the strength leave him.

'You know, Quinn, there's one thing I can't abide. And that's folk who don't credit me with intelligence.'

'I swear I don't know her.'

'I'll pretend I didn't hear that. What I want from you is the answer to one simple question. Was she more interested in Breek House? Or was it all about the firearms? It couldn't be simpler.' A pause. 'Breek House?' Another pause. 'Or firearms?'

There was a rush of blood in his ears. Would Archie try to beat the answer out of him? He'd been in similar situations and knew he could stand it. But was it worth it? Dania's main interest was surely the converted replicas. If he gave up Breek House, would that really matter? In fact, would it not be wise to steer the subject away from the guns?

'All right, Mr McLellan, I'll talk.'

'Ach, don't Mr McLellan me. I'm not into flattery.'

'I'm a police informant. I report directly to DCI Ireland.'

The silence rang in his head.

'The police want to know what your interest in Breek House is,' he continued. When there was still no reply, he added, 'I'm willing to help you. Tell me what you want to know.'

A snort. 'What is this? We're supposed to make nice, now?' A pause. 'You know something? I'm no longer interested. And I don't believe anything you say, anyway.'

Footfalls away to the other side of the room, and then back again.

'I'll tell you what I'm going to do, Quinn, just so's we're clear.' Something cold and hard touched his hand.

'I reckon that's your wanking hand. So curl your fingers round this and tell me what you think it is.'

Quinn moved his fingers carefully, feeling the wooden shaft, the cold slug of metal at the end, the two claws. Fear surged through him. 'It's a hammer,' he whispered.

'The best I could buy at Homebase. Now, I'm just going to move you on to this plastic sheet. And then we can begin.'

He felt the bed lift at one corner. There was a crackling of plastic, and then the other corners were lifted in turn. More crackling. Suddenly, a thick rag was crammed into his mouth, forcing his jaws apart so wide he thought they'd dislocate. He tried to scream but it came out as a desperate mumble.

'Best if you calmy doony, lad. Difficult, right enough, but if you try and shout, you're in danger of choking. And we wouldn't want that. We need to play the game to the end.'

He struggled against the restraints, feeling the room tilt around him. The fingers were inside his trousers again, massaging his limp penis. After a few seconds, Archie removed his hand.

'I'm going to begin with the arms,' he said softly. 'The lower arms, to be precise. Those bones are easier to snap. Then I'll move on to the lower legs.'

Quinn's stomach lurched. After what felt like an eternity, he heard a grunt, followed by a cracking sound. Pain seared through his lower arm, shooting up into his shoulder. He howled like a dog, the sound emerging as a loud rumble.

'How was it for you, Quinn? Good?'

His arm pulsed with pain. He pulled his undamaged arm up as

far as it would go, clenching his fist and trying to break out of the restraints.

'Don't bother, son. You'll only tire yourself out.' A pause. 'So, are we ready for the other arm?'

Quinn thrashed about, not caring that it was futile, because all he wanted to do was to stop the pain, stop Archie, get out of there and as far away as he could.

The hammer came down harder this time. Nausea surged through him. He felt waves of blackness swell and recede.

'Now for the legs, Quinn. It'll need a few goes, I reckon.'

As the hammer came down again and again, he felt his entire body burn. He was no longer aware of Archie or what he was doing. Unable to lift his limbs, he lay shuddering and twitching, hoping the pain would tip him over into unconsciousness.

Archie's voice came to him as though from a distance. 'And now, my lad, what we've both been waiting for. The finishing touch.'

Something sharp was placed against his forehead. A sudden flash of light, numbness in his arms and legs, and he went spinning into the dark.

Marek finished his article and sent it to his editor. That should keep the woman busy for a while. It was Saturday morning, and he wanted to take Danka to lunch at the Dundee Contemporary Arts. A quick phone call confirmed she was free and, yes, she'd meet him at the DCA.

An hour later, he climbed the steps from the car park and pushed through the glass door, savouring the rich smell of food and alcohol. His sister was already seated at a window table, gazing out at the low unbroken clouds. She'd ordered a bottle of

San Pellegrino. The absence of wine or vodka suggested she was on duty.

He leant over and kissed her lightly on the cheek. 'I'm glad you could make it, Danka.'

'Me too. I've been staring at a computer screen all morning.'

He pulled out the chair opposite. 'The Brodie Boyle case?'

'The Breek House case.'

'Anything you can tell me?'

'The victims were found in pairs. I'm wondering if there were people who went missing at more or less the same time, so I've been working through MisPers.'

'Sounds like a thankless task. Any joy?'

'My problem is I don't know how to define "at more or less the same time". We have a ten-year window.'

'Maybe you need a statistician.'

She smiled. 'Maybe I need a vodka. Shall we order?'

He went for the pan-fried rainbow trout and she ordered a salad of pear and grilled goat's cheese.

'What are you up to these days?' she said, as they waited. 'Any further in finding your doctor?'

'I think he may have gone back to Vienna.'

'He's Austrian? Then Harti's your man. He's well connected, especially with the police.'

'I'm in luck. He's offered to help me.' Marek paused. 'The man I'm looking for will be in his seventies or eighties. There's no point asking around or putting up flyers because he moved away in nineteen eighty-five.'

She poured water for them both. 'Have you tried the obvious? An Internet search?'

'I got nowhere.'

'Social media?'

'I didn't think about social media in view of his age. But it's worth a try.'

They chatted about nothing in particular until their food arrived.

'You know, Danka, I've been thinking. If I can persuade Harti and Gerrit to come over in the summer, we could all go on a road trip. How do you feel about that?'

'I'd never get the time off. All I can manage is the odd half-day here and there.'

'You need to find someone. If only because you'll work yourself into the ground otherwise.'

'I'm not the sort of woman men fall in love with.'

'Nonsense. You just have to get out there. Ah, from that smile, I'm guessing you already have.'

'Not quite, but there's someone I'm interested in.'

'Care to tell me who it is?' he said, inclining his head.

She hesitated. 'Not yet. Nothing may come of it.'

'What's he like?'

'Someone I feel comfortable around. It's the first time I've felt like this since leaving the Met.'

Marek didn't press her. She'd always been reluctant to talk about her personal life, even when they'd shared a flat. They might be brother and sister, but they were different people in that respect.

In the way they'd heard the British do when they ran out of things to say, they fell to talking about Brexit. Article 50 had still not been revoked but no one thought the process of leaving the EU could now be reversed. The issue of what would happen to EU nationals like themselves had still to be addressed, but the way the government was going about things left them in no doubt that this was something none of the politicians had thought through.

'I have to run, Marek,' she said, gulping her coffee. She opened her bag.

'I'll get this. You go on.'

She leant across the table and kissed his forehead. 'Thanks. My treat next time.'

'Let's try to keep more in touch. I hardly see you these days.'

He watched her go, wondering who the mystery man was who'd taken her fancy. It would be someone from work. Who else did she have time to see in her high-pressure job? It might be DC Laurence Whyte. He had that shy look about him that women seemed to love. The first time Marek had met the man, he'd hardly made eye contact with Danka. There was interest there but he seemed too timid to do anything about it. Some men were put off approaching competent women. Fortunately, Marek wasn't one of them.

He paid the bill and headed back to the flat.

His mind strayed to something Danka had said. He'd assumed that a man as old as Peter de Courcy wouldn't have a social-media profile, but that assumption might be incorrect. He opened the laptop and did a Facebook search. There were several people by that name but their profiles didn't fit, and they were far too young. But they could be relatives. He left messages, explaining who he was and asking if they were related to the hypnotherapist, Peter de Courcy. Worth a try, although he doubted he'd get anywhere.

He thought again about his Internet search. Perhaps his approach had been too simplistic. If de Courcy had practised decades ago, it was hardly surprising that the web links returned had led nowhere. He would need to dig deeper and do it systematically. Using a website that allowed him to remove the top hundred sites, then the top thousand, and so on up to a million, would give him his best chance. He entered a variety of search terms in English and German. It was early evening before he'd exhausted all possibilities, and himself as well. The first site that looked promising was in German, and carried an article from the newspaper *Die Presse*. It was dated 25 April 1975.

He read it quickly, and then again, more slowly. The gist was that Herr Professor Doktor Peter de Courcy had left his post at the Reisinger Institute after several successful years. It wasn't clear why he'd gone, but the reporter hinted that it had something to do with the death of one of the patients.

Herr Professor Doktor Peter de Courcy stared out of the screen. He was wearing a double-breasted dark jacket and spotted bow tie. The photographer had caught him off guard because he looked both startled and slightly afraid. He had heavily lidded eyes and a shock of dark hair, which grew up in tufts. It was hard to tell from the grainy photo, but it looked as though he had a scar on his left cheek.

Could this be the man Marek was looking for? That particular Peter de Courcy had come to Britain from Vienna in 1975. Could he be the Herr Professor Doktor who'd left the Reisinger Institute in 1975? The year 1975 seemed too much of a coincidence. And there was the physical description. Although the man in the photo wasn't wearing reading glasses, he had a scar on his cheek. And Archie's comment about 'dark hair, all over the place' was spot on. It had to be the same man. Had to be.

Marek did a search on the Reisinger Institute. A private clinic, obscenely expensive, evidenced by the absence of prices on their website, it was one of the oldest in Vienna. The list of treatments didn't include hypnotherapy, but that meant nothing. It might not be offered now but could have been in 1975. And, if so, de Courcy might have practised it. But the article hinted at a patient dying. Surely it wasn't possible to die under hypnosis. Perhaps hypnotherapy was only one of Peter de Courcy's specialisms, and the patient's death was due to something else. It was even possible the death had nothing to do with him, but the institute had needed a scapegoat.

Marek printed off the article. He now had something firm to go on. He rang Harti and left a voicemail, outlining what he'd found, and clarifying what he needed to know. The Austrian would do the rest.

CHAPTER 18

'So what's this diagram, ma'am?' Laurence was saying.

Dania sat back, crossing her arms. 'I've been thinking about those skeletons at Breek House, specifically how they were buried. I'm wondering if each pair of victims was killed at more or less the same time. What do you think?'

'Definitely worth a punt.'

She and Laurence were the only ones on duty, and she wanted to run her theory past him before letting it loose on the others. 'Tech have created this tool for me,' she said, picking up the mouse. 'The horizontal axis shows the time between nineteen seventy-five and nineteen eighty-five. The four hundred and fifty-eight people reported missing over that period, who are in the right height and age group, are represented by dots. There are so many that, on this scale, they form a continuous straight line.'

'And why are there two lines?'

'Pink for girls and blue for boys.'

Laurence grinned. 'Is that politically correct?'

'I won't tell if you won't. Now, if I zoom in, the line breaks up into individual dots.' A couple of clicks and the horizontal axis changed to show data from January to December 1980. 'If I double-click on a dot, a window comes up with the name of the missing person, the date they were reported missing, and any other pertinent information.'

'Wow, ma'am, who set all this up?'

'Louise. I discovered that, as well as being an analyst, she's a stats expert. She had a career as an environmental statistician before she joined the force.'

Interest blazed on Laurence's face. Dania happened to know that he was sweet on Louise. And, according to Honor, Louise was sweet on Laurence. Neither party had made a move on the other, the girl had said, adding that, in the interests of scientific experimentation, she'd decided to say nothing and see how long it was before they realised they were made for each other and got their act together.

'Why are some of the blue dots bigger than others?' Laurence said, squinting at the screen.

'Those are people who did manual work. There are ten.'

'So, if we're thinking about Sites A and B, we need to find pairs of big blue dots that are close together in time?'

'Exactly. But none of the big blue dots is close to any other. They're spread out right across that ten-year period.'

He frowned. 'In that case, shall we concentrate on the other pair? The man and the woman at Sites C and D?'

'Then we're looking for a blue dot close to a pink one. Now watch. With a bit of Louise's magic, I can move the lines so they almost superimpose.'

She could feel Laurence's breath on her cheek as he leant forward for a better look. 'That is totally brilliant,' he said reverentially.

'Let's start from January nineteen seventy-five, and go right through to December nineteen eighty-five.'

She could see he wanted to grab the mouse and do it himself, but rank has its privileges. 'The problem is deciding what constitutes close together in time. What would you say, Laurence?'

He puffed out his lips. 'We could try one week apart? And then widen it?'

She zoomed in and ran the mouse slowly along the screen.

'There!' he shouted into her ear, making her jump. He jabbed at the screen where a blue and a pink dot were almost superimposed.

She brought up the profiles. 'It's a husband and wife. Reported missing in mid-April nineteen eighty-one by their teenage son. The wife went missing first. A week later, the husband.'

The photos showed a harassed-looking woman with soulful dark eyes, and a man with a fat nose and lank hair. His arrogant, brutish expression suggested one explanation for his wife's disappearance. Not many things would force a mother to leave her teenage son but abuse was one of them. 'Let's move on,' she said.

After an hour, they'd reached 1985, having found a large number of blue-pink pairs. She surrendered the mouse to Laurence, wondering if there was a better way.

'Here's a really interesting one,' he said. 'A sister. Reported missing by her brother. And then the brother himself goes missing. I can think of all sorts of scenarios where a husband and wife go missing. But why would a brother and sister go missing at about the same time?' He continued to move the mouse. 'Okay, this pair here is of a totally unrelated couple. He's a teacher who didn't show up for work. Two days later, a prostitute was reported missing by her mates.' He brought up the photo of the tom. Black curly hair framed a face with red lips and wide, vacant eyes.

'How do you know these two are unrelated? Maybe the teacher ran off with the prostitute.' She hesitated. 'You know what I'm thinking? You should go and see Louise and ask her to write a script that will go through the data and pull out these pairs.'

181

He chewed a nail. 'You think she's on shift now?'

'I happen to know she is.' Dania looked closely at the screen so he wouldn't see her smile. 'And, as your shifts both end shortly, maybe you could take her out afterwards.'

'Take her out?' he said nervously. 'Why?'

'To thank her, of course.'

'But I'll freeze up.'

She looked deep into his anxious green eyes. 'Oh, I think she'll defrost you.'

It was just after five thirty p.m. and Dania was on the point of dragging herself home when she remembered she hadn't rung Harry. He might be at work on a Saturday afternoon and be persuaded to stroll into the town centre for a drink. Then again, he might actually have a life and be at home, getting ready to go out. Perhaps this wasn't the time to call. But she'd been thinking about him off and on since running into him in the Overgate and was finding that thoughts of him were now more on than off.

She rang his work number. It was answered after two rings.

'Harry Lombard,' came the confident reply.

'Harry, it's Dania.'

'Dania! How nice to hear from you.'

'I'm just finishing work and wondered if you're free this evening.'

'I'll be free in about half an hour,' came the eager reply.

She was about to suggest meeting for a drink, but something made her say, 'Do you fancy coming round for dinner? I'm making a Polish dish this evening.' That wasn't strictly true. She'd made it the evening before in great quantities because, like most Polish dishes, it benefited from being reheated.

'Polish cuisine? That would be lovely.'

'You're not a vegetarian, are you?'

'There's hardly anything I don't eat. Can I bring something? Wine, perhaps?'

'I've got everything we need. But thank you.' She gave him her address on Victoria Road. 'I'm on the top floor above the carpet shop. There's an entryphone system.'

'Excellent. I'll be there as soon as I've finished.'

She noted the anticipation in his voice. Perhaps he, too, was hoping the evening might turn out to be more than simply dinner.

She was still smiling when Laurence hurried in. One look at his face told her that things hadn't gone well.

He flopped down next to her. 'Louise said she'll have the script ready and run by tomorrow. Monday at the latest.'

'And did you ask her out?'

'She was called away somewhere before I had the chance.' He looked at his hands. 'And then her pal told me she has a smoking-hot date tonight,' he added miserably.

'Ah.'

He looked so wretched that Dania was almost tempted to ask him to join Harry and her for dinner.

Dania glanced round her living-cum-dining room, wondering whether she hadn't made a blunder in inviting Harry. Although the flat was spotless – she was scrupulous where that was concerned – it was a mess, reflecting her current modus operandi. In fact, 'mess' was an understatement. The books were still everywhere, and the packing crates were still pushed up against the wall. And there was no time to do much about it now.

She removed the books from the table and piled them on the crates. From the kitchen drawer, she drew out an old linen table-cloth embroidered with brightly coloured flowers. It was from the

Kaszubian region of western Poland and had been a gift from her grandmother. She rammed the pork dish into the oven to reheat, put the pre-peeled potatoes on, and laid the table.

She was putting her hair up when the entryphone system buzzed.

'Dania?' came the voice. 'It's Harry.'

'Come on up,' she said, pressing the entry button.

Half a minute later, she heard his footsteps on the stairs. She opened the door.

He was standing half hidden behind an enormous bouquet of gardenias.

'Is that you, Harry?'

He poked his head out, beaming. 'These are for you,' he said, handing her the flowers. 'And these too,' he added, thrusting a box into her hand.

'Ooh, Belgian chocolates. Thank you.'

'It's the least I can do. You've been slaving over a hot stove, after all.'

She thought about the thirty seconds she'd spent in the kitchen. 'Would you like a drink? I can offer whisky or vodka. Or Polish beer.'

'It'll have to be vodka, if we're eating Polish.'

'Excellent choice. Come through and take a seat.'

She arranged the flowers in a vase and brought it into the living room. Harry was sitting on the cushioned wickerwork armchair, looking as though he lived there. She appreciated a man who could make himself at home and didn't need to be fussed over.

There was nowhere to put the vase, and the table was too small for such a large arrangement, so she set the flowers on a packing crate. The sweet, heady scent perfumed the air, masking the ever-present smell of damp. If Harry thought the presence of packing crates unusual, he said nothing. He continued to look round the room, taking in the decorated high ceiling and the long windows with their floor-length shutters.

She fetched a bottle and two small glasses from the kitchen. 'This is Starka,' she said, setting the vodka on the table. 'It's made from rye and has fifty per cent alcohol by volume.'

He got to his feet. 'Just the ticket, then.'

She filled the glasses and handed him one.

'Well, bottoms up,' he said. Before she could stop him, he'd downed the vodka in one.

She watched in dismay as his eyes watered, and a deep flush spread across his face.

'My God,' he wheezed, clutching his throat. 'What just happened?'

'You're supposed to breathe in, drink it down, then breathe out. Not the other way round.'

'My throat's burning,' he gasped, sinking into the armchair.

'Shall I get some water?'

'No, no, it's starting to pass.' He wiped his eyes and looked up at her with a little-boy expression. 'I made a mess of that, didn't I?'

She was unable to think of a suitable reply that wouldn't hurt his feelings. He started to laugh. Relieved, she joined in.

'Would you like another?' she said.

'Is that a dare?' He paused. 'Maybe you could show me how it's done.'

'With this vodka, I wouldn't drink it in one go. It has a slight flavour.' She poured half a measure into his glass. 'Now sip.'

'Yes, ma'am.' He brought the vodka to his lips. 'Slightly aromatic. Tastes of apples, actually.'

'If you're used to clear vodkas, it'll come as something of a surprise. And it's not to everyone's taste.' She took a gulp, holding the liquid in her mouth before swallowing.

When she was sure he was taking small sips and not about to

set his gastric tract on fire, she went to fetch bread and plates from the kitchen.

She returned to find him standing staring at a large framed photograph on the wall. 'Where's this?' he said without turning round.

'It's Holy Cross Church in Warsaw. Inside is a crystal jar containing Chopin's heart. You can see it in the photo, in the pillar on the left.'

He looked surprised. 'I thought Chopin was buried in Paris.'

'He is, in the Père Lachaise cemetery. But, when he knew he was dying, he asked his sister to take his heart back to Poland.'

'What an incredibly romantic thing to do.'

'It's not as romantic as you might expect. He was terrified of being buried alive.'

'That's understandable. It must be horrifying to wake up in a coffin. You'd last only two to three hours.'

'A long time to go slowly mad while you're fighting for air.'

'Indeed.' He studied the photograph. 'I'm guessing, as you're Polish, that it's Chopin's music you prefer to play. I noticed your long fifth fingers. That must be a definite bonus.'

'It certainly helps when you have to stretch more than an octave.'

'Were you born in Poland?'

'Warsaw.'

'Then you're a Polish citizen,' he said, with a slight frown.

He left it at that. Like her, he was probably tired of talking about Brexit.

'Do have a seat,' she said. 'I'm about to serve.'

She brought in a bowl of potatoes and the casserole dish.

'Gosh, it smells marvellous,' he said, closing his eyes.

'It's how it tastes that matters. This is an old Polish recipe.' She heaped meat and potatoes on to their plates.

He waited until she'd picked up her knife and fork before piling in. 'Wow,' he murmured. 'Is it wild boar? Where on earth did you get it?'

It was time to come clean. 'I'm afraid this is a bit of a cheat. The ingredients are intended to make pork taste like wild boar.'

A look of amusement came into his eyes. 'In that case, you must give me the recipe. Some friends from my university days are coming to stay next month. This would be just the ticket.' He smiled. 'Did I tell you I have a Polish colleague working with me at the moment? He's always cracking jokes.'

'Poles love doing that. The best are from the Communist era. Here's one. What is the definition of Communism?' Without waiting for a reply, she added, 'The long, hard road from capitalism to capitalism.'

'Ha! That's a good one.' He sipped the vodka, studying her. 'So where did you work before West Bell Street?'

'At the Met.'

'It must be tame here by comparison.'

She thought of her first major case in this city, in which she'd almost lost her life and which had taken the life of her DI. A feeling of guilt that she now had his job would occasionally creep up on her. 'Tame? No, I wouldn't say that.'

As they ate, he talked about CAHID, how he'd always wanted to work in forensics and, after qualifying in medicine, had heard about the work being done there and knew it was the place for him. As soon as there was a vacancy, he'd applied and got the job.

'I've always thought forensics is just another type of detective work,' he said, wiping his plate with a piece of bread. 'You wallow around in the dark for ages and then, suddenly, the dark clears and you see what you've been unable to see before.'

She looked at him thoughtfully. Clearing the dark was a good way of putting it. 'I'm afraid there's no dessert,' she said, gathering up the plates. She got to her feet. 'I'll bring in the coffee.'

'That would be great.'

She stacked the plates in the sink. The coffee made, she returned to the living room. 'Shall I open the chocolates?' she said, setting down the tray.

He smiled. 'They're for you. And I don't have much of a sweet tooth, to be honest.'

They sat at the table, sipping.

'So, are you any further forward with your case?' he said. 'Breek House? You said you were going to look through your Missing Persons database.'

'The problem is that we have several hundred possibles.' Seeing his look of disappointment, she added, 'It could be worse. We could have had several thousand. In fact, we started off that way, but your data narrowed it down.'

He seemed genuinely pleased to have been of help. 'You know, Dania, I'm something of a completer-finisher. I never like leaving things, especially with a case like this. I've been thinking that there's one further thing we could try.'

She wrapped her hands round her coffee cup. 'Oh?'

'Craniofacial reconstruction. The skulls are in good shape. Even the damaged one can be repaired enough for the procedure to give us a reasonable likeness.'

Her thoughts tumbled over one another. Craniofacial reconstruction was always the last resort, once every avenue had been explored. 'The DCI would never agree. As senior investigating officer, she's accountable for the expenses on the case.'

His expression brightened. He reached across and gripped her hand. 'Tell you what, why don't I have a word with my superior and see what I can do?'

188

'A sort of two-for-the-price-of-one deal?' she said, not daring to look at his hand in case he took it away.

'Better than that. I might be able to swing it as a training exercise. We've taken on a couple of new postgrads and they've still to learn how to use the software.' He grew animated. 'If you're willing to let them loose on the remains, it might cost you nothing.'

'Harry,' she said, unable to believe her luck, 'under those circumstances, the chief inspector could hardly refuse.'

He released her hand and sprang to his feet. 'I'll talk to my boss now.' He drew himself up with crusading zeal. 'He doesn't live far from me. And he won't be in bed yet.'

She was about to suggest it could wait until morning, but he was already at the door. 'I'll be in touch as soon as I have a concrete proposition for you to take to the DCI,' he said. He seemed to remember himself then. 'And thank you so much for a smashing evening.' He hurried out.

She sat staring into her coffee, trying to overcome her frustration. The promise of the evening hadn't materialised. Disappointment rose in her gorge, threatening to spoil her mood. But perhaps she'd been expecting too much. She might have misjudged the situation, and Harry was looking for nothing more than friendship. She finished the coffee slowly, wondering if it wouldn't be better to leave things as they were. Yet the evening hadn't been a total disaster. She glanced at the packing crate, seeing the vase of gardenias. And the box of chocolates.

She felt a smile forming.

CHAPTER 19

Marek was at home on Monday morning, sipping his coffee and checking his text messages. Nothing yet from Harti. He opened the laptop and looked through his emails. Same negative result. He launched Facebook. And, as he scrolled down, he discovered that someone had replied to his query about Peter de Courcy. He felt his pulse quicken. The Peter de Courcy who was messaging was sure that Marek was referring to his relative, given what he'd posted about Vienna and hypnotherapy. Did he want to contact him directly?

Marek fired off an email with his contact details and settled down to wait.

A reply was not long in coming. His mobile rang. It was a UK number with an area code he didn't recognise.

'Marek Gorski,' he said.

'Mr Gorski? This is Peter de Courcy.'

The voice was without the trace of an Austrian accent. If anything, it was English, making Marek wonder if this wasn't a wild-goose chase. 'Thank you so much for getting back to me,' he said.

'My pleasure. But, before we go any further, I'm wondering what your interest is in my relative.'

'I've been asked by someone to find a Dr Peter de Courcy who practised in Vienna. This person's uncle was cured by him after a course of hypnotherapy.'

'At the Reisinger Institute in Vienna?'

'Here in Scotland. It was some years ago.'

There was suspicion in the voice. 'And why is your client trying to find him?'

Marek decided this was the time to be completely honest. 'He didn't say. But his father had severe depression and killed himself. As I mentioned, his uncle, who had the same condition, was cured after a course of hypnotherapy. My strong impression is that my client is starting to show the same symptoms and is desperate to find the man who cured his uncle.'

A long pause, in which Marek could almost hear the caller deliberating. 'Are you a private detective?' he said finally.

'I'm an investigative journalist.'

'Hoping to investigate and write about hypnotherapy?'

'Actually, no. I was asked to take this on because I tracked down a paedophile who'd gone on the run. You may remember the case a few weeks ago of the football coach?'

'Vaguely.'

'I was the journalist who ran him to ground. But it was a stroke of luck. I'm not a trained detective by any means. To be honest, I'm a bit out of my depth.'

A faint chuckle. 'Except you managed to find me.'

'Facebook was something of a last resort. I don't have access to the sorts of tools detectives have.'

A pause. 'I like you, Mr Gorski. The last detective who came calling was so offensive that I showed him the door. I told him I had nothing to do with the person he was looking for. Was he also sent by your client?'

'He must have been. My client told me he'd engaged the best private detective he could find.'

A snort. 'Well, he wasted his money. Okay, Mr Gorski, I'm willing to talk to you. I live in Kelso, in the Scottish Borders. Could you get yourself down here?'

'When would suit you?'

'Shall we say Wednesday afternoon?'

Marek made a mental note to cancel whatever he was doing that day. 'What's your address? Or do you want to meet in a café or something?'

'I run the Old Vienna restaurant not far from the abbey. Just ask for me there. I'll be in all day. You may prefer to come in the morning. It's up to you.'

'Thank you so much for your time, Mr de Courcy.'

'Don't mention it. I'm just as keen for you to find him as your client is.'

'Why would that be, may I ask?'

'Peter de Courcy is my father.'

It was nearly midday before Dania got a phone call from Miss Hayes. The morning had been spent poring over the data from Louise and studying the male-female pairs in MisPers. The team were now checking whether any had had links to Archie McLellan. She knew it was a thankless task, not just from their looks but because anyone who'd had links to the Nailer at that time would have done his utmost to hide them. They all recognised this to be a box-ticking exercise but, as she'd pointed out, if they got nowhere, which was what she expected, it strengthened the case for the more expensive analyses such as DNA. She'd said nothing about Harry's offer of free craniofacial reconstruction, as she hadn't yet heard back from him and didn't want to get anyone's hopes up. As for the Brodie Boyle murder, the investigation had stalled. There was nothing for it but to go back to the beginning and work the case again.

So, when Miss Hayes's call came, she was grateful for the distraction.

'Is that Inspector Gorska?' came the voice.

'Speaking.'

'Eileen Hayes. We met at Breek House.'

'I remember.'

'I wondered if you were interested in meeting up for that wee chat.'

'Of course. When would suit?'

'I'm free this afternoon. Two o'clock?'

'Two o'clock would be fine.'

'I can come to the police station.'

'I look forward to it.'

'Aye, me too.'

And with that, Miss Hayes rang off.

'I've never seen the inside of a police station,' Miss Hayes said primly, as they sat in one of the empty rooms. The smell of lemon polish was overpowering in the small room, making Dania wonder if it would ever wash out of the woman's skin, let alone her clothes.

'Is this where you question suspects?' Miss Hayes added, looking round.

'It's one of several interview rooms. We won't be disturbed here.' Dania poured the coffee. 'Milk and sugar?'

'No milk. Two sugars, please.' The woman studied her openly. 'You speak English better than most folk in Dundee.'

'Thank you.'

'Do you find it difficult?'

Dania smiled. 'Not any more.'

'My granny told me the Polish soldiers picked up the language no problem.' She cackled. 'At least, the words they needed to romance the lassies.'

Like many, Dania knew how outrageously successful the soldiers had been with the local girls. In fact, it was the girls who proved to be the best teachers of English, although the pronunciation of the English 'th' defeated most Poles. Dania's mother could never get her tongue round it. 'Birthday' became 'birdsday'.

'Did your granny have a Polish boyfriend?' Dania said, sipping.

'All the lassies did. The Scottish menfolk were none too pleased. But they couldn't compete with those manners, all that heel-clicking and hand-kissing and the like. Do the Poles still do that?'

'Some of them.'

'If the Dundee lads tried that today, they'd get a smack in the puss.'

Dania laughed. 'You know, when a Pole kisses a woman's hand, it's a mark of respect, nothing more. They're not trying it on.'

'I ken that. The soldiers were perfect gentlemen, my granny said. And they could dance like Fred Astaire. My granny loved dancing.' She took a gulp of coffee. 'The soldiers said they'd travelled through lots of countries after they escaped from Poland, but Scotland was way up top when it came to kindness. They talked about holding a big party after the war. It would take place in free Poland. All the church bells would ring when the Scots arrived, and everyone would get well bevvied.' She shook her head. 'When you think how Poland was abandoned.'

Dania wanted to move the woman on to talking about Breek House but guessed it would be counterproductive to hurry her. 'Who was your granny's boyfriend?'

'His name was Romek. He was a braw lad. She met him when she came with a gift of Gillette razors for the soldiers. To begin with, he and his mates referred to the Scots as Englishmen.' She rolled her eyes. 'You can imagine how *that* went down. The folk in St Andrews got their own back by referring to the Poles as Russians.' She paused. 'My granny told me about the day Churchill came to town. Not sure which year, nineteen forty-one, I think. Romek was fair excited. Pronounced the name as "Shurshill". Anyway, the Poles had a march-past. It was chucking it down, but Churchill just stood there in his grey mac, next to the Polish general. Nobody knew what he was thinking as he watched the soldiers.'

'So, what happened to Romek? Did he take part in the Normandy landings?'

'It was the Italian campaign. He was in the Second Polish Corps. Fought in some famous battle, I forget which. My granny kept in touch with him, though. He came back to St Andrews right after the war with tales of his adventures. The soldiers had a bear with them in Italy. Did you know that?'

'That would be Wojtek, the "Soldier Bear".'

'Aye, that's the one,' Miss Hayes said, grinning. 'They found him as a cub, didn't they? Somewhere in Persia, my granny said. Enlisted him in their army with a name, rank and serial number. He used to drink beer and eat cigarettes.'

'There's a new monument to him in Edinburgh. In Princes Street Gardens.'

'A monument?' the woman said excitedly. 'I'll need to get myself down there, right enough. Somewhere I've got a photo of Romek with that bear.'

'And what became of Romek?'

She ran her hands down her pleated skirt. 'He always said he wanted to go back to continue his studies at the University of Warsaw. Asked my granny to marry him and go with him. But she didn't want to leave Scotland. So he went back on his own.

195

And she never heard from him again. The sad thing is that she changed her mind as soon as he'd gone and tried to contact him.' The woman's voice grew hard. 'It was a wee while before she found out what had happened. He'd been carted off to some camp in Siberia. No one could tell her why.'

'I'm afraid it's what happened to many of the soldiers who returned to Poland. The Soviets didn't trust the ones who'd fought with the Western Allies. They were treated as enemies of the people.'

Miss Hayes shook her head. 'Heartbroken, she was.'

'Did your granny also work at Breek House?'

'Just my mother.'

'It was Donnan McLellan who lived there then, wasn't it?' Dania said, refilling the woman's cup.

'Aye. You ken how he died, don't you? Mind you, after what he went through, no one could blame him.'

'What happened?'

'His mind went soft. My mother tellt it all to me. He'd get this glaikit look, and spend hours staring at nothing, moving that great head of his from left to right. Then, for no reason, he'd take to babbling to himself. No one could make out the words.' She took a sip of coffee. 'He'd yell at them to go away. But there was no one there. He just saw them in his head. I reckon that's why he blew his brains out. He wanted to make sure they were dead.' Her eyes widened. The whites were edged with yellow. 'Poor man,' she whispered.

'And who ran the farm when he was like that?'

'His wife and son, Ned. At least they tried to keep things going.'

'Not Archie?'

She sneered. 'He was banged up, wasn't he?'

Dania set down her cup. 'And did Ned and Mrs McLellan make a success of things?'

'They had to lay off some of the farmworkers.'

'I don't suppose you remember any names?' she said, trying to keep the hope out of her voice.

'Ach, I was a bairn then. I didn't ken any of the workers.'

'And the McLellans kept your mother on?'

'Eventually they had to let her go as well. And then they flit house to somewhere in town. Every so often, though, they'd ask her back to do a big clean-up. They seemed to have the odd guest staying downstairs in that back room, the one next to the new gin parlour. I thought that strange as it was on the ground floor, and there are bedrooms upstairs. Maybe they ran it as a B and B. Hard to see anyone wanting to stay so far away from town, though. I ken old Mr McLellan's brother paid a visit now and again.' She lowered her voice. 'One time, when we were skint, my mother went over to the house, hoping they'd have some work. It was night and I was in the kitchen, doing my lessons. She came in and sat down and I could tell from her face that something wasn't right.' The woman lifted a hand to her throat. 'She'd seen something, right enough. Something in that back room.'

'What was it?' Dania said, when Miss Hayes seemed reluctant to continue.

'Her face was white as a ghost and she mumbled something about bad things happening and she wouldn't go back there. Not ever. No, not for a pension.'

'When was this? Can you remember the year?'

'It was nineteen eighty-one. I mind that the news was all about the royal wedding.'

'Did she say anything else?'

'Aye, well, after a wee dram, she did talk a bit. The front door to Breek House had been left open, so she just walked in. There was no one in the living room. But then she heard a howling. Like an animal. She reckoned it was coming from the dining room, but when she got there, she heard it in that back room. There was a light under the door, so she pushed it open a wee bitty and took a keek inside. She couldn't see much, only shapes. Someone was lying on the bed, shrieking and jumping about as though the devil had taken him. A man was hunched over him with his back to her. It was dark, but she reckoned it was one of the McLellan boys. She thought on it some more, and then said she was sure it was Archie. And there was a second person there.'

'Ned, maybe?'

'Bigger than Ned. It may have been old Ma McLellan. What they were doing there she didn't rightly know, as they were living in the town by then. Anyway, she got out of there fast. Said we'd get the rent money some other way. She found work cleaning offices. Did that nights. We kept our heads above water.' The woman paused. 'She never went back to Breek House. And neither did I. Until recently.'

'Would your mother be prepared to come in and be interviewed about this?'

Miss Hayes looked at her sadly. 'My mother passed away last year. Just before Christmas.'

'I'm sorry to hear that.'

'She was only seventy. It was the lung cancer that got her in the end. She smoked untipped cigarettes when she was a lass.'

Dania tried to hide her disappointment. Yet it hardly mattered. She doubted this account would be of any use in a court of law. With no positive ID, it was worse than useless. After thirty-five years, who would believe the testimony of a child who was reporting her mother's drunken ramblings?

'When did you start work there yourself, Miss Hayes? Was it when the council owned it?'

'The council didn't bother much with the place. I started work last year, after the two ladies bought it. I clean at the next farm along. I was leaving work and saw them arrive. So I offered my services, saying my mother had once worked there. They took me on there and then.'

'And how is that going? Are they easy to work with?' Dania said, watching the woman closely.

'The older one is. She makes it clear what has to be done, and what I don't have to bother with.'

'And the other one? Robyn?'

'She's a bit of a haughty besom . . . There's something not quite right about her. I can't put my finger on it. But she's hiding something. I reckon they both are.'

Dania waited, seeing the emotions come and go on the woman's face.

'From time to time I hear them having a wee natter,' Miss Hayes continued. 'When I get near, they stop in the middle of a sentence. The younger one usually has that look on her face, like she's feart. Don't get me wrong, I don't spy on them, but folk have always found me invisible when I'm cleaning. Which is as it should be,' she added promptly.

'Have you seen Archie McLellan there recently?' Dania asked, rearranging the crockery on the tray.

'Why would I?'

'No reason. I just wondered if he looked in on the old place.'

'I haven't seen him for a long time, not since my mother cleaned there. Mind you, I overheard the two ladies talking about him once.'

Dania tried not to appear too interested. 'Oh?'

'Something about money arriving in their account. That was all. They buttoned it when they saw me.'

'What do you think was going on in that back room?' Dania said, after a silence. 'When your mother peeped in?'

Miss Hayes looked at her hands. 'I've thought on it over the years. I've read about Archie McLellan in the papers so I know what he is. If he was the one doing awfy things to some poor laddie, it wouldn't surprise me. It's why my mother kept her mouth shut.'

'Don't you think he'd do it in a cellar or an attic? Somewhere out of the way? Not in a room that any of the farmworkers could walk into?'

'Nah. This is Archie McLellan we're talking about.' The woman's mouth twisted into a sneer. 'When the Nailer does awfy things, he likes everyone to know it.'

CHAPTER 20

Marek was making good time, having left straight after breakfast, and estimated he'd be in Kelso before eleven. The day had started well with only scraps of white in the sky but, as is often the case in Scotland, the clouds had packed together, turning the sky a smoky grey. He had followed the A68 south of Edinburgh, passing St Boswells, and was now turning on to the A699. The road ran on, acre after acre, through farmland and hamlets, reminding him of the countryside around Dundee. All that was missing was the occasional glimpse of the river.

As he drove through the patchwork of fields, he thought again about the previous day's news: the debate in the Scottish Parliament about whether to call for a second referendum on Scottish independence. In the first vote, Dundee had declared its wish to leave the UK by 57 per cent to 43 per cent, but Brexit had muddied the waters and it wasn't clear how the city, or Scotland for that matter, would vote if a second referendum were held. His colleagues never missed an opportunity to bring up Indyref2 and Marek had long since decided it was a subject to steer clear of, as frayed tempers were never conducive to a productive working environment. As if they didn't have enough to worry about with leaving the European Union, he thought wearily.

He reached the stone bridge across the river Teviot and saw the sign to Kelso. The A699 led him over a second, longer, bridge that crossed the Tweed on the southern approach into the town. He followed the road past the war memorial and the ruined twelfth-century abbey and cruised into the main square.

He still hadn't heard from Harti, but he wasn't particularly worried. The man would get back to him in his own sweet time. As he manoeuvred the Audi into a parking spot, he wondered what, if anything, he would learn from Peter de Courcy junior.

This was Marek's first trip to Kelso. He was tempted to let his sat-nav suggest where to have coffee but the brightly painted pub off the square caught his eye. The garish sign above the door showed a young man in eighteenth-century dress, on a rearing horse. Underneath were the words, The Lost Shoe.

The dark interior was made darker by a low ceiling hung with wooden beams and was painted the same shade of red as the carpet and upholstery. Most of the light came from the bar. A smell of fried food hung in the air.

He took a seat at the counter and ordered a cappuccino.

'Anything with it?' the girl said. She had auburn hair and a clear complexion.

He glanced at the array of wilting muffins on the counter. 'No, thank you.'

'I don't blame you. We're not good on desserts here. If our customers want something sweet after lunch, we send them over to Old Vienna for cake. Peter makes them.' She closed her eyes. 'They're absolutely heavenly.'

'Peter de Courcy?' Marek said, trying not to sound too interested.

'You've heard of his Viennese cakes, then.'

'Hasn't everyone?' He hazarded a guess. 'The most famous is *Sachertorte*, I believe.'

202

'Oh, aye, they always have that. And apple strudel. My favourite is the one with meringue and sponge and loads of cream.'

'That would be *Kardinalschnitte*.'

'Just looking at it makes me put on weight.'

He took in her shapely figure. 'Surely not,' he said, raising an eyebrow. 'It's mainly air, after all.'

She smiled coyly. 'On the days I eat those cakes, I make up for it by not eating anything else.'

He laughed. 'Good plan.'

She bustled about at the coffee machine, and brought over his cappuccino.

'Why is this place called The Lost Shoe?' he said.

'Och, it's some story about Bonnie Prince Charlie losing a shoe when he rode through here.'

'He lost his shoe?'

'It was his horse.'

He paid for the coffee and was about to question her further when a loud group of cyclists breezed in, talking and laughing. They crowded round the bar and he realised he wouldn't get her attention again.

He drank the coffee and left.

Old Vienna was a white-painted three-storey building with a slightly canted slate roof and dormer windows. It nestled between a boutique and a charity shop, a minute's casual stroll from the abbey. Only those with hardened constitutions could walk past the double windows without pausing to stare at the confections piled high behind the glass.

Marek pushed open the door, breathing in the blended scents of caramel, cream and sugar. Directly ahead was an archway with the restaurant beyond, its walls painted a vivid shade of peach. On the right a small shop sold cakes and tins of Viennese coffee. A dark-haired woman was serving an elderly gentleman, giving Marek time to scan the menu on the board. Typical Viennese cuisine. If the cakes didn't pile on the pounds, the other food would. He considered staying for lunch after his meeting.

'I'll be with you in a moment,' the woman called over. Her eyes were a faded blue and her skin was like putty.

'There's no rush.'

She threw him a harassed smile and he wondered, from her apron and cap, whether she didn't double as a waitress.

The gentleman paid, pocketed the change and left grinning, clutching a large box.

'What can I get you?' she said to Marek. 'Unless you're here to eat. We don't start serving till twelve thirty, I'm afraid.'

'Actually, I'm here to see Mr Peter de Courcy.'

'Is he expecting you?'

'He is. Marek Gorski.'

'Let me just call him.' She picked up the phone.

A minute later, the door behind her opened, and a tall man in a pale blue denim shirt and dark trousers emerged. He had brown eyes and the same messy dark hair his father had had at the same age. Marek put him in his late thirties.

'Mr Gorski? I'm Peter de Courcy.'

'Mr de Courcy,' Marek said, extending his hand.

The man shook it firmly. 'Let's go upstairs to my flat.' He turned to the woman. 'Yvonne, we're not to be disturbed.'

He led the way up the narrow flight of steps. At the open door, he stood back to let Marek enter.

The overheated flat smelt strongly of tobacco and was sparsely decorated with a few pieces of dark wooden furniture. Nothing lay on any of the surfaces, except a pipe in the ashtray on the sideboard.

De Courcy gestured to the armchairs. 'Please take a seat, Mr Gorski.'

'Thank you.'

'So, you're looking for my father?' he said, when they were settled.

'My client is keen to find him.'

'And are you able to give me the name of this client?'

He thought for a moment. If he refused and was shown the door, it would be the end of his mission. And Archie would be less than pleased that he'd thrown away his best chance because of some outdated notion of political correctness. 'His name's Archie McLellan. Your father treated his uncle, Keith McLellan, for severe depression. Successfully.'

A brief look of recognition crossed de Courcy's face. Perhaps even in the Borders they knew the name Archie McLellan.

De Courcy fiddled with the neck of his shirt. 'And this Archie McLellan is wanting a course of hypnotherapy treatment?'

'That's my guess.'

'But he hasn't confirmed it?'

'Not to me.'

'It's possible your friend has the same condition. I understand there's a genetic cause for some types of severe recurrent depression.'

'Are you an expert on the subject?'

'I'm afraid not.' He smiled ruefully. 'I'm a humble pastry chef. No, my father told me about depression and how best to treat it.'

'You mentioned you were keen to find him yourself.'

'We've lost touch, I'm afraid. And I'd like to contact him.'

'When did you last see him?'

'I can't remember exactly,' he said dismissively. 'About five years ago, maybe. That was the last time we spoke.'

'And where was that?'

205

'Austria. My parents were living in Vienna at the time. Still are, as far as I know, although they've changed address. When I had no reply to my letters, I rang their landline. The stranger at the other end told me she'd bought the apartment from them.' He frowned. 'Which would account for the lack of response to my letters.'

'Didn't that alarm you?' Marek said in surprise. 'Your parents not telling you they'd moved away?'

'Not really. My father never was one for keeping in touch. I usually did all the running.'

'Does he have a mobile?'

'If he does, I haven't got the number.' De Courcy shifted in his chair. 'I get the odd holiday postcard. The last was from Zell am See. Do you know the area?'

'I've never been there.'

'Nor I. But the mountains and the lake look spectacular.'

Marek paused. 'Were all the postcards sent from holiday resorts?'

'I recall that they were. The one from Zell am See was posted a month ago.'

A month ago . . .

'May I see it?'

'My wife usually throws the cards away. She's totally unsentimental and she hates clutter. The flat's not huge. We just live on this one floor.' He got to his feet. 'I'll see if I can find it. If she's kept it, it'll be in the album in the bedroom.'

He left the room and returned a short while later. 'No luck, I'm afraid. All the postcards have been chucked away.'

Maybe Harti could pick up the trail in Vienna. 'Looks as if your parents' last-known address is the place to start looking, Mr de Courcy.'

'I'd be grateful if you'd try. I've done nothing myself as I've always assumed my father would ring if he needed to.'

'May I ask why you want to contact him now?'

His expression softened. 'My daughter's having her First Holy Communion next month. I'd hoped my parents could attend.'

After a silence, Marek said, 'Well, if you could let me have that address in Vienna?'

'Of course.' He pulled out his phone. 'I've still got your number. I'll forward you the details.'

'Thank you.' Marek got to his feet. 'No need to see me out, Mr de Courcy. I can find the way.'

'Good luck,' de Courcy said, standing and shaking his hand. 'And please don't hesitate to get in touch if you think there's anything more I can help you with.'

Marek smiled, nodding his thanks, and left.

Before leaving the building, he bought some cakes. Something to take back for himself and Danka. 'Thank you, Mrs de Courcy,' he said, handing the woman the money.

'I'm not Mrs de Courcy.' She opened the till. 'I just work here.'

'Is Mrs de Courcy around?'

'She's away today.'

As he walked towards the town square, he wondered if he was any further forward. It seemed strange that Peter de Courcy junior wasn't particularly worried he didn't have his parents' address, being content with getting the odd postcard. But then how often did Marek call his parents in Warsaw? Yet he did have their address and would be alarmed if they moved away without letting him know. He couldn't shake the feeling there was more to this than de Courcy was telling him.

He passed The Lost Shoe and decided that driving back on an empty stomach would be unwise.

The same red-haired girl was at the bar, which was empty now, except for a middle-aged couple in the corner. He ordered sausage and mash with garden peas and onion gravy.

The girl smiled. 'Anything to drink?'

'Mineral water. I'm driving.'

She threw a knowing glance at the box with the Old Vienna logo. 'I see you couldn't resist the cakes either.'

'They're for my sister.'

The girl inclined her head with an 'Oh, really?' expression on her face.

'Well, maybe I'll have one. Or two,' he added, when her smile widened.

'Which ones did you get in the end?'

'Four pieces of *Esterhazytorte*.'

'All the same cake?'

'That way we won't fight.'

'I think I've tried them all, but which one is it?'

'Here, have a look.' He untied the ribbon and opened the box.

She leant over. 'I've had those. Lots of almonds. And cream. And hazelnut meringue.'

Seeing her drooling, he was tempted to offer her one, but then he'd have to join her. And that would spoil his appetite.

'Old Mr de Courcy particularly likes those,' she said, straightening.

He paused in the act of retying the ribbon. '*Old* Mr de Courcy?'

'Peter's father.' She thought for a moment. 'At least, I think it's his dad. The age difference looks about right. You don't see him very often, but when he visits with his wife, they all speak German.'

'Would you recognise him from this photo?' Marek fumbled in his pocket and produced the *Die Presse* article. He smoothed out the page. 'This is how he looked in nineteen seventy-five,' he added, trying to keep his hand steady.

She lifted the sheet to her face and squinted at the photo. Her expression cleared. 'Aye, that's him,' she said firmly. 'The scar's unmistakable. His hair's white now but it still stands up all over the place. He was here a few days ago. I saw him in the shop with his wife.' She rambled on. 'I went in to buy my cakes. I get the odd sugar craving. When that happens, I'm totally lost.'

'I know what you mean,' Marek said, inclining his head conspiratorially.

'Anyway, Yvonne left to fetch Peter. He came down and they all went into the restaurant.' She returned the clipping. 'Are you looking for his father?' she said, gazing at Marek with interest.

'A friend of mine knew him a long time ago,' he said, feeling the lie curl inside him. Knowing that the girl might pass on this snippet of information to Yvonne, who might pass it on to de Courcy junior, he added, 'This friend wants to come over and surprise them at their daughter's First Holy Communion.' He put the article away, trying not to seem too interested.

'I'll say nothing in that case.'

He threw the girl his most disarming smile. 'I appreciate that.'

'Take a seat, and I'll bring the bangers and mash over.'

He sat at the window, staring out into the square. The girl's description and positive identification left him in no doubt that de Courcy junior had lied to him. The man's words rang in his head: *About five years ago, maybe. That was the last time we spoke.* Misinformation, intended to throw Marek off the scent. And not for the first time in his career.

The address in Vienna was likely to be a red herring, presumably intended to derail Marek's investigation. Which was why de Courcy junior had suggested the meeting. He wanted to know what Marek knew. Unless he wanted to know who Marek's client was, and why he was trying to find his father. And now he had Archie's name. Would he do anything with that information?

For the first time since he'd taken the assignment, Marek wondered if he hadn't got himself into something he shouldn't. As his food arrived, and he picked at the sausages, his appetite gone, he consoled himself with the thought that he was at least one step ahead of de Courcy junior. The man had no idea Marek knew he'd been lying. And was therefore unlikely to change his plans. Whatever they were.

CHAPTER 21

It was late afternoon when Dania's phone buzzed, telling her that Quinn was trying to get in touch. She pulled it furtively out of her pocket and glanced at the screen. A text message. She was in a press briefing, so it would have to wait. Jackie Ireland, as senior investigating officer, was fielding the questions, leaving Dania and the others on the platform to look intelligent and on top of the case. Dodging the questions would have been a more accurate description. They had made no significant progress with either the Breek House murders or with Brodie Boyle. That the investigations were ongoing was the only message she could give the press.

The briefing over, the officers left the stuffy room. To everyone's relief, the DCI made for her office.

Dania slipped into the Ladies, and read the text from Laszlo: *Lloyd, need to speak to you urgently. I finish at 6.30 a.m. Meet me in Candle Lane.*

Strange. It was just after four and Donnan's wouldn't be open for at least an hour. They could have met now. Unless there was something Quinn needed to do beforehand. She wondered what he had to tell her. Perhaps he'd found a way into Archie's safe, although she couldn't think how unless Archie had left it open by mistake. She returned to her desk and worked through the day's reports without paying them much attention. Her mind went constantly to her meeting with Miss Hayes, and the woman's description of what her mother had seen in the back room at Breek House. *Someone was lying on the bed, shrieking and jumping about as though the devil had taken him.* Dania had discussed the incident with the team, most of whom thought it was superstitious delusion on the part of the mother. Or the drunken ramblings of a woman who'd had more than a wee dram. If she'd seen anything, it was a guest having a nightmare. But not everyone was so dismissive. Hamish and Honor had looked at her thoughtfully.

Dania had set the alarm for five thirty a.m. but woke well before it went off. Pale light was trickling under the curtains, heralding the possibility of another fine day, although nothing about the weather was ever certain. There was time for only a quick shower, as she intended to get to Candle Lane early. She buttered a piece of toast and chewed quickly, then gulped a mug of black coffee. Grabbing her bag, she left the flat.

It wasn't a long walk from Victoria Road to Candle Lane and the streets were quiet at that time of the morning. She hurried down Meadowside, past the site of the old bleaching green where the citizens of Dundee would spread their linen to dry in the sun. Opposite the McManus Galleries, she turned on to Commercial Street and, after reaching the Holiday Inn, headed left and arrived at the entrance to Candle Lane a minute later. Dawn was streaking the sky, but it would be a while before the sun rose above the river and lightened the city.

She checked her watch. It was six fifteen. Quinn would have to use the main entrance to leave Donnan's. Unless he'd found a way through the garage. Was that why he'd chosen Candle Lane?

212

Leaning against the wall, she scanned the gloomy lane, making out the door to the garage, but little else. It had been cold the previous night and the air had a moist, earthy smell, which seeped up from the river. She couldn't see the Tay from her position by the bollards since Dundee's waterfront development had filled the space with shopping centres. Only from City Quay was it possible to glimpse the waters of a dock that had once been home to jute vessels and whalers. A gust of wind lifted her hair and tugged at the edge of her jacket.

A sudden noise came from Donnan's. The revolving doors were sliding round with a whoosh, and people were hurrying out. Her watch told her it was six twenty-five. As Donnan's closed for business at five thirty, these would be the staff. She pressed herself into the shadows and waited for Quinn.

Minutes later, a man she recognised from the nightclub left the building. There was the click of locks as he made the doors secure. So where was Quinn? She hadn't seen the faces of those leaving, but she'd know him anywhere.

Soft footfalls behind her made her turn. Had he come through the garage? She peered into the murky lane.

And then, some distance away where there was a scrap of wasteland, she thought she saw a spark. Yes! In front of the low wall. A sudden flare, which dwindled into a constant point of orange. It would be Quinn lighting a Sobranie. She smiled to herself. The man couldn't go five minutes without a fag.

A glance around, and she pushed past the bollards.

She approached the light cautiously, aware that she couldn't be seen in the shadows, and not wanting to spook him. He was sitting on the ground, leaning against the wall. His black woollen jacket was open, showing his Donnan's waistcoat.

'Bad day in the office, Quinn?' she said quietly, but not so quietly he couldn't hear.

He continued to sit motionless, the only movement the thin thread of smoke from the Sobranie in his mouth. The chocolate-tea sweetness of the tobacco reached her nostrils.

She sat down beside him, wondering why he was so pre-occupied. His right hand resting on his thigh held the pay-as-you-go. His head was bent and he seemed to be studying the screen, which was strange as the phone was switched off.

Wanting to lighten his mood, she said, 'Those things are going to kill you one day, you know.'

He gazed at the mobile silently.

'Quinn?' she said. 'Are you okay?'

When there was no reply, she leant over and placed a hand on his arm. The smell from the Sobranie was now so strong that she felt it at the back of her throat. Except that it was subtly differ-ent. It was overlaid with a nauseating odour. 'Quinn!' she said, shaking his arm.

His head dropped further on to his chest, and the cigarette fell out of his mouth.

With a growing sense of horror, she gripped his arm. Slowly, his body slid towards her, falling into her lap. The cloying stench of putrefaction closed round them.

'My God,' she murmured. She struggled out from under him. With trembling hands, she pulled out her mobile and switched on the flashlight. Steeling herself, she pointed it towards him. Bile rushed into her mouth. His face was bloated, the skin a pale greenish purple. The lips were swollen and pouting, and a thin line of fluid was leaking on to his chin. But it was his eyes that held her. They stared ahead in silent reproach.

She dropped to her knees and, ignoring everything she'd learnt about not touching a corpse, put one hand against his swollen cheek and, with the other, stroked his hair back off his face.

And then she saw the dark hole and the thin lines of blood across the forehead. For a second, she felt such a pressure in her chest that she was afraid she would faint. A few deep breaths brought her back to herself. And to the realisation that whoever had done this to Quinn had done it also to Brodie.

'Oh, Quinn,' she murmured, closing her eyes. 'I'm sorry. I'm so, so sorry.'

As the tears trickled down her cheeks, she held the phone to her face and called the emergency number.

The figure watching a short distance away detached itself from the shadows and loped back in the direction of Dock Street. Aye, he'd been right, he thought triumphantly. Quinn's police handler, Lloyd, wasn't DCI Ireland but DI Dania Gorska. His interest had been kindled when he'd smelt the man's foul cigarettes on her the night she and her brother had come to the casino. After all, no one else at Donnan's smoked Sobranie. His suspicions had been aroused when she'd admitted she didn't smoke. But the fact that she'd responded to his text of yesterday was the clincher.

So what was she after? Intelligence about the firearms, right enough. And what had Quinn found? Nothing. Because there was nothing to find. He'd been careful to leave no trace at Donnan's. The safe, assuming Quinn could have cracked the combination, held nothing that would incriminate him. And the firearms were no longer being converted in the old garage.

But Breek House. Quinn had found the folder in the safe and told Gorska. What was her interest in the place? Was it only to do with those remains found on the land? The press had fallen silent on that, probably because Brodie's murder had knocked it off the front page. But there were things about Breek House he'd rather the polis didn't know. Aye, he'd have to be careful or they'd dig up more than just bones.

He padded silently towards the entrance to the old garage. With a final glance up the lane, he punched in the keycode.

CHAPTER 22

Dania was watching the body bag being loaded into the mortuary van. In view of the advanced stage of putrefaction, Jackson had agreed to perform the autopsy without delay. Behind her, under strong arc lights, the SOCOs were combing the area, although no one believed they'd find anything. It was unlikely Quinn had been murdered there. The state of decay suggested he'd been killed some days previously, and a passer-by glancing into Candle Lane would have found the body before now.

'You all right, boss?' Honor murmured, scuffing the ground with her toe.

'He was my informant.'

It was as if the girl had been slapped, so great was the shock on her face. The bond between an officer and an informant was a strong one, and losing an informant to the job was akin to losing a member of the team.

Dania stared out past the Old Custom House where the rising sphere of the sun was turning the sky a blue shade of grey. 'I sent him to Donnan's undercover, as a croupier.'

'That nail. You think it was Archie McLellan?'

'Who else?' she said savagely. She lifted her hands to run them through her hair, and then smelt the stink of rotting flesh.

'Did you touch him, boss? You need to go home and get cleaned up.'

'I have to finish here.'

Jackson was hurrying over. 'If you ladies are attending the post mortem, I can give you a lift to Ninewells. But we're going now.'

At the mention of the post mortem, Dania breathed in so deeply, it sounded like a sob.

'It'll just be me,' Honor said firmly. She threw Dania a glance. 'The DI has things to do.'

'As you wish. But we need to make time.' He marched off.

'I'll see you later,' Honor said, making it sound like a question. She followed Jackson to where he'd left his car.

Dania gazed after them, knowing what a sacrifice the girl was making. Honor found autopsies difficult when the body was fresh. Quinn's post mortem would finish her off. She was about to shout that she'd go instead when one of the SOCOs called her over.

'These are all we found in his pockets, ma'am.'

The items consisted of a wallet and loose change, a couple of keys on a chain, a pack of Sobranie and a box of matches. 'And we found this in his waistcoat,' the SOCO added.

It was the red and white gaming chip he always carried for luck. Except that his luck had run out.

'And his phone?'

'We've sent it off already.' The girl smiled faintly. 'Did you know him, ma'am?'

'Why do you ask?'

She hesitated. 'Because you're crying.'

'I want you to go home,' Jackie Ireland said firmly. 'That's an order.'

'He was there,' Dania said, pacing the room. 'He sent me the text message and he knew what time I'd be at Candle Lane. He lit the cigarette.'

'Sit down, you're making me dizzy.'

'He wanted me to *know* he was there,' Dania said, flopping into the chair.

'Aye, and that's exactly how the Nailer operates. Don't take it personally.'

'How can I not? He knows Quinn was my informant. He used the agreed codename when he texted me.'

The DCI studied her. 'Take the rest of the day off. There's nothing you can do for the moment.'

'I can go and see Archie McLellan.'

'In your state, you'd do more harm than good. Until we have a time of death, and a cause of death, we can't even think about an arrest. You know that.'

'There was a vital reaction round the wound in his forehead. It suggests the nail killed him.'

'Still not enough to lift McLellan.' Her voice softened. 'Forensics are fast-tracking this one, and they may find something to link him to the scene.' She didn't sound convinced. 'The autopsy report will be in by close of play today. Anything else, and the others can handle it.' She paused. 'You've got a good team behind you. Learn to trust them.'

'And what will I do at home?'

'You can take a shower, for a start. And change your clothes.' She played with her fingers. 'I want to tell you something, Dania. I lost someone when I was in the military. It was entirely my fault she died, I won't go into details, and there isn't a day when I don't think about her. But I told myself that life goes on. My life. I've dedicated myself to putting the bad guys away. Quinn's death isn't your fault. I don't know the details, but I know you don't make the sorts of mistakes I did at your age.'

Dania could see what it had cost the DCI to take her into her confidence. 'All right,' she said quietly. 'I'll go home.'

'And I don't want to see you here before tomorrow,' the DCI said, making a show of tidying her desk.

Dania left the office. It was just after nine, a strange time to be clocking off. She'd told herself on many an occasion that if she only had the time she would do this or that. Now that she'd been given the time, she couldn't think of a single thing she wanted to do.

Marek was working on an article when his mobile buzzed.

'Danka!' he said. 'I was going to ring and have you round. I've got something special for us. And, before you ask, I'm not going to tell you what it is. You're not the only one who can spring surprises.'

'Are you free now?'

His article would be finished by the time she arrived. 'Now is an excellent time.'

'I'll see you soon.'

He disconnected, wondering whether she had the day off. Unlikely, given she was deep in a murder case. She'd sounded strangely distant and not her usual lively self, and the thought crossed his mind that she might have discovered he was working for Archie McLellan. Could she have been suppressing her anger only to unleash it as soon as she arrived? When they quarrelled, he was the one who caved in, not because he couldn't hold an argument but because he hated it when anything came between them. As twins, they were closer than most siblings. He'd have to come up with a convincing explanation as to why he was on Archie's payroll, although anything he rehearsed sounded too tame to bother with.

By the time the doorbell rang, he'd decided he would stick to his strategy of denying any involvement with Archie. Another lie, which would increase his time in Purgatory, but it would be worth the peace of mind it gave them both.

'You're just in time, Danka,' he said, taking her jacket.

'Is that coffee I can smell?'

'It's eleven. Time for my morning break.'

'So what's this special thing you've got?' she said, following him into the kitchen.

He removed a large box from the fridge. 'I was in the Borders yesterday and found a great shop.' He undid the ribbon and pulled back the cardboard flaps.

'What are these?' she said, gazing at the iced layers.

'*Esterhazytorte*. I bought four pieces.'

'You thought ahead, then.'

He studied her. 'Is something wrong? You look terrible.'

'Thanks.'

'Is it something you can tell me about?'

'I lost a colleague.'

He knew better than to press her. Doubtless it would soon be in the papers. 'Why don't you sit down and I'll bring the coffee over?'

She collapsed into the chair and put her hands over her face.

'Do you want to talk about it?' he said gently.

She let her hands drop and looked at him. The expression in her eyes filled him with alarm. 'I can't,' she said.

'I understand.' He busied himself getting plates and mugs. His sister would open up when the time was right.

'What were you doing in the Borders?' she said listlessly. 'Was it to do with this doctor you're trying to track down?'

'It was. I was following a lead.'

'Was Milo any help?'

'The good professor pointed me in the right direction,' he said, bringing everything to the table. 'Have you got the morning off?'

'The DCI ordered me not to come in till tomorrow.'

He poured coffee for them both. 'Because of your colleague?'

'Because I couldn't stop crying. But I'm all right now.'

He pushed a mug in her direction. 'Danka, getting over someone will take time. You need to be kind to yourself.' He lifted out a slice and put it on a plate. 'Better still, let other people do it. Here, eat this. And then you can have another piece.'

She picked at the cake, then ate quickly, finally stuffing the last pieces of almond and buttercream into her mouth. He smiled. There wasn't a Pole alive who didn't have a sweet tooth.

'Take another piece,' he said, refilling her mug. 'Go on,' he added, when she hesitated.

'You're too good to me. I don't deserve you.'

'Few people do,' he said, lifting a second slice on to her plate. She smiled.

'Ah, that's better,' he said. 'Smiling is good for the constitution.' It was a favourite saying of their mother's. 'So, what shall we do today?'

'Haven't you got work?'

'I've finished everything I need to do. And I'm due some time off.' It wasn't strictly true, but he could edit his finished article after she'd left, which he hoped wouldn't be till late evening. He was disturbed by her colour, or lack of it, and wondered who this colleague was that she'd lost. He hoped it wasn't the skinny Londoner who referred to her as 'boss'. From what he'd seen, work-wise they were a match made in Heaven. If that girl had died in the line of duty, Danka would feel the loss keenly.

'We could go somewhere,' she was saying. 'Edinburgh, maybe.'

'Ah, I feel a shopping trip coming on.'

She finished the second slice, more slowly he was relieved to see. 'What about that memorial to Wojtek?' she said, licking her fork. 'It's in Princes Street Gardens.'

'Done.'

'Shall we go now, or after lunch?'

He glanced at her empty plate. 'You can eat lunch after that?'

She stared at him with a serious expression. 'Can't you?'

He couldn't tell if she was joking. A good sign. 'Danka, why don't you play something while I clear up?'

'All right. What will it be?'

'You choose.'

She smiled faintly, and left the kitchen.

A minute later, the sound of Chopin's étude, Op. 10 No. 3 in E major, came from the living room. One of the composer's better-known pieces, it was occasionally played with an orchestral accompaniment. Marek guessed why she'd chosen it: it was known as 'Tristesse'. She played it with great feeling, putting Marek in mind of one of Chopin's quotations: 'It is dreadful when something weighs on your mind, not to have a soul to unburden yourself to. I tell my piano the things I used to tell you.'

She was reaching the end when a buzz came from under the kitchen table. It was her mobile. He considered putting it on silent until he remembered it could be a matter of life and death. He tugged it out of her bag. 'Danka,' he shouted through. 'You've got a call.'

The music stopped abruptly.

She hurried into the kitchen, and he handed her the phone. 'DI Gorska,' she said.

He continued to bustle about the kitchen, his attention not on tidying up but on her half of the conversation.

'And when did this happen?' A pause. 'Okay. I'll be there immediately.'

'Back to work?'

'I'm not supposed to be working, so I can't use a squad car.'

He put down the dishcloth. 'I can drive you.' He saw her hesitate. 'I'll drop you off and wait round the corner, if you like.'

'That might be problematical.'

'Why?'

'There isn't a corner. This place is miles from anywhere.' She made a sudden decision. 'All right, let's go.'

CHAPTER 23

'You're right that this place is miles from anywhere,' Marek said, as they passed through the metal gates. 'Who lives here?'

'The Montgomerie sisters,' Dania said. She saw no reason to keep this information from him, since it had been in the papers.

'So this is Breek House?'

'That's right. Now follow the driveway to the left.'

A minute later, they reached the clearing. He pulled up outside the front door.

'Wow, it's Wuthering Heights,' he said, staring out of the window. '*Absit Invidia*,' he added.

'Pardon?'

'The crest over the door. It means, "Let envy be absent."'

'Hard to see how it can be when you look at a house like this.' She undid the seatbelt. 'Can you just wait here for me?'

She left the Audi and sprinted up the steps.

The door opened immediately and Val appeared. She was wearing a flared turquoise dress, pulled in at the waist with a white leather belt. Her hair was loose but immaculately groomed. 'Inspector Gorska, thanks for coming so quickly.' Without waiting for a reply, she added, 'It would be easier if we took the path round the building.' She hurried down the steps and turned left, seeming not to notice Marek sitting behind the wheel of the Audi.

'It was Dariusz who found it,' she said, over her shoulder.

'Not his dog?'

'He was without Louie today. I asked him to clear the waste-land behind the house. We want to get it ready for planting, you see. I must say the Poles have been brilliant helping us on the land.' She laughed. 'We offer them our homemade gin but they turn their noses up at it. In a nice sort of way,' she added hastily.

'And Dariusz found it when?'

'Just before I called you. It was his lunch hour and he came round to do some digging. As soon as he'd uncovered enough of it to see what it was, he fetched me. He said it might be part of a crime scene and we should call the police.'

'You did the right thing.'

They rounded the corner and headed away from the house towards what was left of the woodland. Many of the trees had been felled and there was a strong smell of sawdust.

'Our plan is to clear all this away,' Val said, picking her way through the stumps. 'The Poles have made a good start. They've even cut up the timber for firewood. Dariusz was working over there, in front of the fence.' She indicated the abandoned spade and the mound of freshly dug earth. 'I let him go, as his shift on the farm has just started. But we can get him back if you want.'

'No need,' Dania said, staring into the hollow.

At the bottom, with clumps of soil sticking to it, lay a rusted red motorcycle.

'I'm here to report a missing person,' Archie McLellan said to the duty sergeant.

'And you are?'

'Archie McLellan.'

If the name had registered with the young officer, his face didn't show it. He must be new, Archie thought.

'I'll just take some details.'

'Ach, don't waste my time. I want to see the main man.'

The sergeant's eyes opened wide.

'Who's the head honcho on duty today?' Archie said.

'It's the DCI.'

'He'll do.'

'It's a woman.'

'She'll do, then. Get on with it, laddie,' he added, when the man continued to stare at him.

'I'm not sure the DCI will see you. Missing-person enquiries are usually handled by the junior staff.'

'The DCI will see me once you've given her my name.'

'Sorry, what was it again?'

The lad had forgotten already. 'Archie McLellan.'

The sergeant called what Archie assumed was the DCI's secretary. He watched in amusement as the lad's face changed and he nearly dropped the phone. 'The DCI will see you in one of the interview rooms,' he blurted.

Which meant that their conversation would be recorded. Not a problem. He didn't have much to say, and what he did could be said quickly.

A uniform came hurrying along the corridor. Seeing Archie, his jaw grew slack. 'This way, Mr McLellan,' he said, letting the words drift.

'Aye, lead on.'

The man took him back along the corridor and opened a door on the left. 'Coffee, Mr McLellan?'

'Not for me, thanks.' He settled himself behind the desk.

The man left, almost running.

A few seconds later, the door opened and Jackie Ireland came in. She'd had the good grace not to keep him waiting, some-thing he appreciated. She paused at the door, then sat down opposite him.

'We meet again, Chief Inspector,' he said softly. 'It's been a few years.'

She held herself rigid. He had that effect on people, right enough. 'And what can I do for you, Mr McLellan?'

'My croupier, Quinn Selby, has gone missing.'

'Your croupier?'

'He was the replacement for Brodie Boyle.'

'And why do you want to see *me* about this?'

'I'm not interested in the hired help. You're in a position to make things happen.' He leant forward. 'And I want something done about finding him.'

'When did you last see him?' she said after a pause.

'Last Saturday. The eighteenth. He was supposed to come in on the Sunday and he didn't show. It's now Thursday. And, before you ask, I had my brother Ned check with his landlord. Quinn hasn't been seen at his apartment for days. And he doesn't answer his phone.'

'How do you know he hasn't just taken himself off somewhere?'

'And where would he go, Chief Inspector?'

'He might have had a better offer.'

Archie smiled thinly. 'I had my men check the other casinos in Dundee. They haven't seen him either.'

'What do you think's happened to him, Mr McLellan?'

Archie gazed at the table, then lifted his head slowly. 'The same thing that happened to my boy Brodie. That lad was killed in a way that made it look like my doing.'

'And how was that?'

'Don't play the daft lassie with me. We both know that nail in his forehead was put there to lead you to me.'

227

The woman's face was set in anger. Aye, she wasn't used to people speaking to her like that.

'Someone's got it in for me,' he went on. 'God knows, I've made enough enemies in my time.'

'And you think we'll find this Quinn Selby with a nail in his head.'

'I reckon you might. I'm telling you this because I don't want you getting your pretty little knickers in a twist chasing me over it.' He kept his gaze on her. 'Because it wasn't me.'

Her voice was hard. 'Is that all you wish to say, Mr McLellan? It's just that I have things to do.'

'So have I.' He pushed his chair back and strode out of the room.

'I can tell you what this is, ma'am,' Hamish said, studying the rusting motorcycle. 'It's a Kawasaki KZ1000.'

'I'd never have guessed,' Dania said, shielding her eyes from the sun. Since the make was imprinted on the metal and visible through the rust and soil, she was tempted to add, 'I can read the name for myself.'

He grinned. 'I've ridden one of these.'

'That's a bonus.' She indicated the back of the motorcycle. 'The rear registration plate has been removed, so we need to find the vehicle identification number.' It would be registered with the DVLA along with the identity of the owner. 'Any ideas where that might be?'

'On this model, the VIN is stamped on the steering head below the handlebars.' He pulled on gloves and leant over the vehicle. A few seconds later, he straightened. 'It's been erased,' he said, in a voice full of outrage.

'Completely?'

'Well enough that I doubt we can identify it.'

'This motorbike has been in the ground for years,' she said wearily. 'I'd be surprised if it's still in the DVLA's records.'

'Why do you think it's been buried? You think it belonged to Archie McLellan?'

'Why would he bury his own motorcycle? No, I think it belonged to one of the bones victims. Whoever put those people into the ground did the same with this.'

'What about the cadaver dog, ma'am?'

'I've sent for him. Just in case there are any remains here. He did go over the entire grounds, but it's possible there's something buried so deep in this spot that he didn't find it. But he may now.' She watched the SOCOs moving around the hole, taking soil samples. 'Let's leave them to it. If there's anything to be found, Nelson will find it. Or Kimmie.'

Dania had sent Marek home as soon as she called it in. She didn't want him hanging around as questions would be asked if he was found sitting in his car, twiddling his thumbs. As she and Hamish walked towards the staff car, she wondered if this find was the breakthrough they were looking for – a motorcycle that had belonged to one of the victims. But any means of tracking down the owner had been erased, so it wouldn't be easy. What else was new? she thought glumly, as they trudged across the grass.

'I told you to go home,' the DCI said firmly.

Dania looked at the floor. 'Val Montgomerie rang me.'

'Aye, and you should have called the station and let someone else handle it.'

She knew this infraction would go on her file. Jackie Ireland was not one to brook disobedience on the part of her subordinates. 'I have to keep working, Chief Inspector. If I sit and mope at home, I'll go mad.'

The woman's expression suggested she understood. But she hadn't finished. 'Carry on like this, and it will hit you badly later,' she said, in a warning tone.

Dania said nothing. She'd seen it at the Met, officers who thought they could cope by throwing themselves into their work, then breaking down at the most unexpected and inconvenient moment. But she knew the symptoms and was sure she'd recognise them in herself. And, if that moment came, she'd take herself off somewhere, perhaps to Marek's, and wait it out.

'Bring your chair round,' the DCI said. 'There's something I want you to see.' She opened a window on her PC. A second later, the image of Archie McLellan being ushered into the interview room filled the screen. 'He came to report a missing person. And he insisted on speaking to me. I reckon the whole nick crowded out the control room.'

Dania watched, baffled, as Archie denied he was involved in Quinn's disappearance, demanding the police find the man.

'You've got to hand it to him,' the DCI said. 'He's got nerve.'

'It's the perfect bluff. By drawing attention to himself, he more or less takes himself off the list of suspects.'

'He did this before, when I first knew him. Came forward before we'd found his latest victim. Raging that the man was missing. Just like now.'

'I take it Forensics are still at Quinn's place?'

'They've just finished. They found his other phone. Nothing much there. A couple of voicemails from Archie, asking where the hell he was.'

'He was preparing the ground. What about CCTV?'

'We're still looking. But there aren't many cameras round Candle Lane.'

'How did Honor make out at Ninewells?' Dania said quietly.

'She and the fiscal watched from the viewing area. Jackson had

230

to wear a mask.' The DCI handed her a folder. 'That's his report. Get yourself a strong coffee in the canteen, and find a quiet wee corner to sit in.'

As she got up to go, the DCI laid a hand on her arm. 'There's something to keep in mind, something that may work for us. Quinn's body was kept hidden for several days . . . You saw the condition it was in.'

Dania drew in her breath. The DCI didn't need to spell it out: wherever the body had been kept, there would be a significant quantity of Quinn's DNA.

Dania stirred the coffee vigorously. She'd put in two heaped tea-spoons of sugar. Not that she took sugar in coffee but she had a feeling she might need it. She opened the folder and went through Jackson's report, hearing his English voice as she read.

Rigor mortis had worn off, and the body was now at the bloat stage. Jackson had helpfully reminded the reader that, under normal conditions, a corpse starts to decompose three days after death, gases in the body and abdomen expand, and body fluids are pushed out of the orifices. Unfortunately, the larger the post-mortem interval – the time elapsed between death and medical examination of the body – the less accurate the determination of time of death. In the case of the deceased, the conditions under which the body had been kept were unknown, and all they could say from the core body temperature and degree of putrefaction was that, depending on the environment, the time of death could have been anywhere between two and five days previously. Although Jackson hadn't specifically drawn attention to the fact, Dania knew that inaccuracy in the time of death would compli-cate identification of a suspect.

She read on, trying to imagine the difficulty Jackson would

231

have had in examining the internal organs, whose appearance and weight were listed in the report. Evidence of restraints round the wrists and ankles suggested the deceased had been immobilised. Death was caused by insertion of a nail in the forehead and would have been almost instantaneous.

Which would have given Dania some comfort had it not been for the final paragraph. She sat up so sharply that she spilt her coffee. The words jumped out of the page: the bones in the lower arms and legs had been subjected to blunt-force trauma of such magnitude that they had splintered. The fractures were sustained shortly before death as there was no evidence of healing.

With shaking hands, she removed the X-ray photographs from the envelope. And, as she laid them on the table and gazed at them, she remembered where she'd seen images like them before.

CHAPTER 24

The revolving doors to Donnan's were locked. Marek ran a hand along the wall, found the well-camouflaged bell, and pressed his weight against it.

The thug with the ace-of-spades tattoo unlocked the doors and beckoned him in. 'We're not open at this time of morning,' he said, in a bored voice.

'I'm here to see Mr McLellan.' When the man looked doubtful, Marek added, 'Believe me, he'll want to see me.'

The thug took out his mobile. 'Gorski is here, chief.' A pause. 'Aye, he's ready for you now,' he said to Marek. He scrolled through his messages, apparently having lost interest in the waiting visitor.

'So, do I find my own way, or what?' Marek said, irritated.

He put the phone away and jerked his head at Marek to follow him.

A few minutes later, they entered Archie's living room.

Archie got to his feet. He was in a navy suit and white shirt, the tie hanging loose round his neck. 'Marek, nice of you to call in. I take it this isn't a social visit.'

'I have some information for you.'

'Excellent, excellent. You can leave us, Col. Can I offer you some refreshment?'

Marek wanted this over as soon as possible. 'No, thank you.'

'Take a seat, lad,' Archie said, dropping heavily into the arm-chair.

Marek lowered himself on to the sofa. 'I found this newspaper article about Dr de Courcy. It's dated nineteen seventy-five.' He handed the sheet across.

Archie glanced at it. 'It's in German,' he said, handing it back.

'Happily, I read German.'

'Then read it to me happily.' Archie sat hunched forward, his hands clasped loosely between his legs, as Marek translated. 'He left this Reisinger Institute after the death of one of his patients?' Archie said.

'The reporter only hints that that was the reason.'

'So it may not be true.'

'Reporters have to be careful how they phrase things in case they're sued. On the other hand, they want their articles to be as sensational as possible. You can't take that comment about de Courcy as gospel.'

'Aye, fine, so did you find the man?'

'I found another Peter de Courcy, who turned out to be his son. We agreed to meet.'

Archie's white eyebrows shot up.

'The man lives in Kelso. At this address.' Marek held out a piece of paper. When Archie didn't take it, he laid it on the coffee table next to the *Die Presse* article.

'And the father?'

'Visits him from time to time.'

'His son told you this?'

Marek knew Archie would get the same lies from de Courcy junior if he went calling. 'He tried to throw me off the scent by telling me he hadn't seen his father for five years. It was one of

234

his customers that said Dr de Courcy visited his son just a few days ago. So we know he's alive.'

Archie's face was expressionless.

'I don't know what his son's trying to hide. Anyway, he gave me his father's last-known address in Vienna.' Marek gestured to the piece of paper. 'I've written it there for you.'

'For me?'

'That's what we agreed. I've found Dr Peter de Courcy. I've kept my end of the bargain.'

Archie shook his head slowly, a smile playing about his lips. 'No, you haven't, laddie.' He leant forward and tapped the paper. 'You just told me his son lied to you about seeing his father. So this address in Vienna's likely to be a load of shite.' He paused. 'Isn't it?' When Marek didn't reply, he added, 'You're not done with this.'

'So when *am* I done? When I bring him to you?'

'Aye, that would do it. If he is living in Vienna, and not Kelso, I reckon my down payment will get you there and back.'

'What if I find him, and he won't come?'

Archie crossed his legs, smoothing his trousers. 'Bring him anyway.'

'You're suggesting I kidnap him?' Marek stared at the man, not bothering to hide his distaste.

'You won't need to. I have something that'll persuade him.'

Archie got to his feet and left the room. He was absent for several minutes, making Marek suspect he'd gone downstairs. When he returned, he was holding a small sealed package.

'Give him this, lad. You can tell him it's for openers, and there'll be plenty more. Now, if you'll excuse me, I've things to do. We're in a wee bit of a bother here.'

'Why is that?'

'I'm not sure Donnan's will be able to open for a while. My croupier's gone.'

'That's too bad,' Marek said, in a tone that suggested he didn't mean it.

'He's the second in a row.'

'To quit?' Marek snorted. 'Maybe you need to improve your working conditions.'

Archie frowned. 'The other one was Brodie Boyle, the lad that was murdered. We got a replacement, right enough. But now he's vanished.'

Marek was put in mind of what one of Oscar Wilde's characters had said. To lose *one* croupier, Mr McLellan, may be regarded as a misfortune . . . But this wasn't something to joke about with Archie. The man seemed lost in thought. No doubt he was more concerned about the loss of earnings of his casino than about the well-being of his croupier.

'I'll be going then, Mr McLellan.'

Archie gazed into his eyes. 'I look forward to our next meeting.' He paused for effect. 'With Dr de Courcy.'

It was always going to be a long shot, Marek thought, as he strode along Perth Road. He hadn't seriously expected Archie to let him off the hook. But it had been worth a try. And Archie had seen he was making progress of a sort. The man was unlikely to bother him for a while if he thought Marek's next port of call was Vienna. But surely he didn't have to make the trip to check on that address. Not when he had Harti. He reached Union Place. Time to give the man a call.

Harti answered after one ring. 'Harti Gassinger.'

'Harti, it's Marek.'

'Marek, my friend, how are things? And where did you get that nice checked jacket you're wearing?'

'My checked . . .'

236

He wheeled round. Harti was across the street, leaning against the wall of a shop that sold wine and whisky. He was grinning broadly. He waved at Marek, put his phone away and, after picking up his small leather suitcase, shambled across the road, assuming, correctly as it happened, that the traffic would screech to a halt for him.

'Marek,' he said, dropping the suitcase and throwing his arms round the other man. 'It's been too long.' He hugged him fiercely.

'What are you doing here?' Marek wheezed, trying to catch his breath.

'I've come to assist you in your enquiries. With Peter de Courcy.'

'I appreciate the help, you know that. But you didn't have to come all the way over here.'

Harti ran a hand under his collar. 'Well, I have another reason for wanting to get out of Vienna right now. Gerrit has decided to give the apartment a complete overhaul. And I mean "complete". New carpets, new wallpaper, new furniture. And she's made it clear I'm not to get under her feet while she organises the workmen.'

'I suppose that's the risk you take when you marry an interior decorator.'

'And this Peter de Courcy is becoming more interesting by the day,' Harti went on. 'I thought he would make an excellent subject for investigation.' He glanced around. 'Shall we go somewhere and talk about it? And this weather,' he added, closing his eyes and lifting his face to the sun. 'I thought it always rained in Scotland.'

It was too soon for a drink, although Harti could put it away at any time of day or night. 'I know a good place,' Marek said. 'It does great coffee.'

'And cake?' Harti said, slipping an arm round the other man's shoulders. 'You know how I like my *Kaffee und Kuchen*.'

'I'm sure the place can run to cake,' Marek said, wishing he had more of the *Esterhazytorte*. When it came to cakes, Harti had certain standards.

The man clapped him on the back. 'Lead the way, my friend.'

Minutes later, they were sitting at the back of Dundee Contemporary Arts, the Austrian tucking into a gigantic slice of carrot cake. Marek, who knew the Pole behind the bar, had had a quiet word with him, the result of which was a double serving for Harti.

'I'm glad you're here,' Marek said, watching him stuff himself. 'Things have taken a turn for the worse.'

Harti looked up from his plate. 'In what way?'

As quickly as he could, Marek told him about Archie McLellan, and the visit to Kelso.

Harti wiped icing from his chin. 'It gets more and more mysterious. Let me tell you what I uncovered about de Courcy senior.' He pulled an iPad out of his suitcase. 'First of all, the de Courcys are an old Austrian family, going back centuries. Our Dr de Courcy inherited a considerable sum. He didn't really need to work for a living.'

'Nice for some.'

'He was born in nineteen forty, so he'll be seventy-seven now. As for education, he went to the prestigious Medizinische Universität Wien, the Medical University of Vienna, where he trained as a psychiatrist.'

'And the posting at the Reisinger Institute?'

'Was his first job, and his only job, in Vienna.'

'Did he practise hypnotherapy?'

'He did, according to the archivist at the Reisinger.'

'What about this patient who died? Was de Courcy involved in any way?'

'On that point, I'm still no further forward. We'll have to wait till I hear again from the archivist, which should be soon.' He rested his gaze on Marek. 'There's one thing that may interest you.' He touched his cheek. 'That scar is a *schmiss.*'

'A duelling scar?'

'When he was young, Peter de Courcy was a member of a *Studentenverbindung*, a fencing fraternity.'

Marek considered this. It wasn't unusual for Austrians of a certain age to indulge in this mostly outdated practice, which was considered a test of courage, and the scar, a mark of honour.

Harti drank half of his coffee in one go. 'That barmaid in Kelso said she'd seen the de Courcy father a few days ago, right?'

'He came to the cake shop.'

'It ties in with what I found. The man no longer pays taxes in Austria. In fact, after nineteen seventy-five, there was no trace of him anywhere on our system. If he had returned to the country, believe me, the government would be after him.'

'We can safely forget about looking for him in Vienna then. And that address his son gave me?'

'Will turn out to be someone else's. Or a petrol station. Or a brothel.' Harti wiped his mouth. 'I think he's living in this country. Can your sister not track him down from his tax returns?'

'I can't ask her. She doesn't know I've taken this assignment from Archie McLellan. I haven't even told her the name of the man I'm looking for. And I'd like to keep it that way,' he added firmly.

Harti shook his head. 'Keeping secrets from that smart woman is not a good idea, my friend.'

'She's investigating McLellan for a murder that took place recently.'

'Don't worry, Marek,' Harti said, tapping the side of his nose. 'Your secret is safe with me. I'll just tell her I'm taking a few days to look around Scotland.' He grew thoughtful. 'Okay, we'll have to find de Courcy on our own.'

'I can't understand what's going on,' Marek said, smoothing

his hair. 'Why does de Courcy junior not want anyone to find his father?'

'That's what makes this case so intriguing. I'm convinced it has to do with what happened at the Reisinger.'

'That was forty years ago. Surely people will have forgotten. And, anyway, if he'd done anything illegal, the Austrians would have started extradition proceedings.'

'Maybe. But remember that the Reisinger had its reputation to preserve. Bad publicity was the last thing they'd want. They may not have involved the police but simply – how do you say it? – let de Courcy go.'

'I still don't get it. What would the de Courcys have to fear in Scotland? After all, Dr de Courcy seems to have had a successful career here. All Archie McLellan wants to do is have the man treat him.'

'I must admit that the whole thing is strange. You said you found the son on Facebook?' Harti pushed the iPad across. 'Show me which is the son's page.'

Marek scrolled down the screen. 'Here. He advertises his café, Old Vienna.'

'And is there anything else on Facebook that might help us?'

'I've already looked. It's all about him, and his wife and daughter. Not a mention of his parents.'

'If the last-known sighting of de Courcy senior was in Kelso, that's where we need to pick up the scent.'

'How do we do it exactly?' Marek said.

'Take up position outside Old Vienna?'

'We may be there a long time. The problem is I have no idea when he'll next be in Kelso.'

But as Harti spooned the froth off his coffee and licked it, Marek realised that, yes, actually he did.

★ ★ ★

'These are the X-rays of the victim's arms and legs,' Dania said, projecting the images on to the large screen.

'Crikey, boss,' Honor murmured, 'what that bastard did to the poor man was brutal.'

'We kept the information about the fractures in the Breek House bones from the press. So it's not a copycat.'

'What about CAHID, ma'am?' Hamish said. 'Could someone there have leaked it?'

'Professor Lombard says no, and I believe him.'

'It's all pointing to the Nailer.'

'I sent Quinn in there to see what he could uncover about the firearms Archie's been bringing in. I'm inclined to think he stumbled across something that ultimately cost him his life.'

'Would Quinn have given up your name?' Honor said quietly.

Dania gazed at the X-rays. 'I know I would have. But Archie's known all along that I suspect him. It wouldn't have come as a surprise that I planted an informant at Donnan's.'

'He won't like that, ma'am,' Hamish said. 'You'll need to watch your back.'

'What did you all learn from the staff at Donnan's?'

'The last time anyone saw Quinn was the morning of Saturday, March the eighteenth,' Honor said. 'A staff member leaving the casino about the same time saw him turn into Candle Lane.'

'He'd have been heading towards the bus station on Seagate.'

'That's my guess, too, boss. And the guess of the staff member. He said Quinn didn't own a car.'

'If you know someone's movements, ma'am, Candle Lane's a good place to lie in wait. Especially in the wee small hours.'

'That's just it,' Dania said. 'You'd have to know his movements. But it sounds as though everyone did.'

Including Archie. She thought of him lying in wait in the old garage, listening out for the footsteps that would tell him Quinn

241

was making his way up the lane. Would he have tortured and killed him in the garage? Unlikely. Quinn's body had been found some days later. Archie wouldn't have taken the risk of keeping it on the premises. Which suggested somewhere out of town. Given the man's vast property empire, it could have been anywhere. But, once they found it, the forensic evidence would convict him. It had to, she thought desperately, since they'd found none in Candle Lane. And Quinn's pay-as-you go had not only been wiped clean, the SIM and SD cards had been removed.

'How we do proceed, boss? Turn Donnan's upside down?'

'We'll never get a warrant. We'll have to approach this another way.' She massaged her temples, feeling a headache coming. 'When I met Quinn earlier this month, he told me that, when firearms are traded at the Howff, it's on a Friday night. I've sent officers there each Friday for the last fortnight. No one showed.' She studied their faces. 'But it's Friday again today. And I've a mind to go there myself.'

The girl looked at her aghast. 'You're not serious.'

'If we can catch someone in the act and pull him in, he might lead us to Archie.'

'It'll never happen. Archie's name is enough to turn people deaf and dumb.'

'We could offer protection.'

They were looking at her doubtfully.

'Let one of us do it instead, ma'am.'

'I need two volunteers to accompany me.'

Everyone spoke at once.

She smiled faintly. 'I think you two got in first,' she said, pointing to Hamish and Laurence. 'Okay, everyone, let's take a break.'

The officers left the room.

'Not going to grab some lunch?' she said, seeing Hamish hanging back.

'I know there are more important things on, right enough, but I thought I'd let you know where we are with the motorcycle.'

With Quinn's death, she'd forgotten. Luckily Hamish had taken the lead.

'There are several motorcycle associations in Scotland,' he said. 'Including some in this area. I've been ringing round to see if they know of a red Kawasaki KZ1000 that was owned by one of their members.'

'That's a good idea,' she said brightly. 'It would be worth checking if they keep records going back a few decades.'

'Aye, I asked them that, too.'

She closed her eyes briefly. 'Of course you did. Just ignore me.'

'All their records are recent, I'm afraid. And Nelson found nothing round the area. At least no human remains.'

She smiled her encouragement. 'That's something, at least. I couldn't face it if more bones were found.'

'Ma'am, are you sure you want to go to the Howff tonight?'

'I owe it to my informant to take the lead on this.'

He said nothing, but the look in his eyes told her he understood.

She watched him go. Her appetite had deserted her. What she needed was something to take her mind off her work.

A few minutes later, she'd reached the Overgate and was making her way towards the baby grand when she heard a familiar voice booming above the general lunchtime hubbub.

'Dania! Is that you?'

Turning, she saw Marek looking embarrassed. Next to him was a barrel of a man she recognised as Harti. He ran over, scooped her up and lifted her off her feet, hugging her hard and planting a kiss on her cheek.

'It's been too long, Dania,' he said, grinning.

'Harti, what on earth are you doing here?' she gasped.

243

He squeezed her again before releasing her. 'I'm touring Scotland. Marek has offered his hospitality so I'm staying with him for a few days. Look, we must all get together. What about tonight?'

Out of the corner of her eye, she glimpsed Harry Lombard. She turned and stared at him. He was watching the scene, frowning.

'Tonight?' she said vaguely, dragging her gaze back to Harti. 'I can't, I'm afraid. I'm on duty.'

'Tomorrow, then?'

'The next few days are impossible.' She glanced at Marek. 'I'll be in touch. I have to run just now.'

She looked towards where Harry was standing. He turned on his heel and walked rapidly away.

'Harry,' she called after him.

He stopped, giving her time to catch him up.

'Dania,' he said, switching on a smile. 'I thought you might be playing the piano this lunchtime. But I see you were meeting someone.'

'Just a friend.'

'Just a friend,' he said coldly.

'He's someone I've known for years.'

'An old boyfriend?'

'No, no, nothing like that,' she said slowly.

'Well, he's certainly behaving as though he is. And letting every-one know it.'

'He's staying with my brother for a few days. Have you had lunch?' she added, when Harry said nothing.

'I have, yes.'

'Shall we get a coffee?'

He ignored the suggestion. 'I was hoping to find you as I have some news about the craniofacial reconstruction we talked about. We're more than happy to set up a training exercise for our new students. At no cost to the police, I should add.'

'Harry, that's marvellous.'

'Perhaps after you've had lunch with your friend, you can come over.'

'I'm free now.'

He smiled unconvincingly. 'Shall we say in an hour? That will give us time to get everything set up.' With a brief nod, he marched stiffly away.

She stared after him, stunned by his change in attitude. Had he really objected to Harti's public display of affection? Surely not. After all, it was how old friends behaved.

She returned to where Marek and Harti were standing watching.

'Everything all right, Danka?' Marek murmured.

'Everything's fine.'

'Shall we have lunch?' Harti said, peering down the ramp at Costa.

She became aware of the smell of burnt coffee and melted cheese. Her appetite returned. 'Why not?'

But as she ate her tuna and cucumber sandwich, listening to Harti's tales of his recent cases, all she could think about was Harry's sudden coolness towards her. And the expression of disapproval in his eyes.

An hour later, Dania presented herself at CAHID's reception. 'I'm here to see Professor Lombard. DI Gorska. He's expecting me.'

The girl picked up the phone. 'Let me give him a call.'

A minute later, Harry arrived. 'Ah, good, you're on time,' he said, somehow making it sound clumsy. 'We're through in the main lab. If you could just come this way?'

She followed him through the maze of corridors, dispirited by his change of attitude. They arrived at a room full of state-of-the-art computers and related technology.

A young-looking lad with curly red hair was sitting near the door, gazing into a screen. On the desk beside him was a skull.

'This is Thomas,' Harry said, smiling at him. 'He's one of our postgraduate students. Thomas, Detective Inspector Gorska.'

'Hello,' she said.

Thomas grinned. 'Hi, Inspector.' He seemed completely at ease, as though this weren't the first time he'd had dealings with the police.

'So where are you from, Thomas?'

'Broughty Ferry.'

'Thomas is here on a scholarship,' Harry said.

She smiled. 'That's excellent.'

'He's been working on one of the skulls found at Breek House.'

'Which one would that be?'

Thomas glanced at Harry as if for confirmation.

'Go ahead,' Harry said warmly. 'This is your show. I'll just sit here and chip in if I need to.'

Thomas cleared his throat. 'It's from Victim B, Inspector. You know which one that is?'

'The second one found.'

'Aye, that's right. Jessica is working with Victim A.' He hesitated. 'Have you had much experience of facial reconstruction?'

'Very little, I'm afraid. At the Met, I saw modelling done in clay, but I understand it's all gone digital now.'

'That's interesting,' he said slowly. 'I've never seen a clay reconstruction.'

'It was a great success. Someone recognised the face. We were able to take it from there, and finally brought the case to court.'

'Cool,' he said, his eyes shining.

She could tell from his expression that he was hoping they'd be able to do the same with the Breek House victims. She glanced at Harry, but he kept his eyes on the screen.

'The two processes are similar,' Thomas said. 'You build up the head in layers. First, the soft tissue, then the facial muscles.'

'I'm sure it's not as easy as you make it sound.'

'You need to know how the muscles are attached, and how they move. There's a lot of dragging about and tweaking. Not so bad on a computer, but I bet if you use clay you get it under your fingernails.'

'We should make clear that facial reconstruction is not an exact science,' Harry said, 'despite what all these *CSI* programmes suggest.' He smiled at Thomas, but didn't extend the smile to Dania.

'Aye, we work with both an artist and a forensic anthropologist,' Thomas went on. 'There's no standard method so two reconstructions will produce two different sets of results.'

Which meant that, on its own, facial reconstruction couldn't be used in court. She would have to find hard evidence before presenting the case. 'So what sorts of problems did you have?' she asked.

'Getting an accurate value for the thickness of the soft tissue, for one thing. The bones were completely clean so we had to do some averaging.'

She was impatient to see the results, but Harry would have instructed his student to explain the process carefully. All part of the training, so she went along with it. She could hardly do otherwise. It was costing West Bell Street nothing.

'And what do you do when the nose is missing?' she said, looking at the skull.

'It's easier if I show you,' he said, pulling on his gloves. He picked up the skull. 'First, we take measurements of the hole where the nose would be. They give us an idea of the length and width.' He turned the skull sideways. 'But see this piece of bone here, the pointed bit? It's called the nasal spine and can give us clues as to the nose's shape.' He set the skull down carefully. 'The lips were a bit of a headache too, to be honest. Their shape depends on the size and position of the teeth, and those were missing as well. Then there's the skin.'

'You need to get the texture right, you see,' Harry said.

'Aye, all we knew was that Victim B had worked with his hands. There are farms around Breek House, so we reckoned he worked outdoors. We added a few wrinkles and gave the skin a wee bit of a tan.'

'And the eyes?' she said.

'You can do a bit with them by measuring the depth of the eye orbit and looking at the shape of the brow.'

'Are eyes that different?' she said in surprise.

'They have different shapes. And some bulge out more than others.' He grinned. 'You just need to look at horror films to see that.'

She grinned back, hoping Thomas would stay on at CAHID so she might work with him again. 'I suppose we have to forget about beards and moustaches,' she said. 'There's no way of telling if he had them.'

Harry slipped into professor mode. 'The unfortunate thing is that facial hair, hairstyle, eye colour and things like scars are what people notice first in a face. We can't determine any of these from the shape of the skull. It's why we'll have to stress to the public that they may not be accurately represented in our reconstruction.'

'If someone comes forward, Thomas, can they sit with you, describe what the missing person looked like and work with you to make the changes?'

'Aye, of course. Better still, if they have a photo, we can superimpose it over the scan of the skull. If it's the same person, the facial features should line up accurately.'

They waited, watching her.

'Show me what you've got,' she said, unable to contain her impatience any longer.

Thomas tapped eagerly at the keyboard. A second later, the image of a reconstructed head filled the screen.

It was a man in his late thirties or early forties. He had a short, flat nose, a stern mouth, tanned skin and deep-set eyes that were neither brown nor blue. His high cheekbones seemed to suck in the rest of his face. That and the cleft in his chin gave him a slightly threatening appearance. Although Dania had never seen him before, her first impression was that this was someone local.

'What do you think, Inspector?' Thomas said nervously.

'I'm stunned by how real he looks. Did you do all this yourself?'

'It was my first go with the software so I mainly watched and learnt. But I'll be more hands-on with one of the other skulls.'

'What does he look like from the side?'

'If you use these gadgets at the bottom of the screen, you can rotate the image. Do you want to have a go?'

She touched the screen, sliding and pinching the controls. The head moved slowly round, giving her a view of the sides. The man's short, mid-brown hair was swept back off his head.

'Could you print some of these images?' she said, unable to tear her gaze from the eyes.

'Aye, okay. But would you like some with different hairstyles? Or eye colours?'

She thought of the column inches available to her in the *Scotsman*. 'These will do for the papers.' She glanced at her watch. 'If I could have them now, I may just be able to get them on the evening news.'

She caught Harry's eye. He smiled at her for the first time that afternoon. But it wasn't his usual warm smile. It was the satisfied smile of a professor whose student has done a good job, a credit to him and the organisation. As she waited for the images to be printed, watching Harry and Thomas chatting like old mates, she had to remind herself that she'd never got anywhere with him, anyway. And, as he took his leave of her at the front door, addressing her as 'Inspector', she realised gloomily that it was unlikely now that she ever would.

CHAPTER 25

'Did you see *Reporting Scotland* this evening, ma'am?' Laurence said. 'The DCI was on, showing those reconstructed images. And they'll be in tomorrow's papers. We were lucky to get them in the Saturdays.'

'I caught the programme in the canteen,' Dania replied. 'She did a great job. Better than we're doing here,' she added, peering into the screen.

She and Laurence were looking through the photos of missing persons. They'd restricted themselves to the ten who'd done manual work and had gone missing between 1975 and 1985. None of the faces matched even closely the reconstructed images from CAHID, although some were grainy and a couple were blurred and taken from the side, and one of those had his eyes closed. They therefore couldn't be ruled out.

'Pity about these two,' she said, pulling up the ones taken from the side. 'Had they been looking straight at the camera, we might have been able to superimpose their photos on the images from CAHID. This one here interests me because of his high cheekbones. Or cheekbone, as we can only see his left side.' She pressed a key and the screen changed to show his details. 'Willie MacMartin. Reported missing by his son, Calum, in nineteen eighty-one.'

'Should we contact Calum MacMartin?'

'If he's still around. But it's worth a try.'

'He might have Willie's passport. It would have to have a better photo than this. I'll do it tomorrow, then.'

She glanced at her watch. 'Hamish should be here soon and then we can go.'

'I'm glad it's tonight and not tomorrow,' Laurence said eagerly.

'And why is that?'

'I finally asked Louise out. And she said yes.'

He seemed so surprised by this admission that Dania couldn't help laughing.

'That's great,' she said. 'I guess the hot date she went on led nowhere.'

He pulled a face. 'That was a total fabrication on the part of the Tech guy. He just wanted to torment me.'

'Where are you taking her?'

'I'm not sure yet,' he said, frowning. 'It has to be a swanky place. Can you recommend somewhere, ma'am?' he added anxiously.

'I'm afraid you're asking the wrong person. I haven't been anywhere swanky for ages. Except Donnan's.'

The door opened and Hamish sauntered in. He was dressed the part, as they all were. Rough, dark clothes. Nothing that would make them stand out.

After all, they were going to buy a firearm.

The Howff, the ancient burial ground a few minutes' walk from the police station, was bounded on two sides by iron railings and stone walls, and was overlooked by buildings on the others. It therefore seemed an unlikely place for illegal transactions. Then again, as Hamish had pointed out while they paused at the bus stop on Meadowside, that very fact made it ideal.

252

It was now ten, and the street was in darkness. Although the sky was clear, the waning crescent moon might not have been there for all the light it cast.

'I used to play here as a lad,' Hamish said, peering through the railings.

'In a cemetery?' Laurence said.

'Why not? The gravestones are just the right size for Hide and Seek.'

'Strange place to put a cemetery. It's right in the middle of town. We're not far from the Overgate.'

'It wasn't always a cemetery,' Dania said. 'There was a monastery here once.'

'When was that?'

'Thirteenth century. But it was destroyed by the English in the sixteenth. It was after that that Mary Queen of Scots granted Dundee the land for public burials.'

'I see you've been boning up on your history, ma'am,' Hamish said wryly.

'I found a website with all this information when I was looking for a plan of the area. The word "howff" means "meeting place". Tradesmen and city functionaries gathered here for a chat.'

'What was wrong with the ale houses?'

'I suspect they gathered there as well.'

'Are people still buried here?' Laurence asked.

'Not since the middle of the nineteenth century.'

'So how do we get in? The gates are locked.'

'Quinn didn't specify that the guns are actually traded *in* the Howff. It's possible it's done somewhere outside.'

'If I were selling a firearm, I'd want to do it away from prying eyes,' Hamish said. 'The burial ground's perfect for that.' He paused. 'There's another gate on Barrack Street. We might have more luck there.'

'Okay, let's try it.'

They retraced their steps until they arrived at the intersection between Barrack Street and Meadowside. The railings disappeared, leaving a stone wall. The cobbled road narrowed, they passed Friarfield House, the location of Dundee's Criminal Justice Services and, before the road swung left, reached the stone arch. The street was deserted. The absence of streetlamps would have made the darkness complete had it not been for the weak light struggling through the curtains of the three-storey building opposite.

Dania pulled out her torch and played the beam over the arch. The light illuminated the paired iron gates and the stone crest.

She pushed against the gates, which opened silently. 'Interesting. Why aren't they locked?'

'I doubt the council would have forgotten, ma'am,' Hamish said quietly. 'I think someone who shouldn't has a spare set of keys.'

'Well, gentlemen,' she murmured, switching off the torch, 'shall we?'

The men stood motionless. She pushed the gates wider and stepped inside.

Laurence tugged at her arm. 'How will they see us?' he said, in a stage whisper.

'They'll hear us, Laurence.'

She moved further into the burial ground, her eyes slowly adjusting to the gloom. Around her were silhouettes of ancient stones, large and small, some misshapen. A few were the box-like coffer tombs for which the cemetery was famous. Behind her, she heard her colleagues' footsteps. Hamish's matched hers in sound and confidence, but Laurence's were more hesitant. As she moved further along the path, she made out the shapes of bushes and the arcs of trees.

Suddenly, she felt something shift in the darkness. She froze and peered into the shadows.

Hamish had seen it too. He stepped in front of her. 'Who's there?' he said gruffly, but without menace.

'Who's asking?'

'Somebody who's looking to buy. I ken this is the place.' He took a few steps forward.

Laurence started to whisper something, but Dania gripped his arm and shook it to silence him.

A figure emerged from the shadows. It was too dark to make out his face or clothes but he was taller than Hamish, although not as broad.

The nasal voice pierced the silence. 'And what do you want to buy fer yersel, eh?'

'A gun.'

'I'm nae selling.'

'Then I'm awa' hame.'

Hamish made to leave, but the man said quickly, 'I can sell you something else.'

'Not interested. I want to buy only what Dougie's selling.' He turned on his heel.

'Wait!'

He faced the man. They would have been close enough to make out each other's features had they not been swallowed up by the dark.

'What kind are you after?' the voice said.

'What kind have you got, Dougie?'

Dania wondered if, in calling the man by this name, Hamish hadn't overstepped the mark. But the voice replied, 'You need to be a wee bit more specific.'

'I want the best. The kind I can buy for three grand.'

'Show me the money.'

Hamish started to pull something out of his pocket when Dougie stepped forward. 'Slowly,' he said.

'Aye, all right.' Hamish drew out the notes and handed them across.

Dania waited, holding her breath. This was the riskiest bit of the operation. There was no guarantee the man even had a firearm, let alone was prepared to part with it.

They heard him counting the money, muttering something incomprehensible.

An owl hooted somewhere behind them, causing Hamish to turn his head.

Without warning, Dougie lifted his arm and brought it down hard on top of the other man. Hamish grunted, his legs buckling.

'Hey, you bastard!' Laurence shouted. Before Dania could stop him, he'd rushed at Dougie.

The man sprinted into the bushes and melted into the dark. Dania didn't hesitate. She raced after him. Had it not been for the running feet and laboured breathing, she would have lost him. She followed the sound, trying not to crash into the headstones.

Dougie was halfway up the railings when Laurence exploded out of the bushes and gripped him by the legs. A quick kick to the head, and the boy went flying, tripping over a broken headstone and falling heavily. There was a sickening crack, and he lay still.

Dania was determined not to let Dougie escape. She'd just reached the railings when she felt a strong hand on her shoulder. She was thrust roughly aside.

'I'll get this, ma'am,' Hamish shouted.

He hurled himself at Dougie, who was flinging a leg over the railings and yanked him down. The man screamed in pain and toppled into the cemetery.

Hamish bent over him, lifted his head up and bounced it off the ground.

'That'll keep him quiet for a wee bit,' he said, ignoring the man's moans. 'You okay, ma'am?'

'It's not me you need to worry about.' She shone the torch into Laurence's face. 'Dear God,' she wailed. 'We need an ambulance, Hamish. Now!'

It was after midnight before Dania and Hamish returned from Ninewells. The news wasn't good: Laurence's injuries had left him in a coma. There was nothing they could do except wait for the results of the tests, the doctor had said. As for the other gentleman, he'd added, referring to Dougie, the rip in his groin wasn't life-threatening. They'd be able to stitch him up, give him painkillers, and send him home. Dania told the doctor that she and her colleague would wait and take the man away after he was discharged. In fact, they'd prefer to stay at the hospital while he underwent treatment. The doctor had glanced at the officers' warrant cards and nodded silently.

Now, back at West Bell Street, they were examining Dougie's effects. Of particular interest was the hinged metal sleeve they'd unclipped from his arm.

'Clever wee weapon,' Hamish said, feeling the thickness. 'Explains why I thought he'd hit me with a tyre iron.' He sifted through the contents of Dougie's pockets. 'Usual junk. Wallet, house keys, bus pass as he's registered unemployed. And this packet of white stuff.' He opened it and sniffed. 'Washing powder,' he said, with a sneer.

But Dania's attention was on the firearm they'd found tucked inside Dougie's waistband.

'This is a Glock 17L, ma'am. The barrel's unmistakable.' He turned it over. 'It's the longest and largest Glock produces.

257

Everything about it is large, right enough. The magazine capacity is seventeen rounds. Hence the name.'

'Is it loaded?'

He released the magazine and pulled back the slide. 'The chamber's clear.' He peered inside the magazine. 'And the mag's full.'

'What kind of cartridge does it have?'

He pulled one out and held it up. 'Parabellum. ZVS on the headstamp.'

'Same type that killed Brodie Boyle. We need to get all this to Kimmie. If she can match this weapon to the one that killed Brodie, we'll have taken a major step forward.'

'Shall I get her out of bed?'

'It can wait till tomorrow. We'll let Dougie stew tonight. It might soften him up for his interview.' She smiled bravely. 'Get some sleep, Hamish. We've a long day tomorrow.'

It was after he'd gone that she remembered Laurence was going to take Louise out the following evening. Someone would have to tell the girl that he wouldn't make it. A sudden wave of anger surged through her. And, just as suddenly, it vanished. She felt her heart constrict. First Quinn, and now Laurence. She closed her eyes, unable to keep the hot tears from streaming down her cheeks. Then, knowing she was alone in the room, she covered her face with her hands and sobbed like a child.

CHAPTER 26

'I don't need a brief,' Dougie growled at Dania.

'Very well,' Dania said. 'For the record, Mr Paterson has waived his right to a solicitor.'

'Can I smoke?'

'You may not.'

'*He*'s been smoking,' Dougie snarled, glaring at Hamish, who reeked of tobacco.

'But he's not smoking now.'

She studied Dougie Paterson, wondering why he didn't want a brief. He had vicious brown eyes, a slit of a mouth and a shaven head. And a gaze that constantly roamed over her body. Perhaps it was just as well he wanted to be questioned without a solicitor. There was a darkening bruise on his forehead where Hamish had slammed his head on the ground, and a brief would make political capital out of that. But maybe Dougie realised the game was up – he'd assaulted two police officers in the execution of their duty, to say nothing of having a firearm on his person. A brief, however expert, couldn't make that disappear.

'Mr Paterson, you were caught in possession of a handgun. That's a minimum sentence of five years. What do you have to say?'

'It was planted.' He jerked his head at Hamish, who was sitting watching with his arms crossed. 'By him.'

'Pish,' Hamish said. 'Your prints are the only ones on the fire-arm. We took them this morning. Remember?'

'They were planted too.'

Dania ran a hand through her hair, wondering at the stupidity of the remark. Was he trying to wind them up? 'A jury will come to a different conclusion,' she said.

'You're doing yourself no favours, son,' Hamish said. 'Where did you get the Glock?'

'What Glock? I don't know what you're talking about.'

Kimmie had confirmed that the handgun was a converted replica, machined to take the 9×19mm Parabellum. The ammunition was live, although she had still to do the test fire to see if this was the weapon that had killed Brodie Boyle. They already had enough to detain Dougie: possession of a handgun, even a converted replica, meant they could charge him immediately. But Dania wanted more. However, until they could get him off the subject of planted evidence, there was no point pressing him on the wider issue of converting replicas and trying to sell them.

'What were you doing in the Howff?' she said.

'I was visiting a grave. I like to show the dead the respect they deserve.'

'At night?'

'Best time.'

'How did you get in?' They hadn't found a key on Dougie, or any means of picking a lock as sturdy as the one on the Barrack Street gates. It meant that someone else was involved.

He shrugged, saying nothing. He was evidently not bothered by the threat of a few years in prison. Maybe he'd been there before and Archie had got him off. They'd have to find a way of making him want to talk. Until they did, there was no point continuing.

She glanced at Hamish, who nodded. 'Interview terminated at three twenty p.m.,' she said.

Dougie smiled condescendingly. 'Does that mean I'm free to go?'

'You're free to go back to your cell.'

He made to get up, then sank back with a groan. 'Christ,' he murmured. He spread his legs and rubbed gently between them.

'Something wrong?' Hamish said, in a bored voice.

'My nuts are still aching from when you dragged me off that railing. Whoever invented pointed iron railings should be shot.' He ran his tongue over his lower lip, transferring his gaze to Dania. 'You wouldn't like to massage some ointment on to my little man, would you, Inspector?'

Dania was at her desk when she got the late-afternoon call from Kimmie.

'Test results, Dania. The Glock's never been fired.'

'You're sure?' Silly question. Kimmie wouldn't have rung otherwise.

'I took it apart and checked every bit. There's no GSR. I did a test fire just in case, but the firing pin and ejector marks don't match those on the cartridge found with Brodie Boyle.'

'And the suspect's clothes?'

'No GSR there either.'

'We can still hold him for possession of a firearm.'

'You must be closing in,' the girl said cheerfully. 'All three weapons – the one used to kill Brodie, the Zoraki he was carrying, and now this Glock – used the same ZVS cartridges.'

'That's something, I suppose.'

A pause. 'How's your officer doing?'

'Honor's just come back from Ninewells. He's still unresponsive. He's got something called a subarachnoid haemorrhage. It's bleeding in the brain.'

'That's too bad. What's the prognosis?'

'She didn't say.' She didn't have to, thought Dania. The look in the girl's eyes had said it all. Laurence was on a ventilator and a drip, she'd blurted, her eyes filling with tears.

Dania had been quick to contact Laurence's parents, who were holidaying in Africa. Whether they would get back in time was anyone's guess. She'd had a more painful encounter with Louise in Tech. The girl, on being told, had gone grey with shock. She hadn't uttered a word, just nodded and left the room. Dania, never good at breaking bad news, considered going after her, but caught the frown on the face of Louise's colleague, a heavy-featured man with spiky hair. He shook his head slowly.

As soon as everyone was in, she'd called them into the incident room and described the events of the previous night. Her heart felt like a stone in her chest as she observed their various expressions. Shock and grief were there, but also anger. And determination. Laurence had been a popular officer, always wanting to do the right thing, and she knew her staff would redouble their efforts.

There was little she could say or do other than abandon them to their grief. She'd walked out of the room, leaving a silence. After hurrying to the Ladies, she'd locked herself into a cubicle, sat on the toilet seat and wept uncontrollably.

'You sound as though you could do with a drink,' Kimmie was saying.

'I can't drink at a time like this.'

'I meant for medicinal purposes.'

'If I'm drinking for medicinal purposes, I've got everything I need in my freezer.'

Dania bowed her head at Sunday Mass, wishing she hadn't drunk herself to sleep the previous night. But the bottle of Wyborowa had slipped into her hand as though it belonged there. She'd tipped a small amount into a glass, taken a mouthful, then another, and finally finished it off. The first vodka had been followed by a second, then a third, and after that she'd stopped counting. Several glasses later, a heaviness settled in her arms and legs, and her head sank on to the kitchen table. In the morning, she woke with her neck stiff and her head pounding. Catching sight of her face in the bathroom mirror, she decided not to bother with make-up. After all, no one at early-morning Mass would know her. But, as the congregation took their seats for the sermon, she glimpsed Marek and Harti on the opposite side of the nave. Her luck was in. They hadn't seen her. She crept out of the church just after Communion.

She was on her way to Ninewells when she got the call. She pulled over and picked up the phone. It was the consultant in the ICU, giving her the news that she was dreading. At the first opportunity, she turned the car round and drove to West Bell Street.

The instant she entered the station, she realised the news had preceded her.

The duty sergeant avoided her gaze. 'The DCI was asking for you, ma'am.'

'Can you let her know I'm on my way?'

'She's left the building.'

Probably to go to Ninewells and talk to Laurence's parents, who would have arrived by now. Dania was glad the woman was sparing her that particular ordeal.

She strode into the incident room with a renewed sense of purpose. They were all there, talking in hushed tones. Honor was smearing tears away while Hamish spoke quietly to her.

'Get Dougie up from the cells,' Dania said to Hamish. 'Now, please.'

'Yes, ma'am.'

She left the room, conscious of their stares. But this was not the time to talk about Laurence. That would come later.

'It's Sunday,' Dougie growled. He glared at Dania. 'Why the hell have you woken me up at this ungodly hour?'

She clasped her hands together. 'To charge you with murder.'

The expression on his face changed. 'What are you mithering on about?' He gestured to Hamish. 'Your officer's still alive.' He tried a grin. 'At least, as alive as anyone can be on a Sunday morning.'

'I'm not talking about DC Hamish Downie. I'm talking about DC Laurence Whyte.'

'Who's he when he's out?'

'The officer you kicked in the head. Do you remember him now?'

Fear registered in Dougie's eyes.

'You put him in a coma. He died this morning.'

The shock on the man's face was nothing short of gratifying. The murder of a police officer in the course of his duty was considered an offence of exceptionally high seriousness, something she was sure he was aware of.

'Do you know what a whole-life order is, son?' Hamish said. 'You stay in prison until you die. No parole.'

Dania got to her feet. 'Book him, Constable.'

'No, wait.' Dougie stared at her, licking his lips nervously.

'What am I waiting for?' she said, when the silence had gone on too long.

'It was an accident.'

'It was intentional. I saw it clearly.' She glanced at Hamish. 'And so did DC Downie.'

Dougie's gaze flew from one officer to the other. And she knew she had him.

'I can tell you about the firearms,' he said, desperation in his voice.

She sat down. 'Talk then, Dougie. Tell me about the firearms.'

He hesitated and, for a second, she thought he'd try to bargain with her.

'Do you want a solicitor?' she said.

'Look, I'm just the middle man. I sell on the converted guns.'

'Like the one in your possession when we arrested you?'

He chewed at his fingers and nodded.

'For the tape, the suspect nodded his head.'

'I pick them up and sell them in the Howff the odd Friday night.'

'Where are the conversions done?'

'In an old garage somewhere. I don't know where. That's the God's honest.'

This had to be the garage at the back of Donnan's. She tried to control her excitement. 'Who gives you the firearms to sell on?'

He took a long breath. 'Mr McLellan,' he said almost inaudibly.

She felt rather than heard Hamish sit up in his chair.

'And it's Mr McLellan who does the conversions?' she said, keeping her voice level.

'As far as I know.'

'Where does he get the blank firers?' Hamish said.

'You'll have to ask him that. All I know is that they come from Glasgow.'

'How does it work, Dougie?' she said. 'How do you advertise you've got guns for sale?'

He shrugged. 'I don't. I go to the Howff whenever I get a new batch. Anyone wanting to buy knows I'll be there on a Friday night.'

265

'Not very efficient.'

'It works well enough.'

'What's your cut?'

'Ten per cent of whatever I make.'

'And Mr McLellan knows how much you make?' She looked at her nails. 'You don't, by any chance, give yourself a bonus now and again?'

'It's a standard rate. Three grand for a Glock, two for a Zoraki and two for a Taurus. They're the ones we've been getting lately. Those models can all be converted to take the nine millimetre Parabellum.'

'And how do you source the cartridges?'

'They come from Glasgow too.'

'How long has this been going on?' Hamish said softly.

'No idea.'

'How long have *you* been working the scam, then?'

'About five years.'

'You must've netted a tidy sum.'

Dougie sneered. 'A man's got to eat.'

Dania was tempted to remark that there were other ways. 'Let's come on now to the murder of Brodie Boyle.'

'I ken nothing about that,' he said promptly.

'He had a Zoraki in his waistband. A converted replica.'

The man looked stunned.

'Did he buy it from you?' She made her voice firm. 'You're doing well, Dougie. Now isn't the time to start lying.'

'He might have bought it from me. I can't say for definite.'

She opened a folder and pushed across one of the posters of Brodie. 'Do you recognise him? Take your time.'

Dougie stared at the photo, his face taut with tension. 'Never seen him. I swear to God.'

'How do you know? It's dark in the Howff.'

266

He considered this. 'I see well in the dark, ken.' He tapped the photo. 'And I've never seen this lad before.'

She gazed into the man's eyes. It was impossible to tell if he was lying. 'Could he have bought the Zoraki from someone else? A competitor of yours?'

'I'm the only one who sells converted replicas in Dundee.'

'Why do you think Brodie Boyle was murdered?' she said, after a pause.

'You're asking the wrong person.'

'Should we be asking the Nailer? After all, a nail was found in Brodie's forehead.'

'Ask him if you like,' Dougie said slowly, looking from her to Hamish with a puzzled expression. 'But none of that's got anything to do with me.'

She slammed her hands on the table, making him jump. 'Really? A murdered man with a nail in his forehead is carrying a converted replica, which you've just said only you sell? And the person who gives you the replicas is Archie McLellan? The Nailer? And you say it's got nothing to do with you?'

Dougie almost leapt out of his seat. His face was ashen. 'Not Archie McLellan! Ned! Ned McLellan!' He was shouting now. 'Archie has absolutely nothing to do with any of this. I never said that. It's Ned who's bringing in the replicas and converting them. Ned! I get them from Ned!'

'Well, we didn't see that one coming, boss,' Honor said, as Dania and Hamish entered the incident room.

Dania ran a hand over her face. 'Ned, not Archie. We've been looking at this all wrong.'

'Not necessarily. Archie may still be involved. Ned does the conversions but Archie sources the replicas. Brodie worked at

Archie's nightclub, didn't he? And there was that nail in his fore-head. Archie has to be involved in this. He has to be.'

She stared at the girl, seeing in her face the same doubt she knew was on her own. They would have to hope Ned had some answers. And they were the right ones. 'We need to get over to Ned's. Can someone get a search warrant from the fiscal? And one to search Donnan's?' She paused, thinking aloud. 'If Ned's not at home, we can track him via his mobile. Anyone know his number?'

'We have it from when he was charged with benefit fraud,' someone said.

'We'll need number-trace authority. And the call logs from his service provider.'

The news, when it arrived, was that Ned's mobile was switched off and had been for some time.

'He'll be using burner phones,' Honor said, chewing a nail.

Prepaid mobiles frequently replaced would avoid leaving a trail. What they needed was the number of the one he was currently using.

An hour later, the warrant to search Ned's house arrived but the fiscal had denied one for Donnan's. The woman's rationale was that there was no evidence Archie McLellan was involved. Dania didn't bother to hide her disappointment. She didn't need to. They all felt the same.

They were about to leave when the duty sergeant rang her. 'There's a gentleman here for you, ma'am.'

For a second, she thought it might be Harry, but the sergeant continued, 'Says his name is Calum MacMartin.'

'I can't see him now.'

'He's most insistent. He's asking for you in person.'

'Did he say what it's about?'

'Yes, ma'am.' A pause. 'The Breek House murders.'

CHAPTER 27

Calum MacMartin was leaning against the desk, chatting to the sergeant. He straightened as Dania approached. She saw a thin man in his fifties with soft brown eyes and greying hair falling over his forehead. There was something about his face that made her think she'd seen him before.

'Inspector Gorska? I'm Calum MacMartin.' He had a deep voice, at odds with his appearance. 'I'm here about the missing-person photographs.'

She felt a rush of blood in her ears. Now she knew where she'd seen those high cheekbones and that cleft in the chin. 'I'm so glad you've come in, Mr MacMartin. Can I offer you some coffee?'

'No, thanks. I've not long had breakfast.' He cleared his throat. 'Thanks for seeing me at such short notice. I would have come yesterday but I had a funeral to attend.'

'Oh, I'm sorry.'

He smiled faintly. 'I'm an undertaker.'

She nodded, not sure how to reply. 'We'll be in the chief super's old office,' she told the sergeant.

Since the start of the refurbishment, the chief super had been allocated a larger room. His old place was now used as a temporary office, an interview room, a place to sit and work quietly and anything else that took the station's fancy. He'd left behind his massive desk, and his old computer, which he'd rarely used. Since policing had gone digital he, like many, had struggled to keep up with the technology.

Dania ushered Calum into the room. 'Please take a seat, Mr MacMartin,' she said, nodding towards the armchairs.

When they were settled, he said without preamble, 'I saw the *Reporting Scotland* programme on Friday evening. And also the reconstructed images in the *Scotsman*.' He seemed to struggle to catch his breath. 'I think they might be of my father. It's not an exact likeness by any means, but I can see similarities. And the height and age are in the right ball park.'

And she remembered that Laurence had been going to contact a Calum MacMartin about his missing father. 'Was his name Willie MacMartin?'

Calum looked surprised. 'Aye, that's right.'

'You reported him missing in nineteen eighty-one, if I remember.'

'You're way ahead of me, Inspector.'

'I've been looking through our database of people who went missing between nineteen seventy-five and nineteen eighty-five. Your father's name came up.'

His expression changed. 'I've wondered all this time what happened to him.'

'We need to be sure it's your father. Have you got a full-face photo? And could you come with me to the lab where the reconstruction was done? The professor in charge can sit with you and change things like the hairstyle and eye colour. He can use the full-face photo of your father to measure and compare the facial features.'

'They can do all that? Aye, of course. I'll help in any way I can.'

'I'll need to arrange a time.' She smiled encouragingly. 'If we can get further evidence it might be your father, and you're prepared to give us a cheek swab, we can get a DNA test done. And that way we can be absolutely sure.'

He dropped his gaze. She guessed what he was thinking. His father had been missing for decades and, now that there was a possibility of discovering what had happened to him, he was reluctant to continue in case what he heard was something he couldn't live with. The location of the remains, buried in a shallow grave, must have made him suspect the worst.

'What did your father do for a living?' she said gently.

Calum lifted his head. 'He was a cabinet maker. Made all kinds of furniture. And restored it, too.'

'And he'd done this all his life?'

'He left school young and got an apprenticeship. Work was good to begin with, right enough, and he made a fair living. But once the likes of IKEA came along and people could buy flat-packed kits and assemble them themselves, it tailed off. Things got hard. We didn't always have bread on the table. He got a wee bit of work making coffins. I think it was watching him do that that got me interested in the business.'

'Did he ever speak about a man called Archie McLellan?'

Calum frowned. 'Not that I remember.'

'Or anyone by the name of McLellan? Would he have done business with a McLellan?'

'I kept all his papers. Would you like me to check the records?'

'I'd be very grateful.'

'May I ask why the interest in the name?'

'Archie McLellan owned Breek House when those people were buried in the grounds.'

Calum's eyes blazed. 'You think he was involved in my father's death? Could this Archie McLellan have murdered him? And those other poor devils out there?'

'That's what we're trying to find out.'

'In that case, I'll look through those invoices as soon as I can.' After a pause, she said, 'What sort of a man was your father?'

He ruffled his hair. 'What can I tell you? He was very gentle. Happy to spend all the hours God sent making furniture. I can still smell his workshop. I used to watch him when I was a wee lad, marking and machining the wood, fitting the joints together. My best times were when he was finishing the pieces, staining them or applying French polish. The process could take hours. He was a perfectionist, which is why he was sought after by folk who needed their pieces restored. It broke his heart when everyone started to buy all that prefabricated stuff.'

'What about your mother? Is she still alive?'

'She died giving birth to me. You'd think my father would resent me but he never did. Or he never showed it. Did his best to bring me up right, and earn a decent living at the same time. It wasn't easy. I think that's what caused his depression.'

'Depression?'

'Aye. Severe depression. The type that makes you feel suicidal. In fact, when he disappeared, that was the first thought that came into my mind. That he'd gone off somewhere and done it quietly. With no fuss. That would have been his way. I used to scour the obituaries, looking for his name.'

'Did he get treatment for his condition?' she said slowly.

'His GP referred him to Ninewells. He saw a specialist there.'

'Can you remember the specialist's name?'

'Not after all these years. Look, everything's in the attic. Stuff to do with the business, letters from the hospital. Why don't I dig it out?'

'That would be brilliant.' She paused. 'Can I ask if your father owned a red motorcycle?'

'He didn't even own a car. There was the company van, but he sold that when money got tight. Why do you ask?'

'We're following a line of enquiry, that's all. There's one other thing I need to ask you. Did your father have any enemies?'

A look of anguish crossed his face. 'What sort of enemies would a man like that have, Inspector? All he did was make furniture, aye, sometimes well into the wee hours. Always delivered and didn't overcharge his customers. He didn't spend his free time getting bevvied because he didn't *have* any free time. And that meant he had few friends. He was a God-fearing man. Didn't work on a Sunday, except when he was behind on a commission.' Emotion choked Calum's words. 'There isn't a day goes by when I don't think about him and everything he did for me.' He was close to tears now. 'I hope you find the man who killed him, Inspector, and put him away for the rest of his life.'

'We'll find him, Mr MacMartin.'

He wiped his eyes with the back of his hand. 'I'll be in touch once I fetch down those papers. I've got a funeral tomorrow, so maybe after that.'

'And I'll arrange for us to meet with the team doing the reconstructions. They're still teaching but I think they'll be able to squeeze us in.' She gave him her card. 'Please feel free to ring me directly at any time.'

'Thank you, Inspector.' He smiled. 'I hope I haven't embarrassed you.'

'Why do you think you've embarrassed me?'

'Aye, well, men aren't supposed to cry.'

'I don't know who came up with that nonsense. It's surely better to cry than to bottle everything up.'

'That's what my dad used to say,' he said sadly.

'Mine, too.'

As they left the room and she walked him to the exit, she had a feeling in her gut that the remains found at Site B would indeed

273

turn out to be those of his father, Willie. And, consequently, a lot more crying would be done.

Calum MacMartin had just left the building when Dania's mobile rang.

'Boss,' Honor said, 'we're at Ned McLellan's place. You need to get yourself over here.'

'Why, what's happened?' Dania said quickly.

'Just come over.' The girl disconnected.

Cholera, Dania thought. She'd sent Honor and Hamish to Ned's, hoping they'd make a straightforward arrest. But things were never straightforward.

She took the squad car and drove to Berwick Drive, a long, sprawling road to the north and east of the city. The weather was on the turn, the wind churning the clouds.

Ned's was one of the last houses on the western approach. There was no fence round the scrap of weed-ridden lawn that passed for a garden. She pulled up outside the two-up-two-down semi, seeing Honor waiting on the pavement, hugging her jacket round her.

'Did you find Ned?' Dania said, getting out of the car.

'There's just Mrs McLellan here.'

'His mother's at home?'

'Hamish is waiting inside with her. There are uniforms covering the front and back doors.'

'Have you searched the house?'

'Not yet, boss. But come and take a look at this.' She led Dania round the back to what looked like a small warehouse. 'When we saw it, we thought we'd better check it out first. It's too large to be a shed.'

'It's been built without windows.'

'And we thought that must be where the conversions are being done. But Mrs McLellan wouldn't give us the key. We had to break the lock to get in. Or, rather, the locks. There were several.'

'What did you find?' Dania said impatiently.

The girl met her gaze. 'I think you need to see for yourself.' She handed Dania a pair of gloves.

'I take it there's an inside light?'

'All will be revealed, boss.'

As soon as Dania pushed open the door, she was hit by the heat and humidity. And the smell. It was heavy and sweet, and left her lightheaded. Rows of black plastic pots filled the available space and growing in them were plants with serrated green leaves. Every inch of wall was covered with foil that gleamed with condensation.

'This is a commercial operation,' Honor was saying. 'See those UV grow lamps? The wall timer switches them on and off at set intervals. And those cans stacked to the ceiling contain fertiliser or root stimulator.'

'What's that humming noise?'

'The ventilator.'

'How come you can't smell anything from outside?'

'There's an extraction system with a carbon filter. This place has been custom built. See the watering system?' At intervals along the walls, there were taps with hoses attached. 'Plants in pots as small as these need regular watering.'

Dania was starting to sweat into her clothes. 'So who's the gardener? Ned? Or his mother?'

'We've still to establish that. But they both live at this address.'

'Then I think it's time we spoke to the lady.'

Mrs McLellan's living room was full of the kind of easily assembled pieces that Calum MacMartin had railed against: a patterned three-seater sofa and matching armchairs, a glass-panelled sideboard, and a chest of three drawers. But pride of place had to go to the pink and white doll's house by the window, one side raised to show the rooms with their miniature furniture. Someone had made the mistake of putting the Swiss cheese plant near the mantelpiece, and its leaves were wilting in the heat from the coal-effect fire. The carpet was covered with good-quality rugs, some of which were threadbare, and Dania guessed that they were the most valuable items in the room. Her gaze was drawn to the mobile phone on the sideboard.

Mrs McLellan was sitting on the sofa in front of the window, wearing her eighty years like armour. Beside her, on the small scallop-edged table, lay a packet of John Player Specials and a half-full ashtray. She was clutching a silver lighter as though it would ward off evil.

Hamish was sitting stony-faced in an armchair, making Dania wonder what he and the woman had been talking about. Honor took up position by the door, while Dania sat down next to Mrs McLellan. The woman shifted her bulk, making the sofa creak ominously. A musty, yeasty smell came from her clothes, as though they hadn't been washed in a while.

'Mrs McLellan, I'm DI Dania Gorska.'

'I ken who you are,' the woman said, in her rasping voice. 'You're the Polish detective who's been coming to Donnan's.'

'Well remembered.'

'So you've found my plants, have you?'

'You don't deny they're yours?'

She stroked back her grey hair. 'Why would I?'

'Cannabis is a class B drug under the Misuse of Drugs Act 1971.'

'Aye, and?'

'You've admitted possession of a controlled substance, Mrs McLellan.'

'It's for my own consumption.'

Dania thought of the half-acre of cannabis plants. The woman would have to consume handfuls of leaves morning, noon and night. And even then there'd be enough left to make spliffs for the rest of Dundee. 'Your own consumption? You expect me to believe that?'

Mrs McLellan opened her eyes wide, the bags under them making her look like a ghoul. 'I need cannabis for my condition, Inspector.'

'And what condition would that be?'

'I suffer from the nerves.' She nodded at Hamish. 'And I don't take kindly to having a male copper babysitting me.'

He spread his hands as if to indicate he'd been behaving like a perfect gentleman.

'Mrs McLellan,' Dania said, 'you have enough cannabis on your property for commercial distribution. That's a category-one offence, regardless of whether only you consume it.'

The woman folded her arms over her ample chest, her attitude defying Dania to prove her wrong.

'I'm afraid we'll have to take you down to the station.'

Her mouth twitched into a smile.

'Where's your son, Mrs McLellan?'

'In his nightclub, I should imagine.'

'I was meaning Ned.'

For the first time, a look of something other than complacency appeared on the woman's face. She pressed her lips together, a hostile expression in her eyes.

'He lives here with you,' Dania went on.

'Ach, away. You're havering.'

She suppressed her irritation. Did the woman really think the police wouldn't have checked who resided at this address? 'Mrs McLellan, I doubt very much that you could tend those plants on your own. That building looks specially constructed to grow cannabis. There's ventilation with an extraction system, to say nothing of a system for watering the plants. Was it Ned who had all that put in?'

'It was already kitted out like that when I bought the place.'

Dania leant forward and said softly, 'Where is he, Mrs McLellan? Where's Ned?'

'I haven't a scooby, Inspector. I've not seen him for days.'

'He's already in a spot of trouble. Benefit fraud. His case comes up next month, I believe.'

The woman turned her head away, a bored expression on her face. Dania wondered how much she knew about her son's activities. Was she aware that he converted replica firearms and sold them in the city centre?

'You're not helping yourself by protecting him. We'll find him eventually. But, right now, we're going to search the house. My officers have shown you the warrant?'

The woman nodded primly.

'Police are covering the front and back doors, Mrs McLellan, so please don't do anything rash, like trying to leave.'

'Why would I leave, Inspector? This is my house.'

Dania motioned to Hamish and Honor, and the three of them left the room. She was the last out and pulled the door towards her but didn't close it.

In the corridor, she whispered to the others to make as much noise as possible. As they clumped up the stairs, she put her ear to the door and listened.

A second later, she heard the creak of the sofa. Mrs McLellan was getting up. Her heavy tread suggested she was making for the sideboard.

Dania counted the seconds, imagining the woman picking up the phone, locating Ned's contact details, and calling him. She pushed the door gently and peered inside. Mrs McLellan was hunched over with her back to her.

Dania crept across the room and, before the woman had a chance to lift her head, snatched the phone out of her hand. She held it above her head, out of reach.

'Give me that back, you little bitch!' Mrs McLellan shouted. She lunged at Dania, who sidestepped neatly, and tripped on the rug, falling face down across the armchair.

Dania hurried out of the room and out of the house, passing the surprised uniform at the front door.

'You may have to restrain Mrs McLellan,' she said over her shoulder. 'Make sure she doesn't leave the building.'

She leant against the squad car and stared at the phone's screen. It couldn't have been better. Mrs McLellan had started a text message: *Ned, the polis are here. You need to*

She cancelled the message and, using her own phone, sent Ned's number to Tech, with instructions to contact the mobile networks and see which one provided a service to that number. And then to monitor it. If Ned kept his phone switched off, they would have to wait for him to call. But she'd put down good money that, when they did locate him, they'd find him converting replica handguns. All in all, not a bad morning's work. But they would have to move quickly.

There was a sudden commotion from the house. She glanced up to see Honor and Hamish escorting Mrs McLellan out of the door. The woman was using the sort of language that would make a soldier blush, but neither officer seemed bothered. She shook her arm free and struck out wildly, landing a punch on Honor's shoulder. The girl swore and grabbed her arm.

'Your officers are manhandling me, Inspector,' Mrs McLellan shouted, seeing Dania. 'If there's any harm done, it'll go badly for you, and no mistake.'

'You're right,' she said. She nodded at Hamish. 'Cuff her.'

CHAPTER 28

'Her phone's ringing, boss,' Honor said excitedly.

'And just as I was about to call Ned.'

'What will you do? He'll know it's not his mother's voice.'

'I won't pick up. He'll either think she's left the house and forgotten to take her mobile, or she's fallen asleep in front of the fire. The main thing is he's switched on his prepaid.' Dania glanced at the officer sitting in front of the large monitor. He was looking determinedly at the data on the screen and seemed to have the tracking well in hand.

'Right, ma'am, we've got him.' He moved the mouse, and the on-screen map changed. 'This is his location.'

'Cripes,' Honor said, peering at the map. 'Auchterhouse. What's he doing way up there?'

'Can you send the details to my phone?' Dania said to the officer.

'No problem.'

'Okay, Honor, let's go.'

Two men from the Tactical Firearms Unit were waiting in the corridor. One carried a battering ram, and both had Taser stun guns as well as handguns, which, thanks to Hamish's tutorial, Dania recognised as Glock 17s. The men had been fully briefed but she wanted to go through it one more time. 'Remember, we need to catch him in the act,' she said. 'Otherwise he'll say he stumbled on the place and just went in to have a look.'

'Won't his dabs be everywhere, ma'am?' one of the officers asked. He had striking blue eyes and a rich, deep voice. And a physique that would turn heads in the street. He was the senior of the two and had introduced himself only as Frank, speaking in an accent Dania recognised as pure Dundee. Like his partner, he was dressed in black, and wore a Kevlar vest.

'So far, he's been careful not to leave any prints behind.'

Frank nodded thoughtfully. 'Any idea how he might respond?'

'Hard to say. But we think he's responsible for the deaths of two men. That means he'll know he's in a corner.'

'And might be tempted to fight his way out?'

'It's why you're here. And I'd prefer him taken alive. You're the experts, but my suggestion would be to park a short distance away and creep up on the place.'

'That sounds like my kind of operation,' Frank replied, with an uneven grin. He handed the women their Kevlar vests.

Auchterhouse, a few miles north-west of Dundee and popular with commuters, sat south of the Sidlaw Hills, less than a quarter of an hour by car from the city centre. A mild haze lay over the jumble of fields, and they were glad of the change in landscape as they approached the village. And that the wind had dropped.

Dania peered at her phone. 'According to the map, he's somewhere in those trees behind us.'

'Then we'll dump the van here and walk back,' Frank said.

There was nowhere to park in Auchterhouse, so they left the vehicle on private land, hoping the residents would see the police notice.

'Right, he's here,' Dania said, after they'd walked a short distance.

Frank motioned to the signpost. 'Dronley Wood Farm. If he's in a farmhouse, we'll have to take special care.'

'I don't get it,' Honor said. 'We passed Dronley Wood about two miles back.'

'Maybe all the land between here and there belongs to the farm,' Dania replied.

Frank removed the handgun from his holster. 'We'll check out what's in those trees. Wait here,' he said to the women. He nodded at his companion, and they hurried towards the wood and disappeared. Seconds later, he reappeared, beckoning to them.

Behind the wood, a dilapidated farmhouse stood well back on the other side of the rutted road. Its windows were broken and part of the roof had caved in. Some distance to the right there was a single-storey brick building. A white car was parked outside.

Frank pulled a small pair of binoculars from inside his vest. After glancing into the sky to gauge the position of the sun, he handed them to Dania.

'That's his Renault Mégane,' she said, studying the car. She passed the binoculars back. 'He's chosen a good place. He can convert his replicas in complete seclusion.'

'What do you think the building used to be?' Frank said, nodding towards the brick structure.

'Maybe a lambing shed.' She remembered Dougie's words about the conversions being done in an old garage. 'Or a place for storing vehicles like combine harvesters.'

'There's someone at home,' Honor said quietly. 'I saw him walk past the window.'

Frank looked at his subordinate. 'Got the ram ready, Gary?'

The man called Gary grunted, which Dania guessed was a 'yes'.

'We'll approach from that direction,' Frank said, motioning to the farmhouse. 'But, first, let's check there really is no one in those ruins.'

'Aye,' Gary replied.

'You two stay here.'

'We're coming with you,' Dania said.

Frank glanced at her. 'Okay, then, but stay behind me at all times. And do what I do. If I go down on all fours, you go down on all fours.'

The men set off towards the farmhouse, crawling on their bellies. Dania and Honor had no choice but to do the same.

One look inside the building told them the inhabitants were long gone. Mould grew on the walls and carpet, slates littered the floor, and beams from the damaged roof had fallen on to the staircase.

Through a break in the wall, they glimpsed the brick building. Frank squinted into the sky, then lifted the binoculars. 'There are windows on either side of the door,' he murmured. 'And the door's not closed. We won't need the ram.'

'Crikey,' Honor said, letting out her breath. 'Bit rash, leaving himself wide open like that.'

'He's not expecting anyone.' Frank continued to gaze through the binoculars. 'That'll work for us.'

Gary put down the ram and removed the Glock from its holster. 'There's no cover between us and him,' he growled, in a strong east-coast accent. 'We'll have to go softly-softly.'

'I have a bad feeling about this,' Honor said, chewing her thumbnail. She looked sick with worry.

'Stay here,' Dania said gently. 'I'll go.'

'I'm not leaving you, boss.' Honor straightened. 'I'll be all right.'

Frank was frowning. He was probably afraid she'd jeopardise the mission. Or lose her life.

The thought had also crossed Dania's mind. 'Go back to the road, Honor. We need someone to keep a lookout. That's an order,' she added, when the girl started to protest.

Honor glanced at Frank, who looked at the ground. She turned and left the way she'd come.

'Maybe just as well, ma'am. I don't hold it against her.'

'We lost an officer recently, a close buddy of hers. We're all still getting used to it.'

'I understand.'

'So, shall we go?'

He threw her an appreciative look. 'And remember. Behind me at all times. It's vital not to be seen through the windows.'

'Got it.'

The men stole out of the building, Dania following. They dropped into a crouch and crept towards the building, taking up position one on either side of the door. Frank gripped Dania's arm and dragged her behind him, pulling her so close that she felt the warmth of his body.

She peered over his shoulder, seeing Gary facing them, a determined look on his face. Both men had their Glocks at the ready.

From inside came an intermittent drilling noise, followed by hammering. She was overcome by a sudden feeling of dread that it would all go badly wrong. Perhaps this was what Honor had felt.

'Stay outside until we've made the place safe, understand?' Frank murmured, looking over his shoulder at Dania.

She nodded, unable to speak because of the constriction in her chest.

He lifted his free hand and made a series of signals. Gary nodded.

Then everything happened too quickly. Frank kicked the door open and he and Gary rushed into the building, yelling.

Dania crouched low, risking a quick peek round the doorframe.

The men had taken up positions to left and right. Ned was bending over a cardboard box, an expression of shock on his face.

His gaze locked on hers, and the expression changed to one of determination.

'I said show me your hands!' Frank shouted. 'Now!'

In that instant, she knew Ned was going to make the wrong move. He stood up and lifted both arms straight out. And then the world exploded in a shower of metal and sparks and smoke. She clamped her hands over her ears and swallowed rapidly.

When the smoke had cleared, she saw Frank and Gary standing over Ned. Frank was holstering his weapon.

He turned and waved to her to come inside.

Ned was lying motionless, his arms resting on his stomach. The flesh of his hands hung in ribbons, the fingers bent into impossible angles or missing completely. The shreds of bloody white material round his wrists suggested he'd been wearing magician's gloves. His face was covered with a film of black powder, the bottom half a slurry of bloody flesh. A thick metal shard was buried in his left eye, which had leaked, leaving a thin clear trail in the powder. His right eye glared at them in barely suppressed fury. Dania had often wondered why the newly dead were able to express their feelings. Perhaps it was after rigor had come and gone that their faces looked peaceful.

She turned her gaze to his green gamekeeper's jacket. It was torn at both pockets and gaped open, revealing an off-white fleecy jacket and baggy jeans. His white trainers were slowly staining red in the spreading pool of blood. These were the clothes he'd worn when he shot Brodie Boyle, she realised then.

'Not a pretty sight, ma'am,' Frank said, watching her.

'What happened?'

'He tried to fire at us, but the gun exploded in his hands,' Gary said. 'He never got off a shot. And neither did we,' he added sourly.

Frank was peering into the cardboard box. 'Nice little stash he had here.'

She pulled on her gloves and lifted out a handgun. It was a revolver with a black handle, and the shortest barrel of any handgun she'd ever seen. 'What's this?'

'A Taurus LOM-13, ma'am.'

There was little trace of what the building had been used for. The farm equipment had been removed, and cardboard boxes of varying sizes were stacked around the room. Ned had installed a modern workbench, which held an array of machine tools for converting replicas to the real thing.

Her gaze fell on the claw hammer. And the bedframe in the corner. Its outline, visible through the plastic sheet, left her in no doubt that this was where Quinn had spent his last hours.

She bent over Ned and gazed again into what was left of his face.

'What are you thinking?' Frank said.

'I'm wondering how I'm going to tell his mother.'

Jackson Delaney took his time getting out to Dronley Wood Farm, citing a string of incidents that had delayed him. No one was fooled. His bloodshot eyes and boozy breath told them he was still recovering from a jolly Saturday night. Miraculously, one look at Ned's corpse and sobriety returned.

'You don't need to tell us how he died, Doc,' Frank said. 'We saw it all.'

Jackson glanced up. 'Well, lucky you,' he said, with a sneer. He turned to Dania. 'The mortuary van's outside. I'll get him to Ninewells without delay. But the PM will have to wait until tomorrow.' He started to organise his staff.

Honor was with the SOCOs, who were photographing everything prior to bagging up the machines.

'I'd hoped there'd be some record of where he sourced the

replicas,' Dania said to Frank, who was watching proceedings with interest.

'Would a man like that keep records?'

'We're searching his house. But I expect what we want is on his mobile.'

'Well, if you don't need us, we'll take ourselves off. Can you get yourself back to the city?'

'I'll ride with the SOCOs.'

'I'm sorry we couldn't take him alive.'

'It was his own stupid fault. You did everything correctly. And that's what I'll put in my report.'

'Let me know if there's anything else you need. You know where I can be reached. *Wszystkiego najlepszego*,' he added, using the Polish phrase to wish her the best. *'Do widzenia.'*

'You speak Polish?' she said in surprise.

'My name's Franek Jagielski.'

'You could have fooled me. You haven't got a Polish accent.'

'I was born in Scotland.' He smiled slowly. 'Perhaps we could have a glass of vodka some time and talk about life in the old country.'

It was late afternoon before Dania returned to West Bell Street. Her first task was to report in to the DCI. Although they still had many unanswered questions, her boss congratulated her on a positive result. As Dania left the office, she prepared herself for her second task.

'Can you bring Mrs McLellan up from the cells?' she said to one of the constables.

He nodded, his expression telling her better than words that he didn't envy her.

She waited with Hamish in the main interview room, rehearsing mentally what she would say.

Mrs McLellan was brought in. She shook off the constable's arm, muttering to herself. 'So, you're not going to cuff me this time?' she rasped, sitting down.

Dania studied the woman, wondering how she would react. 'Mrs McLellan, please prepare yourself for bad news.'

'Ach, what now?' she jeered. 'You've taken my plants away? Is that it?'

'I'm afraid your son is dead.'

The woman cackled with laughter. 'If you think that's going to trick me into telling you anything, you've gone soft in the head.' She leant forward, hatred in her eyes. 'You'll have to do better than that.'

'We caught him in his workshop at old Dronley Wood Farm. He was converting replica firearms.' Dania watched the woman closely. Suspicion had replaced hatred. 'He discharged a handgun at one of my officers. It exploded, killing him instantly.'

The woman drew her brows together. Realisation that the police officer was telling the truth replaced suspicion. For a second, Dania thought she was going to lunge across the table, but she continued to stare, her expression vacant. Dania waited for some sort of reaction. Grief, anger. Anything. Only the hands clasping and unclasping revealed the woman's inner turmoil. She had probably grasped that the text message she'd tried to send her son had led to his eventual downfall.

'I want to see him,' she said in a flat voice.

'I don't think that's a good idea.'

'I want to see him.'

'Mrs McLellan—'

'Listen to me,' the woman said, her voice harsh. 'I want to see him. Or you'll get nothing from me. Nothing. Do you hear?'

Dania glanced at Hamish. He shook his head.

Mrs McLellan had caught the exchange. 'I'll make you a deal. Let me see my Ned and I'll tell you everything. After all, none of it matters now. You have my word on it.' She seemed to consider what she'd said. 'It's the only thing I've got left.'

'This is highly irregular, Inspector,' Jackson said. 'The corpse isn't in a condition for viewing.'

'I'm aware of that, Professor, but the suspect won't tell us what we need to know unless she sees her son's body. This is a special case.'

'For you, maybe,' he said nastily. 'It's going to help you get your next promotion, I expect.'

Dania tamped down her anger. Jackson was probably still smarting from being called 'Doc'.

'He's in the positive-temperature cold chamber because I'm conducting the autopsy tomorrow,' he said. 'You know what that means, I take it?'

'The body temperature is above freezing.'

'And I don't want the woman fainting on to the corpse.'

Dania couldn't imagine anyone less likely to faint than Mrs McLellan. 'I'll take full responsibility.'

He considered this. Then, with a curt nod, he said, 'Where is she?'

'In the corridor with one of my officers.'

'Bring her to the mortuary. I'll meet you there.' He stalked out of the room.

'The professor's given his consent,' Dania said, when she was outside. She studied Mrs McLellan. 'Are you sure you want to go through with this?'

'I wouldn't have made you bring me all the way out here just to change my mind, would I?' she said, her lips curling.

'As you wish. Let's go, then.'

The mortuary was not well signposted, but Dania knew the way. Jackson was waiting at one of the wall shelves with the attendant, a round-shouldered man with a shaven head and blond moustache.

She and Hamish took up position, one on either side of Mrs McLellan. At a nod from the professor, the attendant pulled back the cloth to reveal the face. Even though she'd seen it earlier, Dania felt shock surge through her. The metal shard was still in Ned's left eye, and there was a second fragment, one she'd missed earlier, in his neck. It had severed his artery, staining the collar of his off-white jacket a dark red.

Mrs McLellan stepped forward and bent her head, taking a good look at her son.

Although the credit cards in his pocket identified him as Ned McLellan, they needed a positive ID from a close relative. 'Is that Ned McLellan?' Dania said.

'Aye, that's him,' the woman replied, straightening. And then she said to no one in particular, 'I suppose someone will have to tell Archie.'

CHAPTER 29

They were in the main interview room with the tape running. Mrs McLellan was nursing a huge mug of coffee, looking nothing like a woman who had just seen the ravaged body of her son. Grim determination was etched into the lines of her face and, had Dania not known better, she'd have thought the woman was plotting revenge.

'I'd like you to begin at the beginning, Mrs McLellan,' Dania said.

The woman turned flinty eyes on her. 'Depends what you mean by the beginning.'

'How did Ned get into the business of converting replica firearms?'

'It wasn't Ned who started that.'

'Who, then?' Dania said, her pulse racing. 'Archie?'

'Archie?' Mrs McLellan said, with derision. 'Archie was never involved. No, I ran the operation. In fact, I started it.'

Dania felt Hamish stir. 'You?' she said, stunned.

'I ken people in Glasgow. They sell me the blank firers and the cartridges.'

'Who are these people?'

'Relatives.' The woman smiled. 'Aye, it's best to keep things in the family. They're my sister's sons. I can give you names and addresses.'

'You're willing to give up your family?'

She shrugged. 'I gave you my word, didn't I?'

'How long has this been going on?'

'Ach, I can't remember. But you'll find everything in the house. I keep the paperwork there. Invoices, and that.'

'Are you telling me you keep accounts?'

'I have to, don't I? For the Revenue.'

'Hold on,' Hamish said. 'You make returns to the Inland Revenue?'

'Well, of course I don't write guns and cartridges. That would bring the law down on my head.' She seemed to be enjoying herself. 'The Revenue think I'm running a wee import-export business.'

'What do you put on the return?' Dania said slowly.

'Doll's houses. I make out that I import the raw materials, like the walls and roofs, and put them together and sell them from my premises.' She turned the mug in her hands. 'It's not so big the Revenue come calling. They don't have the manpower with businesses like mine. But if they did, they'd see that what goes in and out of my bank account tallies with what I enter on the return.'

The doll's house in the living room would be there to support her claim in case the Revenue conducted an audit. Dania had the strong urge to laugh. She could imagine how this was being received by the DCI and the rest of the team watching from the control room.

'So Ned just did the conversions?'

'Where business dealings are concerned, he hasn't two brains to rub together,' the woman said dismissively, 'but he's well good with his hands so that's his side of the operation.' She scratched her chin. 'I had to walk him through how to take precautions, use gloves and wipe everything.'

'And it was just you, Ned and Dougie converting and selling firearms? Archie's men weren't in on it?'

'*Those* twallies.' She rolled her eyes. 'Give me some credit. No. Keeping it just to the three of us meant that less could go wrong.'

'Except it wasn't just the three of you. There are your nephews in Glasgow.'

'They wouldn't clype on us. They're blood. And Dougie's loyal, he's like family.' She brushed her hair back. 'The idea to use the Howff was Ned's. He has a pal on the council who gave him a duplicate key. For the gates on Barrack Street, ken. Dougie would tell Ned when he'd next be at the Howff, and Ned would make sure the gates were unlocked.'

'All right. Let's come now to the murder of Brodie Boyle.'

'Aye, that was an awfy business,' the woman said, as though converting and selling guns wasn't. 'If I'd known what Ned was up to, believe me, I'd have throttled him. I very nearly did when he told me what he'd done.'

'How did he meet Brodie?'

'At Donnan's.' A look of scorn crossed her face. 'Ned told me about him, how he gave him the eye. I suppose queers can sniff each other out.'

'Did Ned start up the relationship?'

'He pretended to start up the relationship.'

'He told you this?'

'He told me everything. We were close in every way. Mothers always have a favourite lad. Well, Ned was mine.'

'Why did he pretend with Brodie?'

'He needed something from him.' She took a deep breath. 'You'll want to know it all, I reckon.' She finished her coffee, making them wait. 'On that day, Ned arranged to meet Brodie in a wee hotel not far from that gym. After a bit of hochmagandy, he gave Brodie a gun, asking him to pass it on to someone.'

'And Brodie agreed? Just like that?'

'The lad was skint, something Ned would ken fine well. Brodie

293

agreed to help in exchange for a cut. Aye, a canny lad, he was. He told Ned he could be the courier who delivered to the buyers, and this would be his first gig. A sort of test run.' She looked hard at the table as though afraid of what her expression would reveal. 'Ned took the bus in to Seagate Bus Station and got to that hotel through the back roads to avoid all those cameras the polis keep putting up. He had two guns, which he'd wiped clean. He told Brodie to meet the buyer in a pub on Castle Street. The lad would have to go along Dock Street to get there, and Ned wanted that because it was well close to Donnan's. He left the hotel first, telling Brodie they shouldn't be seen together, and took the back roads to Candle Lane.'

'Why Candle Lane?' Hamish said.

'He'd left his stuff there a couple of days before.'

'In that old garage at the back of Donnan's?' Dania said softly.

'He had the keycode.'

'Archie told me only he has the keycode.'

'Well, Archie was wrong. I've had the code for years. And it's never been changed. Ned went into the garage, put on his black jacket, and picked up the hammer and nail.'

'And then he lay in wait for Brodie, watching from Candle Lane?'

'He saw the lad walk past and followed him.' Her eyes widened as though she could see the events unfolding. 'Ned caught up with him. He called to him and the lad turned round. And then he shot him.'

'Why?'

'To frame his brother. The nail in the head was to make the polis think it was Archie.' She sighed theatrically, as if they were all too stupid to understand what she was telling them. 'Ned was jealous of Archie. Of his success. Even if he worked all the hours the Lord sent, he'd never make the kind of money Archie was making.' She snorted. 'He thought that, because there was a nail in the lad's head, the polis would put Archie away, and he could then take over Donnan's.' She tapped her head. 'Porridge for brains.'

'Are you sure you knew nothing about this?'

'As God's my witness, when Ned told me, I went mental. The eejit hadn't bothered to take the gun out of Brodie's waistband. The wee fact that the polis would turn their attention to the replica business when they found it simply hadn't registered with him. He reckoned he was so smart, choosing a day and time when Archie would be at home with no alibi.'

'What did he do with the murder weapon? Did he bin it, like he binned the jacket and hammer?'

'He got Dougie to sell it. At least he had the sense not to hold on to it.' She pushed the mug away. 'After the shooting, he took the long way round to that old garage on Candle Lane, and waited till everything had died down before legging it.'

'Tell me something, Mrs McLellan. Archie must have wondered what was going on with that nail in Brodie's forehead. Did he never suspect Ned's hand in it?'

'Why would he? Ned told me they did have a blether about the shooting, and Archie reckoned someone was trying to frame him with that nail, it wouldn't be the first time, but he didn't think it was Ned.'

'What did he think Ned did for a living? The man was un-employed, but he always seemed to have money to spend at Donnan's.'

She shrugged. 'He thought Ned helped me with the doll's houses. I have a pension, too. Courtesy of the state.'

'You'd have needed start-up money to get the first lot of the blank firers in. Where did that money come from? Did Archie help you?'

'I wouldn't take money from Archie.' She picked at a loose thread on her sleeve, avoiding Dania's gaze. 'I had a wee bitty saved.'

Dania had seen behaviour like that before. The woman was lying.

'Let's talk now about Quinn,' Dania said.

'Quinn?'

'The man whose body was found in Candle Lane. You must have seen it in yesterday's papers.' She made her voice hard. 'Don't waste your time denying it. We found evidence in the building Ned used for his conversions. It was all over the bed Quinn had been tied to. The DNA will prove it was his.'

Rage flared in the woman's eyes. 'Christ, I told him to get rid of everything.' She seemed to deflate then, her shoulders slumping. 'We suspected he was an informant when Ned heard him using his phone. Ned was in Archie's lavvy at the time.' She smiled grimly. 'Voices carry in that place. Everyone was outside with the fire drill, but Ned was taken short so he sneaked back in. He heard Quinn talking about what was in the filing cabinet. And that he hadn't found any firearms or cartridges. You can imagine how Ned's ears pricked up at that. He called me straight after. We reckoned Quinn was a grass.' She looked directly at Dania. 'I didn't ken at the time that he was one of yours. That came later.'

Dania clasped her hands together to stop herself striking the woman.

'Quinn smoked those black fags,' the woman went on. 'The ones with the foul reek. When you came to Donnan's to play the tables, Ned smelt them on you. My first thought was that maybe you smoked them too. But you came to Donnan's again and I heard Archie offer you a cigarette. And you said you didn't smoke.' She tapped the table with a bony finger. '*That's* when I knew.' She pointed at Dania. '*You* had to be the handler.'

'And because you wanted to be certain,' Hamish said, 'you had Ned kidnap Quinn and torture the information out of him.'

The woman looked at Hamish with distaste. 'Ned didn't need much of a shove. He would ken what was at stake.' She transferred her gaze to Dania. 'Dougie and his pal helped him take your boy. They drove him out to Dronley Wood Farm.'

'Were you waiting there?' Dania said, feeling the muscles of her face tighten.

'I'd told Ned what to do. I didn't have to be around to see it.'

'And the nail? Was that your idea too?'

'Aye, this time it was. You'd already made Archie as prime suspect for Brodie's murder so I saw no reason not to stitch him up for Quinn's.'

Dania clenched her fists. This was not the time to lose it. 'And the text message I got from Quinn's phone?' she said, keeping her voice even. 'To meet him?'

'That was to make sure. You see, Quinn didn't give up your name. He was a brave lad. We wanted to see who came, and it could only be his handler.'

'You were there?'

She shook her head. 'Ned was hiding in the shadows. He said you didn't see him. You were greeting like a wee bairn.'

'And you left the body at the back of Donnan's to make us think it was Archie.'

'Aye. But we didn't do it straight off. We let it rot for a wee bit inside the plastic sheet. That way you'd not get a definite time of death. I've been watching those programmes on telly.'

'Holding on to a body is risky,' Hamish said.

'Sometimes you have to take risks, lad. We didn't ken Archie's movements. He might have had a rock-solid alibi.'

Dania didn't bother to conceal her loathing. 'What kind of a woman are you? You'd implicate an innocent man? Your son?'

'Ned was my son, too,' she spat out. 'I loved him more.' There was venom in her voice. 'Aye, Archie was generous with his money, he'd been left the farm with nothing going to Ned, but his generosity only made it worse. He wouldn't give Ned a living. Said he should make something of himself the way he, the great Archie McLellan, had done. He didn't see what was happening to Ned.'

'And what was that?'

A bewildered expression came into her eyes. 'The same that happened to my Donnan. God knows, I recognised the symptoms. I saw it starting with Ned, although it would be a while before it took hold.'

'What are you talking about?' Hamish said.

'The dark. It took Donnan so that he couldn't stand it any longer. He saw ghosts of people. All the enemies he'd made in his lifetime. Aye, and that was a fair few. He thought they were coming for him. It began the same way with Ned, with nightmares and shouting in his sleep. When I went in, he'd tell me it was dark, even though the lights were on.' She lowered her head. 'Maybe it's just as well that he left this world early.'

Dania stared at the woman, her thoughts swirling. She felt disgust that Mrs McLellan was willing to frame one son for murder to save the other. But, strangely, seeing the woman's defeated expression, she also felt pity, the kind of pity you feel for a beaten dog.

'We'll type up a statement, Mrs McLellan, and ask you to sign it.'

'Aye, well, all right.' She frowned. 'So what will you be charging me with?'

Dania thought of the replica-to-real firearm business, incitement to commit murder, conspiracy to commit murder, defrauding the Inland Revenue. If she put her mind to it, she'd come up with a few more. Although what she'd heard from the woman would put the production of cannabis into the shade. 'There's one more thing I want to ask you, Mrs McLellan.' She paused. 'It's about Breek House.'

The woman looked at her with suspicion. 'You're going to set those bones murders at Ned's door, too?' she said quietly. 'He had nothing to do with it. As God is my witness.'

'I was going to ask you about Archie. He owned the house in the period those people were murdered. Nineteen seventy-five to nineteen eighty-five.'

'He might have owned Breek House, but he never lived there. He was in prison.'

'He was released in nineteen seventy-eight.'

'Aye, but he went to live in town. He moved in with a pal. Hardly ever set foot in Breek House again.' She was silent for a moment, and then she said, 'I've told you enough for today, Inspector. I'm feeling tired. And I think it must be time for my tea.'

They were waiting outside. As Dania and Hamish left the interview room, they crowded round, all talking at once.

'Congratulations, ma'am,' someone shouted.

Dania raised a hand for silence. 'It's not over yet. We may have found Brodie's killer, and Quinn's, but there's still Breek House.' She saw their deflated looks. With Laurence's death uppermost in their minds, they could do with some good news. 'But I think we're close. And, once we've got that sorted, we'll celebrate. And drinks will be on me.'

They returned to their desks in a state of excitement.

'We were wrong about Archie,' Honor said, hanging back. 'He had nothing to do with it.'

'I still think he helped his mother financially when they started converting replicas. We haven't finished sifting through what we found in her house.'

'There'll be no money trail. He'll have covered his tracks. He always does.'

'There's one thing I don't get, Honor. It's about Breek House. I keep hearing conflicting things. Mrs McLellan just said that Archie rarely set foot in the place after his father's death. And yet, when I sat in his office, he acted as though he ran the farm on his release. He talked about taking on casual labourers as and when he needed them. I should have smelt a rat when he told me he'd cleared out the records for the period after nineteen seventy-five. I wonder why he didn't just come out and say he lived some-where else.'

'It would be good to get to the bottom of that, boss. One of them is lying.'

'At *least* one. But if Archie didn't live there, who did? It must have been Ned and his mother.'

'Trying to keep the place going?'

'Or another relative, maybe. Is there anyone else in the McLellan family?'

'There was a Keith McLellan. But I don't think he was a farmer. He's moved away, from what I heard. We'll have to stick with it. Mrs McLellan may open up yet.'

'I'm not holding my breath. But there's one person who has the answers. And, first thing tomorrow, I'm paying him a visit.'

CHAPTER 30

'I want to see Mr McLellan,' Dania said firmly. 'Right now.'

The man scratched at his ace-of-spades tattoo. 'I'll see if he's receiving guests,' he said, in a bored voice.

She injected just enough menace into her voice. 'Whether he is or not, I *will* see him.'

He stared for a moment, then nodded and sauntered into the nightclub, leaving her in the corridor.

A short while later he reappeared. 'Mr McLellan's in his office. I'll take you in.'

She followed him into the nightclub. It was empty, except for the cleaners, who were upending chairs on to the tables and washing the floor. The smell of stale beer followed her into the corridor to Archie's office.

'Inspector,' Archie said, getting to his feet. 'This is a surprise.' He was dressed in black trousers and a zip-up faux-suede jacket. He jerked his head at the man, who left quickly.

Dania realised that Archie couldn't know about his brother. The DCI's press conference wasn't until midday and, as far as she was aware, Mrs McLellan hadn't asked to make a phone call.

'Please take a seat,' Archie said slowly, studying her. 'You're not looking your usual lovely self. I reckon these murders are taking their toll, right enough, and you're having to do overtime.' He sat down, shaking his head. 'You'll do no one any good by working yourself into the ground.'

She took a deep breath. 'There's no easy way to say this, Mr McLellan. Your brother died yesterday.'

His face remained expressionless. Only the twitching of his cheek muscles suggested the news had affected him.

'We caught him at Dronley Wood Farm, near Auchterhouse. He was converting replica firearms. When he tried to shoot a police officer, the firearm exploded in his hands, killing him.'

Archie got to his feet, his gaze never leaving her face.

'It was Ned who killed Brodie Boyle. And also Quinn Selby. Your mother has told us everything.'

He walked to the wall safe and entered the combination. Inside was a single item, a bottle of what looked like whisky. The label told her it was a twenty-one-year-old Lagavulin. He stood it on the desk, then produced two crystal glasses from one of the drawers.

'I'm afraid I'm on duty, Mr McLellan.'

He ignored the comment, poured liquid into the glasses and handed her one. 'I never drink alone, Inspector. And I need a drink now.'

She took the glass and sipped. The whisky had a sweet peaty flavour with spicy undertones.

'Thank you for coming to tell me,' he said. 'A lesser person would have let me hear it on the news.'

'The DCI is holding a press conference later this morning. It will be in the news after that.'

'So you've solved your cases. That's something worth drinking to, no?'

'Not all my cases,' she said carefully. 'There's still Breek House.'

'And how are you getting on with that?'

'There's something that doesn't add up. And maybe you can

help me. Your mother told me you didn't live at Breek House after your release from prison. And yet here in this office you led me to believe you continued to run the farm. You didn't, though, did you? That's why you have no farm records for after nineteen seventy-five.'

He smiled then, a slow, sad smile. 'It hardly matters now.' He swirled the whisky in his glass. 'Aye, I didn't live there. Or try to run the farm. The place had been losing money hand over fist since my dad died. I let Ned and my mother have the run of the place. They had little in the way of income so I turned a blind eye when they took in lodgers. Knowing Ned, I doubt he'd have informed the Inland Revenue. He would have taken cash in hand.'

'And this went on until you sold Breek House to Dundee Council?'

'Aye. Ned and my mother moved to town eventually and the lodgers became tenants. When my brother told me he could no longer find anyone to rent the place, I decided to get shot of it.' He lifted the glass to the light, examining the colour, then brought his gaze down to hers. 'But there were folk there, either lodging or renting, from nineteen seventy-five when my father died until shortly before I sold the place in two thousand.'

The implication of his words hit her – what if one of these lodgers had murdered four people and buried them in the grounds of Breek House?

He'd guessed her thoughts. 'If you want to know who put those bodies into the ground, Inspector, you'll need to find out who the tenants were, right enough.' An expression of sympathy appeared in his eyes. 'I don't envy you. But there's someone who could help you,' he added, refilling their glasses. 'My mother has an excellent memory for names.'

★　★　★

'You're keeping me from my lunch, Inspector,' Mrs McLellan said petulantly.

'I've made sure the cook is keeping it hot for you,' Dania said. It had been Honor's idea to question the woman on an empty stomach. Dania had agreed only if the girl sat in on the interview and they, too, delayed their lunch.

'You asked what we'd be charging you with, Mrs McLellan. I can add one more thing to the list. Defrauding the Inland Revenue.' She smiled. 'The first time you did it, that is.'

'What are you talking about?'

'I'm talking about the tenants at Breek House.'

The woman waved her hand in irritation. 'Breek House again. So what if we had tenants? We needed the money.'

'I'm intrigued you kept accounts for your replica firearms business but not for renting out the property.'

'We didn't put any cash through an account in those days as we needed every penny. Anyway, it was Archie who owned Breek House so, if the tax men came calling, I'd point them in his direction,' she added, with a smug smile.

'You kept no records whatsoever?' Honor sneered.

The woman turned her withering gaze on the girl. 'No, lass, I've just said it wasn't a good idea. Try to keep up.'

'Mrs McLellan,' Dania said, laying her hands flat on the table, 'you're facing a number of charges that will see you in prison for a very long time. We can try to reduce your sentence if you help us.'

'I've told you everything.'

'I doubt that.'

'Aye, well, what do you want to know?' she said irritably. 'The sooner we get this over with, the sooner I can have my mince and tatties.'

'Who were your tenants?'

She rolled her eyes. 'Och, come on. You expect me to remember the names?'

Dania pushed a pen and paper across.

The woman played with the biro for a while. 'Most were workers come to pick fruit,' she mumbled. 'They were from Europe. A whole lot would rent the house for the summer. I don't remember any names because they were foreigners.' She clicked the pen on and off. 'And then there were the regular farmworkers who rented all year round. But I mind now that happened just the one year. And we had to get the house well cleaned after.'

Dania exchanged a glance with Honor. These were unlikely candidates.

'Is there anyone who rented for a longer period? Several years, perhaps?'

The woman looked up slowly. Her expression cleared. 'Aye, there was one.'

'Well?' Dania said impatiently.

'He was a doctor. I remember because he wasn't a big man, but he had a wife who was built like a brick shithouse. They were foreigners too.'

'How long did they rent for?'

'I mind now that they came around the time of the royal wedding. You know, Lady Di's. No, wait, it was the year before, now I think on it. Nineteen eighty.' She nodded, pursing her thick lips. 'It was Donnan's brother, Keith, who arranged it all. I think this doctor had been treating him.'

'And how long did they take rooms for?'

'Five years. The doctor paid a year's rent in advance to secure the house. Each year for five years. No one does that.'

'Why did he want to stay at Breek House?' Honor said.

'That, my lassie, is the one question we never asked. Not with the cash he paid.'

'You just took the money and ran, huh?'

'What was his name?' Dania said, leaning forward so her face was close to the woman's.

Mrs McLellan screwed her eyes shut, pulling the name out of long-forgotten memory. 'De Courcy.' Her eyes flew open. 'That's it. Peter de Courcy.'

Dania and Honor watched Mrs McLellan being led away to the cells.

'What do you think, boss?'

'It could lead nowhere.'

'The time period is right. Nineteen eighty to nineteen eighty-five.'

'Why would a doctor and his wife rent a big house, Honor?'

'To set up a practice would be my guess.'

'In the middle of nowhere?'

The girl shrugged. 'Maybe it was the sort of practice that catered for people with cars. Perhaps the doctor specialised in diseases of the rich.'

'We have a name.' Dania rubbed her face. 'Peter de Courcy. We'll start there.'

'On it, boss.'

She smiled at her colleague. The girl seemed to have a renewed sense of purpose. Just as well someone had. She herself felt as though she'd been squashed and was now two-dimensional. It was time to plump herself up. And the DCI had told her to take the leave she was due. Maybe Marek and Harti were at a loose end and she could persuade them to take her to a cocktail bar.

But when she tried her brother's phone, it went to voicemail. She wondered about calling Harry, but he'd be working. And she was afraid she'd get a polite but lukewarm reply, and she couldn't bear that. Then there was Franek, who'd suggested they get together for a drink. But he'd be working too. And she wasn't sure she should ring him yet. Or even at all.

She didn't want to go back to her flat. The crates were still packed, apart from the one she'd upended to find the hot-water bottle as the heating had broken down. And the unwashed dishes were piling up in the sink. There was only one thing for it.

A few minutes later, she was in the Overgate, playing Schubert's dreamy 'Ständchen', a piece her piano teacher had made her practise blindfold. She was moving into the more turbulent section when part of her conversation with Mrs McLellan filtered into her mind:

The dark. It took Donnan so that he couldn't stand it any longer. It began the same way with Ned, with nightmares and shouting in his sleep. When I went in, he'd tell me it was dark, even though the lights were on.

She stopped in the middle of a bar.

What had Calum MacMartin said about his father, Willie?

It wasn't easy. I think that's what caused his depression. Severe depression. The type that makes you feel suicidal.

Three men who'd succumbed to severe depression, referred to as 'the dark' by Mrs McLellan.

Ignoring the looks of surprise and irritation, she snatched up her bag and ran back to the station.

There was no one in the incident room. After pulling away the map, she picked up the marker pen and, under the heading, THE DARK, drew three circles on the whiteboard and wrote in them: Donnan McLellan, Ned McLellan and Willie MacMartin.

Donnan McLellan and Ned McLellan were father and son. That connection might or might not be significant. Willie MacMartin, on the other hand, had been a cabinet maker with, as yet, no obvious association with the McLellans. But, if Calum MacMartin was correct about the facial reconstruction, it was his father's remains they'd found at Breek House.

And there was the connection. She drew lines from each circle to the centre of the board, and in it she wrote 'BREEK HOUSE'.

'I'm grateful you could see me, Professor,' Dania said, sitting down.

'I think it's time you called me Milo,' Professor Slaughter said in his deep voice, which seemed to have grown deeper with age. 'It's been a while, hasn't it? I don't see nearly enough of you.'

'I suspect we're both workaholics.'

'Wonderful English word. Is there an equivalent in Polish?'

'I suspect there is, but I'm afraid I don't know it.'

'So what can I help you with?'

'I understand you're on sabbatical.'

'That's the general idea.' He smiled. 'But one gets sucked into things one would rather not do.'

'In that case, I'll try not to take up too much of your time.'

'I'm always here for the police,' he said hastily. 'Sabbatical or not.'

'I'm not sure if this is your field, but I wanted to ask you about depression.'

For a fleeting moment, she saw a shadow of recognition cross his face. And then it was gone so suddenly that she must have imagined it.

'What do you want to know, Dania?'

'I'm interested in the kind of depression that makes people suicidal.'

'Ah yes, major depressive disorder. It's the most common form.'

'Is it hereditary?'

'We used to think not, but researchers have isolated a gene that appears in several hundred families with severe depression. By that, I mean that multiple family members are sufferers. We now believe that a significant percentage of those with depression can trace it to a genetic link.'

Which would explain Donnan and Ned, she thought. 'Are there specialists in depression at Ninewells?'

'In our Neuroscience Division.'

'Would you happen to know who the expert was who treated patients in the early nineteen eighties?'

He swivelled his chair to face the computer screen. 'I'll check our archives.'

As he tapped away, she stole a glance at his office. Piles of books and folders littered the room, and several used coffee mugs cluttered the windowsill. She suddenly felt less bad about the mess in her flat.

'Here he is,' Milo said. 'Professor Stuart Sellars. He was both an academic in the Neuroscience Division and a practising physician in the NHS's Advanced Interventions Service.'

'Did he treat a William MacMartin?'

A few more taps and then Milo said, 'Indeed he did.'

'Donnan McLellan?'

More taps. 'He treated him briefly in nineteen seventy-four.'

'And what about Ned McLellan? He'll be down as Edward McLellan.'

'Edward, Edward,' Milo said, scrolling down. 'Easier if I use McLellan as a search term.' A few moments later, he said, 'Yes, he treated an Edward McLellan of Breek House.' His eyebrows shot up. 'And there's also a Keith McLellan.'

'He was Donnan's brother,' she said, her mind racing. 'When did Professor Sellars treat him?'

'Nineteen seventy-eight.'

After a pause, she said, 'When Ned's mother described what was happening to him, she used the expression "the dark".'

'I've heard that term in connection with severe depression. It seems as though the McLellan family has been particularly hard hit.'

'Do you know how successful Professor Sellars's treatment was?'

'I'd need to look up the case notes.' He nodded at the computer. 'I don't have access to them from here.'

'I don't want to take you away from your research,' she said, in a tone that suggested she did.

'Nonsense. It would be a pleasure. Shall I give you a call when I've got something?'

'I'd be very grateful.'

As she left the office, the feeling that this was not new to him returned. It was almost as if someone else had come to see him, asking the same questions.

CHAPTER 31

Tuesday afternoon saw Dania at her desk, reading the reports that had come in that morning. The analyst who'd studied the papers in Mrs McLellan's house had found returns to the Inland Revenue going back to 2005. The name of the business was 'Doll's Houses 4U'. Hardly original, he'd added, commenting that Mrs McLellan was at least smart enough to show she had an income. And, as everyone had expected, there was nothing in the returns that linked the business to Archie. The DCI had looked in on Dania to say that Glasgow CID had picked up Mrs McLellan's nephews, finding a stash of the same blank firers and cartridges they'd found at Dronley Wood Farm. And they were mightily pleased they had Mrs McLellan's confession, which would put those arsewipes away for a long time. As for Ned's mobile, there was nothing useful on it. Like many in his line of work, he bought prepaids which he replaced on a regular basis.

Jackson's post-mortem report was of little interest. The shard that had severed Ned's carotid artery meant he'd have taken several minutes to die, whereas the one in his eye had pierced the socket and entered the brain, killing him instantly. As for the man's general state of health, he appeared to have lived on a typical Scottish diet for his entire life.

There was a knock at the door and Kimmie poked her head

round. She was clutching a folder. 'G'day,' she said, smiling. 'Are you busy?'

'Never too busy to talk to you,' Dania replied.

'You'll want to hear about the DNA first,' the girl said, sitting down. 'We already had Quinn's which meant we could get a quick result. The bottom line is we were able to match it to sweat and urine that had soaked into the canvas bed. And we got good samples from the cable ties.'

'The ones round his wrists?'

'We got nothing from the ones round his ankles as he was wearing socks. There was more evidence on the plastic sheet. My strong suspicion is that his body was wrapped in it for several days, then taken to Candle Lane.'

'Any traces in Ned's car?'

'Nothing but of Ned himself. He must have wrapped the body carefully. Did you ever find his Renault Mégane on CCTV?'

Dania shook her head. 'There are lots of roads without cameras round the lane.'

'His machines and tools were consistent with those used for converting replica firearms. And the boxes were full of replicas and conversions. No dabs anywhere, though.'

'We caught him red-handed,' she said, then remembered the shredded flesh hanging from his fingers. 'Sorry, that just came out.'

Kimmie grinned. 'I'll leave the report with you. I take it that's the case solved?'

'Pretty much. There's just Breek House.'

'Are you getting anywhere?'

'I think I may have found something, but it's early days.'

'Is the Nailer in the frame?'

'He doesn't appear to be, which is the astonishing thing. What I've found is a connection between three – no, four – people. Willie MacMartin and three members of the McLellan family,

312

Donnan, Keith and Ned, were all treated for severe depression by a Stuart Sellars from Ninewells.'

'And how does that link to Breek House?'

'We think Willie is one of the bones victims. The McLellans have owned Breek House for generations.'

Kimmie looked unconvinced, but was too polite to say how feeble the theory sounded.

'I know,' Dania said. 'There are still too many pieces missing. Willie is the one I need to concentrate on. I'm convinced he's the link in all this. Talking of Breek House, did you get anywhere with that red motorbike?'

'The Kawasaki? I'm afraid not. Someone gave it a good scrub before burying it.' A look of concern appeared in her eyes. 'You know, Dania, I've been thinking, maybe when this is over, you and I can go out for a drink. My shout.'

'That would be good.'

'You can meet my new bloke.'

'Ah, a new bloke? How long has this been going on?'

'I've been dropping hints for ages and it's like I was talking to fresh air. Then suddenly, I mean just this morning, he rang suggesting lunch and it all sort of happened then. I don't know whether it's going to last. But he's a real sweetie.'

'I'm glad for you,' Dania said, meaning it. 'Let's get together then when the case is wrapped up.'

'I'd better run,' Kimmie said, glancing at her watch. 'You know what life is. Busy, busy.'

'Thanks for dropping by.'

She left the room, colliding with Honor, who was hurrying in.

The girl flopped down on the chair Kimmie had vacated. 'Right, boss,' she said, out of breath. 'I've got the gen on Peter de Courcy. He and his wife, Anamaria, moved to Dundee in nineteen seventy-five.'

313

'From France?'

'Austria. They have one son, also called Peter, born in nineteen eighty. Now here's the interesting thing. They rented a villa in Roxburgh Terrace where the doctor registered his practice, the De Courcy Clinic.' The girl could hardly keep still. 'But get this. It wasn't a GP's practice. Peter de Courcy was a hypnotherapist.'

'A hypnotherapist?' Dania said slowly. 'Mrs McLellan said he lived in Breek House for five years from nineteen eighty. Did he move the practice there?'

'Not according to the records. Everything shows him both living and working in Roxburgh Terrace. There's no mention of Breek House.'

'So he was paying rent on the Roxburgh Terrace villa. And also rent cash-in-hand to the McLellans for Breek House.' She ran her hands through her hair. 'Why pay two lots of rent? If he had good reason for relocating to Breek House, why not give up lodging at Roxburgh Terrace? It doesn't make sense. And what reason could he have for going to Breek House in the first place?'

'Absolutely, boss. I mean, how much room does a hypnotherapist need?'

'Unless he was doing something else there. Did he move back to Roxburgh Terrace in nineteen eighty-five?'

'He left Dundee altogether. He closed down the practice and he and his wife moved to Carlisle.'

'Where they're living now?'

'We think so. But he seems to have fallen off the radar.'

'Okay, keep checking. You've done well to get all this.'

'Boss,' Honor said, picking at her lip, 'are we thinking this de Courcy had something to do with those remains found in the grounds?'

'Too early to tell. But I think Willie MacMartin is the key. Talking of which, if Calum doesn't phone today, I'll go and see him.'

'Has Harry been in touch?'

'It was his student, Thomas. They've been working on the remaining three skulls. He said to come in whenever we want. But I need to bring Calum.'

Her phone rang.

'DI Dania Gorska,' she said.

'Inspector Gorska? It's Calum MacMartin. Are you free just now? I've been rootling through some old papers and I've found something that may interest you.'

'I'm on my way.' She paused. 'Where do you live?'

'I'm at work at the moment. High Street in Lochee. You can't miss it. My name's on the door.'

'I'll be there as soon as I can.'

She disconnected. 'That was Calum MacMartin phoning from work.' She gazed at Honor. 'Coming?'

The girl pulled a face. 'If you don't mind, I'll stick with Peter de Courcy. Funeral homes aren't exactly my cup of tea.'

And, thought Dania as she shook the jacket off the back of her chair, they weren't hers either.

Lochee had once been a town in its own right, its inhabitants employed by the textile entrepreneurs, the Cox family, who'd made their wealth from jute. The only remnant of their famous Camperdown Works was the chimney known as Cox's Stack, which Dania passed on her way to work. Since Lochee had been subsumed into Dundee proper, however, textiles had made way for the funeral business.

MacMartin & Sons Funeral Directors was hard to miss since the name appeared in over-large letters above the premises. Grey clouds were gathering, threatening rain, as Dania pushed open the door. On the right was a polished wooden desk and chairs, and on the left, a lounge area with a low glass table and deep arm-chairs covered with a rose-patterned material. Illumination came from two standard lamps, one at either end of the room. A coffee machine stood in the corner, and the smell of freshly ground beans suggested it had recently been used. On the wall behind the desk was a blue and white logo telling visitors that MacMartin & Sons was a member of SAIF, the National Society of Allied and Independent Funeral Directors (Scotland).

A young man in a sober charcoal suit rose from behind the desk. 'Hello, I'm Jim MacMartin, the funeral administrator. May I help you?' He had fair hair, cut in a wavy style, and the same soft brown eyes as his father.

'DI Dania Gorska,' she said, pulling out her warrant card. 'I'm looking for Mr Calum MacMartin.'

'That would be my father. He told me to expect you.' He indicated the lounge area. 'Please make yourself comfortable, and I'll fetch him.' He disappeared through the side door.

A minute later, he returned with Calum, who was dressed in an equally sober charcoal suit.

'Inspector,' Calum said, 'thank you so much for coming in. Let's go through to the back.' With a nod at Jim, he ushered Dania into a wide corridor with doors leading off.

'Your son looks like you, Mr MacMartin.'

He threw her a smile. 'Aye, he does, right enough. We're a family business. Jim works at reception and does the accounts. Aaron is a professional embalmer. He also drives the hearse.'

The corridor ended in a door with a keypad entry system.

'We go through here to get to my flat,' Calum said, punching in the code.

'You live on the premises? That doesn't bother you?'

'When you deal with the dead, you lose your fear of them. I suspect it's the same for the police.'

316

The door opened into a large room smelling sweetly of beeswax. The coffins, each on its own stand, were made of different types of wood, which ranged from light-coloured pine and oak to the darker mahogany and walnut.

'This is our display room, Inspector. All our coffins are hand-finished,' he added, with a hint of pride. He laid his hand on the coffin nearest the door. 'This is our most expensive model. The wood is mahogany.' He lifted the lid. 'Take a wee look.'

She peered inside, seeing a pure white material lining the base of the coffin. It was soft and satiny, the type of cloth a nightgown would be made of. But what struck her was the unmistakable scent.

'The lining has been impregnated with essence of white lilies,' he said. 'We find that when families come to view their loved ones, a scent like this can be comforting.'

'I understand.'

'It's the only one of its kind we have,' he said, closing the lid. 'A pity that the manufacturers have gone out of business.'

He opened a door at the back of the room and took her across the small yard that led to his flat. They passed a single-storey building. 'Our mortuary facilities are through there,' he said.

The sturdy building looked nineteenth-century, designed to deter Dundee's resurrectionists, who would find breaking and entering a welcome change from exhuming fresh corpses from the Howff to sell to the anatomists.

'My flat, Inspector,' Calum said, when they were inside the small kitchen. He indicated the papers spread on the table. 'You asked about the name McLellan, and whether my father made furniture for them. Well, I've gone back through the records, and can't find any mention of it.'

'How far back did you go?'

'Nineteen sixty-two. That was when my dad started the business.'

'That's a lot of records. You must have been up till the small hours.'

'Not really. Everything was cross-referenced in alphabetical order.' He studied her. 'So what does the absence of the name McLellan mean?'

'It means that your father would have had no reason to be at Breek House.'

'Aye, I've wondered about that too.' He opened a folder. 'I've also dug out the correspondence between my dad and the specialist at Ninewells.'

She was about to cut him off, as she already had the name, when he said, 'I should have remembered, because I saw him whenever my dad went for his appointment. I used to go with him and wait outside the room. He was called Professor Sellars. He treated my dad for a couple of years or so, but eventually referred him on to someone else.' Calum riffled through the papers. 'Here we are. It was a hypnotherapist in Roxburgh Terrace.'

She stared at him, her mind in a daze. 'The hypnotherapist's name was Peter de Courcy,' she said, almost to herself.

'There you go again, Inspector,' Calum said, smiling. 'Way ahead of me.'

'A lot's happened since we last spoke, Mr MacMartin.'

'So does that help you with your investigation?'

But she'd tuned out. She was too busy trying to join the dots. Willie, who had no business connection to Breek House and therefore no reason to be there, had been treated by Stuart Sellars. Stuart Sellars had referred him to Peter de Courcy, who *did* have a connection to Breek House. He had rented it. And there it was, what she'd been looking for – the link between Willie MacMartin and Breek House was Peter de Courcy. There were still pieces of the puzzle to join together, and many that were missing, but she was convinced she was on the right lines. They'd need to find

Peter de Courcy as a matter of priority. First, though, she needed confirmation that the man whose skull they'd found was indeed Willie MacMartin. If not, her theory would unravel.

'Inspector?'

'Sorry.'

'You were miles away. Was it something I said?'

'Mr MacMartin, are you free tomorrow morning?'

'I don't have a funeral, right enough, although I've things to do.' He'd caught something of her mood because he added enthusiastically, 'But nothing that can't wait.'

'Can you be at the station first thing?'

'Aye, of course. What are we going to do?'

'We're paying a visit to CAHID.'

He seemed to understand. 'And I've got that full-face photo of my dad.'

'Please bring it. But now I need to go.'

'I'll see you out to the high street.'

'Thanks. You've no idea how helpful you've been.'

It was as she was driving back along Lochee Road that the thought slipped into her mind that Willie MacMartin might not have been the only patient Stuart Sellars had referred. Perhaps he'd sent others to Peter de Courcy. And, for some as yet unknown reason, four of them had ended up buried in the grounds of Breek House.

Dania was nearing her flat when her phone rang. She pulled over.

'Dania? It's Milo. Where are you?'

'On my way home. Why?'

'Can you divert to Ninewells?'

'Have you found something?' she blurted.

'I'll see you soon.' And with that, he rang off.

When she finally made it to Milo's office, having dodged the rush-hour traffic, her nerves were in a frazzle. She burst in without knocking.

He sprang to his feet.

'Sorry, Milo. Did I startle you?'

He smiled. 'Only in a good way. Do take a seat.' He sat down and shuffled through his folders. 'I managed to track down the case files for several of Stuart Sellars's patients.' He lifted his head. 'It appears that Sellars referred many of them to a hypnotherapist by the name of Peter de Courcy who practised from his house in Roxburgh Terrace.'

So her hunch that Willie MacMartin hadn't been the only patient Sellars had referred was correct. 'How many patients are we talking about?' she said.

'Quite a number. I'm still going through the files, but so far I've counted a dozen. It appears that Sellars discharged the patients who didn't improve, recommending they try hypnotherapy as a last resort.' His voice grew sombre. 'But there's something else. While I was rummaging in the archives, I ran into an old colleague who's on research leave. We got chatting.' He smiled ruefully. 'As old academics do. I told him what I was looking for in regard to Stuart Sellars. As soon as I mentioned the name, he suggested I talk to the man who was director at Ninewells when Sellars was there. I was able to get him on the phone. To cut a long story short, he told me he remembered Sellars well. He ran the Neuroscience Division until nineteen eighty-five.'

1985. The year Peter de Courcy had left Breek House . . .

'And then, according to the director, Sellars simply vanished. On the day he disappeared, he'd been in a state of great agitation. He confided to the director that he'd run into a former patient and learnt that he'd been treated by Peter de Courcy, but *not* with hypnotherapy. This patient waxed lyrical about a completely different course of treatment, which had improved his condition almost immediately. The improvement was so great that he'd discharged himself.'

'What was this different treatment?'

'ECT. Also known as electroconvulsive therapy.'

She felt her jaw drop. 'Electric-shock treatment?'

'It's also known by that term.'

'Can it help cure severe depression?'

'We could debate the pros and cons until the cows come home, Dania. But the point is this. Sellars told the director he was alarmed to hear that. He'd had no idea de Courcy was using ECT. What turned his alarm to panic was that, a fortnight earlier, he'd referred his widowed sister, Fiona, who'd been suffering from chronic depression, to Roxburgh Terrace for hypnotherapy. When he heard nothing from her, he made enquiries there, but Mrs de Courcy told him that Fiona's hypnotherapy treatment had been unsuccessful, and she'd been discharged. Sellars repeatedly tried to contact his sister by phone and in person. But she'd vanished. There was nothing he could do but report her missing.'

'But when he learnt about the ECT . . .'

'. . . which was a week later, he told the director he was going to see de Courcy and find out what the hell was going on. He jumped on his motorbike, revved up the engine and roared off, not even bothering to put on his helmet. And that was the last time anyone saw him.'

She stared at Milo. The dots were finally joining up.

'I've got to go,' she said, springing to her feet.

He was looking at her strangely. 'Dania, I need to tell you something about Peter de Courcy . . .'

'I can't stay, Professor. But I'm in your debt.'

She ran to the car, thinking about ECT, what sort of equipment you would need, and how big a room. She should have asked Milo. Right now, though, she was heading back to the nick.

CHAPTER 32

'*Elektrokonvulsionstherapie*,' Harti said, looking up from the iPad. 'That's electroconvulsive therapy. Sorry, I forget that you speak German.'

Marek was lolling in the armchair, scrolling through his messages. He put the phone away. 'And that's what your contact said de Courcy was doing at the Reisinger?'

'The good doctor was employed to use hypnotherapy. It seems that he tried electroconvulsive therapy when one of his patients showed no signs of improvement. The patient died as a result.'

'Which would explain the cover-up.'

'And why he left. I suspect he was asked to sign a confidentiality agreement. As were the staff in the Reisinger who knew about the affair.'

Marek gestured to the iPad. 'What else does the archivist lady have to say?'

'Only that she's had to call in a large number of favours and work her ass off over the weekend and I owe her big-time.'

'So how does electroconvulsive therapy work?'

'I've no idea. But the Internet will tell us for sure.'

Marek took a seat next to him. A few clicks and they found a list of sites. Some were from medical journals, others the proceedings of conferences. 'I can't understand any of this,' Marek said.

'Here's an article that's more readable. It's written for the layman.'

They skimmed the text. The gist was that opinion was divided over the treatment's efficacy, some considering it a brutal way of dealing with people who had mental disorders, others swearing it worked where other treatments failed. Many doctors refused to sanction it because the reason it worked, on the occasions it did, was still unknown. It had been in widespread use in mental hospitals across Europe and North America until appropriate drugs became available in the sixties and seventies. After that, use of ECT tailed off, although it was still practised with a small number of patients. It was used mainly to treat schizophrenia and severe depression.

Marek rubbed his face. 'You know, Archie never mentioned ECT. All he said was that hypnotherapy had cured his uncle Keith.'

'Maybe when de Courcy came to this country, he worked only as a hypnotherapist. You need specialised equipment for ECT, which I suspect you can't buy on Amazon.'

'Look at this,' Marek said, gazing at the screen. 'Says here that ECT's a safe, medically controlled procedure, which delivers a small electric pulse to the brain. Brain cells fire in unison and produce a seizure, which can relieve the symptoms of depression. But if patients aren't sedated during the procedure, serious side effects can occur.' He scrolled down. 'They include physical injuries like broken arm and leg bones, caused by the body thrashing about.'

Harti screwed up his face. 'It sounds positively medieval. What other side effects, apart from these fractures?'

'It can cause long-term memory loss.'

'That would be disastrous. Imagine looking at a woman and not remembering if you've made love to her.'

'Maybe that's why it works. It simply wipes out those memories that make you depressed.'

Harti cocked his head. 'This Archie gangster might not be so keen to be treated if he realises he might have his brain fried.'

'That's his decision. My orders are simply to get de Courcy here.'

'Do you think your gangster's suffering from depression?'

'If he wasn't before, he will be now. His brother Ned died a couple of days ago.'

'Another gangster?'

'Not a very good one. The gun he fired went off in his hands and blew half his face off, if the *Scotsman* is to be believed.'

Harti smoothed his forehead. 'You know, my friend, de Courcy and this ECT procedure will make a great article. Even if he tried it just the once.' He tipped his head. 'You don't mind if I pinch the story from you?'

'Be my guest. The only story I'm interested in writing is about Archie himself.'

'A Scottish gangster. He sounds an interesting man.' Harti peered into the iPad. 'Perhaps I could stay and write my article here, and that way I could meet him.'

Marek laughed. 'And steal another scoop from me, you mean.'

'Marek, how can you say that?' Harti said, trying to look scandalised and failing.

Marek glanced at his watch. 'Right, I need to switch on the radio. I want to know what the government has decided.'

And, as they caught the midday news, they heard what Marek had been expecting, and dreading – the United Kingdom had invoked Article 50 of the Treaty on European Union, beginning the formal process of withdrawal.

Harti sauntered over to the sideboard and poured himself a large Scotch. 'You know, my friend, the UK will come to rue this day.' He returned to the sofa. 'They'll spend ten years suffering the consequences of Brexit, ten years regretting their decision, and ten years trying to get back in.'

'That sounds about right.' Marek watched him sip the whisky. 'So, what's our next step?'

'Get ready for our trip.' He shrugged. 'What else?'

Dania was at her desk by seven a.m., having slept badly, which always happened when she had something unresolved on her mind. After leaving Milo late the previous afternoon, she'd returned to West Bell Street only to find the computer system was down and, according to the disgruntled techie, wouldn't be back up any time soon. She'd trudged home and made a start on unpacking the crates.

She was convinced that the Kawasaki had belonged to Stuart Sellars, who had roared off in search of his sister. Although what had made him go to Breek House was still a mystery. But the thing that niggled, escaping each time she closed in on it, had to do with the MisPers data she and Laurence had examined.

Now, with the computer system rebooted, she was searching through the data using Louise's application. It took her an hour to find what she was after and, as soon as she did, Laurence's words came back to her: *Here's a really interesting one. A sister. Reported missing by her brother. And then the brother himself goes missing.*

And it was all there – Stuart Sellars had reported his sister, Fiona Huntley, missing on 15 April 1985, and the director at Ninewells had reported Stuart missing on 23 April.

A few more clicks and she was reading the police report. In the transcript of their interview with Dr de Courcy, he'd stated that, yes, he'd treated Mrs Huntley with hypnotherapy. And, yes, Professor Sellars had arrived at the De Courcy Clinic, wondering what had become of his sister, but he could only tell him that her treatment had been discontinued because it hadn't helped her. No mention of ECT. And no mention of Breek House. With no further leads, the police had reassigned the case as a missing person's.

Dania was still mulling this over when the duty sergeant rang to say that Calum MacMartin had arrived. She left the room and hurried to the reception desk.

'Inspector,' Calum MacMartin said nervously. 'I hope I'm not too early. It's just before nine.'

She smiled. 'I think they'll let us in.'

He was dressed smartly. As though he were going to a funeral, she thought suddenly. She wondered how he would react when he saw the reconstructed face.

There was a taste of rain in the air as they left the building. She'd rung ahead and been informed a visitor's parking space would be reserved on Dow Street, so they took the squad car.

There was no one to meet them at the front desk, but the girl arranged for someone to take them to the main lab.

Thomas glanced up as they entered, his face brightening as he saw Dania. 'Inspector Gorska,' he said, getting to his feet.

She made the introductions, then said, 'Thomas, Mr MacMartin has brought along a photo of his father, Willie.'

'That's great.'

Calum removed a photograph from his wallet. 'It's a wee bit small, but it's the only one I've got where he's looking straight into the camera. It was taken a few years before he disappeared.'

'Aye, that's fine,' Thomas said, examining it. 'In fact, it's perfect.'

They sat round his desk and watched while he scanned in the photo and recast the image, producing something that resembled a cartoon. 'Before computers came along, we'd have to hold a photograph over an X-ray of the skull,' he said. 'But these days we can go one better.' He pulled up an image of a skull. 'This is from Victim B.'

There was a sharp intake of breath from Calum. If Thomas

326

heard it, he pretended he hadn't. With a few deft movements, he superimposed the cartoon on to the image, adjusting the cartoon's size so that the lengths matched. It didn't take an expert to see that the facial features – the eye sockets, nose cavity, mouth and particularly the cheekbones – were in alignment.

'I think we've got something,' he said quietly. He glanced at Calum. 'I can change the hairstyle and eye colour to match those in your photo.'

Calum seemed unable to speak, so Dania said, 'If you would, please, Thomas.'

He tapped at the keyboard, and the reconstructed face of Victim B filled the screen.

'Oh, God,' Calum said, his voice drifting.

'It'll take me a few minutes. Do you want to get a cup of tea while I do this?'

'No, I'd like to see the process,' Calum said stiffly. 'That's if you don't mind.'

'I don't mind at all,' Thomas said, with a kindly smile. 'Right, first we'll change the eye colour to the same shade of blue.' He pulled up the scanned photograph on to another screen. 'I can do a drag and drop and get the match exactly.' A second later, Victim B's eyes were blue. 'The next thing is the skin colour. He's not as tanned as we made him.'

Dania watched, mesmerised, as Victim B's skin grew progressively paler.

'Now for the hair. This will take a wee while.' He studied the photograph. 'His hair's a bit like yours, Mr MacMartin. It falls over the forehead. And it's a darker shade of brown than we gave him.'

'Do you think a time might come when you'll be able to determine hair and eye colour from bones?' Dania said.

'Aye, I suspect we'll eventually get it from DNA.'

He made long, bold strokes with the mouse the way an artist

might use a brush, constantly referring to Calum's photograph. Fifteen minutes later, he sat back, scratching his cheek. 'I reckon there's more I can do, but this should be enough for an identification.'

Calum pulled out a handkerchief and wiped his eyes. 'That's my dad, right enough,' he said, in a ragged voice.

'I'd be inclined to agree.'

'So what's the next step, Inspector?' Calum said bravely.

'We'll get a DNA test done.'

'And when will you release the remains?'

'Not until the case is closed.' Seeing his expression, she added, 'I hope it will be soon. Your information has helped move the investigation on enormously.'

'I'm so glad I could help.' He looked at Thomas. 'And I think you've done a grand job.'

Thomas threw him a crooked smile. 'It's kind of you to say, Mr MacMartin.'

'Are you any further forward with the other three sets of remains?' Dania said.

'We're almost finished.' He nodded at the adjacent table. 'I've got them up for you.' He reached across and swivelled the screens round. 'Jessica and I have done these. We were slow to begin with as we were still learning how to use the software, but we got faster.'

Dania stared at the images of the two men and one woman. She couldn't get over how lifelike they were.

'We've not put the hair on yet,' Thomas said.

'You needn't bother with this one,' Calum said, indicating the screen on the right. 'His hair was cropped close to his head.'

'You recognise him?' she said quickly.

'Professor Stuart Sellars from Ninewells. He treated my dad for depression.'

'Are you sure?'

'It's not an identical likeness, but it's very close.'

She felt a surge of excitement. 'If that's Stuart Sellars, this woman will be his sister, Fiona Huntley.' She turned to Thomas. 'They're Victims C and D? Am I right?'

'Aye, spot on, Inspector.'

A DNA test would confirm they were siblings. And, with Calum's identification, and what Dania had discovered about Stuart Sellars, the DCI couldn't withhold permission for the tests. Her excitement turned to elation. 'Gentlemen,' she said, 'I can't tell you how close we are to solving this.'

'Your excitement is infectious,' Thomas said, with a flush of pleasure. 'I'm beginning to think I should have been a sleuth.'

'You already are.' She gazed at the middle screen. 'The next question is: who is the fourth victim?'

The man had a round face and shallow-set eyes, which stared out at them. 'Find out who I am,' he seemed to be saying. 'And then find my killer.'

'I'd better not keep you from your work,' she said to Thomas.

'Aye, and I'd better not keep you from yours. I look forward to working with you again, Inspector.'

As they left the room, Calum said, 'Is there a men's room anywhere here?'

'Just round that corner.'

'I won't be long.'

'No rush. I'll wait for you here.'

Dania watched him go, suspecting he didn't really need to relieve himself. He was looking for a place where he could have a quiet cry. She didn't blame him.

She leant against the wall, feeling a sense of triumph. The identification of three out of the four Breek House victims was a huge step forward. What she had to do now was—

'Harry, you can't do that here,' came a familiar voice.

'Why not? There's no one around.' A pause. 'I'm just putty in your hands, you know.'

She straightened slowly. The voices had come from the room opposite. She glanced along the corridor, then tiptoed across and put her head carefully round the door.

Harry and Kimmie were sharing a long kiss. His arm was round her waist and the fingers of his other hand were interlaced with hers.

She stepped back before they saw her. So this was Kimmie's new man. She felt a tightness in her throat. But she and Harry had never been an item. They'd had coffee. And dinner. Nothing more. Why, then, did she feel such a crushing sense of disappointment?

CHAPTER 33

'Our priority now is to find Peter de Courcy,' Dania said.

The DCI placed the palms of her hands together. She was taking this well, considering she'd just blown a significant chunk of her budget authorising DNA tests. 'What's your theory, Dania?'

'Peter de Courcy worked as a hypnotherapist from his clinic at Roxburgh Terrace. With some of the worst cases, he gave up on hypnotherapy and decided to use ECT. I've spent the last hour reading up on it. You need equipment, and a room where muscle relaxants and a general anaesthetic can be administered. The treatment has to be repeated periodically and usually involves a stay in hospital.'

'And you think de Courcy did this at Breek House?'

'He rented the place from the McLellans between nineteen eighty and nineteen eighty-five specifically for it. It was ideal. Plenty of room, it's out of the way, and the McLellans had moved out. We've got the testimony of Miss Hayes, the cleaner's daughter. She assumed Breek House was being run as a B and B.' Dania opened her notebook. 'The words she used were "the odd guest staying downstairs in that back room". She found that strange, given there were bedrooms upstairs. In nineteen eighty-one, her mother came to the house unexpectedly. She peered into the back room and saw a figure lying on the bed, shrieking and jumping about. Two people were bent over him.'

'And you think that was the electric shock being administered?'

'Without either an anaesthetic or a muscle relaxant. I've just come off the phone to Professor Slaughter. With a muscle relaxant, the spasms are greatly reduced. But without the relaxant, they can produce serious injuries.' She paused for effect. 'Injuries like the ones in the Breek House victims. Broken or fractured arm and leg bones.'

'Nineteen eighty-one was when Calum MacMartin reported his father missing,' the DCI said quietly. 'That figure on the bed might have been Willie, right enough.'

'Something was going badly wrong with the treatment, and patients were dying, and de Courcy was covering it up. Stuart Sellars was unwittingly sending his patients, including his sister, there. He referred them to the de Courcy Clinic for hypnotherapy, not realising de Courcy was taking them to Breek House. A former patient told him about the ECT and would have told him where he'd been treated. Stuart went over there on his Kawasaki.'

'And got his skull smashed for his pains.'

'That was in nineteen eighty-five, the year the de Courcys left Dundee. Presumably because they took fright that someone had arrived to check up on them.'

'It sounds incredible. What was the man trying to achieve? Instead of curing his patients, he was killing them.'

'We need to find him and get some answers. We don't know who the fourth victim is. We're still looking for his DNA in the database.'

The DCI folded her arms. 'How close do you think you are to finding de Courcy?'

'The whole team is on it. There are several people in the UK with that surname. We're checking them all.'

The woman looked at her with admiration. 'Keep me informed every step of the way.'

It was late Saturday afternoon before the team got their break-through. By a process of elimination, they'd concluded that a Peter de Courcy currently living in Kelso had to be related to Dr Peter de Courcy, the hypnotherapist. What strengthened their case, and what had led Honor to refer to it as a breakthrough, was that the Kelso Peter de Courcy had attended school in Carlisle, which was where the doctor and his wife had moved to.

'It must be his son, boss. He's thirty-seven. The age is right.'

Dania glanced at her watch. 'Too late to go now.'

'We could contact the local CID, ma'am,' Hamish said hopefully.

'Let's go there ourselves. If we leave around mid-morning, we'll be in Kelso by lunchtime.'

'Why not leave first thing?' Honor said.

'Because it's Sunday and I'll be at Mass,' Dania said, her voice level.

'So this is where our good Dr de Courcy lives,' Harti was saying, as they cruised through Kelso. 'The town looks a bit dead.'

'It's Sunday,' Marek said. 'I expect people are at church.'

'Should we check the place out? What was the name again?'

'St Mary's. On Bowmont Street. It's also known as the Immaculate Conception.'

'I'll put it into the sat-nav.'

'No need. We're on Bowmont Street. We'll find the church by

the number of cars parked outside. Look, that must be it,' he said, nodding towards the small stone building with the tall windows.

'It was very helpful of the son to put everything on his Facebook page,' Harti said, excitement in his voice. He was like a child on an outing. 'The date and time of his daughter's First Holy Communion, where the reception is being held, and so on.'

Marek pulled up a little way from the church, and they sat for a while watching people going in. 'Okay, Harti, we can't put it off any longer.' He removed a pair of thick-rimmed spectacles from the glove compartment. After rubbing gel into his hands, he ran them through his hair, drawing it up into spikes.

'What do you think?' he said, studying himself in the driver's mirror.

'Terrible.'

'His son knows what I look like. I can't take the risk.'

'You could have worn a hat.'

'In church?' he said, in a shocked voice.

'I think we should go. The service is due to start in five minutes.'

They left the Audi and slipped into St Mary's through the side entrance. The gloomy church seemed even smaller on the inside with only a dozen pews on either side of the narrow nave.

They sat at the back, keeping a watchful eye open. Suddenly, a group walked in, led by a little blonde girl dressed as a child bride. Immediately behind her were the man Marek had met at Old Vienna and a woman, presumably his wife, both smartly dressed. Marek bowed his head as they walked past.

Harti nudged him. 'Look there, behind them,' he said, in a fierce whisper.

Marek lifted his head. A man in an oversized black suit and black bow tie was bringing up the rear. He had messy white hair and hooded eyes. From where they were sitting, they couldn't see his left cheek.

'And that must be his *Hausfrau*,' Harti whispered. 'The one who looks like a Valkyrie.'

A tall woman in a severe navy suit shuffled at his side, her long grey plait swinging slightly. She had a round, flabby face with a muddy complexion, and was staring straight ahead. Her physique made Marek suspect that she never skipped a meal, and probably consumed her husband's besides.

'We've seen what we need to, Harti. Let's get out of here.'

As the congregation rose for the first hymn, the men crept out of the church unnoticed.

'I've never been to Kelso,' Hamish said, as they drove across the river. 'At least the sun's out,' he added, peering into the radiant blue sky.

Honor was sitting in the back, working her way through a bag of toffees. 'Why are there two bridges? We passed one a minute ago.'

'There are two rivers,' Dania said. 'The Teviot and the Tweed.'

'Crikey, look at that ruin.' The girl peered over Dania's shoulder. 'According to the sat-nav, it's a twelfth-century abbey.'

'Aye, and that's the town hall,' Hamish said, gesturing with his chin at the Georgian building with its octagonal clock tower. 'There's plenty of parking in the square.'

He pulled into a vacant slot. They left the car and took the cobbled road that led back to the abbey.

'This is it,' Dania said, stopping in front of the white three-storey building. Above the door was a crowned two-headed eagle, the coat-of-arms of the Austro-Hungarian empire, and the words, 'Old Vienna', in peeling gilt.

Honor stared through the window, drooling at the piles of cakes. 'Ooh, let's go in, boss.'

'It seems to be closed today. See the notice on the door? There's a private function on.'

'So what do we do?'

'Ring the doorbell.'

After the second ring, the door opened and a dark-haired woman appeared. She had pale blue eyes and sallow skin, and was wearing a waitress's uniform and cap. 'I'm afraid we're not open,' she said, in an anxious voice. 'We're holding a private function.'

Dania pulled out her warrant card. 'DI Gorska from Dundee. I need to speak to Mr Peter de Courcy. I understand he owns these premises?'

'He does, but they're all away at church. Little Lisa is taking her First Holy Communion.'

'And when are you expecting them back?'

'Not till nearer two. It's a full-hour service.'

'Maybe we can wait inside, boss,' Honor said, peering past the woman.

'I still need to finish setting up in the restaurant.' She motioned through the archway. Beyond, a room glittered with glasses and polished cutlery. 'Could you come back later?'

Hearing the plea in her voice, Dania decided not to press it. 'That's fine. We'll be here at two.'

'Peter's not in any trouble, is he?' the woman said, her voice faltering.

'We just want to ask him about something. You wouldn't happen to know if his parents are here for the service?'

'Dr de Courcy and Anamaria? Yes, they're here.'

'And can you recommend somewhere nearby where we can have a bite to eat?'

'To be honest, on a Sunday the town centre's booked up. But I can suggest somewhere a bit out of the way.' She stepped into the street and pointed towards the abbey. 'Go down there, turn left and then right. There's a wee pub called Bonnie Kelsae. It's behind the abbey. You can't miss it.'

'Thanks,' Dania said warmly. 'We won't keep you any longer.'

The woman looked relieved that she could now get on with her work. She disappeared through the archway.

'What now, boss?'

'A quick lunch. And then back here to greet the church party.'

'Aye, and not before time,' said Hamish. 'My stomach thinks my throat's been cut.'

'There it is, my friend. *Altes Wien*. Old Vienna.'

Marek and Harti were across the street, studying the building with the gilded crest. It seemed longer than ten days since Marek had last been there, visiting Peter de Courcy junior and buying *Esterhazytorte*.

'You're saying the doctor and his wife live on the top floor?' Harti said.

'I'd put money on it. The restaurant is on the ground floor, and the son told me he lives on the middle floor. But those are dormer windows in the roof. That means living space.'

'So I wonder whose apartment it is?' Harti said, making his voice mysterious. He stroked his chin. 'We've got about an hour to get in and out by my reckoning. And you say the way up to the first floor is behind the counter?'

'There's a door. But if Yvonne is serving, we won't have a prayer.'

'All right, my friend, just follow my lead.'

337

He sauntered across and peered through the window. After glancing up and down the street, he opened the door a few inches and reached inside, lifting his arm. Marek couldn't see what he was doing but, when Harti pushed the door wide and beckoned furiously, he realised the man was gripping the bell above the door to stop it jangling.

Marek slipped inside, and Harti closed the door, gently releasing the bell. The place was deserted, but the sound of clinking glass came from the restaurant. Marek crept behind the counter and tried the handle. The door was unlocked. They sneaked through and up the narrow stairs.

The door into de Courcy's flat was open. The heat hit them as soon as they were inside. The same dark furniture and smell of tobacco.

'How do we get to the top floor?' Harti whispered. 'Those stairs lead only into this room.'

'There must be a way from one of the other rooms,' Marek whispered back. He gripped Harti's arm. 'Tread carefully in case the floorboards creak.'

Off the living room there was a bedroom with Regency-striped wallpaper and a sagging double bed. A door at the back took them into a small corridor. Three rooms led off: a bathroom, kitchen and a bedroom with a single bed, the daughter's judging by the Disney posters papering the walls. But at the end of the corridor, there was a flight of steps.

'Aha,' whispered Harti.

Marek pulled back.

'Having second thoughts, my friend?' Harti murmured.

'I'm not one for breaking and entering just to get a story.'

'We may have entered, but we didn't break,' he said, lifting a finger.

338

'I'll remember that when the police question me.'

'I'll take full responsibility.' He grinned. 'Come on.'

The rooms on the floor above had a similar layout: a living room, kitchen, bathroom, bedroom, and a smaller room crammed with old-fashioned wooden storage trunks.

'Let's try in here first,' Harti whispered.

The double bedroom was cluttered with modern whitewood furniture. On the wall, among the prints of oil paintings, was a framed certificate from the Medizinische Universität Wien, next to a black-and-white photograph of a young Peter de Courcy. He was in the uniform of his student fraternity, complete with sword, sash and flat cap. The photo was taken before he'd got his duelling scar.

'Marek,' Harti murmured, 'look at this.' He'd opened both doors of the double wardrobe. At the bottom was a large leather suitcase. 'I think what we're looking for is here.' He made to lift it. 'Give me a hand with this. It's heavy.'

Marek helped haul the case on to the bed. 'How on earth did that small man carry this around?' he gasped.

'The Valkyrie would have done it.'

Harti opened the case. Inside a large piece of equipment bristled with dials and knobs. The lettering was in German and included 'KONVULSATOR III' in red capitals. Attached to the front was a power cable. But it was the pair of leads that drew Marek's gaze. Each ended in what looked like an old-fashioned telephone receiver with a metal plate.

'These are electrodes,' Harti said, lifting one out.

'Looks as if your archivist was correct.'

'This is what de Courcy must have had at the Reisinger. And brought with him to Scotland.'

'I wonder if he ever used it.'

339

'Perhaps this will tell us.'

Inside the sleeve of the suitcase there was a thick sheaf of papers. Harti pulled it out and, after a glance, handed it to Marek. He took a small camera out of his jacket pocket, and quickly set about taking photographs of the equipment.

Marek leafed through the pages. There were names, dates and columns of figures. And what appeared to be scientific observations. Not all of it made sense to him, but he understood that what was being varied were voltage and current. 'Harti, you need to look at these.'

'In good time, in good time,' Harti said, snapping away.

Marek laid the papers on the bed, wondering how they were going to get out of the building without being seen. Perhaps there was a way round the back.

Harti had finished with the equipment and was photographing the papers, turning each page over and doing both sides. Marek returned to the living room and peered out of the windows, seeing the tops of trees.

He was about to rejoin Harti when his gaze fell on a large book lying on the sideboard. It was an old photo album, the cover embossed in red and gold. He opened it at the front page and flicked through slowly. The early photos showed a young boy with wild dark hair, standing between a woman in a blouse and dirndl and a man in uniform. The date was March 1944. With mounting excitement, he turned the pages, seeing the doctor grow into his teens, attend university, get married.

The photos at the back had been taken after the de Courcys had come to Dundee. The familiar landmarks were there – the Tay Bridge, the three-masted RRS *Discovery*, the statue of Desperate Dan. The last two showed an unsmiling Dr de Courcy looking into the camera.

In the first, he was on the steps of a grand house, wearing the same double-breasted dark jacket and spotted bow tie Marek had seen in the 1975 *Die Presse* article. But it was the second photo that made the blood pound in his ears. It was a close-up of de Courcy, the scar on his cheek clearly visible. And just as clearly visible was what was carved into the stone wall behind his head.

With a feeling of unreality, Marek stared at the words 'ABSIT INVIDIA'. Let envy be absent.

And he remembered where he'd seen them before. It was the crest over the front door of Breek House. He'd drawn Danka's attention to the inscription when he'd driven her there. He sank into the armchair, his mind in a whirl. What was de Courcy doing at Breek House? Had he treated Archie's uncle Keith, who'd suffered from depression, there?

But why at Breek House and why not at Keith's? That would have been the obvious place. And, as the thoughts chased themselves round his head, he sprang to his feet, dropping the album.

He rushed into the bedroom. 'Harti, we need to get out of here. Right now.'

Harti looked up. 'I'm only halfway through.' He glanced at his watch. 'We've still got time.'

'You don't understand. De Courcy was at Breek House. I've just seen his photo album. Breek House is where those bones were found.'

'You're not making any sense, Marek.'

He gestured to the equipment. 'He killed his patient at the Reisinger. I think he did the same here in Dundee.' He grabbed the papers and started to pore over them. 'God Almighty, look at these dates. It started in nineteen eighty. And the patient was—'

'Marek,' Harti said quietly.

Marek glanced up. Harti wasn't looking at him. He was look-ing towards the living room.

A small man in a black suit and bow tie was standing at the door. He had the photo album in one hand. In the other, he held a pistol. Behind him stood a ferocious-looking woman, her eyes alight with intent.

'Good day, gentlemen,' the man said.

CHAPTER 34

Marek felt the sudden shift in the room. With de Courcy's entrance, the atmosphere had changed. He realised, with brutal clarity, that the Austrian couple must have heard everything. He also realised that, barring a miracle, he was unlikely to get out of the building alive.

He glanced at Harti, who seemed unperturbed. The man took a cautious step forward, putting himself in front of Marek.

'Please stay where you are,' de Courcy said in a smooth voice. 'And leave your camera on the bed. Yes, that's right. And you,' he said, waving the pistol at Marek, 'put those papers back where you found them.'

Marek lifted the lid of the suitcase and bundled the papers into the sleeve.

'Not like that, you idiot,' Anamaria shouted, rushing forward. 'Those pages are precious!'

As she pushed past Harti, he threw one arm round her throat and another round her waist, holding her tight against him. She struggled wildly but was no match for a man's strength, especially a man like Harti. Using her as a shield, he pushed her at de Courcy, who waved his pistol nervously, apparently unwilling to fire in case he hit his wife. He must have appreciated how desperate the situation was because he dropped the weapon and ran.

Harti lost his footing and fell, still holding Anamaria. They rolled on the floor, wrestling. Marek didn't hesitate. He jumped over them and sprinted into the living room.

He was in time to see de Courcy disappear through the window. Without stopping to consider whether it was sensible, Marek squeezed through after him. It was a decision he immediately regretted. Below was a concrete pavement. People were gathering, their faces upturned, mouths open. He recognised Peter de Courcy junior, and his daughter in her First Holy Communion dress, chewing the edge of her veil in fright.

He stood trembling on the window ledge, leaning back and gripping the wooden frame. Where in God's name was de Courcy? There was a sudden scrabbling behind him. Choking down his growing feeling of panic, he turned and clambered up behind the dormer. Peter de Courcy had reached the roof ridge and was balancing unsteadily, his arms out.

Marek launched himself up the roof and landed on the tottering man, his momentum carrying them both over the rooftop. As they hit the dormer window on the other side, he felt a sharp pain in his ribs, but didn't release his hold. They slid down the slates and off the roof, plunging into the trees. There was a loud cracking, and branches whipped up to hit him. He released de Courcy and brought his arms up to shield his face. A moment later, he hit the ground in a shower of leaves and twigs. His first thought was: I'm alive.

De Courcy was lying next to him, groaning. There was a deep gash in his forehead, and blood was trickling into his white hair. He turned and looked at Marek in bewilderment. His mouth opened and he started to say something, but couldn't seem to find the energy. A shudder ran through his body, and he went limp.

Marek gazed into the blue vault of the sky, listening to the cawing of crows, and wondered, not for the first time, what had possessed him to take this assignment.

'That's the worst mutton pie I've eaten in a long time,' Honor said, as they left Bonnie Kelsae.

'You should have had the lasagne,' Hamish said. 'I won't have to eat again for a week.'

Dania looked at her watch. 'It's nearly two. Let's go.'

'What's the plan, ma'am?' Hamish said, as they took the road to Old Vienna.

'I'll know when we get there.'

'Crikey,' Honor said. 'What the hell's going on?'

A crowd had gathered in front of the restaurant. People were milling about, gabbling. Some were looking up at the roof, shielding their eyes from the sun.

'Don't let anyone in,' Dania said to the others. She pulled out her warrant card. 'Police. Let me through, please.'

Inside the building, a knot of people with their backs to her were staring through the archway. She spotted the waitress she'd spoken to earlier. 'What's going on?' she said, gripping her arm.

'Someone's fallen off the roof,' the woman said, shock in her voice. She pointed into the restaurant. 'He's in the orchard.'

Dania peered through the tall picture window. She made out a figure lying motionless. 'What's the quickest way there?'

The woman seemed to remember herself. She ran through a side door into a spotless kitchen, which was full of tables groaning with cakes. A corpulent man in a chef's white coat and hat looked up, startled.

The back door was open. Dania pushed past the woman and ran out.

The ground was littered with leaves and broken branches. Two figures were lying under an oak tree.

One was clutching a broken pair of glasses. 'Hello, Danka,' he said.

'Marek?' she said, almost inaudibly.

He turned his head and looked at the other man. 'I'm afraid he's dead.'

She knelt over the figure, seeing a man with a shock of white hair that was slowly turning red. She gripped the flesh under his chin. 'No, he's alive,' she said. 'His pulse is strong.'

She whipped out her phone and called for an ambulance. 'What in God's name are you doing here, Marek?' she said, disconnecting the call.

'It's a long story.'

'Never mind. Can you stand?'

He sat up, grimacing.

'Where does it hurt?'

'I think I've bruised my ribs.'

'And what have you done to your hair?'

He patted his head. 'I didn't want his son to recognise me.' He seemed suddenly to remember something. 'Where's Harti?'

She glared at him. 'Harti's here too? This just gets better and better.'

'He's upstairs with Anamaria.'

She called Honor, who arrived with Hamish. 'Stay with them,' she said to the girl. 'The ambulance should be here any minute.'

'I'm okay, Danka,' Marek said, hauling himself to his feet.

'Is that your brother?' Honor grinned. 'He's changed his hair.'

He grinned back feebly.

'Call me when the ambulance arrives,' Dania said to Honor. 'Hamish and I are going to find Anamaria.'

'I'll go with you,' Marek said, brushing leaves off his trousers. 'You won't find the place otherwise.'

'Lead on,' she said coolly.

He took them into the building, and up the stairs behind the counter. After negotiating the labyrinth of rooms and climbing another set of stairs, they reached the top floor.

'In here, Marek,' Harti shouted.

'They're in the bedroom,' Marek said. 'It's this way.'

A large woman in a blue woollen suit was kneeling on the floor, scowling. Harti was slouched on the bed behind her, pointing a pistol at her head.

'Dania,' he said, sitting up. He swallowed noisily. 'I had no idea you were here.'

'I can see that.'

He handed her the pistol. 'You'd better take this. It's a Walther P38. It belongs to this lady's husband, but I had to take it off him.'

Dania addressed the woman. 'Are you Anamaria de Courcy?'

'Where is my husband?' she demanded in a ringing voice.

In the distance, they heard a siren.

'On his way to hospital, I'd say,' Marek chipped in.

Dania turned to Hamish. 'Can you tell Honor to go with the ambulance? They're taking Peter de Courcy to Borders General Hospital in Melrose. I'm leaving you to take charge of Mrs de Courcy. We'll need the uniforms here as well.'

'Yes, ma'am.' Hamish gripped Anamaria by the arm and helped her to her feet. She continued to scowl at Dania as she was led out of the room.

'Right. Now that it's just the three of us,' Dania said, crossing her arms, 'I'm waiting for an explanation.'

Marek hesitated. 'I don't know whether to tell you this, Danka.'

'Well you've started, haven't you?'

'Peter de Courcy is the missing person I've been searching for.'

347

She gazed at him, unbelieving. 'You said you were looking for a doctor.'

'He is a doctor. But he's also a hypnotherapist. And he's been using electroconvulsive therapy on some of his patients.'

'Why were you looking for him?' she said, stunned.

'Archie McLellan asked me to find him.'

'*Archie McLellan?*' She felt a sudden pounding in her temples. 'And you didn't think to tell me?' she shouted.

Marek said nothing.

'You complete idiot,' she said, slipping into Polish. 'Did it never occur to you that he might have put you in danger? Which he obviously has. You acted as though you'd never met him when we were at Donnan's. You've been keeping things from me.'

'Well, you've been keeping things from me,' Marek said sulkily.

'I'm *supposed* to keep things from you. I'm a police officer. And you,' she said to Harti, forgetting she was still speaking Polish, 'you're completely irresponsible, coming here and getting my brother into this mess.' She waved the Walther in his face. 'I've half a mind to use this on you. Now get out. Both of you.'

Marek jerked his head at Harti who, judging by the alacrity with which he jumped to his feet, had got the message.

It was after they'd left the room that she saw the suitcase on the bed. And the large metal box with the dials and knobs. A bundle of papers had been pushed into the case's sleeve. She spread them out and looked slowly through them. They were in German but she knew enough to decipher the notes. And, as she turned the pages, her blood slowly growing cold, she realised she'd finally found what she'd been looking for.

Marek and Harti were at the bar in The Lost Shoe, munching the snacks on the counter, which were all that the sour-faced barman could offer, given that it was well past lunchtime and Sunday was their busiest day, ken? And, he added crabbily, for some reason a whole pile of people had come in from Old Vienna complaining they weren't getting their lunch there and he'd had to send them away as he had only two packets of sandwiches left.

Marek rubbed his side, wondering if he'd cracked a rib. There'd be a whopping great bruise, but he was in better shape than he deserved.

'Your sister is very scary when she's angry,' Harti said, opening a packet of salt-and-vinegar crisps. 'Perhaps it's just as well I didn't understand a word of what she said.'

Marek swirled his mineral water before lifting it to his lips. He was thinking not about Danka, who would recover from her anger soon enough, but about what he was going to say to Archie. He'd read enough of de Courcy's notes to learn that many of his patients had died under the ECT. But it was the name of the first patient that had made his spirits plunge.

Harti was studying him. 'You seem pensive, my friend. What's troubling you?' When Marek said nothing, he added, 'Your sister will come round, she has a kind heart. And women never remain angry for long.'

'It's not that that's bothering me,' Marek grumbled. 'It's the money Archie McLellan gave me to pass on to Peter de Courcy.'

'Is it burning a hole in your pocket?'

'It's burning a hole in my conscience. I need to give it back to him as soon as possible. Today, if I can.'

Harti crumpled the empty bag of crisps and left it on the counter. 'In that case, let's go. I hate to see you like this.'

They drove back to Dundee in silence. Marek deposited Harti at the flat with a promise that he'd be back shortly, since what he had to do wouldn't take long. Then they could go out somewhere for dinner and celebrate in advance the success Harti would have when he published his article.

Despite the pain in his ribs, Marek almost ran to Donnan's. They were getting ready to open and the bouncer wouldn't let him in dressed in an old anorak and jeans. It was when Marek informed him that Mr McLellan would be none too happy to learn he'd been denied access that he was reluctantly allowed inside.

Archie was sitting in his office, glancing through papers. He was in a smart navy suit and red tie, ready to receive his guests.

'Marek,' he said, looking up in surprise.

'I've come to return this.' Marek laid the sealed package on the table. 'You said I was to give it to Peter de Courcy.' He took a breath. 'I'm afraid I failed.'

Archie drew his brows together. 'Is he in Vienna?'

'He's in Borders General Hospital.' As quickly as he could, Marek told him everything – Peter de Courcy had stopped using hypnotherapy in favour of ECT and, in the process, had killed most of his patients. He and his wife had been hiding with their son in Kelso; de Courcy senior had tried to get away over the rooftop and he and Marek had fallen. Marek was okay but de Courcy was injured, and unconscious in hospital.

Archie gazed at him. His mouth was working and it seemed an effort for him to get the words out. 'So he stopped using hypnotherapy?'

'There's more, I'm afraid.'

'I'm listening.'

During the return journey, Marek had thought of nothing except how to break the news to Archie. In the end, he just came out with it. 'I'm afraid your uncle Keith was one of de Courcy's victims. In his notes, he wrote that Keith McLellan had reverted so he was going to move him on to ECT. The final entry makes clear that, after increasing the current, and applying it for longer than normal, the patient died.'

Archie turned his head away. When he finally looked at Marek, there was an ugly expression on his face. 'And the wife?' he said quietly.

'She's under arrest.' Marek pushed the packet across. 'I really am very sorry, Mr McLellan.'

'Keep it. I know fine well that you tried, lad. And chasing the man across the roof and nearly getting killed goes above and beyond what I'd asked of you.'

Marek was stunned. 'But I can't take this.'

'Ach, why not? You're an honest man and that's something these days. You could have pocketed it and said you lost it in the scuffle.' He tried a grin, but it didn't reach his eyes. He pushed the package back. 'Just don't gamble it all away in the casino.'

Marek couldn't believe his luck. This would make all the difference to his plans to buy a flat. From the weight of the package, there'd be enough for a down payment. With plenty to spare. And yet he'd got the money for something he'd promised to deliver and hadn't.

'Mr McLellan . . .'

Archie waved a dismissive hand. 'Aye, and I haven't forgotten I promised you an exclusive.' He threw Marek a kindly smile. 'But not just yet. I have things to take care of right now. I'll let you know when I'm ready. You should bring your recording device.'

Marek got to his feet. 'Thank you,' he said, trying to inject as much gratitude into his voice as he could.

But Archie had already lost interest. He returned to poring over his papers.

Marek let himself out.

CHAPTER 35

'DI Dania Gorska interviewing Anamaria de Courcy at West Bell Street police station. Also present is DS Honor Randall. The suspect is being interviewed under caution, on tape, with her solicitor present. The date is Monday, April the third, twenty seventeen, the time, nine-fifteen a.m.'

Anamaria glared at Dania, her eyes full of malice.

'Mrs de Courcy, were you a tenant at Breek House during the period nineteen eighty to nineteen eighty-five?'

The woman glanced at her solicitor. Justin Parkes shook his head. He would have assured his client that paying cash-in-hand would have left no record of the tenancy.

When there was no reply, Dania said, 'For the tape, Mrs de Courcy declines to answer the question.' She paused. 'Mrs McLellan, who lived at Breek House, has made a statement that you rented the building from her during that period.'

'Inspector,' Mr Parkes intervened, 'the record will show that my client and her husband rented a property in Roxburgh Terrace. Mrs McLellan was not the owner of Breek House and hence was not in a position to lease it out.'

'Nevertheless, Mr Parkes, Mrs McLellan has testified that Mr and Mrs de Courcy did live there during that period.'

'Shall we move on, Inspector?' he said, in a bored tone.

352

'During that time, your husband treated his patients with electroconvulsive therapy, also known as ECT. Do you admit that?'

The woman continued to glare at her.

From her folder, Dania removed the sheaf of papers Marek and Harti had found in the ECT suitcase. 'The suspect is being shown a bundle of papers.'

For the first time, Anamaria's gaze displayed something other than malice. Her thick eyebrows curved into a frown. She stared at the pages, her look of anxiety intensifying. It was not lost on Dania.

'Mrs de Courcy, our team of analysts has been working round the clock to examine these data, although it wasn't a difficult task as your husband kept meticulous, neatly written notes. The patients' names are legible, and everything is in chronological order. He is to be congratulated.'

Anamaria's expression softened. 'He is one of the finest scientists of his generation,' she said, with pride in her voice.

'Why did he not publish his research?'

The question seemed to take the woman by surprise. She thought for a moment and then said, 'Because it was incomplete. He had still not found the correct electrode placement, and current and voltage settings.' She rested her muscular arms on the table. 'The electric current can be passed across the whole brain from temple to temple, or across one hemisphere from front to back. The results are significantly different.'

'Please tell me more. I know little about this treatment.'

'Most patients have to continue with maintenance electroconvulsive therapy for decades, or even the rest of their lives. What my husband was trying for was a complete cure.'

'Is that why he discontinued hypnotherapy?'

'He continued to use hypnotherapy at the clinic in Roxburgh

Terrace. Only when the depression was treatment-resistant did he suggest his patients try ECT.'

'Mrs de Courcy—' the solicitor said.

The woman shot him a look. 'This is important. I need to make it clear what we did. There is much misunderstanding about the process.'

The solicitor rolled his eyes as if to signify that at least he'd tried.

'It's normal to administer a general anaesthetic and muscle relaxant, isn't it?' Dania said.

'Well, of course, we didn't have access to that.' Anamaria paused. 'And, besides, Peter was convinced that the patient had to be awake throughout the procedure for it to be effective. It was groundbreaking work.'

'Is the procedure not painful without an anaesthetic?' Honor said.

The solicitor tried to intervene, but Anamaria stopped him. 'Please do not interrupt me again, Mr Parkes,' she snarled. She turned to Dania, who kept her expression interested. 'One of the side effects of ECT is memory loss,' she continued. 'When the procedure is over, the patient remembers nothing of the pain.'

'Doesn't the memory of the pain come back, though?' Dania said.

'Memory loss is one of the things we were researching,' the woman said, neatly sidestepping the question. 'Unfortunately, no matter how the electrodes are placed, the current travels through the tip of the temporal lobes, which is where memory is located. We changed the placement of the electrodes and observed how long the memory loss lasted. Sometimes the patients would forget they'd had the procedure and we would have to tell them all over again.'

Dania smiled her encouragement. Anamaria's use of 'we' rather than 'Peter' would in another age have put the noose round her neck. But Dania wanted more from the woman.

'What are the other side effects, Mrs de Courcy?'

'There are none.'

'If there's no anaesthetic, don't the patients thrash about when they have seizures?'

'One of my tasks was to hold them down to minimise the damage. I am a trained nurse.'

She took in the woman's heavy arms. And imagined the scene in the back room at Breek House. Two people hunched over someone shrieking and jumping about. But the hunched figures were not Archie and Mrs McLellan, as Miss Hayes's mother had thought, but Peter de Courcy holding the electrodes, and his wife doing a bad job of restraining the patient.

'And where in Breek House did you perform the treatment?' Dania said.

'Inspector,' Mr Parkes said firmly. 'My client has—'

'I've told you not to interrupt me,' Anamaria said, banging her fist on the table. 'You are dismissed.' When the open-mouthed solicitor failed to move, she shouted. 'Leave us! Go!'

He gathered up his papers, muttering to himself, and stormed out, a pained expression on his face.

'For the tape, Mr Parkes has left the room,' Dania said.

'Our ECT suite was behind the dining room,' Anamaria continued. 'It was also our recovery area. The patient would rest and take some light refreshment. And then, when we were happy that he was ready, he was free to go. From start to finish, it took between half an hour to an hour.'

'How many treatments did patients receive?'

'It varied greatly. Sometimes we saw differences after two or three. Others needed many more. A few patients were completely cured.'

'Who was your first patient?' Dania said, keeping her voice and body language non-confrontational.

'I can't remember.' Anamaria nodded at the papers. 'It will be there.'

But Dania already knew the name. 'It was Keith McLellan.' She smiled. 'Did your treatment help him?'

'I remember him. We began with hypnotherapy. And it almost worked. He had several sessions over a period of weeks. But he regressed to such an extent that he was worse than before.'

'A candidate for ECT, then.'

'We said we would need premises where he could recuperate after each period of treatment. When he told us about Breek House, it sounded ideal. Away from the city. And they were look-ing for tenants.'

'How did his treatment go?' Dania said softly.

The woman paused. 'After several weeks, he was well enough to leave.'

'But that's not what happened, is it?' Dania picked up the sheaf. 'According to this data, Keith McLellan died as a result of the pro-cedure.' Seeing the woman's expression turn to one of suspicion, she added, 'I can read German, Mrs de Courcy. Your notes state that Keith McLellan fractured his arms and legs and smashed his patella.' She put down the papers. 'Were you trained to deal with fractures and broken bones?'

'You don't understand. It wasn't always possible to hold down the patients. They thrashed around so much. And it was out of the question to tie them to the bed. That would have alarmed them greatly and invalidated the results of the experiment.'

'Experiment?'

'I meant the treatment.'

'And how did you treat the pain from the fractures and broken bones?'

'I administered painkillers.'

'That's all?'

'We had nothing else. I looked after the patient until his next treatment was due.'

'What did you do with Keith McLellan's body?'

'We returned it to his family,' she said, avoiding Dania's gaze.

Dania turned to a section of the notes. 'William MacMartin, who died in nineteen eighty-one after treatment, also had fractured arms and legs.'

The woman glared at her as if to say: And your point is?

'Let's come now to Professor Stuart Sellars. He referred his patients to you.'

A look of fear crossed the woman's face. 'How did you know that?'

'His case notes at Ninewells contain a list of the patients he referred to the de Courcy Clinic. He sent Fiona Huntley to you for treatment. But you didn't know she was his sister, did you? What happened that day he came calling? We know he came to Breek House while you were there. We found his motorcycle in the grounds not far from the house.'

Anamaria looked at her hands. After a silence, she said, 'No, we didn't know she was his sister. We had been treating her for several days. A day or so after we buried her, I was at our house in Roxburgh Terrace when Professor Sellars arrived. He said he hadn't heard from Fiona and wondered how her treatment was going. I told him what I told everyone who came enquiring after patients, which was that we concluded we could no longer help them and discharged them.'

'Leaving the relatives to conclude they'd left the area.'

'And possibly taken their own lives. We did add that their suicidal tendencies hadn't diminished.'

'What happened that day, Mrs de Courcy?'

'We were treating someone who was making so much noise that we wouldn't have heard the doorbell. It was a hot day and we'd left the French windows open. It wouldn't have been difficult for the professor to find the ECT suite by following the shrieks.' She licked her lips nervously. 'I looked up and saw him at the door. He ran out, and I followed him and caught up with him in the corridor. He challenged me, demanding to know what was going on. It was then that I learnt who Fiona was. I simply couldn't let him live. If news got out about the deaths, it would mean the end of our research.' She crossed herself. 'God forgive me, but I picked up the bronze statue of Cupid from the hall table and brought it down on his head.'

'And you left Breek House after you buried him. And the motorcycle.' Dania studied the woman. 'Why did you bury the two of them together? Fiona and the professor? And why so far away from the other two victims?'

'By that time, we were disposing of bodies in a disused septic tank on the next farm. I can't remember now why we didn't take Fiona there. We buried the professor with her, because we thought it fitting that a brother and sister should lie in peace together.'

Dania had pored over the doctor's notes, wondering where all the people who'd died at his hands were buried. Nelson had been over every inch of the grounds and found only the four sets of remains. Now she had her answer: a cadaver dog could alert to a septic tank, but not to one on a distant farm.

'You have to remember, Inspector, that it was only those very serious cases for whom we recommended the treatment. Many of them were going to die by their own hands. They had nothing to lose.'

'Is that how you justified it?' Honor said breezily. 'You must have made a fortune in the process.'

Spots of colour appeared on Anamaria's cheeks. 'How dare you?

We didn't charge. We didn't need to.' She made a visible effort to calm herself. 'The ECT procedure is done in this country as part of standard psychiatric practice, so we told the patients we were subsidised by the NHS. It wasn't true, of course.'

'Let's talk about standard practice, then,' Dania said. 'Yesterday, I showed your test results to Professor Milo Slaughter. He confirmed that what you did at Breek House is *not* standard practice. All ECT treatments use a fixed current of just under one amp. It's the voltage that is varied along with the time the current is passed.' She tapped the papers. 'But that's not what you and your husband did. You consistently ramped up the current. Every patient who died at Breek House did so after receiving a current so large that it would have cooked his brain. The pain would have been unbearable.'

The woman said nothing.

'Why did you remove the teeth, Mrs de Courcy?' Honor said.

'Dental records would have identified them. We burnt their clothes. Anything we couldn't destroy was buried on one of our trips to the Highlands.'

'But you didn't destroy this,' Dania said, lifting the papers.

'Destroy scientific evidence? After all our hard work? Are you mad?' The woman drew herself up. 'You must return those notes to my husband when the trial is over. I am hoping to persuade him to continue his search for the correct settings.'

'My God,' Honor murmured. 'So that's why you kept the equipment. You intended to start up all over again. What kind of a monster are you?'

'These papers will become the property of the court,' Dania said. 'It's up to them to decide what to do.' She tidied the sheets and put them into her folder, out of the woman's reach. 'Personally, I hope they burn them. Anamaria de Courcy, I am charging you with culpable homicide and murder. Have you any-thing to say regarding these charges?'

The woman looked baffled. 'But we were looking for a cure,' she said, as if to herself, 'and we nearly succeeded. Yes, people died, but their sacrifice was not in vain.'

Dania nodded to the officer by the door to take her away.

After they'd gone, Honor said, 'All those people in MisPers, boss. We'll have to cross-reference the names against those the de Courcys killed.'

'And we need to search at that farm, the one next to Breek House. Can you arrange to get Nelson out there?'

The girl nodded. 'Identifying the remains will be a nightmare. Specially if they're all jumbled up.'

'It will keep CAHID going for years.' Dania paused. 'You know, it was that word "experiment" that did it for me, Honor. And she wanted to start it all up again. Unbelievable.'

'I keep wondering whether Ned and his mum knew what was going on. Or suspected. They must have looked in at Breek House from time to time.'

'Looked in and looked away. It's amazing what money can do to one's sense of right and wrong.'

The door burst open and Hamish rushed in. 'It's Melrose Police Station, ma'am,' he said out of breath. 'They've just heard from the hospital. Peter de Courcy has escaped.'

CHAPTER 36

'Well, my friend, I can only say thank you for putting up with me.'

Marek was sitting on the sofa, gulping his coffee. 'Are you sure you don't want to stay longer?'

'I need to get back to Vienna and start writing my article.' Harti smiled ruefully. 'And see what Gerrit is doing to the apartment. I just hope she hasn't painted everything pink. You know what women are.'

Before Marek could reply, the doorbell rang.

'That must be my taxi,' Harti said, getting to his feet. 'So, my friend, this is goodbye. And thank you. I'll send you a copy of my article.' He looked at Marek for a long moment. 'And I'm truly sorry if I've made trouble for you with your sister.'

'I'm sure I'll get over it.'

He picked up his suitcase. 'You must both come and see us soon,' he said, grinning. 'There's a new restaurant on the Herrengasse. Gerrit and I would be delighted to take you there one evening.'

'Done. Although when Danka will have time is anybody's guess.'

'Do you think she will forgive me?' he said nervously.

'I suspect she already has.'

The men clasped hands and clapped each other on the back. And, with a final wink, Harti was gone.

Marek sauntered into the kitchen. He took the package intended for Peter de Courcy out of the drawer and ripped off the paper. Inside was a bundle of money – fifty thousand pounds in fifty-pound notes. He sank into the chair. That mortgage down payment. This, and the twenty thousand Archie had given him when he took on the assignment, would easily cover it. First, however, he was going to do something he'd wanted to do for a long time.

He was going to buy Danka a piano.

'DI Gorska. I'm here to see Mr McLellan,' Dania said to the man with the tattoo.

This time, there was no argument. 'He's in the nightclub,' he said quietly. 'I'll take you in.'

Archie was sitting at one of the blue tables, frowning at something on his laptop screen. He glanced up and, seeing Dania, his expression softened and he got slowly to his feet.

'Inspector Gorska,' he said, motioning to her to sit down. 'May I offer you some refreshment?'

'No, thank you.'

'I take it you've got some news. I reckon there was a reason for the cheek swab I gave your forensics officer a couple of days ago.'

'We were able to match your DNA to that of one of the Breek House victims,' she said, with sympathy in her voice. 'I'm afraid it's bad news. The victim was your uncle Keith.'

'Your officer didn't tell me much. Perhaps you can fill me in.'

As succinctly as she could, she told him what had befallen Keith McLellan at the hands of the de Courcys, and how he had been only one of many victims. Archie's expression suggested it wasn't the first time he'd heard this.

'So Peter de Courcy wasn't treating him with hypnotherapy?' he said.

'I'm afraid not. At least, not after he'd tried it and found it to be unsuccessful.' After a pause, she added, 'My brother told me you hired him to find de Courcy. He was there when we made the arrest.'

'Aye, he came to see me afterwards.'

'It transpired we were both looking for the same man.'

'And neither of you told the other, it seems.'

'We're both professionals.'

'I can see that.' He hesitated. 'Is there anything else you can tell me?'

'Mrs de Courcy has been charged with murder. You'll read about it in the papers.'

'*Mrs* de Courcy? What about *Dr* de Courcy?'

'He was injured trying to escape and taken to the hospital in Melrose. I'm afraid when the nurse looked in on him the following morning, he was gone.'

Archie's face grew dark with anger. 'And how the hell did that happen? Wasn't he under guard?'

'I'd specifically requested a uniform stay in the same room. But for some reason he was sent out. He fell asleep in the corridor. In the morning, the nurse found the downstairs window wide open. A and E is on the ground floor, and they concluded de Courcy must have woken up confused in the small hours, opened the window and climbed out. The hospital are sticking to that story. They searched the grounds but found nothing.'

'Do you think that's what happened?'

'I find it hard to believe that de Courcy managed to leave his room without help. I saw the state of his injuries. As for the window, no one could remember if it was closed and locked, or just closed. His son visited him that evening. It's possible he unlocked

363

the window and came in that way late at night. We've interviewed him but he denies it.'

'And the guard fell asleep on the job,' Archie said, with a sneer. 'What can you expect from local polis?'

'We'll find him, Mr McLellan.'

He nodded, his anger apparently gone.

'Is there anything you want to ask me?' Dania said.

After a moment, he said, 'Will you play for me one last time?'

She hesitated but, under the circumstances, she could hardly refuse. 'What would you like to hear?'

'That piece you played the first time. The slow sad one.'

'The nocturne?'

'Aye, that's the one.'

She got to her feet and went over to the platform.

'Have you seen the Polański film, *The Pianist*?' she said, as she adjusted the piano stool.

'The Jewish pianist who survives the war?'

'You may remember the scene where Władysław Szpilman plays for the German officer, Hosenfeld, the man who eventually saves him. In the film, the actor plays Chopin's Ballade, Opus Twenty-three, Number One in G minor. But Szpilman in his memoir says that he played this nocturne.'

She called up her mental map of the piece and brought her hands down on the keys. She played it slowly, as she always did, lingering on the final note.

When there was no reaction from Archie, she said, 'I'll let you know when we'll be releasing your uncle's remains.' When there was still no reply, she added, 'I really am very sorry, Mr McLellan.'

He was gazing at the floor in silence. It was impossible to tell what he was thinking.

She picked up her bag and left the room.

CHAPTER 37

'Any news on de Courcy?' Dania said.

Honor exchanged a glance with Hamish. 'Nope,' she said quietly.

'He can't stay on the run for ever. His bank account's been frozen.'

'What about his son, ma'am?'

'He's sticking to his story that he didn't help his father escape. We've got a tap on his phone, and his premises are being watched. If de Courcy senior surfaces, we'll have him.' She stared through the window. 'I'm convinced his son was involved. Who else could it have been? If his father woke up confused, and climbed out by himself, he wouldn't have got very far in a hospital gown.'

'Do you think Junior knew what his parents were up to at Breek House?' Hamish said.

'He says no, but I'm not so sure.'

'We've got the doctor's picture up everywhere. His appearance is unmistakable.'

'Appearances can easily be changed, Hamish. A bit of hair dye, large glasses, and it's amazing how different you can look.'

A constable put his head round the door. The DCI was asking for Dania.

She hurried along the corridor to the woman's office. The door was open.

Two men were standing talking to Jackie Ireland. They turned as Dania entered.

'Dania, these gentlemen are from the City of London Fraud Squad,' the DCI said. She made the introductions quickly. 'I'll let them tell you what this is about.'

'It concerns Valentine Montgomerie and Robyn Vannerman,' DI Leonard said.

'Vannerman?' Dania said. 'Is she married?'

'Vannerman is her maiden name. Neither lady is married.'

The implication hit Dania. 'So they're not sisters.'

'Robyn's been using Valentine's surname here in Scotland. I suspect they want to keep their relationship a secret, so pretend they're sisters.' He glanced at his colleague. 'Thanks to DS Welland, we've finally accumulated enough evidence to arrest them.'

'On what charge?'

'They both worked for Montgomerie Investment Bank, started by Valentine's father, Lucien Montgomerie. They stole from the company, cleverly disguising the theft as transactions, which were almost impossible to trace back to them.'

'And the father didn't notice?'

'It was an investment bank, Inspector, and the value of investments goes up and down. He simply assumed it was volatility in the markets, and things would recover. In the end, things got so bad that he wound up the company. He died a year later.' The officer hesitated. 'By his own hand.'

Dania frowned. 'And they used the stolen money to start up their gin business?'

'They used it to buy Breek House. A building that size, along with the land, doesn't come cheap. We've been doing some checking. One of the things we'd like to know is how they found the rest of the money for their start-up. We haven't been able to square that circle.'

'Are you going to Breek House now?'

'We are.'

'Would you mind if I came along? There's a question or two I'd like to ask them. And it might help your investigation.'

'Be my guest. But you should take your own car, and we'll follow you. We'll be heading straight down to London once we've made the arrest. I take it you know how to get there.'

She smiled grimly. 'I know how to get there.'

As Breek House came into view, Dania slowed and signalled in plenty of time. She cruised through the metal gates, took the left turn and followed the drive to the clearing. The yellow Chevrolet and a white van with the word 'Ginspirations' in red letters were parked in front of the dark grey house.

She climbed out of the squad car and waited for the officers. A breeze sprang up, lifting last year's leaves.

'Wow,' DI Leonard murmured, getting out. 'It's bigger than I expected.'

'It seems they're both at home,' Dania said, nodding towards the vehicles.

'It's best we get both women together before announcing who we are. Otherwise one of them may do a bunk.'

'I understand.'

He rang the bell. A few moments later they heard voices, which grew louder. There were footsteps and the door opened.

Val Montgomerie stood on the steps. She was wearing a close-fitting suit in a grey and white check. 'Inspector Gorska,' she said, smiling. She glanced at the men, and her smile faded.

'May we come in, Miss Montgomerie?'

'Of course.' She opened the door wide.

'Is your sister at home?' Dania said, when they were in the entrance hall.

'In the living room. Please go in. You know the way.'

Robyn was kneeling on the floor, surrounded by brightly coloured posters, which she was sorting into piles. It seemed the women were getting their publicity organised. Seeing the officers, she got slowly to her feet, brushing down her dress, which was in a red and white zigzag pattern. A shadow crossed her face, making Dania suspect she knew why they were there.

'I take it this is about the Breek House murders, Inspector,' Val said, closing the door behind her.

'We've made an arrest. It will be in the papers tomorrow.'

'That's a relief,' she said brightly.

'But these gentlemen are here on another matter.'

The men took out their warrant cards. 'City of London Fraud Squad,' DI Leonard said.

She stared at the warrants, frowning. Robyn threw a glance at the door. DS Welland stepped back and parked himself in front of it.

'Fraud Squad?' Val said. 'I don't understand.'

'We have evidence that, over a period of years, you and Miss Vannerman defrauded Montgomerie Investment Bank of a considerable sum.'

At 'Vannerman', Robyn's eyes widened. 'Val?' she said.

'It's all right, darling,' Val murmured, putting an arm round her shoulders. She glared at DI Leonard. 'There must be some mistake.'

'There's no mistake, Miss Montgomerie. We're here to take you back to London.' As he spoke the words of arrest, DS Welland came forward and put handcuffs on Val, then on Robyn. Neither woman spoke. The shock on their faces said it all.

'Before we go, DI Gorska has some questions for you,' DI Leonard said, looking at Dania.

'It concerns Archie McLellan,' Dania said. 'You remember that night at Donnan's, Miss Montgomerie? I was in the lavatory next to his office and heard you talking. What was that about?'

'You may as well know,' she said tonelessly. 'Montgomerie Investment managed Archie's portfolio. When he heard we were thinking of starting up a gin business and needed premises and land, he told us about Breek House, and that the council wanted to sell it. We made them a generous offer to secure it. It was a marvellous opportunity to start fresh.'

'And the money Archie was offering you?'

'He decided we had the makings of a good business and wanted to invest. As we reached each milestone in our business plan, he gave us the next tranche of money. We couldn't have done it without him. Buying Breek House left us with nothing. He was a sleeping business partner. That's all there is to it.'

'Why did you tell me you'd never met him?'

'We were aware of his reputation. If word got around that we were associated with him, the business might suffer.'

DI Leonard looked at Dania enquiringly. She shook her head. She'd got what she'd come for.

'In that case, Inspector, we'll get on the road. We've a long drive ahead of us.'

As they left the room, Val threw Dania a backward glance. Her face was expressionless. Robyn was less composed, her eyes darting from one officer to the other.

DI Leonard gathered up the women's handbags from the hall table. 'Can I leave you to lock up, Inspector?'

'The keys are on the table,' Val said to no one in particular.

Dania picked up the keys, and was about to follow them outside, but something made her pause. DS Welland turned the car round. As he accelerated down the drive, she caught a white-faced

Robyn staring malevolently at her, as though this were somehow her fault. The sound of the engine faded into the distance.

She made her way to the dining room. The still stood silent, its pipes no longer gurgling and steaming. But she wasn't interested in gin production. She opened the door to what had once been the ECT suite.

Crates of bottles were stacked around the room. But, as she gazed at them, she saw only the gentle Willie MacMartin, shrieking and thrashing, fighting Anamaria's attempts to hold him down.

She locked the front door and made for the car. As she drove slowly away, she wondered how long it would be before the ivy claimed Breek House for its own, and the woodland crept stealthily across the fields to screen off the building.

Perhaps it was better that way.

CHAPTER 38

It was Friday before Dania had a chance to visit MacMartin &
Sons Funeral Directors. Jim MacMartin, in the same sober charcoal suit, was at the desk.

'Inspector Gorska, isn't it?' he said, getting to his feet.

She smiled. 'Is your father in?'

'He's in the coffin display room, taking an inventory. Would you
like to speak to him?'

'If I may.'

'I'll take you through.'

Calum was standing entering something into an iPad. His face
broke into a smile. 'Inspector, it's good to see you.'

'How are you? Busy, I see.'

'Aye, we've taken in some new coffins. I'm adding them to our
stock database.'

'I've come to tell you that CAHID will soon be releasing your
father's remains. They'll be contacting you directly.'

'They're not needed for the trial?'

'The DNA results as well as what we found in Peter de
Courcy's notes are sufficient for the prosecution. We've now
identified all four victims.'

What she didn't tell him was that they were still in the process of identifying the new remains discovered outside the Breek

House perimeter. Nelson had worked his magic, finding human bones in a disused septic tank under the pigsty. A quick examination by Jackson had confirmed the presence of fractures in some of the lower limbs.

'I'd like to attend your father's funeral, Mr MacMartin. Will you let me know when it is?'

'I'd be very pleased to see you there.'

'I expect you'll be using that mahogany coffin. The one with the white satin lining that smells of lilies?'

'I'm afraid it's away. Someone bought it the other morning.'

'Can you not get one like it?'

'There's nowhere that makes them. That really was the last, right enough.' He shrugged. 'I couldn't refuse the customer. Remember you asked whether my father had ever done business with the McLellans? Aye, well, it was Archie McLellan who bought the coffin. I read that one of the victims was his relative.'

'His uncle Keith.'

'Poor devil. Mr McLellan was very subdued. He asked for the finest model.' Calum paused. 'The papers said he had a brother who died recently, too.'

'There's only his mother left.' And, thought Dania, she'll be facing a long spell in prison once her trial is over.

'I was wondering how things are going with the investigation. The *Courier* said you've charged Peter de Courcy's wife.'

'We're still looking for Peter de Courcy himself. And we won't give up till we find him,' she added firmly. 'We've contacted Europol and Interpol in case he slipped the net before we alerted the ports and airports, although I can't see how he could have. We moved pretty quickly.'

Calum nodded. 'You found my dad, which is the main thing as far as I'm concerned. I can't thank you enough.'

She gazed at him, wondering whether he would still thank her when the details of what Willie had endured at the hands of the de Courcys were made public.

'Goodbye, Calum,' she said sadly.

Darkness was settling on Dundee as Dania let herself into the flat. Her conversation with Calum had reminded her that she still needed to organise the commemoration services for Laurence and Quinn. She would get on to it the following day. Hamish and Honor had offered to help. They were working well together, which delighted and relieved her. Hamish had appreciated the role Laurence had played in the team and, without anyone noticing, had quietly taken his place.

She dropped the shopping on the floor and collapsed into the wickerwork armchair. Although her work was over, she had the sense of things unfinished. Yes, she'd solved the Breek House murders, but their inability to find Peter de Courcy had soured her triumph. The case closed, it was customary to take the team out for a drink. But, with their prime suspect still at large, the case remained open. Still, the DCI had congratulated her on another positive result. Her star was in the ascendant. So why didn't she feel ecstatic?

In the kitchen, she poured herself a glass of Żubrówka. She was bringing the vodka to her lips when her phone buzzed. It was a text from Kimmie. She and Harry were going to the new cocktail bar in City Square that evening and, if she was free, they'd be delighted if she would join them. She deleted the message.

The crates were unpacked, apart from the one holding the vase of Harry's gardenias. When was it he'd come round for dinner? A lifetime ago. She scooped up the dead flowers and threw them into the bin. Lying next to the bags of shopping was the bouquet of russet-gold chrysanthemums she'd bought in the supermarket. She filled the vase with water and arranged the flowers.

It was Friday night and Dundee was out on the razzle. She could sit and watch the stars circling the sky or . . .

She pulled out her phone and sent Franek Jagielski a text. Would he like to share a glass of vodka, and talk about life in the old country?

EPILOGUE

Peter de Courcy opened his eyes. He'd slept badly, his night a turmoil of vivid dreams. How long was it since he'd woken in a strange room and found a dark figure looming over him, rolling back his hospital gown, inserting a syringe into his arm? Heaviness had settled into his limbs, and oblivion had come quickly.

Since then, he'd lost all sense of time and place. He'd awoken in another room, finding himself unable to move his body or speak because his mouth had been taped shut. Over the course of the next few days, or was it weeks?, someone came and spooned thick soup into his mouth, always making sure the light was off before entering the room, which resulted in much of the soup spilling down the front of his gown. Visits to the lavatory were equally unsatisfactory. He was led in the dark to a foul-smelling toilet and had to perform, with the black-clothed figure, whose outline he could just make out, in the same room.

Given the quantity of drugs regularly injected into his arm, he would have thought he was hallucinating, had it not been for the odd moment of lucidity. Then his blood would congeal with fear at the realisation that he was being kept alive for a purpose. But those moments were rare, and the feeling passed once the syringe arrived.

But the last drug had been different. He was sure he'd slept longer. And he could no longer feel the restraints, or the tape over his mouth. He'd been moved to yet another place because he wasn't lying on the rough mattress but on a bed with soft satin sheets. Under his head was a pillow of similar material. And there was a scent of lilies so strong it made him light-headed. There must be flowers in the room, except that the scent seemed to be coming from the sheets.

So where was he? And why was it so black? Even in the darkest room, there was always some light. He turned over, thinking there might be a bedside lamp, and hit the wall. He stretched out a hand, expecting plaster or paper but his fingers scraped against wood. He tried to turn on to his other side and banged his head. With a trembling hand, he reached out slowly, his fingers brushing wood again. A wave of fear coursed through him. He lifted his hands and touched wood a few inches above his face. It was then that he became aware of the lack of air, the need to breathe more deeply, the slight feeling of suffocation. The sudden understanding of where he was sent adrenalin coursing through his veins. Panic overcame him. In a sweat of terror, he drummed his feet and thumped his fists against the sides. Then, feeling madness creep over him, he filled his lungs with hot air and screamed.

ACKNOWLEDGEMENTS

I owe a huge debt of gratitude to Jenny Brown, Krystyna Green and Annette Zimmermann for reading this novel and suggesting ways in which it could be improved. I am deeply grateful to Hazel Orme for doing such a magnificent job of copy-editing, and for all her advice and encouragement. Any errors in the text are mine, and not hers.

Heartfelt thanks also go to my agent, Jenny Brown, for all the support she has given me, and to Krystyna Green, Amanda Keats and everyone at Little, Brown for taking on the publishing of this novel. I am deeply grateful to both Hazel Orme and Kim Bishop for doing such a magnificent job of editing and proof-reading. Any errors in the text are mine, and not theirs.

377